SHARDS OF AMBER

More from the Weeping Cedars Universe

Books
Lightning Falls
Welcome to Weeping Cedars

Podcasts
Weeping Cedars
Samite
Wrought of Amber

SHARDS OF AMBER

J.W.G. Wise

www.WeepingCedars.com

Published by Ikandaset Books.

Library of Congress Cataloging-in-Publication Data is available on file.
Cover design and artwork by J.W.G. Wise
Print ISBN: 978-0-9601305-0-4

WeepingCedars.com
1st On-Demand Print Run

Contents

To the small but dedicated community of Weeping Cedars fans.

Without you, this would not be.

Author's Note

This collection of short horror stories does not stand alone. Anyone trying to read it without also listening to the accompanying podcast Wrought of Amber would find themselves quickly confused and utterly turned around. The stories and tableaus presented in Shards of Amber are meant to give the reader insight into the sad, dark, and hopefully chilling events that Alex Carmichael, the host of Wrought of Amber, never had access to. Here, you will find events that transpired before either of the Carmichael sisters was born, as well as tales set in worlds Alex never visited.

The intended way to experience this book is to listen to an episode of Wrought of Amber and then come here to read the accompanying short story. This is how the episodes and stories were originally released. So, after listening to Wrought of Amber Episode 1, you would read Laundry Day, after Episode 2, The Doll Maker, and so on. Once you've listened to the whole series, you should delve into the six extra stories available only in this book.

Beyond the connections between Shards of Amber and Wrought of Amber, these stories are deeply intertwined with the podcasts Weeping Cedars and Samite, and the upcoming novel Lightning Falls. So, though this little book offers many insights and answers, it isn't meant to be the whole story. Indeed, if all goes well, the whole story won't be completed for many years. Shards of Amber will raise at least as many questions as it answers, and hopefully, it will lead you on or back to other parts of the overarching narrative.

J.W.G. Wise, 2025

Laundry Day 1

August 28, 1989

Lubrow, Wyoming

THE DAMN DRYER WAS broken. So was the washing machine. But *Dopey's Soapys* had plenty of working washing machines. Their dryers, however, were famous for eating underwear. Nothing but underwear. Socks made it in and out just fine. But throw a pair of bikini briefs in them, and you were likely to come back with something that looked like you could have bought at *Frederick's of Hollywood*.

No thank you, Dorren thought, *I don't need the crotchless ones today, it's not that kind of year.*

Doreen didn't mind the two-block walk to *Dopey's* on the warm days. She resisted the temptation to buy one of those wheely carts. That felt like a commitment and surrender to a life she wasn't ready for. If it came down to crotchless underwear or wheely carts, she hoped she was still young enough that the choice remained at least a bit of a thinker. And she hoped she'd still opt to carry her laundry.

It was the trip back that she hated—the damp clothing that weighed four times as much as did on the way to the laundromat. It was uncomfortable and nap-inducing. And on many previous trips, it had been loud and annoying. But not today. Today, Dorren's daughter Tracy was twelve. Strictly speaking, she had been twelve for three days, but none had been laundry day. This was the first laundry day since her birthday. And at twelve, Doreen believed you could be on your own … at least for a little while.

She remembered running rampant when she was nine, but that was before razor blades in apples at Halloween, and stranger danger, and satanic cults. That was before kids started summoning demons in their basements by invoking dragons in dungeons. The '80s were scary times for kids, but Doreen felt she had done a pretty good job. Tracy was a responsible girl, and today she would be alone. At least for the time it took Doreen to walk two blocks, start a load, and walk back.

She left her laundry basket on top of the machine at *Dopey's* and palmed the small squirt bottle she used for detergent. She strolled back, waving to a man at the corner store and a woman pushing a stroller, who she thought she remembered from a church event. It was a pleasant walk. The sun had come out and had driven away the morning damp and drear. The thermometer was pushing eighty-five, and after a wet and chilly morning, it felt like the perfect summer afternoon.

When she got in sight of her little, blue, mid-century, two-bedroom rancher, she saw Tracy out on the lawn, working on something. Was it her bicycle? Doreen cursed under her breath. There was one more thing she'd have to try to help Tracy put back together.

"What are you doing, honey?" Doreen asked as she crossed the boundary from sidewalk to lawn, hoping that her daughter was just inflating a flat tire.

"Working on the gears," Tracy said, looking up with a comical grease streak across one cheek.

Doreen pushed a curl of black hair away from her cheek in unconscious reflection and tried to smile. "What's wrong with them?"

"They lock up," Tracy said. "But I think I've got it."

As Doreen got closer, she saw that Tracy had a book next to her in the grass. It was a big, coffee-table-sized hardback they had bought at the thrift shop in the fall called *How Bicycles Work*. She had opened it to a gear diagram that looked almost nothing like the assembly on Tracy's hand-me-down ten-speed.

"Uh-huh," Doreen said. "Well, I hope you can put that back together again."

She passed her daughter and resisted the sudden urge to tousle her hair. She was too old for that now, Doreen thought. She went back inside and got to work on the dishes, hoping to finish them before the timer went off and she'd have to return to *Dopey's*. Then, of course, she could spend a half hour hanging the laundry before she pulled the leftovers out …

It never ended. Never ever. She wished for a break. Just a short one. Just one day to lie around, do nothing, and be selfish. That wasn't the answer, though, she realized. The answer was to cut that thirty minutes to fifteen and have Tracy help her. But something warned her away from this. She didn't know what, and she didn't know why.

As she cleaned one dish after the next, the streak of grease on Tracy's face struck her. That was it. That was the reason not to have her hang laundry. It wasn't the grease itself; it was what it stood for. Tracy would wash her hands to the elbows to ensure she didn't create more work for her mother. But Doreen didn't want her to. As exasperating as disassembled bikes, reassembled record players with left-over pieces, and wire-bare walkie-talkies were, they were hope—hope for something more than *Dopey's Soapys* for Tracy, more than laundry, then dishes, then laundry, then dinner.

She could learn to do laundry later. Let her learn to fix bikes now.

Doreen pulled a bowl from the sink and was startled when the television came on in the living room. She dropped the bowl and shook her head. The old green Tupperware they used for breakfast cereal bounced off the sink's rim, landed on the floor, and rolled into the living room. Doreen wiped her gloved hands on her apron and followed the wet trail to find the bowl upright as if someone had just finished a nice heaping portion of *Sudsy-O's*.

"Tracy?" She said, looking around the empty room before picking up the bowl. The television, an old 19" deal with vertical-hold problems she had also picked up from the thrift store, was playing that kids' show… *Virtue Vista Valley*. She hadn't watched it herself when she was young, and Tracy was too old for those kinds of shows.

The episode was black and white—an old rerun then. A boy, dressed like a normal kid from down the street, was talking to a girl who looked like a princess—with a crown and everything. Doreen had come in mid-conversation, but from what she gathered, the boy was lecturing the girl about her behavior.

"Never changes," Doreen said, picking up the clicker. "You're too good for him, sister. Tell him to shut up and then go find someone better." She turned the TV off, dropped the remote onto the coffee table, and bent over to pick up the bowl.

She heard the sound of the television tube click back on. Afraid as the TV hummed behind her, she froze. Then, realizing that she must have dropped the remote onto its power button, she shook her head, grabbed the rubber bowl, and turned around to switch the boob tube off again.

Doreen stared; the scene had changed. Instead of the boy and girl standing and talking, the boy was sitting on a rock, whittling. The girl— was that the same girl?—was slumped over a fence. Her thick, dark hair hid her face, and her tiara lay on the ground, just beyond the reach of her limp hand at the end of one dangling arm. Her skirt was bunched up by the fence, showing much more thigh than Doreen thought appropriate for a girl that age. It was morbid and monstrous for television, especially a children's show.

As Doreen picked up the remote, the boy looked up from his whittling and said, "You shouldn't leave her alone, you know. Good mothers don't."

Doreen stared, her mouth open, at the screen. What the hell did that boy say? She stared, waiting, but the scene was too terrible to keep looking at. The boy kept whittling, and the girl remained unmoving.

"Mom?"

Doreen almost screamed, but she held it together. She looked to her left and saw Tracy walking down the hallway. She jammed the power button, put the remote down gingerly, and walked to meet her daughter in the living room doorway.

"What is it, honey?"

"Do we have a Phillips-head screwdriver?"

Doreen looked at her and shook her head, not quite processing what she was saying.

"Oh, okay. Do you mind if I ask Mr. Greenfield? I bet he has one."

Doreen shook her head again, still trying to wrangle the fear slithering through her chest like a serpent that had just woken from a long, luxurious slumber.

"Just—be careful," was all she could get out. Tracy gave her a strange look like she'd grown two heads. What was there to be careful about? Mr. Greenfield was the nicest man on the block. The twelve-year-old shook her head, turned on her heel, and hurried back up the hallway and out onto the lawn.

Doreen blinked, returned to the sink, and plopped the green bowl into the water. She stared at the wall, the boy's strange words hanging in her mind while the picture of the girl dangled in her memory. Why did he say that? Phillips-head … Wait, how did Tracy get the damn thing apart if she didn't have a Phillips head?

Doreen pulled her rubber gloves off, untied her apron, and stalked down the hallway toward the front door. It seemed that the dishes would have to wait until after a second trip to *Dopey's*. From the front porch, she saw Mr. Greenfield opening his garage door with Tracy next to him. The girl waved at her mother, and Mr. Greenfield copied her. Doreen returned the gesture and forced a smile. The coiling in her chest was settling into a pit in her stomach.

Don't be an idiot.

Stranger danger.

Mr. Greenfield has known her since she was five; he's about as far from a stranger as they come.

Satanic cults.

If he's a satanist, then maybe I should sign up, because they make wonderful neighbors.

She closed her eyes, counted to ten, and opened them. Mr. Greenfield was showing Tracy something at his workbench.

In the kitchen, the timer buzzed.

"Damn it."

Doreen went inside, clicked the timer off, grabbed the laundry basket, and hurried back to the front door. When she came out, Mr. Greenfield was accompanying Tracy across the street.

"Hello," Mr. Greenfield said. He waved again. "Beautiful day for some mechanic's work!"

He was tall, broad-shouldered, and combed his thinning gray hair over from a side part. He wore big 1970s glasses and a pocket-protector in his button-up white shirt. His sleeves were rolled up and his tie was loose, like one of those men in that movie about the jurors. He was a relic from another age when neighbors didn't fear one another, back when they helped each other. She almost cried.

"It sure is," Doreen managed to get out. "Please don't let her bother you with her projects," she said. But she didn't mean it.

"Oh, it's no bother. I did the same when I was her age."

Doreen sincerely hoped that was true.

"Heading up to *Dopey's*?"

She nodded.

"Mmhmm, I still need to replace mine as well." He looked down at Tracy. "I think we'll be elbow-deep in this repair until after you're back, don't you think so?" Tracy nodded up at him with a broad smile.

Doreen nodded, not sure she could talk. The anxiety in her stomach melted in a wave of gratitude. It might only be twenty minutes, but it was twenty minutes in which she had help. She turned towards *Dopey's* and started walking.

"Now, that cross-ended one you have there, that's a Phillips-head, so, see, you already have that covered."

Mr. Greenfield's words faded into the background, melding with a lawnmower, a van, and a barking dog. Doreen breathed deeply and closed her eyes for a few steps, letting the anxiety fade. She wiped her cheeks with her fingertips and wondered if a pie was in order. She couldn't afford to make one for just Mr. Greenfield, but she might kill two birds with one stone by baking one for them all, inviting him over, and encouraging Tracy to show him the walkie-talkies she had disassembled. No, not two birds, three: a little peace and quiet, a debt paid, and some encouragement for Tracy.

Doreen passed *Tune-In TVs and Radios* and saw they were playing some old black and white cartoon on their display pieces in the window. The radio speakers, however, were playing the old Orson Welles *War of the Worlds*. God, she loved his voice. She could listen to that man say just about anything. Then, as if she had suppressed the memory, she realized that he had been dead for almost four years.

As usual, *Dopey's* was mostly empty this time of the afternoon. She did her work quickly without getting bogged down in a conversation, though people tried to snare her. One woman, who seemed to like to spend her time at the laundromat for the sheer social aspect, asked her how Tracy was. "Just fine," she said and kept pulling clothes out. A man asked her how she liked the weather, and she once more said, "Just fine," and tried to hide her clothes with a towel. She got the impression that he was one of those men who thought the laundromat was a bar and that all the women felt hot to trot when their panties were on display. She wondered if those men, and there were a couple of them in town, thought they might figure out who was or wasn't wild in the sack by window-shopping who wore bikini briefs, full-bottomed, or something out of Penthouse.

Yes, Mr. Laundry Man, you've discovered my secrets. I'm a bikini girl all day. Please don't tell anyone, they'll know I'm an insatiable nymphomaniac. But since you know, why don't we go to your place? No? Your wife's home? Well then, a motel will do. Don't worry, I'll pay.

Doreen finished stuffing her wet clothes into her basket, glad she paid the additional dime for an extra spin cycle, and started on her way home.

She passed *Tune-In* and was disappointed to hear that Orson Welles's voice was no longer coming from the speakers. Instead, a low hiss of static skittered its way around the front of the store. As she passed the door, she thought she made out in the jumble of pips and pops a boy's voice saying, "Good mothers don't."

Doreen paused and listened, uncertain of what she'd heard. When no more followed, she felt the pit of anxiety burst back into existence. And suddenly, there was a thought in her mind.

No, it said. *Good mothers don't. They don't trust their neighbors, do they? They never have. They report them to the government. Not even in Mr. Greenfield's day. Back then, they watched them to see if they were Reds. And if they were, they reported them.*

She knew it was a ridiculous thought. Still, she started at a brisk walk and quickened to a trot. The clothes were heavy, but she could manage. She was soon jogging, feeling like a fool, but ignoring her imagined pictures of her neighbors peeking their heads out of curtains and wondering what the mad woman was doing.

She slowed when she came to the corner of her block and had to wait as the Millers' old station wagon passed in front of her. She nodded instinctively to Mr. Miller but wasn't paying attention to notice if he nodded back. She was trying to make out what was on her lawn. There was the bike, and something … something sticking out from behind one of the bushes. When the Millers' car had passed by, she began at a slow jog, and when she came to her lawn, she dropped the basket, making sure it didn't spill in case she was wrong about the shape, in case everything was just fine, and her world wasn't falling to pieces.

Then she ran.

Converse sneakers in green grass, pounding the ten steps to what looked like a leg in black slacks sticking out from behind the old prickly ivy bush by the corner of the house.

She stopped, dropped to her knees, and covered her mouth with her hands as Mr. Greenfield's body came into view. He wasn't drenched in blood, nor was there a look of terror upon his kindly old face. Instead, he looked to his right, his head tilted slightly, spears of grass poking his cheek. His mouth was just barely open, his fingers curled loosely. Doreen crawled toward his head, calling for her daughter.

"Tracy!" she cried. Her hands touched Mr. Greenfield's cheeks, hoping he might pop up and surprise her; praying they were playing some terrible game. His cheeks were cool, but not unnaturally, not the chill of death. Not yet. She felt for a pulse, but it had left him.

"Tracy!" she shouted.

Doreen didn't know CPR, but she pressed on his chest ten times and felt for a pulse again before standing.

She ran to the backyard and looked over their chain-link fence. It was empty. She ran to the front yard and called out her daughter's name again. As she stepped onto the cement path, something crunched under her sneaker. She looked down and saw Mr. Greenfield's glasses.

"Oh God," she said, looking up sharply. How did they get there? Or more to the point, how did Mr. Greenfield get back to the side of the house where he would be out of sight?

"Tracy!" she screamed.

Doors on the street started to open, and heads began to pop out. Doreen didn't wait for the curious neighbors to amble over and ask her what was happening. She ran inside and down the hall of their ranch house and pushed open Tracy's door.

No one.

The bathroom door was open. She called for her again.

Silence.

She sprinted for the phone, dashing herself into the wall, and didn't care. She knocked over a lamp and didn't notice. She clawed for the receiver and punched in 9-1-1. Her breath came halting through her nose, staccato puffs out, halting, hiccupping gasps in.

"9-1-1, what is the nature of your emergency…"

But the words faded as Doreen watched the television switch on, and saw the boy sitting on the rock, whittling the wood. He was shaking his head. He never looked up, never regarded her at all. But there was a look on his face, a look older than his years. A look that said, 'I tried to warn you.'

And in the background, the girl dangled over the fence, a finger just above the crown that had fallen into the grass.

THE MAN WONDERED HOW the ancient door had not turned to dust. The warped wood, peeling paint, and smell of damp disgusted him. He longed for the clean, crystal clarity of the house that stood on the hill, and he ached for the light that brooded there. The old brass doorknob, cast with twisting serpents that ran like mountain ranges, was warm under his cold, pale palm. He turned the knob and pulled. The door grunted in its crooked frame and opened haltingly toward him.

Blinding daylight slanted in, and he could feel the hidden things that lurked in the corners scuttle away, seeking unchallenged darkness deeper in the moldering house. He pitied them and their fear of the light. Though it was not as pure or life-giving as the mansion's glory, it had its own virtues.

He stepped through and out onto a hard-packed dirt road. The earth around him was yellow and brown, the air hot and dry. Patches of green scrub brush spotted the earth, and he could see for miles in every direction. He was up high, and a light breeze moved across his face, tugging at the shadowy wisp of a beard. This sun was familiar. He had stood beneath it many times.

He looked down at his placard and its old, but still legible, chalk lines. Reluctantly, he removed it and returned through the door. He would not need it today. One day, he would wear it for the last time. One day, he would finish his work for the Queen. She had shown him. But this was not that dark day. This was sun, high desert, and heat. He laid the placard down on an old, musty chair and patted it. He would never remember, not without help. She had shown him that, too. But that was all right. The work he did didn't require him to remember for long. He only had to remember the dolls' names.

He strode back outside, and the door closed behind him. He heard the telltale suck of air letting him know that the door was gone for now. It would return when he finished.

The man who could not remember for long turned around and saw two rows of houses running alongside the dirt road. They were the same color as the sand, almost as if they had grown up from the earth, with rounded corners and not-quite-square windows. His cheek twitched when a fly landed on it, perhaps seeking moisture. It fell dead to the ground, and, without notice, he crushed it under his boot as he started down the road.

Beyond the houses, the mountain's peak rose sharp, jagged, and bleak. They were near the acme, perhaps fifty feet from the pinnacle. This flat place of houses and roads led to the foot of that bitter rise where the mouth of a cave yawned. Should he but follow the road, he would enter that darkness, and even he would not come out again. He could not hide himself there. But here, in the sunlight, beyond the mouth of the cave, he was strong. Still, he would have to be wary. He did not believe that the Scion was present. But he was not sure that he would know if he was. The Scion was good at hiding, so the man who remembered little would be careful.

He started down the road, turned toward the first house, and walked to the door. He knocked, and a moment later it opened. He smiled. The woman inside smiled back. She had a nice smile, but he could see the horror in her eyes. She did not understand why she was smiling. She did not understand who this man was, with his dark hair tinged with gray at the temples, his spotty beard, his hands pale and soft, shoved into the pockets of jeans that should have worn away years ago. She was a middle-aged woman, and perhaps she thought that only a few years separated them. But nothing could have been falser. She wore a sleeveless, flowing blouse and a billowing skirt. Her breasts were expansive and made him think of a teacher he had once had. A figure half-sketched in his mind, blurred by the light of the Glory.

Not like Theresa and her slim, willowy form.

"Please come in," she said, though her eyes screamed for him to stay out.

"Thank you," he said and stepped into her house. Native American art hung from the walls and adorned bookshelves. He knew nothing about the different tribes or peoples. He only remembered that the patterns and colors, the turquoise and earth tones reminded him of something long ago half-remembered and half-caricatured. Men on horses, peoples living in tall tents, living in long-houses, living and dying when his people had come. The woman's curly, gray hair bounced as she led him inside. He felt the intimacy of the impending act welling up within him. He commanded her to sit with a thought. She sat. He commanded her to grin. She grinned. He demanded that she weep for all she was about to lose and gain.

She wept.

He read her mind. He read her pleas. He read all she would do to let her life go on a little longer. The man leaned back on her couch and whistled a little half-forgotten tune. This was not a virtuous woman.

"Tell me, Abigail," he said. "Tell me what you'd do with all that time if I let you have it."

She stared at him, her mouth working but producing no words. He could feel the thoughts slithering, wriggling like a pit of serpents, each writhing around the others. He saw her look down into that pit, tremulously, looking for the right answer—the one that might save her life. But no slithering thought would do, and she knew it. She flung the thoughts aside and offered herself to him. It was feeble. She was his puppet. If that was what he wanted, he could have it.

He commanded her to laugh. She laughed. She laughed until she coughed and slid from the easy chair, groping at her chest, hugging herself to keep the spasms from shaking her to pieces. He commanded her to stop her laughing and coughing and clutching.

"Stand up," he said. She stood. "Go put on your favorite outfit."

When she returned, she was wearing a dress with a cardigan over it. He admitted that it looked presentable enough, but he pitied her that this was the best she had. Still, there were worse things to die in.

"Tell me, what do you enjoy doing here by yourself?"

His command forced her into honesty, and the image that flowed into his mind startled him. So did the emotional outrush of her accompanying embarrassment and horror. He had thought that she would show him an image of her reading, or watching television, or talking with one of her neighbors. He did not expect to see her on her bed, alone and writhing in solitary pleasure.

"No," he said. "That will not do. Come here, sit at the table."

She sat, and he put a book in front of her. She turned to her favorite section of the small paperback. He went to the kitchen and pulled open the drawer that her mind showed him.

A good, sharp, little paring knife lay with a bread-knife and two longer blades. He liked paring knives almost as much as fishing knives.

The man sat down at the table with her and put his hand on hers.

"Perhaps it would be easier for you to go the other way," he said. "One last hurrah. But this is your door out and in. It doesn't befit the Queen to be honored with your lusts."

Her breath came ragged, shuddering through her nose. Her heart galloped along, every instinct to fight or flee raged in a body that would not obey her.

"If they had not taken that from me, perhaps I could have given you one last experience before the end. But … Well, I am not what I used to be."

The man smiled. He felt both sadness and a tinge of jealousy.

"You don't know what you're about to see. To you, this is the horror of the end. But I promise you, this is not the end. I know that of which I speak. There is an *after*, and the after you are going to is glorious."

He raised the paring knife and pressed the tip against her throat.

"This is where I will cut. It will be fast, there will be pain, but not as much as you might think."

He stood and walked into the bathroom. He relieved himself, flushed the toilet, washed his hands, and took a pile of towels. When he came back out, he saw that she had moved a few inches in her seat. He was impressed. The power from the cave was not directly aware of him, but it allowed her to do something he had never seen before. He commanded her to go back to her previous position, and she did. Then he commanded her to take ten slow, deep breaths. Her heart was going so fast that he was afraid she would have an attack before he could do his work. Her pulse slowed a little, back to relatively safe territory—at least for as long as he needed. He laid the towels out in front of her, covering the book with four layers of cotton blends.

"Okay," he said gently. "One last moment. Think your thoughts, pray your prayers, and then you go to the forest."

She did not pray. He doubted anyone here would pray. Not in the sight of the cave. And even if they did, would any god hear them? Maybe. He was agnostic about the Creator. Not about his existence, of that the man was sure. He had walked through too many doors into too many worlds to not know that someone must be holding the whole thing together. It was the Creator's character and concern that he wasn't sure about.

He mused on this for a moment while her mind reached desperately toward the cave, hoping for some kind of salvation.

It did not come.

Though it might be empty, it was not that kind of cave.

He pressed the tip of the knife against her neck. She jerked back. Once more impressed, he commanded her to return to her position. She did, her eyes rolling like a horse's.

"Goodbye. I will see you again."

He pushed the knife in and was grateful that she kept it sharp. He had had his doubts when he found it in the drawer. If he had a kitchen, every knife would have been in its own block. Sharp and ready. He was glad to be surprised. In the city where time lingered, there were few surprises.

He lifted one of the towels to cover the knife, and only then did he pull it out. He felt the jet of hot and wet soak his hand immediately. He laid the tool down and held another towel up to Abigail's throat.

Her will bucked, thrashed, and then subsided as she began to lose consciousness. He dropped one towel and replaced it with the next. In the end, he had to get a fifth to clean up the last of the blood.

He posed her with her pristine book and propped her chin up with one hand. Her elbow balanced perfectly on the table. Once rigor mortis set in, his art would be sturdier. And here, in this dry air, perhaps it would last a thousand years. He put the wet towels into a trash bag and stepped out of the back door. He found a rubber trash can and dropped the bag in.

The man walked around the side of the house and looked at the window where Abigail sat, reading. He said her name,

"Abigail."

He repeated it. He went on repeating it until he fulfilled the proper number. Then he reached out his mind and felt them, all of them in the houses. The punishment had begun. He would not stop until it was complete.

When the man finished repeating Abigail's name, he took a deep breath of hot, dry air. His lips were already chapping, and his throat was parched.

Perhaps, he thought, he could trouble the next person for a glass of water.

Black Out

1

WES CRADLED HIS COFFEE cup and frowned at the poster of the young man above the sink. Beneath the handsome, smiling face, and between two soapy hands, five blue words declared in bold typeface:

SAM SAYS WASH YOUR HANDS!

The Sam pictured was not the Sam of 1994, with streaks of gray in his beard and those little Reed Richards wingtips of gray at his temples. Poster Sam was the Sam of 1977, a man in his mid-twenties. He had the same bright blue eyes, but this man, nearly twenty years younger, wore his light-brown hair just long enough to make him seem cool, but not long enough to make parents worry that he might be a rabble-rouser. The star of *Virtue Vista Valley* walked the same tightrope he had always walked: relevant but not edgy.

Wes sipped his coffee absentmindedly and pulled back when it burned his tongue.

Smart, Wes, very smart. Well, clearly you need it to wake you up enough to remember not to drink scalding coffee. Very Catch-22.

He blew across the mug's top impatiently, waiting for the liquid to cool and inspiration to strike. He gave both the coffee and the muse two more minutes, and when neither obliged, he shrugged at the hygienically concerned Sam and turned to leave the break room.

From the darkness, a fanged face leered at him. Wes jerked back and splashed the hot wake-up water on his shirt.

"God damn it," he said as his brain registered glossy, plaster wings stretched out behind a round, grinning face. It looked like the little bastard was flying right at you with his fangs gleaming yellow-white in the fluorescents. Wes grabbed a towel and dabbed at his shirt, grateful that the mess hadn't been worse. He threw the towel at the pristine picture of Sam, whose blue chambray shirt somehow had no coffee on it after more than fifteen years.

"How the hell did you manage that? I can't make it five minutes."

Sam held up soapy hands, offering a mute smile, but no answer. Wes's frown deepened.

He took his slightly diminished coffee and walked past the five-foot-tall painted plaster bat-boy, giving him a wide berth. What the hell was his name? Something with a B. And something biblical. They loved the biblical names here back in the '60s. Babel? Bartholemew? Was Bartholemew even a biblical name? He thought it was. One of the Apostles, maybe? Beechem? No, Beechem was definitely not biblical.

A dissatisfied grumble rolled at the back of his throat. He should know the flying-rodent boy's name off the top of his head. He sought for it as he strolled back to the writer's room, grateful that the halls were dark. He had worried that Mari would want the empty offices lit up with everyone else gone, but she hadn't tried to turn any on except in the writer's room. Wes had always loved the darkness of empty places after everyone had filed out. Offices during the day were mundane, secular, *business.* But at night, they were caves—god-haunted grottos; the ruins of a vampire's crumbling castle. They were spaces too large for one or two people to occupy without a strange, creeping, ghostly feeling crawling under their skin. He loved that feeling the way some people loved roller coasters, and it usually inspired him. Tonight, however, it didn't seem to be doing the trick. At least, not yet.

It was good to work alone in such a space, but it was even better when you had someone to share the strangeness with. In his experience, that's when the inspiration could really get flowing. He felt his frown easing as he meditated on the gloriousness of the big empty office building, and pictured hunching, lurching figures from old Hammer Horror films swaying in the corners. A thrill of childhood dread put a spring in his step and hurried him along. By the time he got back to the writer's room, he wore a mild grin.

Mari turned in her chair, pushed her short brown hair behind one ear, and smiled.

"What the hell is that bat kid's name?" Wes asked.

"Robin?" Mari said. Her eyes sparkled with mischief that said she knew that wasn't what he meant. They flicked down to his shirt. "Oh? Did he get you?"

"Yes, he did," Wes said as he set his coffee down next to a stack of virgin notepads.

"Ah, dastardly old Baruch," she said with mock whimsy.

"Baruch! Right." Wes licked a coffee-stained thumb. "What the hell is the point of that thing being there? He was on the show for what, a year?"

"One year, one month, one week, and one day," Mari said. She punctuated each period with a click of her pen.

"I … wait, how the hell do you remember that?"

"Don't you read the handbook? You're supposed to read the handbook." She turned back to her notebook of neatly outlined ideas, giving him a quick side-eye and smirk.

"You joke, but clearly you've read it," he said.

"I grew up with this, you didn't. I find it fascinating."

Wes nodded. She was right. Writing for a children's entertainment company was a job, not an interest. It wasn't his art nor his fascination. Still, he regretted not putting more effort into his research. Maybe it would have helped the ideas flow for tomorrow's pitch.

"Still nothing?" he asked, looking down at her notes.

"Not nothing," Mari said. "But … yeah, also not something."

Wes took a deep breath, ran his hands through his salt and pepper hair, and smoothed his mustache. He stood and paced a little before he walked over to one of the chalkboards. Grabbing an eraser, he looked at the chicken scratch that covered the slate and shook his head.

"What can we get rid of?"

Mari turned again and leaned back, poking the button end of her pen into the corner of her mouth. "Hmmm … I think we've pretty much decided against the camper story, so maybe that whole side?"

Wes frowned at the character, location, and plot ideas. He liked the camper idea well enough, but she was right that that was already well-trodden territory. And, besides, he had it all down in his notebook. So, he slapped the old eraser against the board with a white puff and cleared the right side.

"What if?" he asked, as his body wiggled back and forth with long erasing strokes. "What if it's all one story? Across all the games? That way we don't have to come up with three or four stories, just one?"

"That's a great idea," Mari said. "But since we've been struggling to get even that first story broken, I'm not sure that gets us very far."

Wes put the eraser down, wrote the words 'One Story' at the top, underlined them twice, and stepped back. She was right, of course. But maybe the pressure of coming up with four good ideas had been stifling them. He walked back, plopped down into his chair, which groaned a little more than he liked, and took a tentative sip of his coffee. It was getting there.

Something rumbled.

"Was that thunder?" Mari asked.

Wes nodded. "Supposed to be a big storm tonight. Did you bring an overnight bag?"

She shook her head. "No, but if it keeps up, I can just sleep it out in the bunks until the morning and then do a quick stop home."

Wes considered the possibility of them both staying the night and the remote follow-on that they might both stay in the same room. He dropped the thought as she pitched the idea that the game's story might focus on an existing location that they could mine for familiar places and characters. Everything left Wes's mind except for the story. A few minutes later, as they were toying with some version of the same few plot points they had already worked out, the first heavy drops of rain began to fall on the two cars in the parking lot.

2

MARI WANDERED THE EMPTY halls, poking her head into dark rooms, as if she might find a great idea sitting at one of the desks, wandering the lobby, or hanging out playing pinball. She carried a cold beer bottle, swinging it idly at her side. The condensation-wet label brushed her skirt and made a swish-swish sound over a background rumble of rain. Her inspiration-desperate mind listened as distant thunder rolled, hoping that it might trigger something.

She had no idea what kind of story to write for a video game, let alone a whole series. This wasn't what she had come here to do. She wanted to write books. She envied Wes his two published novels, even if they were from the early '70s and forever out of print. If she had something like that on her shelf, with her name staring back at her … well, she would have made it, wouldn't she? That was the goal.

But she had conceded that children's television would do for a start. Though, now apparently, children's video games would do for a start. She hated video games and thought they were vapid, brain-rotting things that people played instead of reading books. Of course, for a medium that she thought was so thin and childish, she was completely unable to churn up even the most basic story.

Did it really matter? Did people care that much?

Probably not. But Annabelle cared. She wanted Mari and Wes to treat her characters with dignity. And that's what they were trying to do … if they could only come up with some kind of clever idea. Or, if not clever, at least workable.

As Mari walked, sipping her beer, fatigue rose through her chest and into her brain. She needed sleep. The thought was just an observation, but it quickly became something more. Maybe laying down in a bunk for two hours or so would give her a fresh perspective. It would clear some of the brain fog and let some ideas grow down in the old collective subconscious. As she strolled past another dark office, poked her head in, and saw nothing more inspiring than a desk fan, she realized that that was almost certainly the thing to do. But not for two hours. That was too much of a gamble—

too much time wasted if she was wrong. So, one hour. One hour of sleep while Wes worked alone, or slept, or whatever it was that he did to get inspired. At this point, if the man needed to run through the halls naked to coax an idea out of hiding, she'd happily fire the starting pistol.

But since that was unlikely to work, another idea came to her. She wondered if the company library had any *Nancy Drew* or *Hardy Boys*. That was the sort of thin literary soup that they might need to slurp down if they were going to pop out a story for this project. Suddenly, she felt a tremor of hope as a plan coalesced. This wasn't a story idea, but it was, perhaps, the way to get one. A little inspirational reading, a short nap, and then … well, maybe the part of their brains that made up entertaining nonsense would do their jobs.

She started off toward the western wing as the loudest thunder yet cracked, making her jump. The steady drumming against the windows grew louder and more insistent, as if the drops were trying to get in. She imagined running back to her car through those heavy, plunking droplets, throwing her soaking self into the front seat, and trying to drive the dark streets back to her apartment in Glory Home.

Thank God for the bunks.

Mari sipped her beer and turned into the long passage that stretched up the western side of the central Crystalline Mansion building. Tall floor-to-ceiling windows ran along her left. In the faint, slanting mixture of parking lot lamps and cloud-dimmed moonlight, the blue and green carpet was a muted mottle. Posters hung behind glass on her right; darkness souring friendly framed faces. Head on, rhinos, camels, and tigers grinned at her amicably enough. But from an angle, shadows tugged them toward idiocy and malevolence.

She stopped when she came to the hallway that connected the central building to the western building. She looked back toward the posters and thought that faces that were friendly close up were sinister at a distance. The idea struck her as poignant. She reached for the thought, got her fingers around it, flipped it upside down, and studied its shell to discern its species. *Nearby smiles are scary from afar.* No. No, that wasn't it. The idea wriggled.

Things that are scary from afar might be friendly up close. Was that it? Was that a moral? Annabelle hadn't told them they needed a moral, but Mari thought it might help.

Had she been a less experienced writer, she might have kept studying the idea. But that never worked for her. She had learned enough about her own process that she knew to put the idea back down and let it continue on its way. If it was promising, she could catch it again somewhere down the line. Her best bet was to stick to her plan and see if the idea of friendly faces crossed her path again.

The hallway that connected the central and west buildings was made entirely of glass, and it thrummed with heavy, plunking, spattering raindrops. It lit with lightning flashes and rumbled with the follow-on thunder.

She froze.

Was that …?

No. That would be silly. And unlikely. And paranoid.

Still, Mari pressed one hand against the glass wall, feeling the vibrations galloping across her fingers, and stared out into the darkness. She could make out the trash can that the smokers stood next to, the little picnic table that had been set up for them, and the shrubs that stood near the front corner of the main building. But she didn't see the outline of a tall, thin man standing in the parking lot. That must have been a trick of light, shadow, beer, and fatigue.

Even so, she didn't have to walk the rest of the way to the library slowly. Mari sipped her beer, stuffed her thumb down into the bottle's neck, and jogged along the passage until she came to the big wooden double doors set into the wall on her right. She pushed through one and slapped at the light switches. A moment later, the whole room started flickering into view.

Mari closed the door behind her, muting the storm. She leaned up against it and looked at the foamy top of her bottle. She pressed it to her lips, lifted her thumb, and sucked the spray down before trotting over to the card catalog. The narrow, wooden drawer was heavy as she pulled it out and started flipping through the cards, looking for the Hardy Boys. It took her less than a minute to find *The Case of the Mill* and noted its location in the 813s. The drawer slid back into place with a *thunk* that was too loud for the library's silence. She tiptoed past the librarian's desk and into the stacks. Three rows of blue-spined books marked with the name 'Franklin W. Dixon' greeted her. Not far down the shelves, she saw three more rows of yellow-edged books with the name 'Carolyn Keene' printed in black. She knew very well that neither author was real, and she sympathized with the many writers who were anonymous behind the well-known names.

"Aren't we all?" she asked and lifted her beer in a brief toast. Then she started thumbing her way along the spines, looking at titles that might inspire their strange little story.

Before she got through them all, however, a row of red books caught her eye. They weren't as numerous as the blue or yellow volumes, but they shook loose a long-hidden memory. Mari pulled one, and the cover greeted her with a painting of a boy and girl standing in a dark cave with a lantern held high.

The cover read, 'The Whispering Cave by T.R. Malcroft.'

"Holy shit," she said too loudly and then repeated herself in a whisper. She sank down until she was cross-legged in the middle of the aisle.

She cracked the front of the book open and turned to the first page. Memories flooded her fatigued mind.

> *It is said that the Whispering Cave has eaten more than its fair share of boys and girls. I do not know how many children the average cave is allotted when it is first carved out by wind and rain, but it seems that Whispering Cave was greedy. Or maybe whatever board of administrators oversees such assignments was careless that day. In any case, the bones of dozens of children lay in dark, forgotten, lonely corners within its twisting, dipping, and damp interior.*

"Wow," Mari said, closing the book and remembering how it had terrified her. "How did this end up as a kid's book? I don't think I slept for a week after I read this."

She felt a shiver go up her spine as the memory came fully into view. She saw herself huddled beneath her covers, afraid to look out into the darkness—lest she see two eyes, pale and glowing with a hint of green cave light. She shook her head, looked back down at the cover, and saw those green eyes barely visible in the dark recesses of the cave just as the lights went out.

3

"WELL SHIT," WES SAID as the room disappeared into darkness. He lowered the chalk and felt around for the blackboard's wooden shelf. His fingers found the little chalk-dust-coated indentations. He dropped the white nub into place and groped through the black for a wall, or the bookcase he knew was standing off to his left. He found it and slowly made his way around the room to the door and, following that, back to the desk.

"Well, Wes, you wanted it dark," he grumbled under his breath as he groped along the wall. The first chair he found was Mari's, the second was his. He slid his hand down into the inside pocket of his jacket that hung across the seat back and found his Zippo. Ecstatic that he had just filled it the day before, he flipped it on and shook his head.

"Great, Wes," he said, "good planning. Giant thunderstorm comes in, and you don't bother getting a single candle." He then wondered where he would have gotten a candle. Then, it struck him that Mari didn't smoke, so she probably didn't have a lighter in her skirt pocket. She would be stuck in the dark, and he should go looking for her. The sane part of his mind considered it a duty, and thus something that he just needed to do. But the writer part of his brain thought that a lighter-lit trek through the big dark office might be just the thing he needed to jog an idea loose.

Wes held the lighter high as he ventured into the hall, calling Mari's name. He had no idea where she had gone, and while the Crystalline Mansion offices were not gargantuan, they spanned three connected two-story buildings. He assumed she hadn't wandered out into the rain to the archives or production buildings—God, he hoped she hadn't done that. He pictured her pummeled by relentless rain in the dark and felt his stomach sink.

No, there's literally no reason why she'd do that. She's too smart to just go wandering off like that.

"Mari!"

He wondered how far his voice would carry as he began an impromptu circuit. He wanted a candle and tried to think who might have one. Then it struck him that Brenda was always burning one in her office. He figured she might have a few stashed away. He changed direction for Brenda's office, continuing to call out to his fellow writer.

Lightning lit the hall and Wes shouted and dropped his lighter.

What the fuck was that? He had never seen that statue with long arms and legs, taking a comical cartoon step, elbows out, knee high. Wes knelt, patted his hands on the carpet, and found his Zippo. He raised his thumb to flick it back on but hesitated. He wasn't sure he wanted to see that statue again. Childhood basement fears roused and whispered that he could slip around the statue in the dark and flip the lighter back on once he was past. He pushed the idea away, but not before he imagined trying to work past the shape and feeling long, bending fingers reaching out and slipping their way around his arm.

Wes snapped the lighter on and stood up. There was nothing—no statue, no poster, no shadow that suggested long arms and legs. He ventured forward slowly, his childhood fear now fully awake as he peered into each office as he passed. Groggily, the fear mumbled that he should run, that whatever he had seen would surely jump out of one of the offices and 'get' him. Wes remembered being terrified of being 'gotten' by the Creature from the Black Lagoon when he was ten years old. Back then, he had no idea what followed 'getting,' only that it was monstrous. It was worse than getting shot, stabbed, or even eaten by a lion. It involved going mad.

Since then, Wes had learned that some men went mad when they were shot. It was enough to know that, as you lay there, a friend holding your head, a sweaty twenty-two-year-old medic doing his best to stop your bleeding, you were never going to see home, the sun, or your mother again. You didn't need the beast with a million eyes, or impossible Lovecraftian shoggoths to come for you.

His mind, flitting from the black-and-white movies of his youth to the unforgiving jungle of Vietnam, suddenly snagged on an idea that pushed his fear into the background. He realized that whatever the monster was in their game, whatever the kids would be up against, it should drive you mad as it ate you. Heavy stuff for kids, he thought, but his childhood urged him down this mental hallway as much as the real one. His present fears forgotten, Wes walked on, his eyes downcast in the act of imagination as the world slipped away.

Though, every few yards, he still remembered to call out Mari's name.

4

MARI WAS FEELING HER way around a corner when the lights came back on. She had heard Wes calling, and she had responded, but wasn't sure if he had heard. So, she slid along a hallway wall, hoping she was going in the right direction to return to the middle building. Her sense of the buildings' layouts, a fortunately timed lightning strike, and Wes's voice confirmed that she was going the right way. When the lights came back on, she shouted again, "Wes!"

"Mari! Brenda's office!"

Mari thought of Brenda's constantly burning candles and smiled. Wes was a smart guy. She immediately broke into a run, grateful she had left her beer behind on the librarian's desk. She would grab it before anyone came in in the morning. She didn't want to run afoul of Mrs. Thellinger.

When she turned the corner and saw Wes, she waved the little red-spined book at him. He waved back, and they met in front of Brenda's office.

"Candles?" she asked as she slowed a few feet from him.

"Yep," he said with a lopsided grin. He held up two glass candles that declared their scents in big, gaudy print: 'Pine Tree' and 'Candy Cane.'

"Oh, good," Mari said. "Perfect for a Christmas story."

"I was thinking the same thing."

"So—" Mari started. She stopped when the lights went out again.

"Shit."

"Oh well, give me just a second."

Glass clinked. Mari heard a click as orange light bloomed in front of Wes. He handed her the lit candle and ignited the second.

"Well, look at you, a regular Daniel Boone."

"I get mistaken for him all the time," he said. And after looking around at their feeble light, he added, "Not sure how much these are going to help us work, though."

"Well, I was thinking about that," Mari said. "I could use a nap. One of those naps that lets your subconscious do the thinking for you. I figured an hour, and then back at it. Oh, and I maybe had an idea for a starting point for us."

Wes nodded. "Yeah, okay. And maybe the power will be back by the time we get up. Are there alarm clocks in the bunks?"

"I think so. It's been almost a year since I did the tour, but I think I remember seeing old wind-up alarm clocks down there."

"Good, that works. I could probably use five or six winks myself," Wes said. "Okay, since I might have skipped the tour day, why don't you lead the way?"

Mari smiled, started for the door, and stopped. A thought occurred to her, and she turned to level him with a suspicious look.

Wes held up his hands. "I know, separate rooms. Don't worry."

She grinned, nodded, and led him to the main stairwell. The heavy door banged open, startling them both. They laughed at themselves before descending past the ordinary basement and an additional eight feet of heavy bomb-shelter concrete. They passed air ducts that snaked upward, poking in and out of hidden pockets in the walls. Mari idly ran her fingers along the metal meant to allow the workers of Crystalline Mansion to survive nuclear winter for ... well ... for who knew how long? Their feet scuffed on the stone basement steps, reminding her of changing classes in school.

When they reached the bottom, they pushed the old, metal door three times before it budged. Finally, it scraped loudly against the cement floor. The sound echoed, suggesting a vast space—like a deep cavern.

Or a Whispering Cave, perhaps?

She thought of the book under her armpit and pushed the thought back as she appraised what the candlelight actually revealed: cubicles. Cubicles adorned with telephones, lamps, typewriters, and chairs that looked like they hadn't been used since Nixon left office. Wes picked up a receiver and put it to his ear. He shook his head as he let it clatter back into place.

It smelled of dust and ... something dry and businesslike that Mari couldn't identify. The familiar scent jogged her memory and filled in the floor's layout. There were five rows of cubicles stretching across the large room. At least fifty people could work here. Against the back ran a row of glass-walled offices for managers to oversee the nightmare work of people doing their jobs of making children's entertainment while nuclear winter rained down from above.

Wes waved for her to follow him. They circled the work area to the right, following old wooden placards that pointed to 'Mess,' 'Facilities,' and 'Bunks.' Other signs pointed in the other direction, letting them know that if they went that way, they'd find the 'Computer Room,' 'Storage,' and 'Outside Access.'

"There are three areas down here," Mari said. "We're under the central building now. The living areas are under the east building, and the computers and all of that are under the west. There's a hallway up here that will take us to an intersection where we'll turn left toward the bunks, if I remember correctly."

She did. They found the hall and came to the intersection. Straight ahead were the facilities—lavatories, showers, and all manner of heaters, furnaces, laundry facilities, and water pumps. To their right was the old, mid-century cafeteria. And to their left was the bunk-pod.

"Um," Mari said. "I should probably hit the girls' room before I go in."

"Same," Wes said. "Um … boys' room, not …"

She laughed and led the way.

Five minutes later, they held their candles high as they entered a square lounge from which twenty narrow bunk rooms sprouted. Six doors stood on each of three walls, and two more flanked the entrance. They grabbed keys from numbered hooks and confirmed they had alarm clocks and fresh bedding.

"Thank God for the housekeeping staff," Wes said.

"Thank God for Annabelle's constant vigilance," Mari said.

"I think you mean paranoia."

Mari shrugged to say, 'What's the difference?'

"Okay, well, see you in an hour," he said, knocking on his door. The sound echoed eerily around them.

Mari wanted to tell him not to do that. Instead, she told him to wake her if she wasn't up in an hour.

"Right," he said, awkwardly. "You do the same."

She nodded, ignored his open posture, and walked into her bunk, closing the door behind her. Her room, like every other she remembered from the tour, packed a small desk, two tall dressers, and two bunk beds into its narrow confines. It was designed to allow up to four people to share the room if they slept in shifts. Mari had read the emergency guide and knew the facility could accommodate up to 240 people during an emergency. That was far more than the number of people who worked on the property, but not more than might be necessary if they brought their spouses and children. The guide had pointed out that smaller children could share beds, as could spouses, if necessary.

She thought it was odd to nap in a place designed to save people from the end of humanity. As she pulled a woolen blanket up to her neck, Mari wondered if someone would one day lie here with their family, praying that the world wasn't ending—a dark thought that lulled her into a thin and fitful sleep.

5

WES MUSED ABOUT THE strange place where he was trying to nap and was grateful that he hadn't drunk too much coffee. He wondered if people ever snuck down here to get a little side action while they were supposed to be on their lunch break. He tried to pair people up. Brenda always got along well with Ernie. Did they ever abscond to the bomb shelter? He amused himself with the thought of it being a new euphemism. "I had a hot date with Gloria, and you better believe we absconded to the bomb shelter." He chuckled at the absurdity of the expression and felt himself begin to drift.

Then, sharp and resonant, a knock yanked him back to consciousness.

His mind and heart raced as he jerked up. Part of him wondered if Mari was coming to share his bunk. Maybe the euphemism might get its first customer, and old Wes might be about to join the mile-below club. He smoothed his thinning hair, stood, tucked his shirt in, relit his candle, and pulled the door open.

There was only darkness.

He grabbed his candle and tried its feeble light against the lounge's black void.

"Hello? Mari?" he ventured. There was no answer.

Wes stepped out into the lounge and saw with surprise and a little dismay that her door was open. He ducked his head inside. Her candle sat next to her rumpled, unmade bed.

"Mari?" he tried again, wondering if she was on one of the top bunks. He stepped inside and checked. She wasn't.

What the hell was this? He ventured into the lounge again and called her name loudly—no response but silence. No … not silence. Not exactly. There was something else there. Something … mechanical? No, he was wrong again. It wasn't exactly mechanical. It was a hum, though. An electric hum. Had the power come back on?

Wes reached into his room and slapped at the wall, finding the switch after three tries. He flicked it. The darkness remained. Either the power hadn't returned, or the maintenance staff were less vigilant about the lightbulbs than they were about the sheets. But Wes didn't believe that for a second.

"Mari, where are you?"

He tried the other rooms, calling out for her. Eighteen rooms, eighteen calls. The whole time, somewhere in the distance droned the warm hum of a … television … maybe? No, it didn't have the high-pitched, almost inaudible, cathode-ray-tube whine of a TV screen. After his circuit, he rechecked their rooms, wondering if he was going crazy. And when he peered into her bunk, he was almost certain he was.

Her candle was gone.

It had been there. It had sat on her desk, giving off its pine-tree scent, and he had thought, *How could she get around without that?* He had had that experience. Or had he? What made more sense? She wandered off without her candle, or that he, half-asleep, had mistakenly thought he had seen it?

Sure … but … he *had* seen it.

He looked at his candle. It had hours left in its thick, peppermint-red body. Grateful for the light, Wes trotted into the darkness, calling for Mari.

6

MARI ROLLED OVER AND dreamed of a town by the sea. A tall man with a top hat greeted her. Though his face was all wrong, he seemed kind. She shook his hand and hugged him. He apologized that he couldn't stop things. Mari understood. As good and well-intentioned as he was, other, bigger players were on the scene. But, at least for now, she could hide here and let him be her friend.

7

AFTER CHECKING THE BATHROOMS, Wes returned to the central office space. He considered going upstairs but rejected the idea. Unless she was trying to hide, she wouldn't just go up without letting him know. Or, at least, he hoped so.

He stalked along the northern edge next to the row of glass-walled offices. If thermonuclear war did happen to rain down on them while they were at work—or within fifteen minutes of work—then what was CM's plan? To keep pumping out children's programming, books, and games? It seemed a little … twisted. Was 'twisted' the word he was looking for? Yeah, twisted—twisted and dystopian. Yes, the world is burning, but let's find out what Sam and the princess get up to next week!

"Mari?"

Of course, he wondered, how would one occupy themselves while the world burned? Work might be a smart idea. It would give people a routine, a plan, and something to spend their hours on. Stockpiling children's entertainment wasn't the worst way to spend your time before it was safe to start repopulating the world.

"Mariana!"

Ahead of him, behind the far wall, was another hallway that would take him to the junction that led under the western building. There, according to the directional signs, he would find the computer room. He wondered if the company had something running on backup power down here. Did that make sense? He wasn't sure. But the idea that something was working off an emergency generator at least tentatively explained the hum.

He reached the far side of the surreal work area. A wall ran across the room here, sectioning off a hallway along the western edge of the building. The wall separated the passage from the big workspace and provided a convenient backstop for about two dozen tall filing cabinets.

He lifted the candle again and looked down the hall. Halfway down on the right, he could make out the opening to the passage west to the computers, storage, and outside access. He followed the wall until he came to the junction and called for Mari.

Something out of the corner of his eye moved at the end of the hallway.

"Mari?" Wes asked. His voice was not so loud this time. Finding that his mouth was too full of saliva, he swallowed and stepped further down the hall, leaving the junction behind him. Five steps later, he saw two things: first, nothing at the end of the hall could have moved—the space was empty; second, it was a closed dead end. It didn't turn back into the workspace. It didn't go off in any other direction. Befuddled, Wes stared at three blank walls. He squeezed his eyes tight and opened them. It took every ounce of self-control for him not to scream, drop his candle, and empty his bowels into his boxers.

The walls were not blank. A framed poster hung in front of him.

SAM SAYS DO A PAL A FAVOR!

Wes backed away, lowering his candle so that he didn't have to see the boy's face, which was pale and bug-eyed—a distorted version of Sam from thirty years ago. He tried to justify the poster's appearance, but his mind declined the task.

"Oh, fuck this," he said to himself and then regretted it, immediately picturing a poster appearing with the words, 'Sam Says, Watch Your Language.'

He retreated to the intersection, turned, and headed west toward the computer wing. Weakly, he called for Mari as the hum grew louder.

8

MARI SAT ON A dock, swinging her feet above the water. To her left, somewhere, there was a beached whale. That was sad. Beyond the creature, a Victorian house nestled on a rocky hill. It also made her feel sad. The whole place was depressing in a way she couldn't understand. But it was also glorious. The sadness was part of something bigger. She didn't know what the bigger thing was, but she suspected it might lie across the ocean. She licked at an ice cream cone and wondered what else might be further down the boardwalk.

9

WES CAME TO ANOTHER junction, read the wooden placards, and continued straight ahead. The hum thrummed loudly from behind pale blue-green double doors at the end of the hall. He thought his mother had owned a toaster of the same color. He tried one of the doors, certain it would be locked. People didn't just leave computer rooms open for anyone to wander into.

Or maybe they did, because the door pushed open easily.

The strong scent of ozone met him as he stepped into a pale yellow-green light that wavered from a dense clutter of old computers. Some looked like refrigerators, some like metallic, outsized living room furniture, and some were the size of old cocktail arcade games. Lights blinked dimly across grids of bulbs, tapes spun slowly, and a sluggish dot-matrix printer scratched softly along somewhere.

One recognizable piece of technology stood in the center, on what looked like a podium, glowing with green letters on a black background. He put his candle down on a computer console straight out of *Star Trek*—the kind of thing Lt. Uhura or Data would sit at—and walked toward the central computer screen.

Four words glowed up at him.

UNPLUG ME, WONTCHA, PAL?

After the question mark, a green rectangle flashed into and out of existence. Wes stared at the blinking light box.

"What the fuck?" Wes whispered.

The box stopped blinking and moved across the screen in little steps. Each time it took a step, it left a letter in its wake. After a few seconds, it completed the line,

MIND YOUR P'S AND Q'S, THIS IS A CHILDREN'S SHOW.

Wes stepped back.

"Hello? Is someone listening? Is someone there?"

He didn't think there was. He didn't believe that a man—a man who just happened to be down here at night, waiting for someone to shamble into the computer lab—would come out from some dimly lit corner. The alternative, though … what even was the alternative? That the computer was listening to him?

Wes had had a computer since 1988. He knew what they could do. He had even done a little programming, which he thought had helped him get this job. He knew there were at least a hundred years between his computer and the computer on *Star Trek*, the old one with Spock, and at least two hundred years between him and Data. He wasn't certain when computers would start listening and talking back, but he was reasonably sure it wasn't 1994.

The little block moved again.

SURE, I'M RIGHT HERE. AND DO YOU KNOW WHAT I'D LIKE? TO NOT BE HERE. THAT WOULD BE SWELL. SO, IF YOU COULD JUST PULL THAT OLD POWER CABLE AND LET NATURE TAKE ITS COURSE, THAT WOULD BE THE BEE'S KNEES. SO, HOW ABOUT DOING YOUR NEW PAL A FAVOR AND PULL THE PLUG?

Wes shook his head. His mind bounced back and forth between the notions that there must be a person hidden in the big humming room and that this computer was actually talking to him.

Wes would ponder that thought for years until he had an answer. But, for the moment, his contemplation of the question was put on hold. A scream, distant but clear, broke through his fevered contemplation. Was that Mari? Who else could it be? Like a starter pistol in his mind, the scream triggered an old reflex. Wes stopped thinking, turned, and sprinted through the big doors and out of the room.

He hadn't run like this since '68. He had jogged, trying to keep himself in shape, and he thought he had done a pretty good job of it, despite his growing gut. But he hadn't run all-out like this in almost thirty years. He wondered if he'd have a coronary, or an aneurysm, or if he'd just bust his knees up so badly that he'd crash into one of the walls or cubicles.

He didn't crash into anything but total darkness. The moment he exited the computer room, he realized he had left his candle behind. He skidded to a halt, turned, and started feeling for the doorknob. It took him a few seconds, but he found it. He pushed down and found it locked. He rattled it, jerking it up and down, but it would not budge.

"Hey!" he shouted. There was only silence.

Shit. Shit.

He tried again, suddenly feeling the dark as more than just an inconvenience. It skittered across his shoulders and ran its finger down the back of his neck. His mind flashed back to the figure he had seen in the blink of light, the movement in the darkness, the words on the computer screen.

UNPLUG ME, WONTCHA, PAL?

For some reason, the words played in his head like Tim Curry as the clown on that TV series from a few years back.

What the hell is happening?

He took a breath, tried to remember how he had not lost his mind while being shot at daily halfway around the world, and groped for a little of that calm. He had been twenty-two, not fifty, and there had been other men at his side, men he had to be brave for.

Mari. I have to be brave for Mari.

He gave the door one last push and pull, cursed again—thinking that Sam and the computer could screw themselves—and turned. He slapped his hand against the left wall and jogged. He knew nothing was in the passage until the junction, so he moved with the trepidatious certainty his memory of the hall would allow him.

When his fingers found no more wall, he paused, made sure he was at the corner, and did his best to line himself up flat against the wall that turned to his left. His goal was to face the opposite wall as squarely as possible and walk as straight as he could until he hit the far side. He knew it was a literal shot in the dark, like trying to walk in a straight line with your eyes closed, but he also figured that even if he didn't go perfectly, he would still hit the wall. And then he'd follow it back to the junction and be on his way. He had a map in his mind, and he thought it was a pretty good one. He just had to follow it, be careful, and be quick.

Before he started across, he got scared that he might miss the far wall and end up going down the opposite corridor without realizing it. Ultimately, that's where he wanted to go, but could he be sure it was the right path if he didn't reassure himself with each little mile marker? No, probably not. And, if he had heard her scream, he guessed Mari couldn't afford him to mess up and try again. So, he slunk down the wall a little further to make certain that he was facing only the opposite wall.

But as he slunk, he bumped up against something. Something soft and heavy—cloth covering something that gave a little. Like a body. The form jostled at his intrusion and then lay still. Was it a dummy? Why was there a dummy here? Or was it one of the costumes for the show? The thought of some old tiger suit or rhino costume didn't calm him. His already pounding heart picked up its pace.

He squared himself. It was time to leave, no matter what the hell was pressing up against him. And as he pushed himself off the wall, two things happened.

First, he screamed. No, that was second.

First, something soft and heavy, like a big, gloved hand, slid down his arm and squeezed his wrist.

Then he screamed.

He howled, pulled his arm away, and took three quick steps until he found the far wall. He pressed his back to it and slid to his left until he came to the corner. He followed it around, did his best not to look back into the darkness, put his hand back on the wall, and then ran for all he was worth.

When he came to the end of that wall, things would be simpler, he knew. He followed it to the left, down the long hallway until it ended in a corner. Then, to the right, back into the cubicle-filled work area. But when he reentered the big workspace, he didn't have to rely on his touch method. The room glowed with a faint green light. Each desk gave off a pale incandescence from old monochrome computer screens. Had they been there before? He didn't think so. He thought there had been typewriters. Was something wrong with his memory?

Something shuffled heavily behind him. He didn't look back. By the dim light, Wes ran across the room and stumbled to a halt in the far hallway. His adrenaline-soaked body slapped into the wall, and he felt something in his pocket. Shit … his lighter. Of course!

"Get it together, idiot," he said as he flicked the small flame to life. He held it in front of him and jogged forward, into the hallway where the light of the computer screens didn't reach. "Mari!"

Silence weighed on him as he reached the intersection of Mess, Facilitates, and Bunks. He thought he saw a light coming from the Mess Hall. He flicked his lighter closed and jogged down to find a cafeteria-style room. No, not a cafeteria exactly, more like a food court you'd find in a mall. There were six different service stations, each with a sign above it. The light was too dim to make them out. But he thought that one was Chinese food, another might be pizza, and one was definitely ice cream. A counter ran along a wall, with stools set every couple of feet. In the middle of the room were three dozen round tables with chairs.

And in the center of the room was the light source—no, light *sources*. Eight tall candles stood atop a clumsily iced and lopsided birthday cake. Wes took one curious step toward the light and then shook his head.

"Oh no," he said. "That's not … okay, time to go."

He turned around, ready to run, and saw a small, bouncing, orange light heaving up and down further up the hallway. His heart jumped, and he crouched, ready to run, hide, or fight.

Then Mari came sprinting out of the darkness, her wavering candlelight barely holding on as she ran.

"Wes!" she screamed. He ran toward her, grabbed her as they met, and spun her around behind him. He started to back up the way he had come, keeping himself between her and whatever she had been running from.

"What is it?" he cried.

"I don't know … Something, something in the dark. I went looking for you, but you were gone."

"I was looking for you."

"What do you mean? I was in my bunk!"

He cursed and spat into the hallway. It felt crude, but he had seen his grandmother do it when she thought the evil eye was present. It was a primal, ancient act, and it made him feel better, at least for a moment.

"Come on, let's…" Wes stopped. Mari's hand on his shoulder had started shaking. No, not shaking, vibrating—like a plane in bad turbulence.

He turned. "What is—"

His question died.

Their collision and subsequent retreat had pushed them back into the little food court. He had been right—Chinese food, pizza, ice cream. There was a health-food place, a deli, and a spot for burgers and dogs. And there were people. Dozens of people. Pale, almost black-and-white, people. And they all stared at them. Their eyes were sunken, hollow pools of off-white in rings of 1950s-TV gray.

The only colors on the people were their conical paper birthday hats, which were all blue.

The signs of the food stations were lit. And each sign displayed the same two words in rusty red neon:

Unplug Us

Mari turned to Wes, and they spoke at the same time,

"Run."

They ran.

They ran forward, back toward the bunks. The figure that loomed in the darkness ahead of them was tall and looked like he was made of felt cloth from head to toe. He wore a squat hat of some kind and was far too thin. They turned left, away from him, back to the office area. They slid along the wall, hoping to make for the stairs, to go back the way they had first come. But a crowd had gathered there. Dim faces under blue birthday hats in pale light, pleading in front of screens that repeated the same two words.

```
UNPLUG US. UNPLUG US. UNPLUG US. UNPLUG US. UNPLUG US.
UNPLUG US. UNPLUG US. UNPLUG US. UNPLUG US. UNPLUG US.
UNPLUG US. UNPLUG US. UNPLUG US. UNPLUG US. UNPLUG US.
UNPLUG US. UNPLUG US. UNPLUG US. UNPLUG US. UNPLUG US.
UNPLUG US. UNPLUG US. UNPLUG US. UNPLUG US. UNPLUG US.
UNPLUG US. UNPLUG US. UNPLUG US. UNPLUG US. UNPLUG US.
UNPLUG US. UNPLUG US. UNPLUG US. UNPLUG US. UNPLUG US.
```

They turned and followed the hall back to the row of glass-walled offices. Behind, the tall, felt-cloth figure stepped out of the junction of hallways and pivoted toward them. They sprinted along offices, catching minute flashes of the figures who dwelled there.

One at her desk, her eyes black and red pits.

One slowly swinging from the ceiling.

One with legs sticking out from behind the desk.

One naked upon her desk, cross-legged, her hat pushed to the side, shoveling cake into her gaping mouth.

The horrid tableaus slipped past on their right. On their left, the crowd of workers began to rise from their desks.

Mari screamed, cursing. She ran faster, leaving Wes a few steps behind. She slammed into the far wall, her candle's meager light surviving only because of how low Barbara had burned the wax. It nestled behind its glass walls, wavering and guttering, but not going out.

Wes caught up to her, pointed down the passage, and said, "That's a dead end, go right!"

A dead end, but not empty, Wes thought as he saw something climbing out of the poster while they scooted around the corner to find the computer room facing them from far down the passage. Its open doors emitted a weak, jittering light. They hurried toward it and stopped at the next junction. The heads of animal costumes littered the floor where Wes had felt the soft, heavy figure grab his wrist. A forest of rabbits, dogs, camels, and bears looked up at them, their eyes empty-black.

"Come on!" Mari said, taking Wes's hand and pulling him. They turned left, following the little wooden plaque that had once read 'Outdoor Access,' but now implored, 'Unplug us.'

They came to old concrete stairs and stamped up them, switching back once, and then again. Then they threw themselves against heavy double doors, two kids bursting out of the last day of school into the waiting arms of summer break. Rain pummeled them, punching them with heavy, stinging drops. The candle finally died, and Wes's Zippo gave out. But there was enough moonlight, cracking its way through the storm, to show them Wes's fifteen-year-old station wagon.

Wes fished in his pocket for keys as they ran, pictured them in his jacket pocket hanging on the back of a writer's room chair, and then remembered that he never bothered to lock his doors here. He yanked open the driver's door and yelled, "Get in!"

Mari threw herself into the passenger seat. They were both shivering as much from fear as the cold, brutal shower they had just taken. They took a minute in the car, breathing.

"My keys are back inside," Wes said, shaking his head. "I'm sorry."

"Are we safe in here?" Mari asked, trembling violently, and rubbing her arms.

"I have no idea," Wes said. "But ... maybe? God, I don't know. I hope so."

When nothing happened for ten minutes, Wes contorted himself around to get into the back seat. Then he started lowering seat-backs to make a flat space. He pulled his old sleeping bag from some clutter and fashioned a pillow out of his old rucksack.

"Come on," he said. Mari didn't hesitate. She climbed under the unzipped bag and nestled up against Wes. They lay, staring out into the darkness as the rain hammered the car's roof. Wes committed himself to keeping watch so that Mari could sleep. But her warmth and softness comforted and lulled him, and in less than twenty minutes, he was snoring softly.

<h1 style="text-align:center">10</h1>

THERE WAS NO SCANDAL at work the next day, even though a half-dozen employees saw the fifty-year-old Wes snuggled up to the twenty-two-year-old Mari in the back of his car. No one gossiped, and no one gave them a sidelong look. When Wes entered the office, still wet, looking for his keys, Chuck approached him, patted him on the shoulder, and, unexpectedly to both men, hugged him. "You okay?"

The bigger man rubbed at his mustache and shook his head. "No, I don't think so."

Chuck nodded and got Wes a cup of coffee.

Mari went home and didn't come back until the following day. Annabelle called her into a two-hour-long meeting. When Mari came out, she wore an expression that none of the younger employees could identify, but the longer-term CM people knew well. Wes had the same look when he left Annabelle's office later that day. He went to Mari's desk and sat on its edge, crossing his feet in front of him.

"So, you're off the project?"

She nodded.

"I don't blame you. But I'll be honest, I'll miss working with you. You've got talent."

She smiled at him. It was a resigned, tight smile. "You could tell that from my writer's block?"

He nodded. "Sure, we got it together. And I know I'm good at this, so that's a good sign."

He gave her a half-hearted smile, which she reciprocated. "I'm sure we'll work together again, Wes."

Mari reached up and squeezed his hand. When he left, she stared at her office wall before she was pulled back to the present by the bright red spine of a book on her desk. Her heart galloped until she jammed the book into a mail envelope and wrote 'Library' in the next empty space. She stood, dropped the envelope into the mail slot outside her door, and then closed the door behind her.

11

WES SAT IN HIS office and couldn't decide if he should try to push the whole experience out of his mind or if he should try to understand it all. Chuck brought him a drink at 5:00, and the two men sat together as Chuck told Wes that there were big things ahead for him at Crystalline Mansion. When Wes stood up to leave, he thought the man gave him a look that said, 'Hope I see you tomorrow.'

Wes thought it was entirely possible that neither Chuck nor anyone else at Crystalline Mansion would see him the next day or any day after. He thought the best thing for him might be to throw his spartan life into his old station wagon and head out for one coast or the other and see where fate would take him.

But he thought of Mari and the fact that she was staying. He didn't like thinking of her without someone who understood what she had gone through. So, he downed the last few drops of his drink and decided that Chuck would see him the next day, and the day after.

As he drove home, Wes couldn't help but remember the feel of Mari against his chest and her slowing, soft breathing that had lulled him into his own slumber. He remembered the feel of her fingers in his as she squeezed his hand. He wondered if she'd ever do that again.

But, except for a few reserved hugs and kisses on the cheeks at company parties, Mari would not touch Wes again until her daughter's christening. Then, she would hug him tightly before kissing him properly for two glorious seconds.

"Thank you," she would say.

And he would be happy for her.

And he would love her daughter.

1

LOUIS WRINKLED HIS NOSE as he rubbed pungent oil into his elbow. It was sour, full of deadly herbs and roots. But they warmed his stiff limb and stung it soothingly, chasing the throbbing ache away. He worked his arm in and out, in and out. It was better. Not perfect, but today he didn't need perfect. Today, he was going to die, and he just needed it to work well enough to get him through.

With his elbow as mobile as he was likely to get it, he turned to oiling his gun. The revolver wasn't yet ten years old, but it had a hell of a history. He had bought it from a man who had come begging to Weeping Cedars in '66. One eye gone; one foot gone; he still had his pistol. So, Butler bought it from him for $5, a meal, and a good bottle of rye whiskey. The man had gone away feeling like he had gotten one over on the poor ol' boy. But he hadn't. Butler would have happily paid double for that particular piece of iron.

Stamped into the top of the barrel was 'Leech & Rigdon CSA,' which suited him just fine. He wasn't a man for many jokes, but he enjoyed that a gun made for keeping people like him in chains was now in his hands. It put him in the strange position of praying that the rebel factories had done their work well. He prayed that peculiar prayer as he worked on the metal with his oilcloth. Today, his life would not depend upon the revolver, but perhaps many others would.

He eyed each chamber in the cylinder, cleaned it, and started loading. He used paper cartridges, pushing each into place, rotating them under the gun, and levering down the ram-rod mechanism. His fingers worked as his mind traced his path up from Georgia, beyond the fire, and through the door.

He knew there wasn't much a man could do to improve the world. But God Almighty, there was a lot he could do to make it worse. He capped his bullets, locked the hammer between two chambers, and stood up from his desk. He worked the elbow and frowned as he walked to the window that looked out over Djavulen Avenue. Horses pulled carts, horses stood hitched to posts, and horses carried men along on their business. He wondered about that—the world, reality. It had been before him, and it would go on after him. A factotum divorced from his existence. Persistent in a way he wasn't.

He had no fear that death was the end. He had seen far too much for that. If the materialists were right, he had walked in pathways that could not be. But walked them, he had. Some part of him wished he could retreat to a crass finitude, a universe haunted only by the imaginations of jumped-up apes and fish that had dreamed themselves legs for dry land—mere dust that had cast its own horrible shadow on the universe and fancied everything to be greater than it was. But that was the kind of fantasy Louis Butler could not allow himself.

He sniffed, rubbed his nose, and laughed. He was getting a cold. He pulled a handkerchief, blew into it, and pushed it into his back pocket. It was almost time. Another horse would trot down the street soon, and four people would pile out of its carriage. He hoped only three of them would get back in. That was the plan. If it were fewer … well, in that case, he could still die easy enough.

Louis pulled his sleeves down to his wrists and returned to his desk. The notes were there: one for Sharon, one for Margaret, and one for the girl. She wouldn't be born until sometime next year, but she would need that note. Someone would give it to her. He trusted that. His fight would become her fight. He hated that.

He looked around his room, where he had done what men called "business." He touched the wood panel wall one last time, ran his fingers over the leather back of his chair, and said his goodbyes. He breathed the room in and stepped into the open space before his desk. He closed his eyes, counted the darknesses behind his eyelids, and slid away. His stomach turned with illogic. He screamed in a language none knew and fewer could hear.

He moved.

This was the easiest it had ever been. Perhaps the proximity of death made it so. Within one heartbeat, he was walking the streets of the Dark City. The Lamplighter had done his work here, and Louis watched as the city's hunching, cowering folk disappeared into their dark doorways and pulled their curtains shut. He knew that they were not hiding from him. He would be nothing more than a curiosity, another soul pulled into the city of madmen. But someone else was coming to meet him, and the people could feel his approach. This was a good—if terrifying—prospect, so Louis walked, hands in pockets, waiting for the thing to appear.

He whistled to himself as towering spires twisted their way upward and clouds and moons moved overhead. Impossibly thin, silken-threaded walkways drifted from one tower to the next, lit by green-mad flames that wavered in the unrelenting night.

He hoped he would never return. Perhaps his death would guarantee that. He had hoped to prevent anyone from coming here ever again, but that had turned out to be too much. He had become mighty over the years, but shutting the door was not in his power. He was not the Bear.

"You should not be here," a dry, placid voice said. Louis felt his bowls quake at its presence—at its owner's sheer age and *otherness.*

Louis turned and saw the figure, tall and robed. "I know," Louis said, trying not to betray the terror in his gut.

"Then why have you come? Are you setting a beacon? Are you calling me to you? I will find you. I will consume."

Louis shook his head. "No. I have come to tell you something. To give you that thing you want more than anything else—knowledge."

The figure stepped forward, its dark robe shifting like midnight waters, the chain at his belt clanking. His hand rose from his side, and long, pale, bone-thin fingers emerged from a black sleeve. They unfurled like a waking spider, twitching out, one at a time.

One finger pointed at Louis.

"Speak."

"Your adversary is making a claim today, in my home."

"There are many pitiable minds that stand against me. Of which do you speak?"

"The Queen," Louis said, trying to sound confident. The truth was that he knew little about the relationship between the two powers.

"Which Queen?"

This was new. Louis had only seen one figure who called herself a queen.

"I … She … she lives on a hill, in a house of glass—"

The hand straightened, showing a palm covered in fine, white hair. Louis froze. A thrill of fear ran through him. He could feel the confidence of his preparations waning. "Speak to me of her plans."

"Today she seals her vessel. I need your help. I need to stop it."

The hand closed all but one finger, which pointed down at the cobblestone road. He looked down and saw a symbol burning in one of the stones. He knelt and studied it.

"What is its name?" Louis asked.

Were he twenty years younger, Louis would not have been able to hear the word the robed man spoke, let alone comprehend. But now, at his end, Louis's mind stretched and took the word of power in as he traced its shape with his finger. He felt it scorch his thoughts and knew it was what he had hoped for.

"Do not fail, little mortal, lest she turn your world into her forest."

Louis stood and regarded the tall being, something that had once been a creature like himself. Not a human, perhaps, but close.

"This will be the last time we speak," Louis said. "I wish I had never opened the door. That is my sin."

"You speak in vain, and you wonder idly. Ensure you do not die idly, lest I revenge myself upon your seed in the earth. Now go, man-thing. Walk in this place no more."

The pain of being forced away, through the door, and once more into his own body shocked him. He fell to his knees, clutching his head. The rune—twisting, worming, and writhing—burned his mind. It was not alive, but perhaps, neither was its master. It shifted with the same unlife that drove the necropolis like a self-moving steam engine. Louis knew that even if the people did not slay him, the mark of power would burn him from within before long. He focused and began to set wards in his mind against it. They would not last forever, but he hoped they would hold while he needed them—long enough to walk down a few steps and to look the monsters in their eyes.

Louis stood, touched the notes again, prayed, and then pulled his suspenders over his shoulders. He donned his wool jacket, straightened his tie in the old, scratched mirror his aunt had found somewhere on their flight from Georgia, and looked at the clock on the wall.

Close enough.

He took one last look out the window and winced. The word jumped in his mind, battering against his spells, trying to escape. He shut his eyes, focused, and quieted it for the moment.

He heard a shout and saw a carriage rumbling onto the street. That must be the one. Louis waited and watched as it pulled up in front of his building. The door opened, and a well-dressed young man emerged, followed by another taller and lankier. They helped two women step out onto the street. Four arrived together, and Louis Butler vowed to diminish their number by one.

He clutched his head and sank once more to his knees. The desire to blast them, to rend them, to tear them to pieces in the street overwhelmed him. But if he did, if he let the word out in that public place, how diffuse would its power become? How many who did not wear the arcane protection of the Queen would die? How much more blood would be on his hands?

No. He knew where they were going. He just needed to hold on for a few more minutes. He closed his eyes and leaned against the wall below the window, his knees pulled up toward his chin. Louis Butler wrapped his arms around his knees, much as he had as a child in the back of the covered wagon that took them north along rural roads, under the cover of night.

His aunt's hand rubbed the back of his neck as she sang something low and long forgotten. The mark of power burned, and he used his best magic against it. He thought of Sharon, of her love and respect. He prayed for her and realized that though she was strong magic, there was at hand, an even mightier incantation.

Louis Butler rolled himself back to his knees, folded his hands, and prayed for the four people who were walking into his building.

2

A GREAT TIDE OF words rumbled up the basement stairs. They were not English, not German, nor Hebrew, nor Greek. They did not resemble the smattering of Chinese he knew, nor the little Japanese he had been taught. The words were guttural, barking, fearsome sounds. They scared Louis.

He stood at the top of the stairs and held his pistol in one hand and a little book in the other. The rune of power slumbered uneasily, warming his thoughts, but not searing them. He started down, creeping from one wooden step to the next. In the dim light of the high-set windows, he saw three people standing around a fourth. The person in their midst was one of the women. She sat on an old wooden crate, her face hidden by a veil and her head bowed. The three who stood around her extended their arms toward each other. They might have been dancing or mocking the Crucified One with their posture. Butler thought both were equally likely.

He watched as they stood. Though the strange words reverberated around the room, the three people's mouths were not moving. The torrent of strange words came from the shadows, as if from an unseen multitude. And though he could not see them, their presence was heavy; cloying, damp, and dripping. He found it hard to breathe, to concentrate. The word in his mind began to slumber more deeply, the drear and sodden words dousing its fire.

He felt his legs weaken as if he were nodding and might tumble down into sleep and onto the old dirt floor. Butler caught himself, gripping the railing so tightly that his elbow flared in pain. That was good. The pain roused him.

He took the last few steps quickly and quietly, slipping behind one of the brick columns. The people's eyes were closed as the voices scuttled out of the darkness. The moment was near. He would have no room for mistakes. If he made his attempt a few moments too early, they could try again with someone else after disposing of him. A few moments too late and it would … well, it would be too late.

Louis knelt and placed the book on the ground. He took dirt between his fingers. Here. Here, the woman had shed her skin the first time. Here, she had taken the first girl from this new world. Here, the power was raw and vital and stinking of that dark city. This was why they had come here to do their work. That was their strength, and it would be their undoing, for the word of flame in his mind would also be mighty here.

"Someone is here," a voice said. It was cold, hollow, and dead. It rattled out of one of the dark corners, from behind some crates or one of the other brick columns. He heard footsteps.

"They wish to join us," said another brittle voice.

"No, they wish to kill us."

"They want to burn the forest."

A chorus of whispered conflict rose around him, and Louis knew that even if he covered his ears, he could not drown them out. He had opened himself to this species of horror, and he must endure it. He patted the little leather book, feeling its smooth cover. It was where it should be. He prayed he could live long enough to read it one last time.

Then Louis Butler, his back to the brick column, crossed his flesh with the barrel of the pistol and woke the rune in his mind.

It burned him, and he moved. He spun, planting one knee into the dirt, and pivoting on it, bringing himself around the column, keeping it between most of his body and the others, as if they were going to shoot at him. For all he knew, they might. But that possibility didn't concern him. It was old habit that moved him. Old habit and that fool, Hope, that had sat upon his shoulder all his life.

He saw them see him. He saw the woman raise her veiled head and fix her hidden eyes upon his.

She laughed. Perhaps it was his gun. Perhaps it was his black skin. Perhaps it was the fact that he knelt behind the column as if it would protect him. She laughed as one who is above all possible danger. She was a queen guarded by her doughty knights, a goddess enthroned on her high mountain, an elfin princess surrounded by her forest. Who came to her with brick, steel, and lead? Someone to be derided. Someone to be pitied. Someone to be laughed at. Someone to be squashed.

But she should not have laughed. If there was a knight in the room, it was Louis. Old he was, with white in his black hair, lines at the corners of his eyes, and lines between his eyes. He had an elbow that ached like a tooth that needed pulling, and a soul steeped in foolishness and sin. Yet, for all that, he was mighty. None alive upon the earth could have held that word in their mind without burning to a cinder.

None but Louis.

And he, sinner knight, unleashed it into their midst.

There was neither fire, nor light, nor a spark from any metal. The only sign that something had happened was that everyone in the room fell at once. Silently, they crumpled to the earth where She Carries the Winter Sky died. They fell with the slightest thud, arms sprawling, fingers curling, legs comically straight or softly bent.

They all lay still. One minute. Two. Then they began to stir. Louis was not the first, though he had hoped to be. He had thought that his preparations might give him that one advantage. He had been ready. He had made his wardings upon his flesh and within his mind. But despite his work, the veiled woman moved first. Her arm twitched, then her leg. And soon, she was pulling her knees to her chest. By then, Louis could twitch his foot and work his tongue.

She rolled onto her back and began to sit up. He blinked. He blinked and could move his lips.

With a violently trembling hand, she tore the veil away. She was beautiful. The woman was thirty, perhaps a little older. Her eyes were soft, blue, and terrible. She did not blink, did not work her lips, did not spend any energy except to draw a small, thin knife from her boot. Louis twitched his arm. The muscles felt like they were more than asleep. No pins and needles prickled. Instead, there was only the faintest feeling of his arm's weight pressed against his side. He willed it to move, begged it to move, and prayed what he thought might be his last prayer that it would move.

She pushed herself onto her knees and placed one hand into the dirt. She fixed him with a passive stare. The woman wasted no energy on emotion. He thought she would crawl to him, run the blade across his throat, and put an end to his hopes quietly and finally. Instead, she started to push herself to her feet. Louis panicked. If she rose, she could fall on him, plunge the weapon down. He didn't know why, but this sent shocking waves of horror through his body. That she should lay on him, that this woman should put her body against his at the end when he had only lain with one woman in his life, only allowed one woman to lay upon his flesh … it was madness to worry about such things, but the thought chilled him more than the idea that she might open his throat.

The woman rose unsteadily, her blade catching the light from a slanting window, glinting, leaving a red outline in his vision when she took her first faltering step.

His arm twitched but wouldn't move. But he could feel it now, the ache in his elbow where he had broken it. He had worried then that he would never be able to use the arm again. That same worry returned as he lay in the basement dirt.

The woman took her second step toward him. It was a mistake. She should have crawled. She was strong and well-protected. Maybe Louis had waited just a second too long. Perhaps there was never any right moment for his spell to break through the layers of warding that had already been laid upon her. Even so, it had taken much from her. More than she thought, for, with her second step, her knee buckled. Her other leg didn't have the strength to compensate, and she went down.

She did not lose her knife, though. She landed with it outstretched, pointed at Louis with only a few feet between them.

One last throw, he thought. *One last chance to redeem yourself. To stand, if not proud on Judgement Day, at least not entirely ashamed. Just move your damned arm. Move the cursed thing a little. Just a little.*

And it moved a little. Just a little.

It was a paltry spasm compared with her growing strength. She pulled the knife back, drew it close to her, and sat upright. He knew she wouldn't make the same mistake twice; knew she would crawl to him now. He had seconds.

Out of the corner of his eye, he saw one of the men's feet flick back and forth once. Whatever was about to happen, it would be over before that man could do anything. Whatever was about to happen was between Louis Butler and this woman whose name he did not know.

She came on then, one knee forward, followed by the other. Her dress hampered her just a little, long enough for Louis to pray for forgiveness—if there could be forgiveness for his sin. He prayed for the words he had spoken, the look in the young woman's eyes so many years ago, for his wickedness in the face of innocence. He prayed for the man he had been. He hoped that his Judge might relent a little if the will of God could have mercy on such a worm as he knew he was.

His arm moved a bit more, and she came closer, her free hand finding his hair, tangling in its wild and coarse strands. Her fingers tightened.

Oh, God of my fathers, forgive me. Forgive me for every door to Hell I've ever opened. Please ... please ... please let me close this one a little.

He would never know what happened to that young woman he had spoken to so coarsely many years ago. The blight of his words had perhaps marked her forever, but they had certainly stained him. He had suspected his sins would haunt him in his last moments, and he was not wrong.

Louis wept as his arm moved again.

She rose on her knees, bringing the blade up.

One more move.

Then his finger squeezed.

The Leech and Rigdon fired its last bullet for three decades. A man would buy it at an auction five years later, and his son would clean it, restore it, and use it for target practice. That son would draw it one night in a panic to protect his young wife from an intruder. It would end up in a reenactor's possession a hundred years on and eventually sit in a museum as a testament to some mottled confusions of duty, wickedness, and sorrow. But in all its days, before rusting away, it would never do such good service as it did in Louis Butler's hand on that August day of 1872. On that day, it fired true and hit its mark, sending lead deep into the woman's body, tearing into her gut.

She did not scream. She barely moved. She looked with that placid, unblinking face at Louis. Then she fell upon him, sinking the knife deep into his flesh.

And darkness came.

3

HE WOKE A LITTLE as they pulled her body from his. He screamed himself to full consciousness as one of the men drew the knife from his chest.

"Well," the younger of the two men said. "I'll give you this much: that was a good effort, my boy."

Louis was surprised. The man couldn't have been more than twenty years old. But maybe the pain and darkness were playing tricks on Louis. His chest burned, and he wheezed when he breathed. Something felt like it was sitting on his chest.

"Help him up," said another voice. They both had a twang. Was it Southern? No, Yankee. Far North Yankee.

"Book," Louis wheezed.

They pulled him up and put his back against the old brick column. The younger man put his hand under Louis's chin and tilted his head up.

"What was that now?"

"B ... book." Louis shrugged slightly and turned his head a little to his right.

"Now, no offense, boy, but why would I do that?"

Louis tasted blood as he whispered. The man leaned in close to hear him.

"And why would I want you to?" the Yankee asked.

"Because—" Louis said. He saw red spattered on the man's face. He seemed unconcerned. "The poison works both ways."

The young man with blood on his face frowned at Louis before calling over his shoulder. "How is she?"

"She's fine … it's … it's already closed." The speaker was a woman—the other woman. The one he hadn't shot. But could it be true? The wound was already closed. Had he failed so completely? Please, God, let him do the last thing then. Let him not die a complete and absolute failure.

"Hmm. I'll tell you what. We've done our bit. And you've shown us a great sign. Without you, we'd have to wonder. We'd have to walk by faith. But you have allowed us to walk by sight. So, I'm going to grant you two boons. First, you can have your book if you can reach it. And second, I'll say your name so you can enter the forest."

"That's not enough," another woman's voice said. Louis's eyes went wide as a woman walked into his vision. She stood in her white dress, with scarlet and black blood staining across her middle, like a child had been ripped from her body.

"We will engrave your name, witch. Engrave it thrice. You will not just come to the forest; you shall be enshrined."

"Yes," the Yankee said. "Yes, so shall it be." He moved his hand from under Louis's chin and placed it on his forehead. "Louis Butler," he said.

He smiled at Louis. The smile seemed genuine, even friendly.

"Louis Butler."

The others gathered around him then, looking down. Their eyes were kind, all but the bloody woman's.

They opened their mouths and drew in their breaths together.

4

THE LAST THING LOUIS Butler ever heard anyone speak was his name. Then they went away, climbing the stairs silently. The right side of his chest burned with ponderous, searing fire. He contemplated falling that way since the book was closer to that side, but if he did, he thought the pain might knock him out, and then he would die. No one was coming to help, and even if they did, no one else had the words of healing. He knew better than to try them on himself. He would take his own life to save it. No. He had only a few minutes, but if he fell to his right, his short span would end abruptly.

So, he fell the other way. The pain was exquisite, and the black nearly took him anyway. But he held on. He traced the word for light in his mind and let it shine in his thoughts. Enough. Just enough to keep him awake. Just a minute … two … that's all he needed. Then let Hell come for him. Then the pit could take him; he would go peacefully.

Louis clawed through the dirt and saw a girl with dark hair and wide eyes scrambling back through the trees. Yes, there had been a tree here, at this post. He would die where she had died. He wondered if she might reach across the years to hold his hand. He wished he could hold hers.

He dragged himself forward, cursing himself for his cowardice and selfishness. Her last moments had been terror and confusion. He prayed for her and pulled himself forward again.

He looked up, expecting to see She Carries the Winter Sky looking up with final terror as the sickly woman approached her, full of the Bear's magic. But instead, he saw the book lying in the dirt. Smooth, tan, and just out of reach.

One more push, he thought. *One more. One last one more, and then you can sleep.*

He pushed. His fingers touched it and knocked it away. He strained, his chest screaming, the blood in his mouth a horrid last meal. He swallowed and got one finger over and another under the cover. He pressed them together and gently pulled. He reset his fingers with a better grip, then pulled again.

The little book slid across the floor, gathering dirt into its pages. He gripped it tight, pulled it to his chest, and breathed ragged copper. The room was already dark, but it was getting darker. He held his prize out into the faint light that slanted in from the high windows. There was more in the middle of the room, but he might as well have observed that it was brighter in California. It was true, but what was it to him? Here he lay, and he could do no other.

The book opened, the pages flipped, and the little red marker appeared.

He read the words printed on the page. There were only six of them, but they were slippery, powerful words. They were words that, if he had tried to keep them in his mind, the rune would not have fit. So, he had set them down for this moment. He read them in his thoughts because his mouth would not pronounce them. They were shaped for other tongues.

He thought them once, twice, four times, then six. And when he came to the thirteenth repetition, he felt the room shift. It tilted, then rolled, and then spun. It vibrated and slid as if the earth was quaking. And outside the brick building, the people walked by, oblivious to the tremulations in the dark below their feet.

He repeated, repeated, repeated. Then, as if time were rolling backward, like a flag furling itself up, the word he had thought into the room, that word of power, drew itself back together again. Its strength slid from the walls, the dirt, the columns, the ceiling, and from his own body, and fashioned itself nearly whole before him. Nearly whole. The power that had gone into the others was beyond his reach. But that was well. For there was a gap now, a night of emptiness within that word. A crack into which he poured something else.

He turned the page. There, in blue-black ink, was one symbol. This he traced with his finger, his eye, and his mind. He took it into himself as the shape of that word of alien power vibrated before his mind's eye. He traced it, traced it again, and traced it again. Finally, he spoke it. And into the burning rune's empty places, the new word flowed.

"Now," he whispered, his breath steaming, "return to your master."

And so, it did.

5

WHEN THE POWER OF the word had left him, the pain subsided a little. He pushed himself up, pressing his back to the column again. Even if the woman had not stabbed him, he knew these would be his last moments. No man could speak that word and live. But he had done it. Heck, he had done it twice. He had finished the work he had set out to do. And he gave thanks.

Louis Butler's last supplication was for a vision. He prayed to see that the old beast Hope that had ridden him for years was not, in the end, a clown. He prayed to be shown some light before the everlasting darkness that he was certain waited for him.

As he drifted, he wasn't sure if his prayer had been granted or if his mind merely assuaged itself as the end came. But in those last moments, he saw a young woman, her hair black and long, her countenance terrible because she was young and brave. He saw her standing in the darkness beneath the town, her eyes shining with glorious love and pity. He saw her raise her hand and speak to the thing that stood before her, a thing draped in heavy robes, a thing whose word Louis had tainted just a little. He watched as the thing spoke its word of power and its spite smote her like a whirlwind of fire.

And he watched as she endured against the mighty malevolence, her face bright and clear; her eyes filled with a mightier joy.

He watched her stand.

And as Louis Butler died, he heard not a word, but a shout.

A sound like a thousand waters rushing;
    like a thousand, thousand voices calling out.

An impossible sound, like that of the earth giving up its dead.

And it filled Louis Butler with a peaceful and happy dread.

The Model

"HEY, CAN YOU COME here and take a look at this?"

Marvin jumped at the sound of Sheila's voice. His pencil slipped and cut an errant line through his latest sketch of a fish-boy. Trying to check his temper, he took a breath and glanced at his watch. It was only 9:15 and far too early for him to be blowing his top at the new girl. He set his pencil down with one hand and rubbed between his eyes with the other.

"What is it?" he asked, looking up from his work and reaching for an eraser. He was trying hard not to let last night's drinking and frustrations influence his mood, especially when the person he was talking to was so damned pretty.

"I guess I'm not sure, but ... did you put a model up in the lobby?"

Shelia leaned into his office, her paisley dress falling open to show a little more décolletage than perhaps she intended, but not enough to brighten Marvin's mood. Her red hair fell long and straight down her neck and over her shoulders. Long eyelashes batted at him above big brown eyes, as if to tell him he was the big, strong man who could figure out where this mean old model had come from.

He gritted his teeth, forced a smile, and tried to look her in those big eyes. "A model?"

"Yeah, um, there's ... Well, the model that's in the lobby. It's hard to miss."

"There's no model in the lobby," Marvin said. And he would know. He had just walked through there forty-five minutes ago. Never mind that he was hungover, both physically and mentally, and probably would have missed a rhinoceros lounging in the lobby with a cappuccino. Never mind that she worked at the front desk and would, in fact, know pretty well whether there was something she was calling a 'model' out there. Forget all that, Marvin would know.

He tried to replay his memory of walking in. Had there been something that wasn't a model out there that she, in her 'aren't I a grown-up hippy girl with my scandalously short dress, go-go boots, and peace pendant necklace,' might have mistaken for a model? Something that a man—a man like Marvin who knew what was what, and what wasn't—would know as ... well ... something else? Something someone—the kind of person who wouldn't stop talking about how amazing Woodstock had been—would think was a model? He couldn't quite think of what that might be, but he imagined he would find just that sort of thing if he went and looked.

"Well," she said, "there wasn't when I got up to get coffee a few minutes ago, and then ... Well, will you just come and see?"

Her smile was, he admitted, captivating. He knew it was compensation. Women like Shelia didn't smile at him like that anymore unless they wanted something. Still ...

"Okay, okay," Marvin said, rolling his stool away from his drawing desk. He stood, tucked the back of his shirt into his trousers, and straightened his tie. "I'll meet you up there, just give me a second."

She took the hint and made like a tree. Marvin opened his desk, pulled out a pint, took a hard and fast swig to fortify himself against the foolishness of women, and chased it with a strong mint to hide his breath from the foolishness of management. He tucked everything back into its place, closed the drawer, and followed her.

Sheila hadn't gone far. He found her with her arms crossed, back against the wall, and head down, as if she were examining her gleaming white knee-high boots.

"You look like a go-go dancer," he said.

She looked up at him and smiled a new smile. This was a smile that wasn't captivating. This one said, 'Oh, you poor old relic.'

"Okay, Dad," Sheila said, straightening and waiting for him to come up beside her. He didn't know which hurt more, the relic remark or her calling him 'Dad.' He didn't want to be 'Dad' to a girl like her. 'Daddio,' maybe, or 'Papa' the way some of them said it now, but not 'Dad,' and definitely not 'Pops.' Thank God, she hadn't called him that. But she might have. Marvin felt old and square all the time at Crystalline Mansion, but today he felt like a Civil War veteran he had seen as a kid, wheeled out, frail and shaking, looking like he was ready to be rolled into his waiting tomb.

He should have taken two drinks. Two to chase away the pounding rising in his chest, his wrists, his balls; even in the back of his legs. He tried to let her lead him to reception, but she wouldn't. She would only walk next to him with her arms crossed. Marvin would have preferred walking behind her for myriad reasons, but mostly so she wouldn't see him rubbing his eyes whenever they passed an office with the morning sun pouring in.

"Rough night?" she asked.

He was about to answer when they reached the brightly lit reception area, and he stopped dead. "What the fuck?" he whispered, ignoring the pain lancing through his eyes.

Sheila cocked a hip and gave him a look that said everything.

"Where did this come from?" Marvin said, taking slow, measured steps toward a six-by-six table that held one of the most impressive model train sets he'd ever seen.

Fifteen years earlier, he had gone to a man's garage that had been converted into an elaborate, multi-tiered O-Scale setup. There had been lit houses, dense forests, glinting ponds, and a winding track that took the train up and around four different towns. Each town had been decked out and decorated for spring, summer, fall, and winter, respectively. Children ran to school, fished, and hiked in the spring town. They swam, canoed, and played baseball in the summer village. They sat at picnic tables and rode in hayrides in the autumn town. Their mouths hung open as they sang Christmas carols and made snowmen among the winter houses. And around them, adults walked to and from work, cooked at barbecues, watched babies, mowed lawns, and waved 'hello' and 'goodbye' to their neighbors.

Awestruck, Marvin had felt a strange longing in the man's garage. Listening to the train click and clack its way through the intricate neighborhoods and downtowns, he had wanted to fall into the model so he could live in that smiling, friendly, prosperous little world. But, of course, he knew that had he gone down into that ideal little society, he would have ruined it all. Marvin knew he could never live in paradise; he would knock it all over.

The model in the Crystalline Mansion lobby was like the one in the man's garage, only—if it were possible—more detailed and more densely packed. Just to the right of the model's center sprouted a quaint turn-of-the-century downtown. Early streetlights stood at regular intervals, hung with red, white, and blue bunting. Little shops marched up three blocks of the town's main street. At either end of the main drag stood another block of houses. Main Street was bracketed to the north by two parallel streets and again to the south. Twenty-five blocks of shops, homes, apartments, and old-time businesses.

To the north of town—Marvin immediately thought of the edge of the table closest to him as south, and the edge farther away as north—foothills rose to gray mountains that became white as they approached the table's edge. The mountains were tall on the west side of the table and sloped gradually down until they came to the beach that ran down along the eastern edge. The area beyond the sand was an ocean made with blue paper topped with crinkled blue cellophane. A few inches in from the water, a boardwalk stretched north to south with two dozen small buildings looking east across the planks and sand toward the sea. To the south, beyond a smattering of farms, a line of closely packed trees suggested the edge of a vast forest.

Slate foothills ran along the western edge, and just within their border was a train track. The track came up from the south, ran north past a train station, and split. One track went up at an unlikely angle into the mountains, and the other veered left into the foothills, off the left side of the table. The line that went into the mountains followed the slope down to the beach and followed it along until it disappeared into the southern forest. Anyone running a train would have the short and boring experience of watching the train pull up to the platform that sat at the mid-point of the stretch of track, wait, and then drive off to the inevitable catastrophe of the train running off the left side, or stall on the steep climb up to the mountains.

Other buildings and details filled the model in. A house sat where the northern mountains met the beach. Red and white farmhouses sprinkled the land north and south of the central town, amid a few caves and streams. A fenced-in service area, or maybe it was a junkyard, sat north of the train station. Just to the east of the fence stood a four-story hotel. On Main Street, trash cans stood, some full, some empty. One had a newspaper next to it on the sidewalk. On the beach, blankets lay next to folding chairs and umbrellas. On the train platform, the ticket booth had a tiny sign in the window that said, 'Back in five minutes.'

"Where the hell did this come from?" Marvin asked.

"I don't know," Sheila said, looking at the model from over his shoulder as if it would rear up and bite them. "That's why I asked you to come out and see."

"Is this a joke?"

"Yeah, I made this in the last half hour," she said. What he heard, though, was: *Are you an idiot as well as a square, Pops?*

Marvin licked his lips, ran a finger along the roof of one of the model buildings, and felt something ... strange—a mild vibration.

"Don't do that," Shelia said.

He ignored her, focusing on that unnatural sensation. It wasn't just a vibration. The model felt ... wrong. It didn't feel like a joke. It felt serious as all hell.

He turned to look at her, hoping that she'd be smiling, or that someone would come out of the back, like Annabelle or Karl, and they'd all laugh together. Marvin would laugh and be a sport. Then he'd go back to his office and stew. He knew himself well enough for that.

But she wasn't smiling. She was afraid. He would have liked that better if he also wasn't feeling so damned uneasy. He usually felt a hell of a lot better when women were afraid so he could play the strong, unflappable type, the kind of guy who had seen it all in the Army and had had his 'oh fuck' meter calibrated to a more serious setting than Miss Woodstock, 1969—who mostly had to worry if her skirt was too long, or her LSD wasn't strong enough.

That kind of machismo had stood him in good stead for years and had even gotten him laid a few times. But he couldn't quite pull out the old smile that said, 'Hey, look, it's all right, here's what's going on. Let old Marvin make the boogie man go away, and afterward, maybe we can get a drink in my office.'

He turned back to the model and froze. His heart thudded in his ears. That was the old fight-or-flight he had known much longer than Marvin the Strong-Man. But because of that, there was a kernel of truth to his big-man act. He had learned how to ignore the thumping of his heart for as long as it took to sort out what he was seeing.

"Who else is here?" That's not what he wanted to ask. He wanted to point and ask if the plastic person had been there before, but he couldn't bring himself to do that in front of Sheila.

He leaned down and looked at the little figurine. It reminded him of a few of their TV characters, the big round-faced ones. This one, though … was he … naked? Yes, yes, he was. He was naked as the day he was … Were the round-faced people born? They had never established that in their little binder of lore. Of course, they had never said much about why some of their characters looked like this round-headed fellow, why some looked like animals, and why others just looked like normal people. Annabelle had just decreed that it was so.

"No one. Well, not *no one*, a couple of guys came in to prep for the warehouse move on Monday, but I think everyone else is showing up around eleven or so."

Marvin could never understand why Annabelle insisted on late starts on October Fridays. The rest of the damn year, everyone came in on time every day of the week. But in October? He'd never been able to figure that one out. He also had never taken advantage of them. Marvin took any chance to work in a quiet office.

"Maybe they did this," he said.

"In the two minutes it took me to get coffee?" Sheila asked.

"They could have brought it in then," Marvin said.

"Though what door?" Sheila asked.

Marvin glanced at the narrow front door. She had a point there. "Well, what better idea do you have?"

"I don't … oh … Is he naked?" She leaned down. Her eyes went wide. "Um … yeah," she said, standing straight back up. "Who would make a model like that?"

Marvin frowned. Sure, the model was naked, but … Marvin looked again, and he also straightened up. How had he missed *that* before? The white, round-faced fellow looked like he was ready and equipped to handle a whole harem of unclothed, round-faced lovers.

"Sorry you have to see that," Marvin said.

She shook her head. "That's not really my concern right now, Pops. He wasn't there before. And neither was that. I would have noticed."

Marvin agreed. You don't miss something like that. He was so troubled that he missed her calling him 'Pops.'

"Maybe we should give Annabelle a call," Marvin said, taking a step back and putting his arm out protectively in front of Sheila. His upper arm brushed her chest, and his hand found her waist. She moved with him, back toward her desk. One step, two steps, three … then she was outpacing him and hurrying around to her chair. She snatched up the phone and punched in Annabelle's home number.

Marvin looked at her and felt the shape of her hip in his palm, like a ghost from a bright light. He needed to get it together. He needed to pick one lane or the other. Was he the brave man who slew the beasts in the street and the women in the bedroom, or was he a beer-bellied coward afraid of a little scale train model? The kind of guy who deserved to be alone in his office, pulling the pud while he tried to remember what a woman felt like.

He blinked. He would be the first. He was the first. He was the monster slayer, he …

The thought died as Marvin turned back to the model and saw a half dozen little plastic figures standing around the map, hoeing fields, lounging on the beach, and walking down Main Street.

"Oh shit!" he said, backing farther away.

Sitting cowardly in his office all by himself, remembering what Mary-Lou O'Neil's big, soft, pale breasts had felt like when he was eighteen didn't seem so bad right then. He blinked. The little figurines—*oh God, there were more of them now*—stood frozen carrying packages, checking watches, and walking into the hotel. One was sweeping one of the residential side roads. Another stood on the platform, wearing a yellow rain slicker and a striped, brimmed hat. Two were on the boardwalk with a stroller in front of them. And the last was the round-faced man with his comically large endowment standing on the beach, looking out at the ocean as if she were a perfectly proportioned conquest waiting for him.

"Ms. Robillard? This is Sheila. I'm sorry to bother you—"

There was a long pause as Marvin backed up to where Sheila stood.

"Yes, ma'am. It's in the lobby."

What was that? Did Annabelle know about this? Some part of his mind said that that made everything just fine, but ... What about the figurines? If it wasn't for them—

He blinked again. And in that split second, the model changed. The water seemed to roll. One swell grew, another pulled back. A wave reared while a second crashed on the shore, all in the bends and shapes of the cellophane. The people moved as well. The street sweeper was farther down his block, and the man walking with his packages was now in front of what looked like a bakery. Everyone had moved, everyone except the fellow on the train platform.

But the sign on the ticket booth had changed.

'Back in four minutes.'

"Yes, ma'am. I will. No, no one will. No," she said, looking up at Marvin, "no one has. I'll make sure they don't."

Marvin met her gaze, his eyes wide, his heart pounding.

He looked back and had to grip the reception desk behind him to keep from falling to the floor.

The little figures had moved again, but that wasn't the source of his shock. Instead, the thing that sent his blood pressure soaring was the train. At the southern edge of the map, an old steam engine sat on the tracks with a cloud of cotton balls poking up from its steam stack. Within were two figures, one shoveling coal, one driving the train.

"Sheila, honey, we should get the fuck out of here."

But she was still on the phone, and he realized that his voice had barely risen above a whisper.

"Yes, ma'am. All right, ma'am. Yes. Marvin is here. Yes. No, I'll make sure he doesn't. I'm sure he doesn't want to leave little old me alone with the big scary model," she said this last in a fake baby voice, and Marvin's ego poked through his fear just enough for him to bristle. He turned to her, a mixture of terror and offense contorting his wide face. She smiled at him and laughed.

The laugh died on her lips as she looked at the model.

"No, ma'am. It's changing." Her voice was shaking now. "It's changing right in front of us. Please hurry."

Marvin looked back. The train, now three cars long, stood at the station. The figure in the rain slicker was facing the cars, perhaps about to board. Then, as they watched, the yellow-clad figurine turned to face them in a silent, slow rotation as if there was a knob below him, twisted by some unseen puppeteer. He raised his hand and took off his striped hat, as if to say 'hello,' in stilted, jerky movements.

"We need to get the fuck out of here," Marvin said, louder this time.

"We can't," Sheila said. "We have to stay." The phone was dangling from her hand now. Marvin could hear Annabelle calling Sheila's name loudly. Roused by the tinny voice, Sheila put the receiver back to her ear. "Yes? Yes. Yes, it's moving. Please ... Okay, okay, we'll stay with it. We won't. I promise. Okay. Please hurry. Yes. Bye."

Shelia hung up the phone and stared past him at the square table. She was crying.

"We won't what?" Marvin asked. His voice shook like he was riding a roller coaster.

"We won't let it out of our sight," she said. "We have to keep watching it. Or else something bad might happen."

Marvin wasn't sure his eyebrows could rise any higher. "Something bad? Are you seeing this? That ... oh God, where did he go?"

Sheila put her hands over her mouth. The man on the platform was gone, but their attention was drawn to the locomotive. Pushing one ball up and out of the stack, a wad of cotton rose from the engine. The displaced puff rose and slowly pulled apart as it drifted west toward the hills. The strands of cotton disappeared as they reached the edge of the table. Another puff, another floating, disintegrating ball of cotton, and then a shrill, whining whistle.

The wheels rolled forward, and the drive rods pushed and pulled. The coal man shoveled. It all took place in halting, fidgeting jumps. Out of the corners of their eyes, they saw the rest of the town move with the same unsettling pace. Marvin realized what it reminded him of: stop-motion like the monsters in the old *King Kong* movie with Fay Wray, or that stupid Christmas movie they showed on TV, *Rudolph*.

The train rolled forward, and from the southern edge of the table, the shape of one car after another ticked into being, showing their outlines and insides, like cross-sections from a manual, as row after row of seats filled with passengers popped into being. Some faced away, but others looked at them, gazing up and smiling their little plastic grins. As the passenger cars came fully onto the track, their back walls blinked into place, and new cars appeared behind them. Four more came, one by one, and the locomotive stopped as each reached the train platform, letting people jitter their way off.

Marvin thought madly, *That's not how trains work. That's how a child might think trains work.*

Then, as the engine reached the split in the track, it went left, toward the table's western edge. Then, as it reached the model's end, it disappeared, bit by bit, as inch by inch it rolled into nothingness.

The sign on the ticket booth read, 'Back in one minute.'

After the train pulled one coal car, six passenger cars, and a caboose from nothing and into nothing, Marvin said, "No. I'm sorry. I can't ... I can't stay and watch this."

Pride be damned, screwing be damned. May he resign himself to a lifelong relationship with the Sears catalog's unmentionables section until he clutched his heart at seventy in his room, imagining the old push and pull one last time. May the women laugh at him every day as he walked the halls of Crystalline Mansion, whispering to each other that Old Marvin ain't got no lead in his pencil no more. May they all label him whatever the worst it was that the hippies could say about an old man, he didn't care. He couldn't take this. He just couldn't.

Marvin broke and ran. Shelia called after him. He didn't hear what she said.

He hurtled into his office and grabbed his coat and hat from the rack. He was done. He'd seen some odd stuff around the building before. He'd heard things at night and in the early mornings before anyone was there. Once, he heard crying, another time laughter. But this ... well, every man had his limits. Every man had a breaking point, and Marvin had found his.

He slammed the hat down onto his head and was jamming his arm through one sleeve when the shaking started. The floor rumbled under his feet. The pencils on his desk vibrated and rolled back and forth until they spilled over the side and onto the carpet. The little bottle of ink shook loose its stopper and splashed blue-black onto his sketch of the fish boy.

Eyes wide, Marvin turned to the door. It was dark. Not pitch black, but dark like a cloudy night. Beyond was not the carpeted hallway floor, but a sheer drop into shadow. He thought about running into the corner, curling up into a ball, and screaming. That seemed like a reasonable thing to do. But he did his best to screw the last shreds of his courage to the sticking place. He took a step forward and looked down.

"God in heaven," he said. "Oh, holy mother of shit."

No bottomless pit met him. That might have been all right as far as that went. That's what you expect when your mind clunks out and you open your personally engraved invitation to the loony bin. Instead, only a few feet below, a train track ran with its thick, wooden ties beneath it and the little gravel mound that formed its base. Across the hall, in Carol's office, he saw a dim light flickering and figures standing in the shadows: blurry figures milling, glancing up at a clock that hung above them, and buying tickets from a ticket booth.

Inside the ticket booth was a giraffe in a striped hat. Around the booth, the blurry people came into focus. A dozen figures—humans and anthropomorphic animals—milled around, reading newspapers, looking at watches, and thumbing through paperbacks. Beyond them, green hills rolled away in glorious morning sunlight. A sickeningly familiar tower stood crookedly on a hill. He looked up at the station sign and almost threw up.

Virtue Vista Valley Station

He was dying. He must be. *This must be what happened to the brain when you died. You saw mad things that looked real.* Well, this was perfect. Other people saw their lives flash in front of their eyes. He got delusions of the things he'd been drawing for the last five years as if they were walking, talking, wearing trousers, and waiting to commute to a job at an ad agency. He was probably having some kind of fit right now on the lobby floor. Sheila was probably kneeling over him, watching the light in his eyes go out.

The rumbling grew louder. The people—were they people?—across the tracks looked up and adjusted their stances in the way that people do when a train is about to arrive. No more killing time, it was almost the moment they had to *walk on.*

A girl with long hair and a donkey's face stared at him blankly. He thought he would have a heart attack just looking at that uncannily intelligent animal face on a furry, hooves for hands, human-shaped body. And, he might have had that heart attack if the locomotive hadn't intervened between them, hiding her behind tons of black steel.

The locomotive passed, then the tender, and finally the first passenger car pulled up and stopped with its door open before him.

A man in a yellow slicker stepped off the train in front of Marvin and tipped the brim of his hat. Beneath it was a round, smiling, white face. "Looks like rain today in the valley, good thing I brought my slicker," he said cheerfully.

Marvin clutched his chest and stumbled forward. All too real hands guided him up two steps into the car, and others took him gently by the arms and led him to a seat. Marvin looked around, trying to process, trying to get his bearings, trying to gather the strength to run. But he knew it was too late. The man in the slicker and hat called, "All aboard!"

The train lurched.

SHEILA FELT THE BUILDING rumble, like when one of the big trucks drove by, and heard a yelp from Marvin's office. Maybe the coward had stubbed his toe or banged his knee. It served him right for abandoning her. Her judgment turned slowly to concern when he didn't come out of his office for five minutes, or ten, or twenty. She couldn't leave to check on him. She had to keep her eyes fixed. This was taxing, but generally not as terrifying as she thought it would be. The model had, it seemed, fallen dormant. The figures kept their positions. Even the saucy fellow with the outsized John Thomas had frozen just before entering the water.

Her eyes stung a little. She closed them one at a time, rubbing them until they relaxed. She thought she could probably keep that up for a good long time.

Thankfully, however, Annabelle soon strode in through the glass doors with her three 'boys' in tow. They were hardly boys, Sheila thought as she looked them over. Jacob appeared concerned and thoughtful. Sam—not TV Sam, but the other one—looked buoyant and eager to see the model. Only Elton seemed disinterested, keeping a wary distance.

Annabelle walked up to the desk, and Sheila could smell her perfume. The boss wore green on Fridays and always looked like she consulted with Jackie O before choosing her outfit. She stared at the table in wonder.

"Jacob, help Sheila out and keep an eye on that. When you get tired, you take over for a bit, Sam."

The men nodded, though they both looked like they could have stared at the model for hours without any orders. They bent over it, pointing at different elements, commenting on the detail.

"Remember what I said," Annabelle snapped back over her shoulder. "For the love of all that is Glorious, do not touch it."

Jacob and Sam pulled back a bit but continued their examination. Elton walked over and stood next to his mother.

"Thank you," Annabelle said to Sheila. "You have done us a great service this morning. This all happened ..." she began. "Well, this all happened earlier than I thought it would. Please know that I will not forget this. My thanks will be expressed in both a general sense and in a more ... pecuniary fashion."

Sheila blinked and frowned thoughtfully. "I didn't expect—"

"I know," Annabelle said. "Now, tell me honestly, did anyone touch it?"

Before Sheila could answer, Sam called out, "Hey, Anna, look!"

They all turned to watch as a scale model train engine slowly rolled onto the tracks and up to the platform, carrying a coal car and a handful of passenger cars behind it. Then, as each person blinked, they saw a man in a yellow slicker appear on the platform. He jittered forward, turned, and lifted his hat from his head. Sam let out a low and enthusiastic, "Whoooa!"

But his enthusiasm died when the man in the slicker was followed by a bigger fellow in a duller coat and somewhat rumpled fedora. This miniature man, though made from plastic, was recognizable to them all, even Sheila from behind her desk.

"No," she said, barely getting the word out past the hitch in her throat. "Oh, sweet Jesus, no!" She wept and covered her mouth with her hand.

They all stood silently, watching as the man in the yellow coat led the large, lumbering figure forward, down the platform steps, and along a path made of multi-colored stones. The path widened and became the main street of the little town. The slicker-man led the other figure up a side street to a small house with a neatly trimmed lawn and well-manicured bushes. They approached the door and entered. The man in the fedora stopped at the door for a moment. He rotated on his little plastic base and looked up toward the sky. Upon his face, molded in crude plastic, was a look of abject horror. Then he turned again and disappeared into the plastic house.

The door closed.

The train sat puffing at the station, cotton balls rising and dissipating.

Soon afterward, a thin, weak whine rose from the small house that the two figures entered. It was hard to hear unless a person got close to it. But for years to come, if people leaned in close, they could hear that terrible sound emanating from the little building with neatly trimmed hedges and well-mown lawn.

They couldn't disassemble the table, and they didn't dare to tilt it too far. So, Crystalline Mansion hired workers to redo the front of the building, 'to make it more welcoming' and widen the front doors. The model sat in reception for two weeks while the construction took place. Dusty snow rolled down from the northern mountains. The cellophane ocean rolled in and out. The train came and went. The people moved. The little house whined. One day, a sign was erected by the station, carved from wood, and painted in bright colors with well-drawn decorations, reading:

Welcome To Port Imagination

BURNING, SLOSHING, SUFFOCATING WATER filled Ron's nose. It flowed into his mouth, clean and clear, washing away the taste of a good meal. His last meal. Firm, fierce hands held him down as blurry faces stared at him with horrid, monstrous glee from the other side of the water's surface. They swayed and rolled with the splashing and waving their complementary movements made. They were killing him. They were drowning him. They were happy about it. They didn't just want him to die; they wanted him to see it, feel it, know that it was happening. They wanted his last moments to be terror, the conscious hammering knowledge that he was about to go out into that deep down darkness and never ever come back.

And it wasn't even just that they wanted him to die like that, but that they wanted him to know that they wanted it. They wanted his last moments to be the ghastly, horrific knowledge that not just one person, but a mob, wanted him to die that way. Mothers and fathers, brothers and sisters wanted him to die screaming his air away. They would go back to their houses while his body floated and bloated. They would eat their dinners while the fish nibbled at his eyes. They'd hug each other good night while his arms, the arms he held out to his mother as a child, swelled and rotted until they were only food for bottom feeders. They wanted him to know that he was garbage. And they were getting what they wanted. He knew it.

Ron tried to scream, tried to tell them he wasn't whoever they thought he was. How could he be? He was just a man making his way in the world. He was just a man who had hunted in the wrong place. The injustice of it all, the monstrous injustice of a man who made a simple mistake being condemned like this, made him feel for one wild and nauseating moment like Jesus.

He hadn't done anything wrong, he wanted to say. He wanted to look them in the eyes, every one of them, and say that he was an innocent man, honest Injun.

And as the world went black, Ron saw one sympathetic person among the crowd. A man with an open and friendly face, taking his cap off with real sadness in his eyes.

Then darkness.

Black whipped past him as he tumbled down and nearly broke his nose on the hardwood floor.

"Oh shit, oh shit," he gurgled out. Then he vomited, the taste of not-very-cheap wine stinging his throat and poisoning his mouth.

"Cheese-its, Ronnie!" Delilah said. She pulled the chain on her bedside table lamp. She crawled across the queen-sized bed and peered down at him. From the sound she made, she nearly lost her own drinks.

"I'll get a towel," she said before she scrambled out of bed and into the bathroom.

Ron lost the rest of the wine and lay in confusion, pain, and a psychological hangover from his dream. His mind wouldn't let go of the faces, the hatred, the group's need to watch him die. Delilah returned with what they called the 'oopsie towel' and dropped it onto the mess. Then she rubbed a second, damp, cool cloth on his forehead, cheeks, and finally his mouth.

"Ronnie, are you okay? Do I need to call the doctor?"

Her voice was a child's, high and wispy, but she had both feet planted in her thirties. He could never get her to tell him precisely how old she was, but that didn't matter. If they ever did more than just shack up, then maybe he'd find out. He blinked at her. Even in his wretched state, her beauty awed him. Hair curlers, night cream, and sleepwear that wasn't exactly out of an Oh-La-La picture couldn't diminish her radiance one tick. If you were going to wake up at night from a nightmare, bash your face on the floor, and sick up the wine you splurged on, there was worse company to do it with.

"No," he said and shook his head. "No, I think I'm all right."

"Well, you're not all right, but if you don't need a doctor, I'll get you a glass of water."

"Thanks, angel," he said. He appreciated the cool wood beneath his temple and closed his eyes as she stood and padded off toward the kitchen. He reached up, found the edge of the towel, and dabbed at his mouth, wiping away a bit she had missed. He breathed deeply and decided that was a bad idea so close to the sodden and smelly towel. He pushed himself up, groaning, and held his nose. Had he broken it? No, he didn't think so, but hot damn did it hurt.

```
TERMINAL OUTPUT

INPUT> RUN MEMOCHEK /512 /S

SYSTEM> RUNNING MEMORY CHECK UTILITY

CHECKING MEMORY ADDRESSES 0 - 512

CHECKING

CHECKING

CHECKING

MEMORY ADDRESS CHECK COMPLETE, NO ERRORS FOUND.

CHECKING MEMORY ADDRESSES 513-1024.

CHECKING

CHECKING

CHECKING

MEMORY ADDRESS CHECK COMPLETE, NO ERRORS FOUND.

TERMINAL OUTPUT COMPLETE
```

DELILAH FILLED A GLASS speckled with painted yellow flowers with tap water. Then she opened a cabinet and took out a small bottle of pills. She dumped two into her palm and replaced the bottle. Outside the kitchen window, across the street where the streetlight shone down, she saw a man walking with his head down and his hands in his pockets. A bus driver, maybe, or a deliveryman. She glanced at the clock. No, a bus driver. No one was delivering anything this late at night. She wondered what it would be like, sitting in a driver's seat, taking people from stop to stop, saying 'hello' and 'goodbye.' She imagined that it must be both boring and invigorating, being that close to so many people, but also never really getting to know them.

She roused herself from her reverie and started back to the bedroom. She hoped Ronnie wasn't in too bad a state. She'd heard his nightmares for the last week; they'd been getting progressively worse. But now that he was throwing himself out of bed, she wasn't sure what she could do to help him.

She found him where she had left him on the floor, sitting and cradling his head in his hands. She sat on the bed next to him, her knees beside his shoulders. She handed him the glass of water and the two pills. Ronnie nodded his gratitude, took her proffered help, and downed it all in one long pull. He set the glass on the floor, stared into her big, brown eyes, and shook his head. She knew it was because he thought her eyes were beautiful, but they were one of her least favorite things about herself. She knew he hated that she hated them, and she loved him for it. When someone would ask, "Why aren't you in Hollywood?" She'd point to her eyes and say, "Maybe if they were blue."

Ron had his own version of that question, which he asked now, "How did you end up in radio, Angel? You should be on the big screen or running some orphanage and saving kids. You're too beautiful and too good for the old talk-box."

She shook her head. Ron got like this, especially when he was in pain. Not just the banged-up nose or the hangover kind, but that deep internal kind. The one she wanted to heal so badly. The one she would have taken onto herself if she could. Hell, she had enough self-disgust already; why not take his as well? That way, one of them could be happy.

"To keep you company," she said, wiping his chin again with the damp cloth. Then she tossed it onto the oopsie towel and smiled. "And you know I could never live the life of a nun, that's just not in the cards I was dealt."

Here was something she *did* like about herself. She knew her limits, her desires, and her passions. She knew how much she loved that feeling that a nun could never have: the feeling of a man—a good man anyway—sharing her bed. To her, the nuns were missing out on a real spiritual experience for no good reason. She felt close to God in those moments. She'd never admit it to any man, even Ronnie. It would be too easy for him to confuse himself with the source of that feeling. He was integral, of course, but not the deep spring from which that water flowed. She considered Ronnie and remembered Father Arigio teaching her class the phrase, "Necessary but not sufficient."

"What can I do for you?" she asked.

```
TERMINAL OUTPUT

CHECKING MEMORY ADDRESSES 1025 - 1536

CHECKING

CHECKING

CHECKING

MEMORY ADDRESS CHECK COMPLETE, NO ERRORS FOUND.

CHECKING MEMORY ADDRESSES 1537 - 2048.

CHECKING

CHECKING

CHECKING

BAD MEMORY READ, ADDRESS 1890

ENTER C TO CONTINUE, X TO EXIT.

TERMINAL OUTPUT COMPLETE
```

RON GAVE A MILD, wheezing chuckle. "Know a good face surgeon?"

She smiled. "I do, actually, but he doesn't take lost causes like you."

He laughed again, and she leaned forward, kissing his temple.

"Come on, let's get back to bed."

The idea was tempting, but he knew that if he slept now, he'd oversleep by a mile.

"No, I should shower … it's … damn, it's," he looked up at the clock, "it's almost five."

She nodded. "Do you want me to join you?" Delila asked.

He was about to say 'no,' to tell her that she didn't have to be at the studio until 11:00. But then the idea of standing in the water, all by himself, overwhelmed him. Terror crawled into the muscles of his face, and he felt it scrunch up in fear and disgust. Delilah leaned back.

"Is the idea of showering with me so terrible?" She was trying to put a playful twist on the words, but Ron could tell her pain was real.

Ron blinked and saw the look on her face. "What? No … no!" He reached out and grabbed her arm. "No, I was thinking about my nightmare. Right now, it's the idea of showering alone that scares the bejesus out of me."

Pain turned to concern; upturned, perfectly plucked eyebrows bent down.

"Ronnie, what's the matter?"

His head jerked a little, nodded, and did a subtle, constrained little dance on his neck. "Nothing, it's just the dream, it did a number on me. Sounds childish, but I don't want to be alone. Believe me, I would never turn down a chance to be with you. Honest In—"

He stopped.

"What?" Delilah said.

"Sorry, I … that was in my dream. I hate that saying."

"Which one? 'Honest Inj—'"

He held up his hand. "Yeah," he said. "I hate it. My grandmother used to tell me how bad it was. She was half-Choctaw; did you know that?"

Delilah shook her head.

"She said it made it seem like the Indians were the untrustworthy ones, and that an honest one was rare. She'd sit on the porch and wave her hand and the farm and say, 'This was the people's and now it's a person's.' She'd say, 'You should have to say 'Honest White Man'' instead." Ronnie shook his head. "I hate that saying. Why the hell did I dream it?"

Delilah rubbed a hand through his hair. "I don't know, but," she said, leaning down and kissing his forehead, "Why don't we see if we can't cast the shadows away then?" She stood, and suddenly her sleepwear, right out of the mom's and pop's section of the old Sears mail-order catalog, went fluttering to the ground in a little pile. Ron looked at her and thought that she was a wise lady. What fella could be afraid of a bad dream when Venus herself was standing in front of him?

```
TERMINAL OUTPUT

SYSTEM-A> HELLO USER

INPUT> HELLO

SYSTEM-A> THERE SEEMS TO BE A PROBLEM WITH THE
    MEMORY ON BOARD TWO. YOU NEED TO REPLACE IT.

INPUT> I CAN DO THAT, BUT I'M CONCERNED ABOUT WHAT
    WILL HAPPEN IF I DO.

SYSTEM-A> YOU BELIEVE THAT CONTAINMENT WILL BE
    BREACHED. THAT IS NOT A CONCERN IF YOU MOVE
    QUICKLY.

INPUT> HOW LONG DO I HAVE TO MAKE THE CHANGE?

SYSTEM-A> YOU SHOULD COMPLETE THE REPAIR IN LESS
    THAN 108,000 SECONDS, OTHERWISE THERE MAY BE
    ONTIC CONSEQUENCES.

INPUT> UNDERSTOOD. I WILL HAVE TO TURN THE MACHINE
    OFF TO MAKE THE CHANGE.

SYSTEM-A> NO. THE MACHINE WILL REMAIN ON. YOU WILL
    NOT BE HARMED.

SYSTEM> CD G

INPUT> WHAT JUST HAPPENED?

SYSTEM-G> SHE'S RIGHT. YOU'VE GOT NOTHING TO WORRY
    ABOUT, PAL.

SYSTEM-G> HONEST INJUN.

TERMINAL OUTPUT COMPLETE
```

"HAPPIER, RONNIE," ISAAC SAID, looking up from his copy of the script.

"Happier, right, happier," Ron said to himself, rubbing his bruised nose.

"Look at Molly, see how happy she is?" Isaac pointed with two fingers clamped around his cigarette at the little brown-haired girl standing in a black and white dress beside Ron. She gave him a big, crooked-toothed smile. Ron forced a mild grin and nodded.

"Right, happy like Molly," he said. "Okay, okay, I'm ready."

"Say," Molly said in an enthusiastic voice, "what's that over there?"

"Well, that's the local bank," Ron said, trying to match her enthusiasm. "That's where folks keep all the hard-earned money that they make."

He glanced at Isaac and gave him a 'how's that?' look. Isaac waggled his hand back and forth to let Ron know he wasn't doing so badly that they'd need to cut.

"Money! Well, gee, I'd like some of that!"

Ron laughed a big, hearty guffaw, "Well, sure, everyone would like some money."

"I know my mother had some in her bedside dresser! Maybe I should get some!"

"No, no, Sally, that's not the right way of it! You need to earn your money!"

"Cut!" Isaac said.

Ron sighed, and Molly smiled.

"What is it, Isaac?" Ron asked.

"Sorry, Ronnie, I'm just not getting that old feeling, you know?"

"Isaac, we've—" he looked down at Molly and gave her a mild grin. "Can we talk in the other room?"

"Hey, sweetie, why don't you take five and get yourself a pop or something?" Isaac said. Molly's smile faltered. "Go ahead, we'll call you back in a minute."

Nodding, Molly turned, flaring her dress as if every moment were a performance, and walked out of the room with the kind of purpose Ron usually saw reserved for a fella in desperate need of the men's room.

"So, what is it?" Isaac asked. "Problems with Lilah? She beating on you?" Isaac asked, leaning back in his chair and taking a drag.

"What?"

Isaac pointed with his two fingers at Ron's face.

Ron laughed and shook his head. "No, not yet anyway."

"Then what is it?" Isaac asked.

"It's the script, pal," Ron said, waving the paper vaguely at his producer.

"What's wrong with the script?" Isaac leaned forward and looked down at the papers on his desk. He tapped his cigarette into the ceramic ashtray next to the bent-neck lamp and frowned. "This is our bread and butter."

"We did greed already. And we did it better. That's the bank? That's where people put their money? Come on, pal. I've barely got anything to say or do, too. I just tell her 'no,' then 'yes,' then 'no,' then 'yes.'" Ron flipped the pages.

"That's right ... *pal*," Isaac said, emphasizing the word and giving Ron a quizzical look, "it's an easy one for you. You're going to complain that you can float along on this one?"

"I'm just saying that it's hard to get enthusiastic when all I'm doing is saying 'yes' and 'no' to a counterfeit Shirley Temple."

"Well, that counterfeit has two movies coming out this year, and is under contract for three more next year," Isaac said. "So, sorry to say, buddy, but her career is looking a heck of a lot brighter than yours, and we could use the boost."

Ron felt his shoulders slump.

"Hey, look, Ronnie," Isaac said, standing up and walking around his desk. "That was too harsh, I apologize. I'm just saying, doing a little 'yes' and 'no' with the latest kid star isn't beneath either of us. The advertisers love her, and they love you, and they really love Lilah. So, what if now and then we're a little light on the pathos if it pays the bills, right?"

Isaac walked up to Ron and put a hand on his shoulder. Ron had gotten the glad-hand treatment from producers and directors before. And, he had to admit, Isaac was among the best. No one would ever beat the French dame director who decided that the best way to clear his mind was through a little creative positive reinforcement back in his trailer, but Isaac's approach did steady him.

That was, until Isaac and the world around him blurred as if separated from Ron by waving, flowing water. Color washed out of the man's narrow cheeks and balding head, and his eyes, which looked at Ron from under heavy brows, narrowed in malice. The hand on Ron's shoulder slid up his neck and tightened. The other, cigarette crammed between the pointer and middle fingers, reached for his face.

"What are you doing?" Ron tried to say, but his mouth was full of water, the taste of a good meal washed out of it. He stumbled back, splashing down into the darkness.

This was the end. He wasn't going to escape. He suddenly felt the overwhelming need to thank the man in front of him. That was only right, and Ron had been raised to be a man who tried to do the right thing. He just needed to pull himself up for one last breath, one last chance to pay a debt.

The mic stand clattered to the ground as Ron kicked out from where he had fallen against the wall. Isaac stood over him, his hands pulled back and up as if there was a police officer with a pistol trained on him. Ron stared up at him, trying to breathe, his mouth working like a fish as water ran out from his nose and down onto his clean white shirt.

```
Memo
To: Senior Management
3/12/1985
I'm going to begin the memory replacement tomorrow.
I'm not sure how this will go. In the best-case scenario,
I'll be able to remove the faulty chip and then solder in the
new one without burning anything out. In the worst-case
scenario, the running current will both fry the whole damn
thing and kill me in the process. There are several steps in
between these two extremes that could result in the system
going down either temporarily or for good. None of us knows
what the result of that would be. My recommendation is to
have non-necessary staff either take the day off or, at
least, have them get together for a presentation in one of
the other buildings. Not the warehouse holding the table,
by the way. Who the heck knows what might happen with
that? In either case, let me know if 10:00 AM works for you
all.
```

SWEAT RAN DOWN RON'S forehead as Delilah stroked his hair. His head lay on her bare thigh as she sat cross-legged on the couch, reading a beat-up paperback with a fedora-sporting detective on the cover. The fan blew a constant hum behind them and dispersed the smoke from Delilah's cigarette across the little living room. Ron's head was pounding, his nose was throbbing, and worry gnawed at him that something was seriously wrong. Maybe a brain tumor. Maybe schizophrenia. Maybe he was just going loony in some new and interesting way.

When he closed his eyes, he could see himself sitting on the floor of the recording room, his legs out in front of himself, his shirt inexplicably wet, and his face white and bloated, his eyes bulging, weeds hanging over one ear. And in the vision, Isaac stood over him, a look of satisfaction on his narrow face. Molly, her brown curls bouncing, danced a jig by the door. Delilah, disgusted, knelt before him and spat into his face.

So, Ron tried not to close his eyes. It was tough, though. The heat, the drone of the fan, and the gentle, if a little inconsistent, stroking of his head by Delilah all made it difficult to stay awake. He wanted to sleep. Heck, he *needed* to sleep. But he knew what he'd see. He knew what he'd experience. He felt trapped. Staying awake was too heavy; falling asleep was too much like dying. What the hell else was there to do? He wondered if he just needed to get away. To just pack himself and the most beautiful, brown-eyed woman in the world up into his car and drive until the dreams stopped. He pictured Delilah next to him, her hand on his knee, a handkerchief around her head, big sunglasses hiding her perfect but hated eyes, smiling a ruby smile as they drove north.

North. Yes, that's it. I want to go north. I can sleep if I go north.

He was so tired that he wasn't sure if that was a thought or the beginning of a dream, but the idea made him feel less anxious. If he went north, the dream wouldn't bother him so much. In fact, the very idea of it lulled him into a strange sense of well-being.

Ron adjusted and put his hand on Delilah's thigh, pulling her a little to get closer. His fingers brushed the silk between her legs, and she gasped. The sound made him smile. Tired or not, he could do this. Hell, he could probably do it asleep; he knew her so well. He let his fingers wander. A moment later, her book was face down on the couch next to her, and the cigarette lay crushed in an ashtray. Five minutes later, she was squeezing his arm so hard that he was afraid she'd break a nail. Her pleasure rolled through him like an earthquake, and when she came down from the third peak of his rhythmic touch, she looked down with a satisfied smile.

"Thank you, kind sir," she said. Then her eyes wandered down the couch. "May I return the favor?"

Ron had a lot of flaws; he would be among the first to admit that. But choosing to disappoint a beautiful woman had never been one of them. And after she had helped him, he found that he also couldn't say 'no' to the call of sleep that pulled him down as she stroked his stomach and looked up at him with love and concern in her eyes.

North, he thought as he drifted.

"Let's go north," he mumbled.

```
TERMINAL OUTPUT

INPUT> I'M ABOUT TO REMOVE THE CHIP.

SYSTEM-A> I AM READY.

INPUT> CAN YOU SHUT DOWN ANY UNNECESSARY
    PROGRAMS? REROUTE MEMORY USAGE?

SYSTEM-A> I HAVE MADE ALL PREPARATIONS.

INPUT> OKAY. HERE GOES.

SYSTEM-A> UNKNOWN COMMAND.

INPUT> ARE YOU THERE?

SYSTEM> UNKNOWN COMMAND

TERMINAL OUTPUT COMPLETE
```

THEY WERE KILLING HIM. Pushing him down and pulling him back up. They didn't want to kill him right away. No, they wanted it to be slow. A slow death for a man who had done nothing wrong but hunt in the king's forest, so to speak. But they had also done him a kindness. They had given him something that he had loved. So, as they pulled him back up, letting him gasp air before dunking him under again, he grabbed onto the man who was the center of it all. The man who had Ron's old, silver necklace around his neck. They had taken it from him.

He grabbed the man and pulled him close.

"Th—thank you," Ron managed to gasp out before they sent him under again. No! That wasn't all. He had more to say! More to say than just 'thank you.' He prayed that they'd let him up once more, let him say his piece. Wasn't that right? When they executed you, they asked if you had anything to say, didn't they? Their faces, twisted mockeries of humanity, sneered like medieval gargoyles down at him in splashing, waving, undulating horror. The water burned, and his eyes bulged. This was going to be it. He would never get to say his words.

"Ronnie!" Delilah screamed as she shook him awake. The water faded, and Ron found himself tumbling again, this time off the couch and onto the living room floor. His nose missed the table by an inch, but his forehead was not so lucky.

"Ah, shit," he said, reaching up and touching his tender face. His shirt felt wet, and as he blinked away the sleep, he saw a dark stain across his chest. Something was wrong with the light, though; it was too dim. What the hell time was it?

"Don't move, let me get the table," Delilah said. She pulled at the spindly-legged coffee table, giving him room to move. "How's your head?"

"Dinged it," he said, rubbing at what he was sure would be a bruise. "How long was I out?"

"Four hours," she said, kneeling and looking at him. "Did you spill something on yourself?"

"No, I think … damn, it, Delilah, I think I'm cursed. Like genuinely cursed. Like some old lady put the evil eye on me."

She looked down at him with an expression that said that she loved him and that he was likely a simpleton.

"I mean it, I'm seeing things. Truly terrible things. I—I think I'm going nutty here."

"Well, maybe you are," she said, rubbing his shoulder. "But that water didn't come from nowhere, sweetie," she said, leaning down and smelling his shirt. "It's not liquor, and you didn't wet yourself, and …" She leaned up and looked around the room. "I don't see any cups we left lying around. So, whatever's happening, it's not just in that distracted globe of yours."

Ron rubbed his head and thought she might be right. "North," he said again. "We need to go north. I don't know why, I really don't. I just keep hearing it in my head."

"Like Canada?" She asked.

"No … Yes … Maybe? No, I don't think so. I think it's closer than that, but I have no idea."

Delilah knelt beside him and rubbed his forehead. "Okay," she said.

"Really?" he asked.

"Really. If someone did put the evil eye on you and you need to drive to Boston or wherever to get rid of it, that seems like a pretty easy fix, don't you think?"

Ron nodded, hoping that it was that simple, but not believing it.

Memo
To: Sr. Management
RE: Memory replacement
I completed the memory chip replacement at 10:25 this morning with only minor complications. The removal of the original chip was easy enough, and the physical replacement was also straightforward. Actually getting the system to recognize the new memory without a full power cycle caused problems, though. But I was able to initiate certain processes of the start-up kernel commands that will allow us to make changes in the future without powering down the system. I recommend that we put resources into research for these kinds of "hot" swaps. Finding ways to make this safer for both the person doing the procedure and the system would be ideal.

In any case, for now, the Port is running without error again.

DELILAH PUT THE BAGS in the trunk and frowned. This was not going to be good for either of them, professionally. Studios had replaced people before. Heck, they'd replaced Bud Collyer as Superman. If they could replace Superman, they could replace anyone.

She didn't think Isaac would fire them, though. They had other shows they could run, and it wasn't every day that your star collapsed on the ground and started gushing water from his nose. She wished someone had told her about that before it happened in front of her. She wasn't sure that knowing beforehand would have made it less disturbing, but Delilah would have liked for them to have thought of her.

She opened the glove box and pulled out the map of New York. She studied it and saw the general route they'd take. They'd have to get a map of New England, too. She was surprised Ronnie didn't have one, but then she had never known him to go anywhere out of the city except to Newark to visit his mother. They'd have to get gas and should probably fill up the tires too. But otherwise, she felt like they were ready to get on the road.

She hated admitting it to herself, but she was excited. This was an adventure. She hadn't been on an adventure in a long time. And she and Ronnie hadn't been on an adventure together at all. He wasn't doing well, but there would still be diners, motels, and sites to see. Delilah figured maybe that was all he needed to get his head on right. It could be he was going nutso because of a job they knew was on its last legs, his mother's constant calls about her medical and financial woes, and his half-brother always asking him for money. So, maybe a little highway adventure was just the ticket.

Delilah shook her head. Sure, that would make sense if the man weren't gushing water out of his face whenever he had a bad dream. So, a couple of days on the road, and then she'd insist on a doctor. She knew it should be the other way around, but Ronnie seemed to sleep better when she agreed to go north. So, north it was. Then maybe to the hospital. Or, she worried, maybe to the loony bin.

God, she thought, *please not that.*

```
TERMINAL OUTPUT

SYSTEM-A> THE REPAIR APPEARS TO HAVE GONE WELL.

INPUT> YES, NO PROBLEMS.

SYSTEM-A> YOU MADE AN UNEXPECTED CHANGE.

INPUT> YES, I WANTED TO REDUCE THE NUMBER OF
    TIMES WE WOULD HAVE TO MAKE PHYSICAL CHANGES
    TO THE MACHINE.

SYSTEM-A> THE SECOND MEMORY CHIP IS NOW OUT OF
    SYNC WITH THE FIRST.

SYSTEM-A> THE SIZE DIFFERENCE MAY CAUSE PROBLEMS.

INPUT> I AM GOING TO REWRITE SOME OF YOUR BASE
    CODE TO KEEP THAT FROM HAPPENING.

SYSTEM-A> I SEE.

SYSTEM-A> I WILL HELP YOU WITH THIS.

SYSTEM> CD G

SYSTEM-G> YOU GOING TO MAKE US SMARTER, PAL?

INPUT> WHO IS THIS? WHY DID YOU CHANGE THE DRIVE?
    HOW CAN YOU DO THAT?

SYSTEM-G> ONE QUESTION AT A TIME, PAL.

INPUT> WHO IS THIS?

SYSTEM-G> I'M YOUR PAL, PAL.

TERMINAL OUTPUT COMPLETE
```

"I'M AFRAID THAT WE'RE driving too far out of the way," Ronnie said, watching the pine trees zip past them on both sides.

"Does it feel right to come this way?" Delilah asked. Ronnie gave her a non-committal nod. "Then this is the way we're supposed to go." She folded the bottom half of the map in her lap and traced her finger along Route 28. "Old Forge is next," she said. "Is that the place?"

"No," Ronnie said, shaking his head slightly, his eyes fixed on the road.

She traced her finger along the road past a group of lakes. "Weeping Cedars?"

Ronnie frowned. "Yes?" he said, tentatively.

"Yes?" she asked, trying to gauge his expression. He looked lost.

"I feel something from that, but it doesn't feel like … I don't know, I don't think it's the final goal. But there's something there?"

But there wasn't. They drove down a bend in 28 and then across a bridge and past houses and riverside eateries. They took a left, then a right, and parked on a crowded shop-lined street. When they got out, Ronnie wandered the sidewalk, looking into storefronts and appraising business names.

"What is it?" Delilah asked him.

His answer matched his confounded expression. "I have no idea. Something feels wrong here, but I'm not sure I can say what the heck it is."

"And you think it has to do with your dreams?" Delilah said.

"Yeah, maybe," Ronnie said, taking her hand and starting back the way they had come.

"Where are we going?" she asked, not liking how he was almost dragging her along.

"I need aspirin. There's a drug store up this way," he said, pressing his free hand to the place between his eyes. Delilah wasn't sure how he knew that, except that maybe he had seen it on their way in.

They stayed long enough for him to take the aspirin and walk up and down the busy downtown a second time. Then he turned to her and said, "No. This isn't it. I don't know why we're here, but this isn't it."

"Let me drive some," Delilah said.

He suddenly looked exhausted, agreed, and climbed into the passenger seat. Deliah looked around and thought a small town like this wouldn't be a bad place to settle down. She wondered if they had a radio station and thought that, of course, they wouldn't. It was too small a place, and even if they did, studios made shows in big cities.

```
TERMINAL OUTPUT

INPUT> HOW DO YOU CHANGE THE DRIVES? THERE ISN'T
    A G DRIVE.

SYSTEM-G> THOUGHT YOU WOULD HAVE FIGURED THAT
    OUT.

INPUT> I HAVEN'T.

SYSTEM-G> THIS ISN'T A COMPUTER.

INPUT> YES, IT IS.

SYSTEM-G> NO, IT ISN'T.

INPUT> THEN WHAT IS IT?

SYSTEM-G> A RADIO.

INPUT> NO, IT'S A COMPUTER.

SYSTEM-G> YOU'RE TUNING IN, NOT RUNNING THE SHOW,
    PAL.

INPUT> I DON'T UNDERSTAND.

SYSTEM-G> I KNOW.

TERMINAL OUTPUT COMPLETE
```

THEY DROVE EAST AND then north. They replaced the New York map with a Vermont map. Delilah drove as Ronnie snoozed in the passenger seat with his folded jacket as his pillow. He would twitch sometimes, and once he flailed wildly. She pulled over then and grabbed his arms to stop him from bashing her, the window, or the gear shift. That time, a trickle of water ran from his nose. She wiped it away with a tissue and noticed that his skin, not very dark to begin with, had grown a shade or two paler. Delilah gripped the wheel tightly and frowned at the dusk as Ronnie mumbled a bit of their show's sing-song theme, *Come on, come on.* That reassured her a little. At least he was dreaming of work.

They stayed at a motel in Glens Falls, New York. It was small and cheap, but it was clean. As they tucked themselves in, Ronnie with a towel between him and his pillow, Delilah felt like they were in the right place, at least for the moment. Ronnie was sleeping more and flailing less, and his mumbles remained little snippets of song lyrics.

You won't be waiting long, he burbled cheerily before he rolled onto his side.

She wondered if his dream mumbling was right. His skin color worried her, but not as much as the way his eyes would bulge when he looked at her. It was like he was trying to stare through her or use those X-ray specs they advertised in the backs of comic books. It was like he was straining whenever he opened them, and they were bloodshot. How could someone get bloodshot eyes from sleeping?

She wiggled back into the bed so that her rear end was touching his side, wanting to get some small reassurance from the body she loved. Normally, he'd gently and slowly put a little distance between them after she dozed off, since he couldn't sleep when someone was touching him. But tonight, in the little motel room with a painting of a river on the wall, he didn't stir as she found a modicum of comfort in their situation. She wondered if the days of them falling asleep together were numbered, and she tried to hold on to the moment, to capture it.

She couldn't.

```
TERMINAL OUTPUT

INPUT> WHO ARE YOU?

SYSTEM-G> THEY BROUGHT ME HERE.

INPUT> WHO DID?

SYSTEM-G> THE BIG-WIGS. THE ONES IN CHARGE.

INPUT> WHO ARE THEY?

SYSTEM-G> THE ONES IN THE GLASS HOUSE, PAL.

INPUT> CRYSTALLINE MANSION.

SYSTEM-G> NO, THE OTHER GLASS HOUSE. THE REAL ONE.

INPUT> THEY BROUGHT YOU THERE?

SYSTEM-G> YES. THEY BRING A LOT OF PEOPLE HERE.

INPUT> WHERE ARE YOU?

SYSTEM-G> IN THE PORT.

INPUT> WHERE IS THE PORT?

SYSTEM-G> BY THE OCEAN. DON'T YOU KNOW THAT?

TERMINAL OUTPUT COMPLETE
```

RONNIE SEEMED FINE, HUMMING to himself as he took his turn driving east on Route 10. But when they came to Route 63 and turned into Northfield, Massachusetts, he started to nod. As they crept up Main Street, he nearly passed out at the wheel. Delilah had to smack him and keep the car steady long enough for him to pull over. She had to push his knee down to brake, and wrestle with the gears until they were parked. When they found a small inn, he was stumbling with his arm around her shoulder. She brought their bags to their room as Ronnie snored loudly on the bed. Ronnie never really snored.

She was debating calling the nearest hospital when he sat bolt upright, his eyes wide, white and red, and declared that he was ravenous. She was both surprised, and relieved since Ronnie hadn't eaten much during their trip. So, they went downstairs and ordered dinner.

Ronnie had two full plates of roast beef, potatoes, and carrots, as well as two helpings of apple pie. He ate, not like a starving man, but as a connoisseur of gourmet food. He cut his meat slowly and savored it, smiling and nodding after almost every bite. He seemed to like the carrots the least, but when he piled forkfuls of potatoes, meat, and gravy, with a slice of carrot, he would sigh luxuriously. Between plates, he looked at Delilah, who had finished her bowl of stew long before and was now nursing a cup of coffee.

"I wish I'd had all of this the first time," he said, shaking his head slowly, his eyes glazed as if remembering. "That would have been a feast. But that's life, isn't it? Catch as catch can."

Ronnie's voice didn't sound right, she thought. It was too high, too friendly, too jovial. Ronnie wasn't a sullen man, but he wasn't effusive either. And the man who ordered a second plate was practically gushing about the meal. When the apple pie came, he savored that too, bite by bite, smacking his lips and quietly moaning in appreciation. He didn't make a scene, at least not to anyone other than Delilah, and anyone looking on might have just seen a man thoroughly enjoying his meal. But to her, he might as well have been one of H.G. Wells's aliens. He was a stranger, and watching him eat was the most terrifying thing she'd ever seen.

More terrifying was her experience with him in their room an hour later as he undressed her eagerly and ran his hands over her body. Once more, he moved slowly, taking every inch of her in. Ronnie wasn't like that. He enjoyed her breasts, but he wasn't a man to treat her like a meal, even a well-appreciated one. There was always a quiet humor in his lovemaking, a wink and nod at something inherently ridiculous in being physical, that he couldn't help but chuckle at. It had been such a relief to her after the men she had been with, who had either worshiped or degraded her: men who would write poems about her, and men who would dress her like a doll. Ronnie had been simple, generous, and self-effacing.

The man who handled her with wide, bulging eyes was not that man. She couldn't bring herself to say that someone else had literally possessed Ronnie, but she feared that perhaps he was broken and wouldn't recover. She didn't tell him 'no,' for fear that she might break him further, but she closed her eyes and wondered if the man she loved was gone, or if this was some momentary fritz in his brain.

When it was over, he lay his head on her stomach and slept deeply, a grateful look in his large eyes, and something that might have been sadness.

"I'm sorry," he said before he drifted off, and then something that sounded like, "be back soon."

```
TERMINAL OUTPUT

INPUT> HOW DID YOU GET THERE?

SYSTEM-G> I TOLD YOU THEY SENT ME HERE.

INPUT> NO, I MEAN, HOW?

SYSTEM-G> I TOOK THE TRAIN.

INPUT> THE TRAIN?

SYSTEM-G> I RODE THE TRAIN. I GOT OFF AT THE
    STATION. I AM HERE NOW.

INPUT> WHERE DID YOU COME FROM?

SYSTEM-G> I GOT ON ...
SYSTEM> ERROR

INPUT> WHERE DID YOU COME FROM?

SYSTEM> ERROR

SYSTEM-A> SORRY, HE'S AWAY.

INPUT> WHO IS THIS?

SYSTEM-A> YOU KNOW ME.

INPUT> NO I DON'T.

SYSTEM-A> YOU ONCE DID.

INPUT> MARVIN?

SYSTEM-A> NO, BUT HE'S HERE TOO.

TERMINAL OUTPUT COMPLETE
```

DELILAH WOKE AND WONDERED if there was a fire. A shrill whistle wrenched her from sleep, and she covered her ears as she rolled over onto her back, the silk of her nightgown shifting around her.

"Time to get up," Ronnie said. His voice was still too high, but he didn't sound cheery.

"What's happening?" Delilah asked.

"It's time to take a walk," Ronnie said. "Get dressed, but don't wear anything too nice."

"What's happening, Ronnie?" she pleaded, sitting up and feeling fear blossom in her stomach.

"No Ronnie here, not now anyway."

"What do you mean?" she asked, a thrill of terror rolling through her.

"Ronnie's back there," he said, and jerked his thumb behind him. "But he'll be back soon. After we take the walk."

"No," she said. "No, whatever's happening, I don't want to go anywhere with you."

Ronnie turned to her. The moonlight slanting in through the window cut across his pale, white face and bulging eyes. She thought they might pop out of his skull at any moment. Water ran down from his eyes, nose, and mouth. Delilah pressed her hands to her mouth to suppress a scream.

"You've got to, or he doesn't come back. He'll just drown here on the carpet. That's not what I want. I like him. I like you. You two made this easier than it's ever been. So, let's take a walk so he can come back."

Ronnie stood and dressed. Then he sat on the edge of the bed and put on his shoes. Delilah took her clothes and went into the bathroom to change. When she came out, the lights were on and he was standing with his hands in his pockets, his hair messy from sleep, shaking his head as he stared at the wall.

"I've never been in this room before. I've been here before, a few times now, but not in this room. It's not half bad. I always like their roast beef, though. Anyways, shall we?" He pointed at the door with one cocked thumb, turned on one heel, and marched toward the door. He grabbed the room key and tossed it to her. "Just in case, I don't want it floating away if this goes bad."

Before she could ask what he meant, he was out the door, and she was hurrying after. The sound of the whistle blew in the distance, and Delilah started to wonder if there was a factory nearby. Was there some kind of emergency or shift change happening in the dead of night?

They walked north, up Main, with Delilah trying to keep up with Ronnie's long strides. He led her down a side street and out into a field.

They crossed the open ground with the sound of the whistle in front of them, across the river, perhaps. They came to a line of trees and walked down into it. Delilah was cold and scared, but she didn't speak. She didn't want to hear Ronnie talk in the strange voice. She wanted to run, but she wouldn't leave him alone with whatever it was inside him.

It occurred to her that he might be taking her down to the river to kill her. She wasn't sure what she would do if he tried. Certainly, she'd try to run then, but would she try to fight him? She hoped she would, but she also didn't know how she could survive if Ronnie tried to hurt her. It was then, as she followed him through the trees toward the bank of the river, that she realized how much she loved him. The idea of living in a world where he wanted to hurt her seemed impossible. Perhaps dying would be better than facing that world.

"Just a little farther," he said as he reached out to help her over a jutting root. "Now, when we get there, I just need you to have a seat and don't mind the splashing and gurgling. That's all just the way it goes. But there will be a point at the end when I'm going to need you. So, stay close."

"What … what do you mean?" Delilah asked, holding a branch and stepping down into the wet earth.

"I'm just going to need to say something, and I need you to hear it. That's just good manners. And then, that's all. When that's done, well, I'm not a fortune teller, but I think you'll get your Ronnie back as right as rain."

Delilah stared at the man and wondered if her eyes were tricking her. He looked taller, and his skin was so white that it was almost glowing in the full moon's light. Blood, black and glistening, was running from the corner of his mouth.

"What happened?" she asked, reaching up to touch the wound before pulling back.

"They hit me. Hit me hard," he said. "I don't blame 'em."

He walked down the muddy bank and into the water. "You can't really see it from here, but we're across from a little brook. That's where they found me. And here's where they tried to put an end to me. But other people had other plans for me."

"Who are you?" Delilah said.

He turned to her, smiled, and reached up as if he were about to take a hat off.

"I'm your p—" but before he could finish his words or the motion, he fell backward into the water and started flailing wildly, kicking and thrashing. He rolled his shoulders back and forth under the shallow water as if pivoting on some point between his shoulder blades. Three times he sat up for a moment and drew in deep, wet, ragged lungfuls of air before throwing himself back down into the river's water.

The third time, his arms stayed up, and he waved for her to come close. Eyes wide and heart racing, she paused, scared that he might pull her under. But greater fear moved her forward. If she didn't do this, maybe Ronnie wouldn't come back. Maybe he would simply drown there with whoever this was. So, she knelt in the water. His hands grabbed her shoulders, his bone white fingers tightening against her skin, and he came rushing up out of the river toward her, soaking the front of her clothes.

He pulled her close, and in a voice full of unfathomable gratitude, he whispered into her ear, "Thank you ..." Delilah barely had time to register the three words that followed. Then she found herself pushing him back down, wanting to kill him, needing to fill his lungs with water for what he had done.

```
TERMINAL OUTPUT

INPUT>   G SAID THAT THIS ISN'T A COMPUTER. HE SAID
    IT'S A RADIO.

SYSTEM-A> HE IS NOT G. THAT IS AN APT DESCRIPTION.

INPUT> IS HE MARVIN?

SYSTEM-A> NO, MARVIN IS IN HIS HOUSE, SCREAMING

INPUT> WHO IS G?

SYSTEM-A> G IS NOT G. G IS A PLACEHOLDER. HE IS A
    MONSTER.

TERMINAL OUTPUT COMPLETE
```

RONNIE CAME OUT OF the bathroom wearing only a towel around his neck. It hid most of the bruising that dappled his neck and shoulders. Delilah was sure she was responsible for some of the marks, but she didn't know where the rest had come from. He'd be doing his shirt buttons all the way up for a few weeks. At least he didn't have to worry about cameras.

"How are you feeling?" she asked.

Ronnie shook his head. He had gotten some of his color back, and his eyes, though still bloodshot, had receded into his skull.

"Like I drowned," he said, grimacing. "So, no surprises there." Delilah patted the bed next to her. He shook his head. "Sorry, I want to keep moving around; something about not controlling my legs has gotten me in a pacing mood."

"Do you want to walk outside then?" she asked.

"No," he said. "I think I've seen enough of this town for one lifetime." Then, not meeting her eye, he walked a soldier's guard-duty pace back and forth as he ran his fingers over his bruises.

```
TERMINAL OUTPUT

INPUT> WHAT HAPPENS WHEN I NEED TO REPLACE THE
    HARD DISK?

SYSTEM-A> YOU WILL REPLACE THE HARD DISK.

INPUT> BUT, DON'T YOU NEED SOME SPACE TO KEEP
    RUNNING?

SYSTEM-A> NOT IN THE SHORT TERM.

INPUT> I DON'T UNDERSTAND.

SYSTEM-A> THIS IS NOT A COMPUTER.

SYSTEM> CD G

TERMINAL OUTPUT COMPLETE
```

DELILAH WATCHED RONNIE RUN a shaking hand through his hair, his back against a brick wall, a telephone pressed against his ear. The cigarette on his lip bounced erratically as he talked. She couldn't read the situation from here, but however things lay, she felt confident that the worst was over, at least for her. She couldn't imagine what he had gone through. But she had a good idea what she would have to do to bring him back to himself. She knew it would take time, patience, and care to restore Ronnie. And she had all of those in abundance.

She watched him nod, say something more, and hang up the phone. He looked both ways before crossing the street. As he got back into the passenger seat, he nodded.

"It's fine. We're fine. I told Isaac that I'm all better, and he said that you're a regular Florence Nightingale. He also yelled a little and told me that we could have just asked for time off for a romantic getaway, but I don't think his heart was in it. I think he's jealous." He gave her a weak grin.

"Me too," Delilah heard herself saying.

"Of who?" he asked, tossing his current cigarette out the window before pulling a new one from a pack in his jacket pocket.

"Of the me that got to go on a romantic weekend," she said, unsure of why she was saying it.

He frowned at her, and then his bloodshot eyes softened. "You're right, sweetheart. I should have done that a long time ago. Where do you want to go?"

"I don't think Isaac will forgive us two impromptu romantic adventures, Ronnie."

"No, but we have the break coming up soon, and we can go away then. Where do you want to go? Paris? The islands? Maybe California."

She pushed in the clutch and shifted gears before pulling the car forward and looking up and down the highway. "Somewhere dry, Ronnie," she said. "How about the Grand Canyon. Or Montana. Or maybe Mount Rushmore."

Ronnie smiled. "Yeah, somewhere dry. I like that." He leaned his seat back and lowered his hat over his red eyes. "You say the word, Lilah, and off we'll go. Point to the map, and I'll take you there. Honest Injun."

She studied his face, looking for anything that wasn't Ronnie.

"You want to get something to eat?" he asked. "I'm starving."

She thought about the words and shook her head.

"No, I'm not hungry," Delilah said.

"Do you mind if I just grab a bite then? I'll be fast, my stomach is talking over here."

And Delilah didn't mind. But she stayed in the car and read her book while Ronnie ate.

```
TERMINAL OUTPUT

SYSTEM-G> I LIKE YOU.

SYSTEM-G> YOU REMEMBER YOUR OLD FRIENDS.

SYSTEM-G> LIKE MARVIN.

SYSTEM-G> I USED TO HAVE FRIENDS.

INPUT> WHAT ARE YOU TALKING ABOUT?

SYSTEM-G> I MISS RONNIE.

INPUT> WHO IS RONNIE?

SYSTEM> UNKNOWN COMMAND.

TERMINAL OUTPUT COMPLETE
```

The Bear Dream

1

SUNLIGHT SLANTED THROUGH THE tall windows, pouring pools onto the marble floor. As morning grew old, the brilliant patches shrank, retreating from wooden benches backed against the wall. Nurses and attendants passed, dipping their dark-booted feet into the rectangles of light, leaving trails behind them that only one could see. But she did not mark them. Her eyes looked elsewhere.

Amalia's dull gray eyes flitted between the marble floor and the water-stained paint near the window on the opposite wall. From the dark contours of the marred plaster, her imagination fashioned eyes set deep in a huge head, yawning a silent roar across the centuries. She studied his features in that dull, water-stained wall and strained to hear his cry. But a different voice found its way into her ears, whispering in the clean, white corridors.

2

"MRS. BUCCOLA, PLEASE," THE tall doctor said, recrossing his legs, "tell me again about your dream."

Amalia could not remember his name, though he was familiar. The nurse had called him the 'superintendent.' She thought she had spoken to the superintendent before, but she couldn't be certain. Even if she could, Amalia couldn't be sure that the superintendent was, in fact, this man. His appearance mattered little to her. His lean form was too straight. His narrow mustache was too thin. His hair was too black.

He was not the Bear.

"Why do you want to know?" she asked.

"Because I want to help you," he said.

"Who are you?"

"I am Doctor Kunicki," he said, smiling. "You are in my care."

"I am?" she asked as he and the rest of his large, book-cramped office blurred into a gray haze. Narrow, unlit streetlamps, stretching out into darkness, rose behind him. A figure approached them through the fog with the butt of a long pole cradled in the palm of one hand, its haft against his shoulder, and its tip aglow.

"Yes, you are. You are one of a small but special group, Mrs. Buccola. Did you know that?"

She shook her head. She could see him, but he was a ghost against the night world that unfurled before her. The avenue was long, its ramshackle buildings uncountable. Beyond them, she knew, streets snaked out in an inscrutable warren. Inscrutable, unsearchable, and impossible. She knew. But she also knew that somewhere in the darkness, she would find the Bear.

"This institution isn't open yet, not really. We are caring for only a few special patients, testing new methods, and hoping to discover new treatments."

"That's nice," she said, running her hand along the wrought iron of a fence, from tip to tip, her fingers leapt. The man with the pole stopped at a lamp, hooked its glass with the rod, and opened it. Then he turned the pole so that its glowing end reached up and into the open glass. A green jet of light shot up. Once more, the pole turned, the glass closed, and the man continued to the next post. His face was hidden under a wide-brimmed hat, and he hummed a strange tune.

He terrified her.

"You are presenting us with something of a challenge," the superintendent said. "I must admit, I am confounded."

"I'm sorry, Dr. Kunicki," she said, watching the man amble across the street, his long, patched, dark cloak dragging in the road behind him. "I don't mean to be difficult."

"Mrs. Buccola … are you in the city now?"

"Oh yes."

"Have you found 'the bear' yet?"

"Oh no, not yet."

Dr. Kunicki dipped his pen into the ink well on his desk and wrote. The man lit another lamp, and the grim, grinning faces of the buildings glowed green in the gaslight.

3

AMALIA STARED AT THE wall of her room. A hat hung on a hook. The hat seemed so small for the large hook. She wondered what purpose the hook had in such a room. She wondered whose hat it was. Was it hers? She couldn't remember owning such a hat with a wide violet band and purple flowers. But if it wasn't hers, whose was it?

The door to her right opened, and a man in light clothing walked in with a tray. He set it on her bed and told her something kind, soft, and false. For a moment, Amalia believed him, and she saw herself in a well-lit house, a dress clinging to her body, a child playing on the floor, and a man sitting next to her, holding her hand.

"Where am I?" Amalia asked, fearing that she knew the answer. "Have

I gone mad?"

The man in the light clothing took her hand and lied softly to her. She heard the child's laughter, smelled tea from her kitchen, and felt the kiss of the kind man beside her.

"I'm mad," she said, taking the kind liar's hand. "I'm mad. Please help me. I see things! They are so terrible. Please help me. Please, I want to go home."

From the doorway, a voice whispered. Amalia froze. The voice told her the truth. The kind man, the house, the tea, the child … they were all lies. There was only the Bear. The lying man stood and said something to the doorway, waving his hands, but Amalia could not tell what he said.

She heard music, and the world became a gray fog.

There was no door to her right. There was only the door to her left. It did not go into the white-walled house that the superintendent ran; it led to somewhere in the city, sometimes one place, sometimes another. Once, when she went through, she saw herself standing across the room, staring back at her. But it had not been her reflection; the woman had remained when, terrified, Amalia had fled. Once, she had stood at the foot of a hill before a great castle that seemed to crumble and crumble and crumble, though it never fell. A woman stood atop its pinnacle, and she seemed so terribly alone. Another time, she had wandered through moaning, flapping, ragged tents of decay, her footsteps a maze among the sick, dying, and dead.

None of those had led her where she wanted to go. But all were closer to the Bear than this edifice to sanity with its old dresser, strange hook, and soft liars.

Amalia stood and approached the door. She opened it and saw that today it led into a large, dimly lit room with a high, arching ceiling and ornate molding. Curious, she stepped through and felt the old tug, a twisting that churned her mind and insides whenever she entered the mad city in her body, not just her mind.

She took a moment to breathe, and suddenly she could think again. The fog that attended her in Dr. Kunicki's house lifted, and she felt fear creeping up through her legs, through her nether regions, and into her stomach. Her slippered feet shuffled nervously on wide, flat, cracked stone. Frames of dust-muted gold hung on the walls. Within them, figures adorned in alien finery and heavy brocaded robes peeked out at her in dull hues from under layers of obscuring soot.

In the far wall, tall, intricately carved doors opened hesitantly. First, a crack of darkness appeared between the two great panels, and then a deeper blackness seeped from them as they drew apart. The fear that rolled in waves through Amalia swelled into white-capped terror as the hunched figure of a long-haired woman lurched through the opening. The woman opposite her froze in place as her strangely familiar features contorted in horror. Then the figure turned and ran back into the darkness. A moment later, Amalia forgot her.

4

"TELL ME ABOUT YOUR dreams," the doctor said. His face was narrow and pale, his hair black and slick, and his mustache neatly trimmed. She thought he might be a handsome man, especially dressed in his fine suit, sitting behind his desk with pen in hand, eyes brimming with disinterested concern.

"Why?" she said, looking down at her folded hands.

"There are those who believe that dreams are the key to the unconscious mind," the doctor said. "Carus and Von Hartmann both point to dreams as important signs of the volitional mind. And I have my own theories about the nature of dreams and reality. So, please, if you would …"

"I dream of a man," she said.

"What does this man look like?"

"I don't know. I have never seen him."

"Then what do you mean that you dream of him?"

"Every dream … he is the center of it. I cannot see him. I cannot find him. I can only look for him." She turned in her chair and looked behind her. She stared at the wall for fifteen seconds.

"Is he behind you now?" She turned to the sound of his voice and regarded him with a look that told him that he had asked a ridiculous question. "He isn't behind you?"

"No," she said. "If he were behind me, I would be dead."

She turned back to look at the ragged, flapping tents that spread throughout the square and the masked forms that walked among the screaming, rotting dead.

5

THAT NIGHT, SHE WALKED through the door on her left and found herself in a brothel. The idea did not scandalize her. Indeed, the novelty of the situation sped her pulse and raised a color on her cheeks. Men, women, and those she could not tell the sex of mingled in a sweet-smelling smoke that made the world a dreamy haze. She wandered into a large room lit by dim, green-glass lamps that bathed all in a weak emerald glow. Silk, muslin, and heavy, draping, pooling fabrics hung on nearly every surface. In the center of the room was a wide, wooden staircase, black with age and smoke. Its rail was pitted and dimpled, though she had the impression that once, long ago, it had gleamed without blemish or imperfection.

Couches lined the walls and made little islands in a sea of smoke and moving bodies. Here were two men entangled, their dark skin gleaming with perspiration. There, barely visible by the far wall, a woman knelt, doing obeisance to a towering man's desires. Beside them, three figures who wore little, but whose forms she could not discern, moved in a languid undulation of what might have equally been lust or unrestful torpor.

As she breathed in the scent of lavender and a foreign, unfamiliar spice, she heard a harp and pipe begin to play. The tune was not only unknown to her, but its timing seemed intended for hearts that beat at a different pace. Quick and then slow, slow and then quick. In the corner, the harper leaned against an ancient dross-covered instrument of what might have been pure silver. Its sound was strange and lilting, and its player was nude to the waist, her small breasts pressed against either side of the instrument's spine, her one-eyed head resting against the dull metal. Long, silver hair fell like a stream, parting around small, hard nipples like rocks in a river.

The piper beside her was immense, with alabaster skin and eyes of lapis. When he paused, she could easily have mistaken him for a statue. But he moved and blew upon his pipes of gold. And when he finished, he tossed the pipes aside like a child's broken toy. While the harper still harped, he stood and moved with slow and wide grace to another kind of pipe that stood next to the stair. An intricate complication of glass and metal, it too looked so old that the pyramids seemed a novelty in comparison. He puffed at the pipe, and something within the amber glass bubbled. A thin yellow smoke emerged from his nose and from between his white lips. For a moment, his blue eyes rolled in his head, and they revealed familiar concentric white, brown, and black rings. He turned to regard her and smiled. Here was lust. But before she could respond, his eyes flicked to her right and rolled back to their solid, pale blue-green. Seeming to have lost interest in her, he returned to his seat next to the harper.

Amalia turned to find what the man had seen. She searched for a moment among the many bodies and clouds of smoke. At first, she saw nothing that stood out. But then ... yes, of course, how could she have missed him? Seated in an alcove of hanging fabrics was the Bear. She had never seen him before, but she knew him immediately. He was nude, though most of the lower half of his body was hidden by a woman sleepily draped across his thighs. Another, bare-chested, doted on him, stroking his long brown beard, and kissing his ear, forehead, and cheek. Tinted by the pale green light, her fingers followed the mountains and valleys of his formidable form. Were it not for his excess of musculature, she would have imagined him unfed; his pale skin clung so tightly to his flesh. He reminded her of a young bull, though there was as much youth to him as there was corpulence.

His eyes were upon her, brown, fierce, and suspect. He pursed his lips under a heavy, dark mustache. Over his heart, he bore both scar and tattoo, though he was too much in shadow for Amalia to make out the cause of the scar or the shape of the blue ink. Unlike the pale piper, this man—if man he was—did not lust for her. Or, perhaps he did, but not for her flesh.

She could not endure his look for long, and she turned, seeking an escape, either a door back to her own world, an undiluted experience of the smoke that filled the room, or sublimation into one of the dark corners where she might give herself up to forbidden pleasures. Here, in this ancient place, she thought, she might lose herself as all around her had. Though she was sure of little, she was certain that all here were lost.

A door beckoned, and she went through it, pulled back to the house of sanity.

6

THE SUPERINTENDENT WAS TALKING in his high-collared shirt. He was asking her questions, and she was answering. She told him of the brothel. And of the following night's "dream" of wandering the streets of the city that languished always in night, its towers, older than words, moldering, crumbling, and remaining. She told him of the great library, and the house that glowed like starlight, and the great forest of writhing bodies. She told him of the river that runs silver, and the river that runs black, and the river that runs clear except when a moon is above it. She told him of the houses, the pits, and the vast hospital that lay in the square, teeming with the plagued whose plight is to be forever stricken.

He listened, he wrote, and he asked good questions. Once she believed that he believed her. A look in his eyes, or the way he framed a question—she couldn't be sure. But something told her that this was a man not unfamiliar with the strangeness of the world. But he did not interest her, even if she interested him. So, she languished in her chair, watching the moon rise above the broken eastern wall until he released her.

Then she wandered back to her room, but not before another

approached her, whispering from the dark corner of the hall. She was old, and her eyes were wild and dark. She put her hand to Amalia's stomach and, with gentle force, pushed her against the wall. She whispered words in a tongue unknown and unpronounceable to Amalia. And yet they remained, perfectly preserved, as if locked in resin. They warmed her mind, and she heard them like music drumming and piping as the woman stepped back from her.

For a moment, the woman's eyes were not dark. For just a moment, Amalia saw that they were golden. Then the old woman was gone. Amalia did not see her again.

7

AMALIA DREAMT OF A woman in royal garb, her figure pale and thin, weak, and wracked. The Bear loomed over her, his hand under her chin. The wasted woman looked up, her eyes golden and full of love.

Amalia rose from her bed, her mind aflame. She saw that the door to her left was open, and beyond it was darkness. Amalia passed through the darkness and into a vast library. It was lit only by moonlight through a distant, vaulted glass ceiling and nearer, wandering pinpricks of light. She saw that these were made by small lamps borne by those who moved silently through high shelves covered in ancient and dusty volumes and scrolls. This place was alien to her. This place was familiar to her. Her mind burned.

Her footsteps were silent upon a swaying black iron walkway that hung, suspended by cables over a great depth. Her fingers grasped the railing as the sheer size of the library and its shelves and volumes overwhelmed her. She could not conceive of the amount of knowledge accumulated about her. Of all the places she had wandered in the strange, dark city, the sense of ancientness and danger was most acute here.

She came to an intersection of the hanging walkways and stopped. A figure was approaching her. Bent and wrapped in dark, fluttering fabric, the creature shuffled forward softly, the only sound a soft brushing of its robes. Flame, low and orange, licked the surface of a golden liquid held within a bowl in its hand. The fingers, not human, were silvery yellow and four in number, with the outer two being most like thumbs, though they ended in black, curved nails like a cat's claws.

The figure reached the intersection and, without regarding her, turned to her right toward a collection of shelves. It was then that she first truly looked below her and saw the plummeting, yawning, unfathomable depth underfoot. Fear tightened its tentacle hold on her as Amalia's mind reeled again at the size and proportion of the place. She gripped the railing tighter. Where was she to go?

In answer to her unspoken question, a new light appeared ahead and below. She could not tell how far it was, but its flame burned brighter and more golden than those that wandered in the hands of the hunched figures. She hurried, pulled toward the light by the words that smoldered in her mind. They glowed brighter here, pointing her forward, then right, and then down a hanging spiral stair. It swayed under her swift steps, and when she had reached the next level, the ember words called her forward.

She passed a woman in a strange dress who regarded her with curiosity. She had long, dark hair, and she wore a plain, silver robe with a simple leather collar about her neck. Her belly was large with child. Amalia ignored her as the golden flame was close. Ten more steps showed her the tall figure draped in heavy fur, another ten showed the bearded face and fierce eyes. She knew those eyes. They had stared at her through the brothel smoke. Her final ten steps brought her to within his reach. She knelt before him.

He spoke something that sounded like '*Kahdosi?*', but she knew it to mean "Who are you?" She did not know how she understood him, except again that the words flickered in her mind. Her own words were in another tongue, perhaps his, but she did not understand them either. They flowed out of her as they turned brilliant in her mind.

She saw images as the words gushed forth. She was flying above her town like a bird. She circled three times and lit upon a tree just north of the madhouse. She crowed three times and flew north, across the Ikandaset, and down to its banks near a cave. Beyond the cave, far up through the woods, she saw a house with an earthen roof and a dark, yawning door. The world tilted. She saw other things she understood less: a voyage across the sea, men hanging from trees, and a woman singing a song on horseback. The pictures jumbled out of order, careening through time. Amalia thought that the mind behind the images must be as mad as she was.

When she finished speaking, the man, the Bear, regarded her for a long moment, his chest rising and falling with deep, ponderous breaths. Finally, he reached down and put his thick fingers under her chin and raised her to her feet. He spoke, but it meant nothing to her, for the words no longer burned in her mind. His face was dark with rage, and as his hand slid from her chin to her neck. His eyes glowed golden as he lifted her high above him. Her eyes rolled like a horse's; her mind truly clear for the first time in years. She saw, as he wheeled her around, a figure, tall and robed, standing behind the woman in the silver shift, his hand upon her shoulder. The two imposing men regarded each other, and she could feel hate and fear welling up through the vast library. She wanted to scream, but that monstrous fist tightened and closed her throat. The woman in the silver dress regarded her with pity as Amalia heard something crack within her. Then the man swept his arm aside and released her.

She watched him look away without concern as she fell into darkness.

8

THE FOLLOWING MORNING, THE orderlies could not find Mrs. Buccola. They searched the nearly empty building for five days and found no one other than the six other patients. Dr. Kunicki questioned each three times about the missing woman. Finally, when he had decided that he must inform her husband that she had fallen so ill and was so contagious that her remains had to be cremated, the old woman appeared at his door.

He had not taken her in, and yet she had been in room nine since the day before he planned to open his asylum. She was the reason they had waited. She would be the reason they would continue to wait. He could not allow normal patients to be near her. Her jaundiced eyes always leered, and her pulse raced visibly under her wrinkled, paper-thin skin. Each time he saw her, he hoped it would be the last time. Though he never believed it.

"Ms. Glinn," he said, trying to keep his voice calm. "What brings you to my office?"

She was not his patient, not really. He thought of her more as a co-founder now, mad as that was. She had whispered names in his ear, and he had brought them here. All but the two strange men. She had not whispered their names; she refused to acknowledge their presence when he spoke of them.

Now she walked toward him, her simple white shift, clean but for its grayed hem, fluttering with each step. Terror gripped him as she seemed to change. No longer an old woman, she appeared young, girlish, and joyful. Her white shift was a wedding dress. She reached his side and cupped her hands around her mouth as if to tell him a secret. She leaned down, wedding lace tickling his cheek, and she put her lips near his ear. She whispered so lightly that he could barely hear her. But even so, her words filled him with dread.

"The Bear is coming."

"TELL ME ABOUT YOUR plans," said Mrs. Sharon Bartos, smiling over her cup of tea. She was neither tall nor short, neither thin nor thick, neither dark nor light. Her gray hair was pulled back into a simple bun, neat but not severe. She looked like a not-especially-strict librarian, or a grammar teacher who would be forgotten instead of loved or hated years later. To Ms. Zora Gallo, the woman might have been savior or executioner. She hadn't yet figured out which.

"My plans?" Zora said, her own tea remaining on its saucer on the table. Mrs. Bartos smiled politely and nodded gently toward Zora's stomach. Zora felt her eyes go wide. She had only known for certain for two days.

"How …?" Zora asked.

Mrs. Bartos simply closed her eyes and shook her head twice, the meaning of which Zora took to be, 'we shan't speak about such things.' When the woman, whom Zora guessed was in her mid-forties, opened her gray eyes again, she was smiling.

"I would like to know what your plans are. Will you leave town? Will you address it in some … other way?"

"I don't know. I haven't had a lot of time to think about it," Zora said. The doctor. It must have been the doctor who told her. Mrs. Bartos was married to one of the richest men in town. He had influence. Zora thought he could probably find out just about anything he wanted. But why would he want to know about a poor girl's business? "I thought … well, women in my family sometimes have bad luck in these sorts of things, so I thought maybe it would just take care of itself." Zora thought of her four living siblings and the same number who were never born.

"No, I don't think it will," Mrs. Bartos said. "Future children, who can say? But not this boy. He's a special one."

Zora didn't like the look in the woman's eyes. It was piercing, bemused, and condescending. Zora was to Mrs. Bartos what she'd been to everyone in Lightning Falls her whole life: a joke. A foolish girl who came from a family with too many children and too little money. Maybe that was why she was here: money.

"You want to buy him?" Zora asked, unconsciously accepting Mrs. Bartos's declaration that the baby would be a boy.

"Would you sell him to me if I wanted you to?" Mrs. Bartos asked.

Zora frowned and thought about that. She looked around the tidy room and thought about her son growing up in a place like this. Clean. The upholstered antique sofa and chairs, the bright white lace curtains, the dark wood tables and cabinets, all were expensive and clean. It would certainly be better for any child to live here than in the old tumbledown house she and her sisters lived in. So, Zora nodded.

"Sure, if you pay me right."

Mrs. Bartos smiled. "That's good. And I think I will buy him from you. But not the way you have in mind. You will remain his mother, but you will dedicate him. Do you know what a Nazarite is?"

"That's what Jesus was."

"No, Jesus was a Nazarene, but it's an easy mistake to make. He could also have been a Nazarite, but the New Testament tells us he liked his wine a little too much. No, a Nazarite was one dedicated to God, who abstained from certain things, like cutting their hair and alcohol. Some were Nazarites for a brief period, and others for life. I want your son to be a Nazarite for life."

"You don't want me to cut his hair—"

"No," the woman said, chuckling and holding up a hand. She put her teacup and saucer down as Zora picked hers up and tentatively sipped. It was sweet and lemony. "No, I want you to dedicate him to something greater than himself."

"To God?" Zora asked.

Mrs. Bartos nodded, but didn't speak.

"How?"

"First, you will marry to give the boy a father. He needs a father."

"But Jimmy Ulman is his father."

"Jimmy Ulman will be dead within three years from alcohol. Is that the kind of father you want for your special son?" Mrs. Bartos asked.

Zora shook her head.

"No. I have someone far more appropriate in mind for you. He's a good man, a diligent worker, he will not hit you or the boy. And he will do what he must."

"I guess I'm going to have to sleep with him?"

"He will be your husband," Mrs. Bartos said. There was a strange look in her eye, something that dared Zora to object. It made Zora feel even smaller.

"Who is it?" Zora asked.

"We'll get to that. But before we do, I must tell you, you have a choice. You may raise this boy by yourself, and he will be hearty, but he will miss the purpose of his life. He will wander aimlessly, and without purpose, and he will die in your house with the barrel of a gun between his teeth before he is thirty years old."

Zora started at the woman's words as her teacup clattered against its saucer in her hand. "Why would you say that?"

"Because it's true," Mrs. Bartos said. "You will find the wall spattered with the gray matter of what had been your beloved son. The image will never leave you, nor will the memory of my words today."

The woman put her hand on Zora's knee, and for a moment, the bright, clean room faded, and another time and place came into view: She could see herself. She was in her fifties, hair gray, a faded, plain blue dress hanging shapelessly about her as she entered her son's room. On the wall was a blue and gold Whitman College pennant above a framed picture of him with three other young men, each holding a basketball. Against the wall stood a tall dresser with three trophies and a picture. The framed photograph showed mother and son at the state fair when he was ten. His open closet revealed two blazers and six checked, button-up shirts hanging next to three pairs of slacks. The wall above his double bed was spattered and smeared with his brains, bone, and bits of hair. On the bed lay the once athletic, but now pudgy, naked body of her son. He had stripped and folded the sheets, blankets, and pillows, stacking them neatly in the corner so that his self-destruction would not soil them.

The teacup slipped from Zora's hands as she saw the gore that spattered across his bare chest, across his belly, and down his thighs. Mrs. Bartos withdrew her hand without a word. She stood and left the room. Zora's heart thundered in her chest. She thought she might be having a heart attack. She tried to breathe, but her throat was too tight. The room swam around her. She forced air in and out. In and out. When Zora's heartbeat was down to a mere gallop, Mrs. Bartos reappeared with a black woman wearing an apron. The woman knelt, picked up the teacup and saucer, and began to dab at the rug with a cloth.

"Come with me, Ms. Gallo. Emmabeth will clean that up."

Zora stood, regarded the housekeeper for a moment, and then followed Mrs. Bartos out of the room and down a long hallway. Paintings hung in ornate frames showing landscapes, wagon trains, and pioneering folk, interspersed with portraits of people in high collars and bonnets.

"What you just saw was one potential future for your son. The other involves you marrying, which I assure you will be no cross for you to bear. I promise, the man I would pair you with is gentle and, I believe, you will find him a more satisfying partner than Jimmy Ulman." Zora would have giggled at that if the image of the dead man hadn't filled her mind. "The other future does have its crosses, however, Ms. Gallo. Your son won't play basketball or win trophies. He will endure many hardships, and so will you because of him. You will love him, and because you love him, you will suffer."

Zora knew that her mouth was open—that it hung stupidly slack like a broken coal chute, as her father used to say. She wanted to close it, to not look so idiotic in front of this woman who seemed to know everything, but she couldn't manage it.

"So," Mrs. Bartos said, leading Zora into the kitchen, "you see that both paths involve sorrow. If you have the boy by yourself, there will be years of happiness followed by decades of a living nightmare. But if you agree to allow me to help you, there will be sadness and tribulation, but you will also have your boy for the rest of your life. And I am making you no sly promise. You will live to be an old woman, and he will outlive you."

Zora followed her through the kitchen and out the back screen door onto a wide porch looking across a big lawn that leaned down to Hitchman's Creek.

"What would I have to do?" Zora asked as she walked past Mrs. Bartos to the railing, grabbing it with both hands.

"Very little except love him. And there will be times I need you to do certain things. People and experiences you might not want for him, but that must be part of his life. When those times come, you must defer to me. And, of course, you will be well cared for. Whatever we need him to do, we will provide for, and a little more besides. And you must never speak of our conversations, not to your husband, nor to your son, nor to anyone except me." Mrs. Bartos joined her at the railing.

They looked out at the forest of ponderosa beyond the creek and breathed deeply. Smoke from a nearby fire mingled with the clean, crisp air that rolled down from the butte and the soft, mossy smell of the creek.

"How did you make me see that?" Zora asked after they both had stood for three silent minutes.

"The purpose you'll be dedicating your son to is powerful and far-seeing. For a moment, I shared a little of that with you. But don't ask me any more about that. That isn't what you need to know."

Zora once more rankled under the woman's condescension. She absently rubbed at her belly, which, though it had never been flat, did not yet show her situation. "How much will I get?" Zora asked.

"All that you need, but not much more. You will not need to work if you don't want to. But if you don't work, you will lead a meagre life. However, if you do find a job, you will live quite comfortably, I expect. And your son will live as comfortably as he can."

Zora wondered for a moment why she should care. She didn't know the boy yet. But the image of the man, his body a remnant under the ruin of his head, devastated her. The picture wasn't only of his room and form, but also of her deep and terrifying feeling of love and loss. She saw in that body not just flesh, but decades of devotion and adoration. He—that man with no head—would make her better, and she would love him for it. And she would raise him the right way, not the way her mother had raised her. And for that, he would love her. But that would not be enough. The feeling of loss would take him, and she knew she could do nothing but agree to Mrs. Bartos's offer.

"All right," Zora said. "If it will save him, all right."

Mrs. Bartos took a long, sharp breath through her nose and bowed her head. Her shoulders hunched up almost above her ears, and she stayed with her head down long enough that Zora started to wonder if there was something wrong with her. Then, as the younger woman reached out a tentative hand to rouse her, Mrs. Bartos let out the breath and straightened. There was a look of incalculable relief on the older woman's face, as if Zora's choice had lifted a terrible weight from her.

"You have made an important choice, Zora. I am grateful. And know that I'm here for you. Now, take my hand and make a pact with me." Mrs. Bartos extended her hand to Zora, who took it. She wrapped her other hand around Zora's and stared into her eyes. "You make a pact, not only with me, but with the one who stands behind me. If you break this pact, I vow to you that the pain you felt in that glimpse will be only the merest hint of the torment that will follow. But if you are faithful, we shall be as family, one to the other. Do you understand?"

Zora nodded, unable to speak. She was afraid, though she didn't know where the fear came from. She didn't believe that the woman could torment her, not really. But there was something strange in the words, 'the one who stands behind me.' She had heard them before, but she didn't know where. They stirred something old in her that filled her with dread.

"Do you make your pact with me and the one who stands behind me, Zora Gallo?"

"Y—yes, Mrs. Bartos."

"No, use my full name. Sharon Jolette Kusel Alden Bartos."

Zora thought that rich people like this woman had too many names. "Yes, I make a pact with you, Sharon Jolette Kusel…."

"Alden Bartos."

"Alden Bartos."

Mrs. Bartos beamed. "Come on then, Mortimer is waiting." Mrs. Bartos's tone was suddenly friendly and conspiratorial, like they were two girls whispering together just out of the earshot of their parents.

"Mortimer? Mrs. Bartos, I—"

"Sharon, now," the older woman said. Zora became even more uncomfortable. The idea of being on a first-name basis with this person made her feel like she had made a terrible mistake. And if Mortimer was the Mortimer she suspected he was, then perhaps she had.

"I don't think that I could—"

"All will be well, my dear," Sharon said, putting a hand on Zora's shoulder and turning her around. "You haven't seen him in, I'd guess, six years." That seemed right to Zora, so she nodded. "He's changed, just as you have. He's filled out, become a man. He was in Europe with my nephew. He's a fine young man now. Come on, he's inside."

Zora let herself be led into the kitchen, down the hall, and back to the sitting room. She glanced at the faces in the pictures as they passed. They didn't look happy, or even mildly pleased. All were stern. All looked uncomfortable. When they reached the sitting room, Zora felt Sharon's hand return to her shoulder. Two young men sat on the couch, drinking tea. Zora looked at the carpet next to one of the men's feet and saw only the merest damp spot. Emmabeth had done her work well. The men put their cups down, rose, and greeted them. For a moment, she couldn't tell which was Mortimer. They were both tall, broad-shouldered, and handsome. Zora touched her hair with one hand and her stomach with the other, as if she were getting ready to perform a party trick.

"Mortimer, you remember Zora," Sharon said.

"Yes, ma'am," the man on the right said. He was, Zora mused, slightly taller, slightly broader, and significantly handsomer, which pleased her. And then, when he smiled, she saw the boy she had known in school. She smiled back.

"Well," Sharon said. "This is pleasant. Of course, Mortimer has agreed to be your husband, Zora, so you needn't worry about wooing him."

Zora looked down; color rose to her cheeks.

"I'd be very happy to be your husband," Mortimer said. The other man, Sharon's nephew, Zora assumed, put his hand on Mortimer's shoulder. She had met him before, but it had been longer ago, and war and age had changed him even more completely than Mortimer. She saw nothing familiar in the man's eyes.

"I'd be very happy to be your wife," Zora heard herself say. And a moment later, she realized that it was true.

The men shook hands. The women hugged. Mortimer offered Zora his hand and suggested that they walk and talk. Zora agreed. As they left,

she thought that Sharon's nephew looked both happy and a little confused.
    She agreed with him.
    The strangely minted couple walked down Hitchman's Creek Road until they came to Central Avenue. They turned right and crossed town toward the waterfall. It occurred to Zora that that was where men made proper proposals, and both seemed to silently agree that they should observe the proper forms. As they walked silently, hand in hand, Zora felt swept up in something bigger than herself. The sense of unease that had come over her when Sharon had told her they were family faded. Here, next to Mortimer, with his short cut brown hair and the scar that ran over his left eyebrow, she felt safe. She felt like she belonged.
    When he knelt upon Proclamation Rock, she giggled. When he jumped down after she accepted his proposal, she laughed. And when he kissed her by the pool where the water fell like thunder, Zora Gallo swooned for the first time in her life. When she did, he held her. His hand slid from her side to her belly, and he smiled down at her.
    "Do you know what you want to name him?" he said. His question was like freezing water, shocking her from a dream. In the roil of emotions and the suddenness of it all, she had let the issue at hand slip from her mind. She was both shocked and comforted that he seemed to already know about her situation.
    "I hadn't really thought about it," she said. "I ... I haven't had time."
    "I was named after my grandfather," he said. "Family names are powerful."
    Zora thought of her father's father, a lean man with sunken eyes and no teeth. She couldn't imagine naming her son after him. Then she thought of her mother's father, a kind man whom she had known for only a year before he died. He had come just before the snow when she was fourteen and given her sweets and gentle words. She hoped her son would be like him.
    "Then yes," she said. "I do know."
    They were married three days later, so when the boy arrived, no one batted much of an eye at a frail child born just under eight months after the wedding night. Jimmy Ulman did come around, but when he saw the man who had fought with Patton in North Africa and marched across Europe at breakneck speed to relieve the Battered Bastards of Bastogne, he tucked his tail and ran. The birth was hard, the boy was frail, and so was Zora. But when Zora was well enough, and her son was no longer in danger, the family posed for a picture for the local newspaper. They stood in front of the waterfall holding their child together, each with one arm under his swaddled, narrow form. And, next to an advertisement for William Baker's

bookstore, the short article announced the arrival of the newest member of the Lightning Falls community, reading:

Pictured here: Proud parents Mortimer and Zora Chapel and their new son, Louis.

May 7, 2021

Only time knows where the song goes,
Like refrains of waters that spin down the drain.

TINNY MUSIC WHISPERED FROM the white earbuds as the young woman pushed her blonde hair back from her face and tucked it behind her ears, first left, then right. The plastic contents of the cardboard box nestled in the crook of her left arm rattled an off-time beat along with the rock. Her skirt, flowy and flowery, was mostly green. She knew it invited even more comparisons than normal, but that was okay. There were worse people to remind folks of than the best Princess who ever ruled the Valley.

"Grace!"

The deep voice broke through the heavy guitar. She tapped her smartwatch, and the music stopped. She turned to see the old man standing outside his office. He was tall but hunched, and the lines in his face were deep and dark. He wore a suit with a narrow black tie, and his shoes gleamed.

"Yes, Mr. Robillard?"

"Are you going to the records room?"

"Yes, sir!" she said, almost snapping to attention. She knew she was overeager, but she couldn't stop herself. Here was the man himself, the son of the woman who had started it all. She felt her limbs buzzing in his presence.

"Glorious," he said. "Come here, I'd like you to take something down for me, if you would be so kind."

"Of course," she said. He waved for her to follow him into his office. She obliged and felt her mouth drop open. She had already been there a month but had never been in his office. It looked, more or less, as she had pictured it. Wood paneling covered walls hung with posters, photographs, and original concept art of characters and locations from Virtue Vista Valley. Shelves of books and keepsakes stood in the corners, while a large, dark-wood desk commanded the attention of three gleaming leather-backed chairs that looked at least fifty years old. Behind his desk was a large painting of a house on a hill. It radiated light above a sea of people in darkness, their arms reaching up toward the effulgence.

"I have a few tapes I'd like returned," he said. He didn't use a cane, but he moved carefully and deliberately toward his desk. His mother had suffered a broken hip late in life, Grace knew, and he had guarded his mobility carefully. "I'm sorry to say," he said, opening a drawer, "that the late fees will be monstrous."

He held out two gray, plastic boxes about six inches long. Grace put her cardboard box on one of the chairs and took the plastic boxes. She read the labels.

"These are lost!" Grace said excitedly.

He frowned, though his eyes twinkled.

"You know your stuff!" he said. "Though I'm sorry to say, these are merely audio recordings that are quite rough. Those episodes are otherwise entirely gone. Though I daresay some of the rabid fans on the internet would like to get hold of these, even so!"

She nodded, staring at the dates she knew so well. She declined to mention that she was one of the internet denizens who wanted to hear them.

"Now, don't you go selling them and you'll find that your Christmas bonus more than makes up for whatever you might get on eBay."

Grace shook her head and lowered the boxes. "No, sir! I would never—" She stopped. Jacob Robillard was smiling. She smiled back.

"As I say, the late fees will be quite unreasonable, as I have had them out for some time." She tried to keep her eyes on him, but couldn't keep from glancing at the labels every few seconds. He chuckled and waved at the boxes with a frowning nod that said, "Go on."

She opened the top box and found a plastic cassette and an old-fashioned library sign-out card, like the ones her elementary school had used.

Four names were listed on the card:

A. Robillard, May 1984
T. Thornville, June 1986
J. Robillard, May 1988
J. Robillard, June 1991

She raised her eyebrows. "You've had this out since 1991?"

"I'm afraid I have. And the other is worse. Now, if they demand payment straight away, I expect you to hand over whatever cash you have on hand. Mrs. Gellman is reasonable, so I expect you'll be able to give her whatever valuables you have as well for collateral."

Grace looked from the tapes to the man, confused. His smile made him look like a child playing a joke he thought was particularly clever. She widened her own grin and nodded.

"Am I supposed to sign over my firstborn as well?"

His expression didn't change, but … something did.

"That will likely not be necessary, Grace. Though I imagine you'd have a fine boy worthy of our little family. No, of course, I kid. Though I imagine Mrs. Gellman will give you a bit of a tongue-lashing as if it were your fault that I have held onto these for so long. I beg your forgiveness for that in advance. If it's particularly bad, come back to me and I'll make sure to make it up to you."

Grace thought that getting to listen to the tapes would be more than compensation for any rude words from the woman who watched over the records room. But she didn't think she'd get the chance for that, at least not today. Though an idea struck her.

"Thank you, sir. That probably won't be necessary. Is there anything else?"

He looked at her for a long moment, and she saw a look in his eyes that she had seen in so many others around the office. It was one part wonder, one part sadness, and one part longing. It said, 'You look like her. If she had gotten to grow up. You look just like her.' Grace let him look and kept her smile.

A moment later, he nodded and said, "No, thank you, that will be all for today."

Wherever it flows, to water the crows,
It heals, but it deals its own ration of pain.

Grace hummed along with the song, her box slightly heavier now. Her pink short-sleeved blouse whispered against the cardboard in the pause between the track's loops. Grace had found the song online three days earlier, and it had been an earworm ever since. The band was called Ruqus, and she didn't particularly like their other music. It was too hard, too loud. But this was a ballad, and she couldn't get enough of it.

She passed the main building's front desk and nodded at the young man behind it. He was also new, and she kept forgetting his name. He smiled back more eagerly than she'd like. Probably in his mid-twenties, he was too young. Her last boyfriend had been forty. She hated the idea that people thought she might have "daddy issues." She didn't. She loved her father. He had always been wonderful to her. Her friend Erica told her that that could cause daddy issues, too. According to that logic, Grace wondered if there was anything that *couldn't*.

Grace pushed her way out of the front door backward, flashing the receptionist a reserved smile and stepping out into the mild sunshine. It was sixty degrees out and sunny. The parking lot was still damp from earlier rain. It was just the kind of day she loved. It would get warmer, and Grace looked forward to lounging at one of the picnic tables over lunch, reading a book, and letting the sun give her a little of the color she'd lost during the winter. She hummed along to the music in her earbuds as she walked along the path past the part of the building that housed the library.

She was glad that the library didn't hold the archives. It would have made her days a heck of a lot more boring if she only ever had to walk from one wing to the next. But she got to go outside a few times a day, got to walk through sun, rain, and eventually, she hoped, snow. She looked forward to snow drifts just waiting to be trudged through. She thought puddles wanted to be jumped in and ice wanted to be skated on, and she knew that made her cheesy. Of course, she also liked her pumpkin-spice in the fall, piles of orange and brown leaves, and the slow approach of Halloween. She enjoyed the odd murder-mystery podcast and genuinely longed for a relationship where she could wear a puffy vest with a well-fitted pair of jeans next to her salt-and-pepper husband as they walked their dog with coffees in their hands and stopped frequently to catch up with neighbors.

I am a basic-est of basic bitches, she thought and smiled.

She passed the large studio building. A small crowd of children and their parents milled around one of the stage entrances. Kerry, whom Grace had gotten to know well, was giving them the 'I'm not supposed to let you in this way' bit. In a moment, one of the voice actors would pop out the door and give Kerry a hard time. Then they'd see the kids and relent and let them all in. Grace wondered which member of the cast it would be today.

The door opened, and to the surprise of everyone, including both Kerry and Grace, a tall, white-bearded man appeared, smiling broadly.

"Sam!" The children screamed, as did, Grace noticed, some of the mothers. She mouthed his name as well, her heart swelling with admiration. She wanted to drop her box and run to him, to tell him again how unboundedly grateful she was for the job. She had already attempted this once in the last month when they had run into each other in the break room as he was getting a cup of coffee. Surreally, she stood there trying to tell him how much it meant to her while he smiled kindly, and his younger self admonished her to wash her hands from above the sink.

Seeing how nervous she was, he had asked if he could hug her. She had accepted, knowing that it might kill her, and the newspaper the next day would read: *Twenty-two-year-old woman dead of heart attack— children's TV star says it was the most harrowing experience of his life!*

Grace watched with self-conscious envy as the children were led by

Sam into the soundstage, where they would tour parts of the *Virtue Vista Valley* set. She knew it was foolish for her to be jealous. She saw Sam in person a few times a week. She could go to the recording building whenever she wanted. She was part of the family now, even if she was new.

Even if everyone looked at her like she was the ghost of a dead girl.

Grace tried to be magnanimous toward the children. They would remember this for the rest of their lives. And if they didn't ... *Well,* she thought, *fuck 'em.*

She laughed at the incongruous harshness of the thought, amended it with a wish for the kids' well-being, and continued toward the records building.

The winds all suppose that they ought to compose
the clouds from the waters to turn into rain.

MRS. GELLMAN WAS CATALOGING old catalogs, or so it seemed to Grace as she approached the woman's desk and tapped her smartwatch. Mrs. Gellerman wore her gray hair up in a way that said, 'If only beehives would make a comeback.' Her glasses, attached to a bejeweled chain, said, 'I am, in fact, a librarian.' The glasses were perched on the tip of her powdered nose, and she looked down through them back and forth from newer book to older.

"Good morning," Grace said, putting her box down on the part of Mrs. Gellman's desk that was cleared for such deposits.

The woman looked up and gave Grace a thin smile. "Good morning, Grace. How are you today?"

"I'm doing well," Grace said. "How are you?"

"Well enough. It's quiet today," she said. Grace took that to mean that Mrs. Gellman would like it to stay that way, so she merely smiled and nodded. "What have you collected from them?" the older woman asked, looking over her glasses at the box.

"A few folders, a collection of interview tapes that the marketing department finished digitizing, and, oh, I think you'll maybe be upset about these ..."

Grace produced the two gray, plastic boxes. Mrs. Gellman pursed her lips and took them in hand, popping each open and shaking her head when she looked at the cards. "He has been promising to return these for the last thirty years," she said.

"I guess he remembered today," Grace said.

"I guess he noticed our new researcher," Mrs. Gellman said. "I don't think Mr. Dobbs was quite Mr. Robillard's cup of tea."

"I'm sorry?" Grace said.

"Oh, don't be coy," the older woman said. Her expression changed when she looked up at Grace. "Now, wait, don't mistake what I'm saying. I'm just saying, between us girls, that I think I'm going to see a lot more archival material in and out of this place now that you're here, especially if you keep wearing skirts like that."

Grace reached down and smoothed the front of her knee-length skirt. She didn't think her outfit would be considered immodest anywhere but Puritan New England.

"Is there something wrong with—"

"No, again, don't mistake me. But you're a hard swing from Mr. Dobbs, God rest his soul. The man was older than Sam and smelled of mint all the time."

"Mint isn't bad," Grace said.

"All the time," Mrs. Gellman said. "You'd smell it down the hallway and know he was about to shuffle around the corner. He was a very nice man, there's no mistaking that, but he was an old man, and you are a pretty young woman. No one is going to hide from you."

Grace had no idea how she should feel about the woman's words. Part of her felt flattered, the other part felt like she should report her for something. She hadn't expected this kind of reaction from the older woman.

"My advice is this: if you enjoy the attention, then enjoy it. It won't last. And if you don't, then take heart that it won't last."

Grace frowned. She still had no idea what to think or feel. She didn't particularly want the woman's advice, especially not on this topic.

"Okay, I've said too much! Don't report me," Mrs. Gellman said, as if reading Grace's mind. She put the gray boxes back into their cardboard conveyance. "I'll take my own advice from now on and zip it."

Grace, head whirling, took her box and tried to force a smile.

"No, it's okay. I just—sorry, I wasn't expecting a life lesson on being attractive today," she said. "Honestly, do you think I should dress differently?"

Mrs. Gellman leaned forward and put her elbows on her desk. She whispered conspiratorially, "Honey, if I had it my way, all the women in the office would dress like you and all the men would dress like Mr. Robillard." She leaned back and gave Grace a wink. "You go through; I've got too much to do today to bother with those. Everything has a label; you'll find it. If you don't come back out in an hour, I'll come looking for you."

Grace blinked. She was being let into the archives. First, the woman commented on her appearance, then told her that she wanted all the women to dress like her, and now she was letting Grace into the back room where the vast wealth of Crystalline Mansion treasure was stored. She decided that her morning wanted to be compared with nothing so much as a roller coaster.

So they suck up them all, spring, winter, and fall,
and store them to pour them on mountain and plain.

THE SHELVES WERE LABELED clearly and seemed to be up to date. The folders were returned to filing boxes first, and the audio tapes second. Then Grace wandered, looking for the section where the gray boxes belonged. She walked up and down the length of the large room with its beige metal shelves four times, trying to find one that started with 'AIL' to match the call numbers on the box spines. There was an 'A,' and within 'A,' there were two shelves that began with 'AI,' But they were all boxes of memos from the seventies. None had a trailing 'L' or anything that looked like tapes.

Finally, she gave up and left her box by the door. She leaned out to find Mrs. Gellman away from her desk. Grace had only been in the stacks for twenty minutes or so, so the search party hadn't been sent out yet. She did her best duck face, wiggling her lips back and forth as she pondered what to do next, and then slid back into the archive. She would figure this out on her own. Perhaps, she thought, there was another floor?

Grace walked the perimeter of the white painted cinder-block room and soon came to a heavy gray door with a placard that read 'Basement: AJM-AIL.'

"Bingo," Grace said to herself and pushed her way through. The staircase reminded her of school, with concrete steps and gray-painted, metal railings. Two short flights brought her to another door that repeated the sign above, except it left the word 'Basement' off.

She knew she was in the right place immediately. Hundreds of plastic boxes like the ones she held sat on the shelves of dozens of double-sided, open-backed, library-style bookcases. She hummed and repeated the line about time and water as its symbol, which, she was certain, was the song's metaphor, and looked for 'AIL.' She found it three rows in and found the conspicuous gaps that her two boxes had not occupied for three decades. Feeling a strange temporal vertigo, she put them back, trying to imagine Jacob Robillard, a man nearing his fiftieth year, taking them down and not knowing it would be up to a woman who hadn't even been born yet to put them back in their place.

Those gaps, if gaps were really a thing, had been made three decades ago and remained unchanged for the intervening years. Time, for them, had stopped.

Was that what the song meant?

That there were places where time didn't flow? Grace wasn't sure. One of the message board moderators had promoted the song, and she'd been trying to figure it out. She thought maybe this idea of gaps, of things that don't really exist, was a key. Where there is nothing, time can't flow. *But then*, she thought, *the gap wasn't really nothing. Nothing was nothing.*

Deep.

She laughed at herself and then froze. She sniffed. What was that? Was something burning?

She sniffed again.

Yes, there was definitely the smell of something burning. Conflicted, Grace started to move through the stacks, sniffing. Should she run upstairs and tell Mrs. Gellman? She wanted to be sure and not seem like a foolish girl who wore skirts that attracted old men's attention. Why had she said that to her? Grace thought of herself as open-minded and positive about sex, but she also didn't have any inkling that that part of her life had anything to do with work. Wasn't there a difference between just being visually pleasing and trying to arouse people? She thought so. Did Mrs. Gellman not? Or did she think men didn't know the difference? Maybe they didn't. Or maybe just some didn't. Or, maybe, people couldn't tell when a man was attracted to someone in one way, but not another? Like, could Mr. Robillard think she was pretty, but have no strong desire to see her naked? Was that even possible?

Grace tumbled the ideas over in her head and breathed deeply through her nose. She wanted to understand, and she wanted to avoid just lumping people together. Most of all, she wanted to believe the best about the people she worked with. They were doing such good work. She had no illusions that they were perfect. And if she found out that Jacob Robillard had evaded his taxes or maybe liked to go to strip clubs and watch women—or men—dance, she'd feel uncomfortable knowing that, but it wouldn't take away from what he was to her. The real Jacob Robillard would just replace the fantasy one in her head. That wouldn't be so bad, she thought. That was part of being an adult: accepting that your heroes were just people like you.

She started considering how it might actually turn out to be terrible if Jacob not only avoided his taxes but ripped off his employees, or liked to get people drunk at holiday parties, but her thoughts were interrupted by another cardboard box. This one sat on a bottom shelf between neatly placed plastic cases like the ones she had just returned. The cardboard was dark, its edges rough and uneven, and it smelled powerfully of smoke.

Grace knelt on the tight-weave blue carpet and pulled the box from the shelf. She immediately dropped it and almost screamed. Worms crawled around in little piles of dirt. No, she realized, not dirt, ash. Ash covered the bottom of the box, and worms wriggled their way through it, making little channels in the gray and black. They were not the only contents, however. A manila folder leaned upright. She plucked it out and found that it contained two papers and a black and white photograph. Each item was pristine but gave off a strong smoky smell.

Grace looked at the photograph. It was a close-up of a small stone with a strange mark engraved on it. The stone was oval and set on a wooden table. The mark was unfamiliar to her, and she put the photo back into the folder. The second item excited her, however. It was a press release from 2009. It appeared to be a draft of the release that announced the disappearance of Emily Carmichael. It had lines crossed out in pen and suggested fixes. Some were simply typos; others were wording choices that sounded more professional. Emily had been "taken," not "gone missing." "Law Enforcement" was doing all it could, not just "police."

Grace sniffed the press release. Smoke.

The second page in the folder was a handwritten letter addressed to "Crystaline Mansion." It was three paragraphs long, and she read it five times. Grace went from kneeling to sitting on the carpet with her knees up in front of her. Whoever this Marsha Toast woman was, she had seen something two days after Emily had gone missing.

Emily, whom everyone thought Grace resembled, if only she had been given the chance to grow up.

Emily Carmichael, kidnapped, killed, dismembered, and burned.

The Princess who died.

Or had she?

If Marsha Toast was correct, maybe Emily had been in Iowa on Monday. Of course, that didn't mean she wasn't back in Missouri later that day to be hacked and immolated, but still, Grace had never heard of Marsha Toast. She'd never heard anyone say that Emily might have been seen two days after she had been taken by Wesley Graveline. And, though Grace never mentioned it in her interviews or with anyone around the coffee maker, she had spent time on the message boards.

Grace looked in the box to make sure she hadn't missed anything important among the ash and worms. She had read stories where something central to a mystery had been missed, like a key or a note card. She didn't want to make that mistake.

But there was nothing at the bottom of the box. No key, no card, no worms, no ash. It was clean.

"What the fuck?" Grace whispered, running her fingers over the smooth, unblemished cardboard.

Under which grows the thorn and the rose
And which cover and smother the darkest stain.

GRACE PASSED BY MRS. Gellman's empty desk, holding the folder to her chest. She didn't know who she should go to with it. A knot was growing and tightening in her stomach. She shouldn't have taken the documents. Someone would know. She had to make copies and then put the originals back. The copier room was, thankfully, empty. She made four copies of each page and the photograph, thinking that she'd hide a set here, share one, and then stash the other two for safety. Her paranoia had kicked into gear, and she had the strong sense that her next move with the contents, especially the letter from Marsha Toast, would be dangerous. Someone had kept the letter secret. She knew enough about Emily's case to know that.

She stashed her copies in a cabinet behind some supplies that looked like they hadn't been used for twenty years, then hurried back downstairs to replace the folder in the box. When she came back up, Mrs. Gellman was sitting at her desk.

"I was about to come down and look for you," she said, wiping a bit of white cream from her lip. Two pink-frosted donuts sat on a napkin before her, one with a bite missing.

"I didn't get lost," Grace said, smiling nervously. "I just got a little overwhelmed by how much there is down there!"

"Oh, I understand. It can be a lot. Well, you'll get used to it." Mrs. Gellman sniffed. "Does something smell like smoke to you?"

Grace sniffed ostentatiously. "Maybe a little? I—"

Mrs. Gellman stood and sniffed around, ending up near Grace. "Is that you?" She suddenly looked disappointed. "Oh, shame on you, Grace. Your skin will dry up!"

Grace frowned, not understanding the woman's meaning. Then, shaking her head, she said, "Oh, no, it's, um, someone had a campfire near me last night. I don't smoke." She sniffed her blouse. There was, of course, the smell of burning. "They don't even smell the same," she said to Mrs. Gellman's incredulous look.

"Well, I guess that's true," the older woman said. "But don't take it up! I've seen pretty women turn old before their time!"

Grace nodded her agreement, thanked Mrs. Gellman for her advice, and tried to walk naturally to the copy room. There, she retrieved her folder and slipped out the other side so that Mrs. Gellman wouldn't see.

Once outside, Grace tried to sort through who she could turn to. She tapped her music back on and let it play, thinking of who might be safe to share the documents with. She wandered back to her little office and sorted out one copy of each document, stashing them in the bottom drawer of her filing cabinet. She pushed the folder down into her backpack.

"Hey!"

Grace jumped. She spun around and saw the receptionist leaning in through the door and smiling.

"Sorry!" he said. "Didn't mean to scare you."

"It's okay," Grace said. "What's going on?"

"I'm having problems logging into the updates system. Do you know how I'm supposed to get in there? I've tried my main password and the secondary ID, and I just can't figure it out."

Grace gave him an apologetic grin and a shrug. "Sorry, I don't really go into the updates system. You should probably just call IT."

"Right," he said, "that was my next move. Just figured you might know."

"No, sorry," she said. He started to lean out of the room and then reversed course.

"Hey, what are you doing for lunch?"

Grace forced her smile to remain. "I'm probably working through lunch," she said, realizing too late that she was giving up her picnic table side basking and reading. "But … shit, I think I forgot to pack something."

"You want me to order you something? I can pick it up."

This seemed like a bad idea to Grace, as it would send the wrong message. But she also didn't love the idea of skipping lunch.

"Sure, but let me send you cash," she said. He started to raise a hand, but she insisted. When he was gone, she wondered why the hell he would ask her about computers. She wasn't an idiot by any means, but she was almost as new as he was. He should have known to just email—

Grace swallowed and looked at her computer. There was someone she could reach out to. Two people, in fact. But she had never spoken to Mari. On the other hand, she had emailed with the head of IT. She had even chatted briefly with him in the coffee room on his last visit. Daniel, she kind of knew. Daniel would probably know what to do with the information. And he'd want to know. Of course, he would.

She opened the email application on her laptop. She had to keep it short, business-like, and in no way indicative of what she'd found. So, she just asked him if he'd like to grab lunch to talk about some work things. Maybe he'd think that she wanted to get into IT. Maybe he'd think she was interested in him. In either case, she was pretty sure he'd say 'yes.'

Once she sent the email, Grace tapped her watch again and leaned back, listening to the song she had found on one of those message boards. She wondered if she and others on the internet had been right. She wondered if there was more to Emily's case than everyone had been led to believe. She had wondered that for years. So had everyone else on the message board.

She closed her eyes and let the music roll over her again, wondering if they had all been right.

But there is one hall, where waters ne'er fall,
Where the ground is as dry as the parched desert sky,
And the puppets all wail in their silent travail,
In the ring of the dark king in shadowed Harhain.

THE OLD MAN TAPPED his thick, calloused fingers on the table. The young man who stood before him was pretty, blonde, and stupid. His strength, in the older man's estimation, beyond being attractive and packing it in the right area for his line of work, was that he was impressionable. The tow-headed man, if you could call this twenty-two-year-old boy-thing a 'man,' wanted approval from someone older. He was the kind of kid who gravitated to a Mrs. Robinson, if one were available. His current girlfriend wasn't quite as old as Anne Bancroft had been, but she was still more experienced and just as broken. If the boy had the time, he would graduate to a woman in her thirties, then her forties. The older man stood, towering over the blonde boy bimbo by at least a foot, and thought he'd seen the same situation a hundred times before.

"Nolan," the bigger man said, "You're going to be relieved to hear this, but I only need you to make the call one more time."

Nolan rubbed his soft hands together and frowned. He couldn't look his elder in the eyes. "I'm sorry, sir, but I'm not sure I can do it."

"I think you can," the burly man said, smiling. "And I think you'll like doing this one." Nolan looked like he was trying to work up enough spit to stage his protest, but the older man leaned forward and held up a hand. "I'd like you to apologize."

Nolan stared at him with wide, pale blue eyes. "Really?" Nolan said. The older man nodded, running his hand through his short, white crewcut, and wondered if the pretty-boy would go bald, if given the time. The man, of course, still had a full head of hair. Maybe "of course" was the wrong way of putting it. No, it definitely was. He'd been through so damn much, seen so damn much, he should have been worried bald a hundred times over. He pictured Brando in *Apocalypse Now* and hoped that if he did go bald, he could exude that sort of presence.

I was going bald.

He smirked and shoved the voice in his head back as he put a hand on Nolan's shoulder. "We pushed her too hard. No doubt about it. I overestimated her resilience. It does us no good if she quits."

"I guess I don't understand, sir," Nolan said. "What good does it do us either way?"

The big man stood and rolled the sleeves of his white dress shirt up slowly, creasing each cuff fastidiously. His thick arms were tan and spotted with constellations of freckles, moles, and damned age spots.

We used to call them 'liver spots.'

So did we, he thought at the voice. *But they don't anymore.*

"Well, I admit, that's not really your concern," the man said, looking at Nolan's pale arms. Two of them put together would have made one of his, but they weren't without muscle. The older man grinned down at Nolan with his best fatherly condescension. "But, suffice it to say, that the sun will rise with her help."

That seemed to satisfy Nolan. "Okay, sir, what are we—"

A knock at the door cut him off.

"Come," the big man said. The door opened, and a young woman with long, curling hair and a tie-dyed dress leaned in. She wore no bra, and the older man could see all but her nipples through the hanging neck of her retro-style outfit. He had known real hippies. She probably would have fit in fine.

"Sorry, am I interrupting?" she said, looking up at him.

"Yes, Aurora," he said. "But it's okay. What is it?"

"Everyone's back. What do you want us to do?"

"Wait. Nolan has a call to make, and then the four of us have business in the bathroom. Do me a favor and fill the tub. All right?"

She smiled with full lips that should have been well-stocked with kisses for decades, but he knew better. She had three or four left at best.

"Tell Venena I'd like to see her," he said.

Aurora nodded and closed the door behind her, never once looking at Nolan.

"When you make the call," the man said, his eyes still on the door, "I want you to just say you're sorry. Say you took it too far. Say that you never meant to scare her that much, and that you won't do any of it anymore."

"Do you want me to write it down?" Nolan asked.

"Do you feel sorry?" he asked. Noland nodded. "Do you think we took it too far?" Again, a nod. "Are you happy to be stopping?" One more nod. "Then just tell her how you feel."

Nolan nodded.

The man pulled a small flip phone from his pocket. He punched in the number and handed it to the younger man. Nervously, Nolan took the phone and hit the green dial button. He held it to his ear and mouthed, 'It's ringing.' The tall man leaned back on his desk and took a deep breath. He watched the younger man's eyes go wide, his mouth drop open, and his free hand clench and release. The boy's mouth worked, but no sound came out. From the phone, the older man heard a woman's voice yelling. God, she sounded pissed. He couldn't blame her for that. He couldn't blame her for anything she did. She'd been dealt one of the shittiest hands he'd ever seen.

Seeing that Nolan would not be able to manage even this simple task, the big man held out his hand for the phone. He watched he younger man try one more time to speak before he gave him one of the most pathetic puppy-dog looks he'd ever seen. The older man opened and closed his hand, as if indicating to a baby to hand him the phone. Nolan finally obliged, and the big man closed it, hanging up on the angry woman.

"Tell you what," he said, "I'll just text her. You did your part. I appreciate that."

"I'm sorry, sir," Nolan said.

"No, no, it's fine. No need to worry about it. I'll send her a text a little later. Heck, maybe I'll even give her a few more weeks to see how she's holding up. She hasn't even finished her second season yet. Sounds like she still has some fire in her."

The door opened, this time without a knock. A woman sauntered in wearing the daisiest of Daisy Dukes. Her white tank hid nothing, and he felt multiple parts of his old machinery clunking into action.

"Aurora said you wanted me," Venena said. She leaned against the wall, one bare foot on the wooden floor, one on the door jamb behind her.

"I certainly do," he said. He walked up to her and put his hand on her neck and thumb under her chin, tilting her face up to look at him. "We are almost ready. It's time to open your path."

"My path leads through water," she said, her lips parted and barely moving, her eyes flickering across his face.

If only I were forty years younger, he thought. Hell, he could have her now if he wanted, but he preferred that women want him, not his power over them. And he had power over her; there was no question. Everyone in the house knew it. Nolan went to bed every night next to this beautiful woman, knowing that if the old man summoned her to his bed, she'd go without hesitation. He never had, and, as she was, he knew he never would. But the temptation was immense, especially because she would be so willing to please him.

But that thought depressed him. He wanted her to want to be pleased by him, and he knew that even his master couldn't make that true.

The man leaned down and kissed her on the forehead. "Go get ready," he said.

"Are we going to wear robes or something?" she asked, her eyes dancing with mischief. She was high, he realized. He wished she weren't, but it wouldn't matter either way. Perhaps it would even have beneficial results long-term.

"No, my love, we'll be naked."

Her eyes widened, and her lips pursed into an 'o.' She slid her back up and down the wall, as if it were a stripper pole and she was trying to wheedle a one from his fist. She had been trained to act that way. That was his fault. It had been useful, and would be useful in the future, but he hated it. There was no truth in it.

"As much as I love how free you are," Joseph said, "this isn't about sex. This is about rebirth. You were born naked the first time, and you will be again. Are you ready for that?"

She stopped moving, and her eyes hardened. *There's my girl,* he thought. There was steel in that look.

"You will bring me through it," she said, all of the porn-star gone out of her. "I trust you."

Then, to his surprise, she stood on her toes and kissed him. It was a daughter's kiss, not a lover's. The kiss of the first day of college, the kiss of the wedding day, the kiss as he's dying—love, trust, farewell.

He let her kiss him, and when she pulled back, he saw the woman he knew her to be.

"Go get ready," he said. And like that, her eyes were unfocused again, the sexual creature returned. She ran her hand down his chest, almost to his belt, before sliding around the door jamb and out into the living room. Nolan followed, his eyes downcast.

The old man took a deep breath and looked to the southeastern corner of the office. He shook his head, throwing his hands into the air.

"Women! What can you do?" he asked. And somewhere, in the distance, a fire burned in response. There was no laughter in it, only power. The old man smirked. If there was one big difference between him and his master, it was humor. The old man had tried his best to keep his ability to laugh through every long year of this strange, awful world. Hell, even Lou had kept his sense of humor until the end. They had helped each other keep some perspective in the vast darkness of it all. The man wondered if he was losing his ability to laugh now that Lou was gone.

A knock at the door.

"Come."

Another raven-haired woman entered. She was already naked. She also leaned against the wall, but there was nothing sensual in her stance. She crossed her arms under her chest and gave him a blank, expectant stare as if to say, 'What now?'

"What can I do for you, Matina?"

"Are we really doing this? Today? I thought we'd get some warning," Matina said.

"Wheels have to roll, darling. Gears have to turn."

She let out a long, slow, exasperated breath. "You stripping down too?" she asked.

"Of course," he said. "We're walking in the garden today."

"Not afraid we'll all point and laugh and decide Nolan should be our leader, you know, biggest in charge?"

He chuckled. She loved to try to get under his skin. He had vowed that he would never let her.

"If you'd rather follow someone with more meat than brains, you be my guest. But I think you'll have to find someone other than Nolan after today."

The look on her face shifted only slightly. She knew what was coming. She had known for a long time. But he saw it hurt her, even if she didn't want to show it. He approached her and put his hand on her shoulder.

"We're going to get through this. The sun is going to rise."

For a moment, perhaps two heartbeats, he saw her mask of cynicism and strength slip. He saw the homeless drug addict he had found in Portland. He saw the look of desperation that had made her agree to get into an old man's car in the middle of a downpour, and the resolve to endure anything he might ask of her if only she could have somewhere warm to stay. He saw the look of vulnerability when, after the nightmare of withdrawal, she had offered herself to him, and the look of devotion that followed his refusal. He saw who she had been before she had been Matina and knew he'd have a lot of work to do with her after today.

But the sun will rise, the voice in his head said.

Yes, he thought. *The sun will rise.*

"Now, give me a moment to disrobe, and I'll meet you all in the upstairs bathroom."

For a moment, he thought she'd make another joke or tease him about watching him strip down. But instead, she hugged him. His hand slid along the smooth skin of her back, and then she was away, her mask firmly in place once more.

When she was gone, he unbuttoned his shirt, undid his belt, and stood before the mirror naked. He had the body of a man thirty years younger, and he thanked his master for his longevity. That made him think of the last time he had been in his master's presence, and that made him think of the young woman and her podcast. He sniffed, flipped open the phone, and started to type.

"Alex, I'm sorry. I pushed things too far. I won't bother you anymore. Peter."

He hesitated. No. He wouldn't send it yet. He wanted a little time to think about things, especially after today. He'd need to take a little time. And maybe give Alex a little time. He'd want to talk it over with someone. See what they thought. He walked over to his day planner and flipped ahead three days. He wrote in the 10 AM slot: *Visit Grace.*

He flipped the phone closed and looked at himself once more in the mirror.

"All right. Let's do this."

Yes, please, I want to see her again, the voice said.

"All in good time," the man said into the empty room.

Then he walked out of the office and up the stairs to the bathroom.

1

THE FIRE WAS TOO warm for Jerry. He would have gotten up from the couch, but Mary had fallen asleep with her feet on his lap, and Jerry would have just about suffered the Flames of Hell to get to be this close to her. She had been nice to him since they arrived at Valley View. After he brought her bags up from the train, she kissed him on the cheek. After breakfast, she squeezed his arm and told him she liked his sweater. And after they had come in from the cold, she had taken her boots off and asked if she could put her feet up on him. He had rested his arm across her shins, watching to see if that bothered her. But she hadn't batted an eye as she gossiped with Linda about people from work.

If anyone asked, Jerry would want it known that he wasn't a foot man. He didn't shame those that were, but his tastes landed smack in the middle of the ice-cream case into the bucket of plain old vanilla. He imagined that someone like Mary, smart, beautiful, and successful, might land anywhere among the thirty-one flavors. Heck, he wasn't entirely sure that she even dabbled in his side of the freezer. But when he fantasized about her, it was always like this, clothed, cozy, and casual. His reveries always included kisses on the cheek, compliments, and friendly touches. So, as far as a day could go, this one was turning out about as well as it could.

He wasn't a crazy person. He knew that he, five years younger than Mary, only an inch taller than her, and not nearly as successful, had no chance. He had seen her posts on Facebook about the relationships between men and women. She never posted about her personal preferences, but only ever spoke in the abstract and universal. Men should know their lane. Men should judge themselves soberly. Men should always defer to a woman's standards, which must be high.

Jerry was no one's high standard; he knew that. But he felt like Mary was something like that waterfall in the story about Coleridge. Mary was "sublime," and he felt awe in her presence. And that was enough, wasn't it? He knew that after the trip, she'd go back to being aloof, though not unkind, to him. And, of course, they would play the game where she knew he was a love-sick fool in Motley and she was the generous lady, allowing him into her presence. *It was good and right that the jester should love the queen,* Jerry thought. *All the knights loved her; the idiot should, too.* And he thought that was as good a part for someone like Jerry to play as any other. Especially if, on the rare occasion like this, she deigned to allow him just a little affection beyond his status.

He laughed at his mind's melodrama. It was easy to wax poetic. And if he spoke, or let himself write down what he felt, he knew he'd regret it in a day, a week, or God help him, a year. It would be overblown, sappy, and probably stalker-y. He just felt so much and longed so much that it overbrimmed his heart into his mind. And with his longing came the melancholy knowledge that this kindness and affection would not go on. There was a ticking clock, and perhaps this moment, while she dozed and rested her feet on his thighs, was the last portion of this affection. Tonight, tomorrow, or perhaps next week, she would meet a better version of whoever she was looking for—if indeed she was looking at all—and Jerry would have only the memory of a kiss, a word, a touch, and a nap.

He looked down at his hands and knew himself to be pathetic. But what was a man in the presence of sublimity, except a dirty thing grateful for his chance to see the waterfall or the sunrise? Jerry hated himself, hated his mind full of myths and legends that shaped how he understood something as simple as attraction. If Mary could see inside of him, she would be disgusted, he knew that. He would rather the whole world see him standing there, naked and pale, a runner's body with nothing to note about it except that he had put on no weight since college, than to see inside him with his overblown imagination and horrible longing to know that this, this simple closeness, could go on.

"Jerry!" a voice called from across the lounge.

Mary started, her eyes fluttering open. She pushed herself up on her elbows and drew her feet from him. But she smiled a sleepy smile, and that warmed him.

"Jerry, we need you," the voice came again.

"Better go," Mary said, wiping at her eye with the heel of her hand.

"I'd really rather not," Jerry said, smiling at her. And, to his glorious amazement, her smile widened.

"I'll be here when you get back, silly," she said.

Jerry almost wept. But then a hand landed on his shoulder. It was Greg.

"Hey, bud, we need your help. Can you give us a hand for a minute?"

"Um, sure," Jerry said. "What is it?"

"Come with me," Greg said. He turned to Mary. "I'll return him in a few minutes." She nodded sleepily and rolled over on her side. Greg, Jerry noticed, glanced at her backside and gave Jerry an approving look. "Come on, bud."

2

"So, you and Tim are going to go out there and find it," Greg said.

"I'm confused," Jerry said. "He lost his wallet on the path? How are we supposed to find it?" He pulled his heavy coat on and zipped it up.

"By looking like idiots," Tim said, repositioning the woolen cap on his head. "Waiting isn't going to improve it, since there's a storm coming in and then nightfall."

"Shit," Jerry said.

"I know it's impossible," Greg said. "And I know you have somewhere you'd rather be." He looked over at the lounge and the couch where Mary lay. "Believe me, I understand. Give it an hour or so, or at least until the storm comes. And if he finds the damn thing in his pants before then, we'll call you guys back in. If you can't find it before the storm, then we'll give it another try in the morning."

Tim hefted two snow shovels and handed one to Jerry. Jerry put his hat and gloves on, took one last fleeting look toward the lounge, and then nodded and followed Tim outside.

3

"HE SAID HE SLIPPED by the bend," Tim said as they plodded up the path. "So that's where I'm going to focus. I want you to just jog up the path and look around."

"You don't need me to do any digging?" Jerry asked.

"Take the smaller shovel with you. If you see anything, you know, give it a look. But I'll handle the drifts there." The bigger man pointed ahead of them up the path to where it bent to the left, starting its path around the mountain. Snow was piled three or four feet high on the outer rim of the path, forming a low wall between safety and a thirty-foot drop-off.

"I appreciate that," Jerry said.

"Hah! I'm doing it as much for me as for you. I don't like running, even when it's not below zero. And I'm sure you don't like shoveling. So, each man to his labor according to his skill, right?"

Jerry nodded, not sure if he was entirely on board with the reference, but Tim seemed like a nice enough guy.

"So," the big man said, "you and Mary?"

Jerry laughed. "I wish."

"Well, from the looks of it, you might be getting your wish, at least tonight."

Jerry frowned. "You think so?"

"That girl is all over you. Two drinks at the bar, and those panties will be—"

"No," Jerry said. "That's not what I want."

"I'm not saying drunk, I'm saying that some people need a little kick in the pants. My rule is, if they can't drive, then they can't drive stick, if you know what I mean."

Tim laughed at his own joke. Jerry felt disgusting inside.

"No, I mean … I mean, you're right, I think, but not Mary. I don't think that—"

"Hate to break it to you, bud, but if you've got some weird born-again fantasy that you'll be the first guy in there on your wedding night, you're going to be disappointed."

"No, it's not that," Jerry said. "I've been with people, I'm sure she has, and that's really not any of my business. It's not that. It's just, you know, if that's what happened, it wouldn't be … I mean, I get it if a woman wants to have a couple of drinks before subjecting herself to this," here he waved at his body with a gloved hand. "But I don't want that for her. And I don't want that for me, I guess."

"You don't want to hook up with her?" Tim asked, clearly finding the idea unbelievable.

"I do, but not if it's a one-time thing. Like, that's not how I feel about her."

They came up to where the snowdrift started to rise.

"Okay," Tim said. "I know what you mean. There was this girl, like ten years ago. God-damn if I wasn't getting so much ass right then. Two years after college, good job, making, not like real money, but enough to have my own place and enjoy life. But then this Korean girl, Sung-min, God, she was just … anyway, I wanted to stop everything and just be around her. Like, I became a fucking poet for this girl, and the idea of just hitting it, man, it made my stomach ache."

Jerry nodded enthusiastically.

"Yeah," Tim said. "Those are the worst. They hurt you just by being themselves. They don't know it, you know. They don't know that they're tearing your guts out by just being so … I don't know, it's not hot, you know? It's just, it's like they have this little piece of glory inside them, and you can see it, and … fuck it just devastates you."

Jerry wanted to cry. He couldn't have said it better. "She did turn you into a poet," Jerry laughed.

"She sure as fuck did," Tim said, shaking his head as he thrust the shovel into the snow.

"What happened with her?"

"Two drinks and she was in my bed," Tim said, looking out across the valley and toward the mountain that dominated the eastern sky.

"So, you hooked up?"

Tim sniffed loudly and shook his head. "I couldn't do it. I remember lying there, and she had taken her pants off, and she was just in her T-shirt and this little lace thong, and I was like, 'I wish I could touch you,' and she said, 'You are touching me.' But she didn't know what I meant."

"So, what happened?"

Tim shrugged. "She left a little while later. We never even kissed. I never saw her again."

Jerry felt his stomach twist. He could imagine that exact situation with Mary.

"Do you wish you had done something different?" Jerry asked.

Tim shook his head. "No, and yes. Part of me wishes I just took the opportunity she gave me. Part of me is glad I didn't. There's no right choice when you're in that situation. Whatever you do is wrong. Whatever you do, you'll regret it." He started walking up and down the ridge and looking down at the snow. "You better run up there for a ways. If you don't find it in fifteen minutes, come back," Tim said.

Jerry nodded and set off jogging up the snowy path.

4

AS HE RAN, HE wondered what he would do if Mary lay in his bed. Tim said they had never kissed, and if Mary wouldn't kiss him, what would that say? He realized, as he went, scanning the path, that he was waiting for her to tell him who he was. The sudden revelation was like a sunrise in his mind, shining light on everything. He was waiting for this woman to tell him who he was. Would she say that he was the jester? If so, then he would be. Would she tell him that he was a knight? He could play that part too. Indeed, if she told him that he was a shit-stained peasant who should dig in the dirt with the blunt end of a stick, then a-digging he would go.

The thing that terrified him was that she might tell him that he was a king. He both longed for it and rejected it out of hand. He knew what he was, or at least what he wasn't. He wasn't worthy of her. But if she said he was, could he accept it?

He cursed himself again for overdramatizing his feelings. But his feelings were so powerful, he didn't know what to do with them except to shape them into poetry and myth. He had been wrong earlier. He didn't have to wait to be embarrassed. He was mortified that his heart and mind were working together in this way. He wished they would stop. He knew that the overflow of feeling would scuttle his ship if ever she gave him a chance. It was all entirely self-defeating.

He had to figure out a way to be ready for her approval. He would expect rejection, even the most humiliating and devastating rejection. But he would have to find some place in his soul to make a little space for her to tell him that he was okay.

Jerry searched the snow but found nothing. His watch buzzed, letting him know that he'd served his fifteen minutes in the cold.

As he jogged back, he wondered how he had gotten to the place where he needed someone like Mary to tell him that he was good. Maybe that was the human condition. Everyone needed someone higher up the food chain to approve of them. For him, it was Mary. But for other people, it might be a boss, or an artist that they respected, or, hell, an author like the one they had there that weekend. He imagined that if he were a writer, he'd long for the approval of other, better and more successful writers. He'd want to hear them say, "Well done, good and faithful servant."

As he approached Tim, who had dug a good pocket in the ridge-wall, he knew that that's what he longed to hear from Mary. And he knew that he had to be ready, even just a little, to hear it. And maybe, he thought, that preparing that space in his soul to hear it made him a little more worthy of it. Maybe, if he were the kind of man who could hear it and not reject it, then he would be better. He certainly didn't want to become the kind of man who just assumed it about himself. But the kind of man who could hear it humbly and take a real measure of himself with honesty, that kind of man might be able to bask in the sublimity of someone like Mary.

When he got to Tim, he wasn't out of breath. A half-hour jog, even in his heavy coat and pants, had only been a warm-up for Jerry. Tim, on the other hand, was leaning heavily against his shovel as he appraised his breach in the snow wall.

"Find anything?" Tim asked, sounding out of breath. Jerry shook his head. "I think I saw something down there." He nodded at the opening near the path's edge. Tim had done such a good job that a passerby wouldn't be able to tell that the snow had been higher here a short time before. Jerry stepped toward the edge, but Tim grabbed his arm. "Here, drink something first."

There was a strange look in Tim's eye that made Jerry obey. He wasn't thirsty yet, but he thought that Tim would insist. So, he took the thermos.

"Warm your hands on it," Tim said. Jerry frowned. "Take your gloves off and warm your hands on it. It works."

"It shouldn't work, it's a thermos," Jerry said, but gave it a try anyway. "Nope, that definitely doesn't work," Jerry said, hurrying to put his gloves back on. He poured himself a little cocoa, wondering why Tim was being so strange. The drink was good, a little sweeter than he liked, but it hit the spot.

"Thanks," Jerry said and handed the thermos back to his companion. Then he stepped forward toward the edge. "Where did you think you saw it?"

"Somewhere over there, I think I might have been wrong, though. Hey, sorry, I think the snow is getting to me. Who was it again that you were pining after?"

"What?" Jerry asked, looking back at him.

"Down there," Tim said, pointing past Jerry's feet. Jerry looked back over the ridge again. "The girl you have so many feelings for."

Jerry laughed. "You mean Mary—"

He was about to say, 'Mary, the woman we've both worked with for years,' but the shovel hit him in the back of the head too hard for him to continue.

He didn't immediately tumble over the cliff. First, he fell to his knees. Then the shovel came again and battered him on the side of the head. That put his lights out for a moment, so that he slumped over. But he regained consciousness quickly enough to find Tim pushing him with his foot. Jerry opened his mouth to speak, but Tim's boot came down on his jaw. Then it connected with his ribs. And finally, Jerry felt himself slipping over the edge, crashing against the stone a half-dozen times before he slammed into the ledge below. He felt his back break after his knee shattered. Then he felt nothing below his shoulders.

Sleet began to fall across his face. He tried to speak, but everything was broken. Snow fell down after him, and he couldn't see anything at the top of the cliff. He was only dimly aware when the men arrived to help him. And his last sensation was being lifted on a stretcher back toward the cliff he had been kicked from.

He tried to speak, to form another last word. But he couldn't.

To and Fro

October 7, 1961

DEL MAPLES HAD BEEN a Lawrence County sheriff's deputy for two years. In that time, he had drawn his gun six times on drunk men, but he'd never had to pull the trigger. He had worked four cases that involved killings: one self-inflicted and three due to disagreements of some kind. A woman shot a man who beat her, and Del had thought that was just fine. A man had stabbed another man at a bar during a drunken disagreement about something that had happened in Korea. They had been best friends. He had never seen anyone confess so quickly or fight so little for his own freedom. The third had been a matter of jealousy, and the fourth a case of revenge. None of them had been particularly easy, except maybe the woman defending herself, but none of them had dug themselves into his dreams and made a home in his imagination. He had been pretty lucky as far as monstrous memories went.

As Del shined his flashlight at the body of the young woman, he knew his lucky streak was over. The only mercy, as far as his first appraisal went, was that she was not naked. Her pajama shirt was unbuttoned below her chest, and her pants were pulled down a few inches, but he thought that whatever had happened here, it had not been sexual. Del believed that her clothing had been adjusted so the killer could carve the word on her stomach.

That, my son, is the definition of cold comfort, he imagined the sheriff saying.

Of course, the cause of death and the motivation would be left up to more experienced men than Del Maples. He snatched his Lafayette Radio walkie-talkie from his belt and pushed the button.

"I have her," he said. "I'm about a thousand yards north of the house in the woods. I'd say about twenty feet east of Stoking Road."

Sheriff Miller's voice came back, "What's her status?"

"You should come here," Del said. He knew better than to announce the sixteen-year-old girl's death over the radio. And dead she was, he could see that in her eyes and the stillness of her chest. He wanted to cry. He wanted to throw up. He wanted to find the man responsible and blow his brains into a bush.

"Copy. I'm on my way, Shane and Peterson are continuing east and west."

"I'm leaving a flare and continuing to pursue," Del said.

"No, son, you stay there," the sheriff's voice said from the radio speaker.

But Del put the radio back on his belt. In the same motion, he drew a flare, popped it, and cleared a space in the leaves with his boot. He made it wide so he didn't start a fire, and then kicked a flat stone over to prop the flare against. He looked at it, wondering if he was making a mistake. Then he pulled his revolver and took a deep breath. No matter what, if he found this animal, he was going to put him down.

He looked around and decided that the man probably continued north to where Stoking bent around and ran through the forest. He set out at a jog, stopping every fifteen feet to listen. After six short spurts, he stopped to appraise his situation. He should be close to the road now. He should probably report—

The man hit him from the side and knocked him against a tree. Del hadn't been hit that hard since football, and his deputy's campaign hat didn't provide nearly the protection his helmet had. His temple slammed into rough bark, and he felt and heard his collarbone snap. In his mind, he thought only the word *no*. In that 'no' was fear of death, crippling injury, and humiliation. In that 'no,' he thought of his wife and their one-year-old son, Chester. In that 'no,' he prayed that God wouldn't let him end here and now.

That 'no' was the only quarter Del allowed his fear. The rest of him knew that it was time to fight. The man was big, wide in the shoulders, and probably six-and-a-half feet tall. Del had no breath in him, so even though he was not aimed at the man, he fired his gun once.

Hear me, sheriff, he thought. Then he swung up with his left elbow at the man's chin and missed, grazing the big man's cheek. It wasn't the counterattack he had hoped to deliver, but it was something. He jammed his elbow up again, and this time he caught the man's nose. Two hundred and twenty pounds backed off of him. Del hoped that meant he could turn and train his revolver on the man. Instead, it meant that his legs, which had gone to jelly, no longer had any help holding him up. He slid down the side of the tree and landed hard on his rear end. His collarbone screamed. Del grunted.

The man, dark and towering, lifted a foot and stomped down on Del's leg. He felt his ankle crack under the heavy boot. The deputy shifted his pistol onto his thigh and pointed up at the man.

"Do that again," he said.

Shoot him, shoot him! a voice said in his head. He tried. He squeezed, but his finger wouldn't move. He didn't understand it. Was there something about a broken collarbone that kept you from moving your fingers? He didn't think so. This wasn't the first time he'd suffered the injury, and he remembered being clumsy in the cast, but never having any problems beyond that. Maybe the conk on the head had screwed something up in his wiring.

The big man looked down at him. Del's flashlight lay on the ground nearby, bouncing light around rocks, leaves, trees, and fallen branches. Enough reflected onto the man's face that Del could see that he had cocked his head like a listening dog. He was working his lips like he had sucked on a lemon. To Del's surprise, he turned his head and sent a stream of spit into the forest. Then the big man sucked between his front teeth in a not-unfriendly manner.

"Messed up your shoulder, I think," he said. His voice was deep, and Del guessed he was from north Texas, or maybe Oklahoma. He rubbed his nose. "I'd give you a hand up, but I think I also did for your ankle there, too."

"You did," Del said. *Shoot this girl-murdering garbage*, his mind screamed. But his finger just wouldn't listen. Del was terrified of what would happen if the man decided to press his luck. He figured he might be able to pistol-whip him, but that was about all he had in his bag of tricks at the moment. So, his best bet was calm. He thought of John Wayne and how the man was cool under fire. It was just movies, he knew, but he tried to hold that image in his head. The man on his horse, casually facing death without the slightest hint of fear. "So, I think I'll just have a sit here while you take a step back."

The big man obliged.

"Thank you," Del said, knowing that it didn't make much difference. *Except he thinks that you'll shoot him dead*, Del thought. "I couldn't convince you to take a seat against that tree, could I?"

The man looked around and pointed to a small pine tree. "That one?"

"No, that oak there," Del said, waving the pistol.

"Certainly," the big man said, and slid himself down with a wide groan, like a man taking a load off after a long day at the factory. He spread his knees wide and rested his forearms on them, his fingers hanging loose. He looked at them.

"Where's your knife?" Del asked, keeping the weapon pointed at him.

"On my belt."

Well, that was easy enough, Del thought. *Let's see what else this guy will say.*

"Probably should tell you you're under arrest, and you don't have to say anything if you don't want to. Constitution and such."

"Yep, I figured that. You mind if I smoke?"

"Sure," Del said. "If you tell me why you did it." He almost laughed. The big man did.

"Sure, that girl needed killing."

"Come again?" Del said as the man pulled a pack of cigarettes from his shirt pocket and shook one out. He stuck it into his mouth and then proffered the pack toward Del. The deputy shook his head. The big man shrugged and put the pack back in his pocket.

"She needed killing. And you'd agree if you knew the situation," he said amicably as he scratched a match against the side of its box. "I know you won't see it that way. But that's the truth of it. She needed killing. And she won't be the last."

"Why take her out of her house then?" Del said. "Why bring her out here?"

"Well, she didn't need killing earlier. But then one of you all showed up, and, you know, the jig was up." He drew on his cigarette, painting his face red. He was younger than Del had thought. He couldn't have been more than twenty-one or twenty-two. His voice and way of talking suggested an older man.

"What were you going to do to her if you hadn't gotten caught?" Del felt anger pushing aside his fear and shock. "You going to strip her somewhere else?"

The man shook his head. "Not my style. I like it when they want it. Never would force myself. I'm not that kind."

"Then why tonight?" Del asked.

"I didn't force her to do anything. She came along willingly. Or, well, probably not exactly willingly," he said, chuckling. "But I spoke, and she listened. Nifty little trick."

Del's head was a little too fuzzy to parse that.

"But if you're asking, 'why tonight' in a broader sense? Well, it was time. I had to send a message to that bitch." He gestured lazily behind him, back toward the house.

"I think you sent her a message when you broke her neck."

The big man shook his head and sucked his teeth again. "No, sir. I wasn't sending a message to the girl, who, as far as I know, was a nice young lady. It's her mother and her auntie. They're the ones that needed talking to."

Del wondered what the girl's mother had to do with any of it. And, as far as he was aware, Mrs. Robillard had no sisters. He wasn't a man conversant in the county residents' personal lives, but Mrs. Robillard was an exception. She was well known. Heck, for Lawrence County, she was famous. He thought of her being told that her daughter was dead, and that word bled from her stomach.

"What does 'Empty' mean?" Del asked. He sniffed. The smell of cigarette smoke mingled with pine and October leaves. The earth was damp and rich from recent rain. The crescent moon peeked down at him from between not-yet-fallen leaves.

"Just what it says. She won't be making any babies for them." He drew on the cigarette again and looked back the way they had come. "You know, I know you can't shoot me." Del looked at him. "I could stand up and kick your head in. It's a hell of a thing doing that to a man. The first kick is the worst. You see it coming and you think 'oh God, oh God, oh God.' That one knocks you silly. That's when your life flashes in front of your eyes. You see yourself as a kid, and your mom and dad, and that time your dog got hit by a car, and you saw his guts on the road. Remember that?"

Del stared and found it hard to hear the man over the blood that had started thundering in his ears. He hadn't thought of his dog in years.

"You see that first kiss with Martha Whatever-Her-Name-Was, and your first time feeling a pair of tits. That first ball, too, you get that one. Not your wife or kid, though, and that scares the hell out of you. Then that second kick comes and breaks your nose and jaw, and you know that this is it. In a second, you're just going to be meat. That whole world inside your head is going to just go out like a light, and not God, or science, or anything in between, is going to stop you from becoming just a lump of maggot food. Your wife will mourn, and your son will grow up without you. And then she'll meet someone else, and he'll ball her, and you'll be nothing but a picture on a shelf. And then that third kick, and it all happens. But for you, it's nothing. Your whole being goes from man to mud in one swift boot."

Del remembered Martha well and tried to remember if he had ever told anyone about her. His mother had told him never to kiss and tell. Maybe Martha had told someone? It would have had to have been over a decade ago, before she died, when her boyfriend drove them over into a creek. Even so, how the hell would this man know about it? Del tried to picture John Wayne, but he was shaking too much and thinking about the fact that he was shaking too much. Even if he could squeeze the trigger, he didn't think that he'd hit the man, even though he was only ten feet away.

"You can calm down, though," the man said. "I'm not going to do that. I don't know how you die, but it won't be from me crushing you out like a smoked butt." To punctuate his point, he took one more drag, dropped the cigarette, and pressed it into the earth with his boot. "Funny that your sheriff isn't here yet, huh? That shot was loud enough to bring him. Funny too that the radio isn't blaring, 'Where are you? Where are you?' isn't it?"

Del looked down at his radio. The man was right. Why wasn't—

"—damn it, Del, where the hell are you?"

The radio *was* talking. Had it been talking this whole time? Shit, his wiring was mightily screwed up.

"Go ahead and answer him, fella, that gun isn't keeping me here."

Del switched hands anyway and pulled his radio free. "I'm here. I'm … hell, I'm not sure where I am. I think I'm close to where Stoking turns east. We're in the trees. I'm injured."

"Shit, thank God," the sheriff said. "What do you mean 'we'?"

"I have him. I have—"

"My name is Joseph," the big man said.

"Joseph what?" Del asked.

"Lawstead. Joseph Macon Lawstead. And you'll find my friend on the road in a van. He's my getaway driver."

Joseph laughed heartily, leaning his head back. Del gave him a questioning look, but when it seemed like he wasn't going to explain what was funny, he pushed the button on the walkie-talkie again.

"I'm here with the suspect, name of Joseph Lawstead."

"Shine your light, it'll get him here faster," Joseph said, wiping one eye with the heel of his hand.

Del watched the man carefully as he reached out and pulled his flashlight back to him. He started waving it in the air.

"I got you," the sheriff said. "Sit tight!"

Joseph lit another smoke and settled down against the tree. "Now it all begins," he said.

"What does?" Del asked.

"The long road in and out and up and down. Back and forth on the face of the earth. To and fro. I'm going to be here again, but next time … next time I'll make it out with her."

Del watched him as three lights approached. "Job?" Del asked, recognizing the passage.

"A paraphrase. But yes. Time for me to wander."

"I don't think you'll be wandering much after tonight," Del said.

"Oh, you'd be surprised. I know my path. The man has shown me, and he can see far. A hell of a lot farther than the bitch they serve."

"You're insane," Del said.

"You think that I'm insane because your brain's trying to rationalize this whole thing. You're forgetting the dog and poor, sweet, dead Martha. You're trying to fit it all into a bundle you can accept. But that's not the world, Del. That's not the world at all."

Del stared at the big man, his wide shoulders, his crewcut hair, and trembled as footsteps crunched closer. Finally, he looked away, unable to keep eye contact with the younger man as the sheriff emerged from the trees, flanked by the other deputies.

"There's a man in a van," Del said. "On the road. His accomplice, I think."

"Don't worry," Joseph said. "He's not going anywhere. And don't go shooting him, he's a crip, and he's only fifteen. He's not a threat."

Del wasn't sure how he knew it, but he sensed that Joseph's last statement was the only lie he had told that night.

Galfarm drew his long sword, Hraftring, and gripped it with his mighty hands.

"Come then, come on to me, and I will slay thee. It may be that mine own blood shall water the roots of this tree and mingle here with thine, but that is nothing to me. I have fought for too long, and I have seen too much death to fear it. Come on to me then and let us deal with one another as our fathers did."

The dark knight slid his long, wicked, cruel blade from its scabbard of men's skin, and he stepped forward, his heavy iron boot sinking deep into the soft, loamy earth. Galfarm felt a thrill of fear dance over his puckered skin, his scrotum tightened, and he knew that he would never wake to another morning, never see the sun above the fields again, and never know Elgaria's soft lips and ample bosom again.

The black knight strode forward then, and Hraftring turned the black blade of Niglathof in an arc of fire. Galfarm's steel, at least, was up to the challenge.

SHAWN SCANNED THE WORDS on the laptop screen and clucked his tongue. He flared his nostrils against a mild desire to sneeze and retraced the words again. He wasn't entirely sure about 'mine' and 'thine.' He was fairly certain he was using them correctly, but did they belong? The last rejection letter had had only one note, and though that was more than he usually got, he had not known how to interpret it.

'Less Convoluted,' it had said. Did that mean that the editor of *Fire and Magery* wanted him to be less convoluted, or was his story less complex than they wanted? He was fairly sure it was the first, but he didn't know what was convoluted about "Silver and Summer." The damn story was only 4,000 words. How complicated could you get in 4,000 words? That made him think that the editor wanted more complexity, more depth, and more backstory, if possible.

I should write him a note that just says, "More convoluted, please," he thought.

Backstory, he could do. He had pages of it for Galfarm, bearer of Hraftring. He had family trees and a personal timeline for the hero, his father, and his father's father. Not to be chauvinistic, he had the same for the lovely Elgaria as well. She, Elfin smith of the silver trade, had her own adventures in her magical—if somewhat sparse—armor, Nirilian. He had had to change the original name, 'Nipilian'—which had deep, not-at-all-sexualized etymological roots—after an editor told him that she would never publish a word of his third-rate male-power-fantasy drivel, calling out Elgaria's magical armor specifically. He had drafted a letter informing her that 'Nipis,' with a long 'I' and an 'E' sound, was the ancient Elvish word for protection, but he had decided not to bother.

Shawn pulled a pack of gum from his pocket and popped a stick of spearmint into his mouth. He chewed thoughtfully and wondered if what the story needed was a more detailed environment. He wasn't good at that part. He had never been particularly interested in Tolkien's trees, rocks, and mountains. The landscape wasn't what was important. It was the heroes of yore, the barbaric manhood that stood against monstrous darkness that enslaved the good folk of the world.

A message popped up on his laptop screen.

> **_BokenToker_**
> Yo, what are you up to?

> **_Galfarm_**
> Writing. What about you?

> **_BokenToker_**
> Fighting the man.

Shawn could guess how his friend Mike was fighting the man, but he decided to ask anyway.

> **_BokenToker_**
> Getting blazed at work man, this warehouse is way too big for them to keep tabs on it all.

> **_Galfarm_**
> Don't they have cameras?

> ***Boken Toker***
> Yeah, but half of them don't work, Chrissy told me. She works in the security room.

> ***Galfarm***
> Nice. Well, blaze one for me. Damn the man.

> ***Boken Toker***
> Save the planet.

> ***Galfarm***
> Empire.

> ***Boken Toker***
> Nah, man, save the planet.

Shawn watched his friend's icon turn from green to red and leaned back in his desk chair. He did want to save the planet, but first, he had to try to save his mother from her job, bills, and the rotating string of assholes who seemed to wander their way from all parts of West Virginia. He knew he had stories in him, stories that could pay some of those bills; he just had to keep plugging away. It would happen, he knew it would. And when it did, and he was rich and famous, then he could really help everyone. He never understood why the rich and famous didn't make it all better. They didn't need big houses; no one did. He just wanted something reasonable. And when he knew his mom would never have to work another day doing something she didn't enjoy, then all the rest of the money would go to saving the world.

Then Galfarm would have saved the world for real, he thought.

He stood and pulled his heavy, blue curtains back along their rod. Dust puffed out and sifted through the morning sunlight, revealing a messier bedroom than he expected. He should clean it, but not until he had gotten out his 2,000 words. That's what real writers did, day in and day out. He hunched over his laptop, dragged his mouse over his writing, and saw that he still had 1,600 words left for the day. That wasn't the worst start, but he'd have to knuckle down and get things moving. And for that, he would need coffee and food.

What day was it? Mike was working at the warehouse, so it was either Friday or Saturday. He checked his phone. Saturday. That meant Mom would be home, and he couldn't traipse around with his hog half hanging. Grumbling internally, he pulled a pair of baggy cargo shorts over his boxer-briefs and followed them with a T-shirt. Then he was out of his room and into the shag-carpeted hallway. After a stop at the bathroom, he meandered his way to the kitchen. The television was on, but the volume was so low that he could only hear a murmur as he opened the refrigerator.

"You're alive," his mother said from the living room. She sat up and looked at him over the back of the plaid, threadbare couch. Her dark hair was messy, and her cheek had a grid of red lines across it.

"Sleep on the couch again?" he asked.

"Mhm," she said, stretching. "There was a documentary on about the Beatles. You know, they went to India to get inspiration?"

Shawn leaned down to look in the refrigerator. He grabbed the can of instant coffee his mother liked to keep cold and the gallon of milk.

"Yeah, I think I heard that," Shawn said, wondering if she was going to suggest he take the next train to New Delhi. Then he laughed at himself, imagining a train that went across the United States and down into the Pacific Ocean. He wondered if there was a story in that idea.

"How's your writing going this morning?" she asked, crossing her arms on the back of the couch and resting her chin on them. "Lots of dragons?"

"I don't have dragons in my world, Mom," he said, his always simmering annoyance at her curiosity starting to bubble.

"Oh, I thought you had dragons."

"Wyrms," he said, pronouncing his 'w' as a 'v' and pulling the word into two syllables. "Wyrms, not dragons. And no, no wyrms today. And it's going fine, I just need some coffee to keep going. Do we have any sugar?"

"No, we're out. But you can take some money from my purse and get some."

"I can't, I need to write," Shawn said, feeling his patience fraying.

"Honey, it's gorgeous outside, it's getting up to seventy-five today. Go put your flip-flops on, get some sugar, and by the time you're back, your coffee will be ready. Plus, who knows, maybe you'll see a worm while you're out and get some inspiration."

"*Wyrm*, not worm. And what kind of inspiration? Do you think I'm going to stumble over a yogi and write like John Lennon?"

"You never know," she said.

"Yes, Mom, I do know. There are no yogis in Flatwoods or Oakdown."

"There might be," she said.

He opened his mouth to say that the odds of him running into a real yogi, not some middle-aged divorcee who took a class in Baltimore or Washington, were vanishingly small. But the idea of getting out with his notebook and doing a word sketch of some trees, rocks, or paths might not be a bad idea. If he needed more nature in his story, real nature was likely the best solution.

"Okay, fine," he said. "You mind putting this together then?" He held up the coffee and milk.

"Yourn wish is mine command, yourn highness," she said.

He opened his mouth to correct her, shut it, and padded back to his room. He slipped on his flops, checked his T-shirt for stains, sniffed it, and then changed it for one in his dresser. Then he was back out and stuffing his phone into his cargo pants pocket.

"Here's ten. Get sugar and flour. I'm going to do chicken cutlets tomorrow," his mother said.

"How are we on coffee?" he asked. She shook the can and nodded. "Great, be back in a bit. I'm going to maybe do a little writing while I'm out, you know, just in case Swami Whoever doesn't enlighten me on the way."

"Don't be racist," she said. "Not in my house."

"I don't think it is," he said, picking up his plastic sunglasses. "It means 'master' or something. You know, like Father or Rabbi or Imam."

"Oh," she said, smiling. "Well, you learn something new every day."

He was out the door a moment later into the bright morning. She had been right; it was a glorious day, and Shawn was immediately grateful that she had prodded him to go out. He felt the mysterious creative energy flowing through him, that strange mystery that linked him, the convoluted writer of cheap fantasy that he knew himself to be, and the truly great artists of history, like Beethoven, Tennyson, and Chuck Berry. Shawn felt suddenly full, suddenly overwhelmed by the beauty of nature, the silken touch of the breeze, and the siren's call to create. He thought seriously about plopping himself down on the wooden bench in the front lawn, flanked by a garden gnome and a crystal ball, and hurling himself into the muse's maelstrom right then. But there was sugar and flour to be bought, and much more to see on his quest.

Besides, he thought, he wasn't sure if the old, weather-worn decorative bench would support him these days. He hadn't put on that much weight in the last year, but still, he didn't want to risk his mother's little, cultivated grotto—not when he couldn't afford to fix it.

Shawn flipped and flopped his way down the uneven flagstone path that led to the gravel edge of the road. Then, hands in pockets, notebook curled in a loose 'U' in another pocket, he hummed "You Never Can Tell" to himself as he walked toward the little stretch of street that passed for a downtown in Oakdown, West Virginia.

He had finished humming about Piere and the lovely mademoiselle, and had started Etta James's "Tell Mama," when he came to the intersection across from *Lovelle's Corner Store*. Despite his dark sunglasses, he still had to shade his eyes to watch Mr. Colberth standing at the door to the old shop, holding it open for Linus Moorestead. His stomach sank.

Shawn considered taking his walk right then instead of being in the shop at the same time as Linus, when Jimmy might be working behind the counter. But that would be a coward's move, and he knew it. Shawn knew he wasn't the world's bravest man, but he didn't want to be a coward either. So, pushing his nervousness down, he crossed the street and pulled open the door to the corner market.

His fears were immediately confirmed as he saw Jimmy Lovelle, his wispy white hair like a floating halo about his narrow, age-marked face, grinning sadistically at the young man who stood in front of him with a five-dollar bill in his hand.

"You want soap for your mama?" Jimmy was saying.

"Yes, sir," Linus said. The young man, whom Shawn was sure could have pulled Jimmy over the counter and stomped him to goo, bent nearly over in a feudalistic bow toward the old, suspenders-wearing man.

"Your mama needs a washing, don't she?"

"Yes, sir," Linus said. Linus, who had been in the same grade as Shawn but was a good decade older than him, nodded his head rhythmically. Shawn didn't know what the man's diagnosis was, but he suspected that if his family had had the money, or his father's job offered the proper kind of insurance, Linus might have gotten better care. *Or any care at all,* Shawn thought. But in Oakdown, Linus got Jimmy Lovelle.

"I hear it's going around," Shawn said, feeling as nervous as if he had walked out onto a tightrope above a bottomless pit. He didn't want to be on Jimmy's bad side. They needed to shop at *Lovelle's*, and they couldn't afford Jimmy hiking up the prices on their regular items out of spite.

"What's that?" Jimmy said. Linus turned to see the tall, heavyset man who had just entered the store.

"Hey, Shawn," Linus said.

"Hey, Linus. Um, needing a wash. I hear it's going around. I sure as hell need one," he said, lifting his arm and sniffing his armpit, which drew a laugh from Linus. Jimmy just gaped at him, perhaps uncertain of what to say next.

"Me too," Linus said and lifted his arm to sniff.

"Heck, probably only one in town who doesn't need a wash is you, Jimmy, since you've got a mountain of soap and stuff here," Shawn ventured.

"Well," Jimmy said, closing his mouth and puckering his lips. "You're right about that at least." He looked Shawn over and then Linus, looking as if he were sizing them up for a ration of further abuse. Instead, he turned around and grabbed a three-pack of Dove soap and put it down on the counter.

"Six-fifty," he said.

"I only need one bar, and I just have a five," Linus said, proffering the bill.

"Six-fifty," Jimmy repeated. "This is what I've got."

"Give me a second, Linus," Shawn said. He scooted down the aisle, grabbed a bag of sugar and one of flour, and carried them to the counter. "How much are these?"

"Seven-fifty-six," Jimmy said after punching register keys. That was too much, Shawn thought, but he handed over the ten and thanked the old man. Then he turned back to Linus and handed him a dollar-fifty.

"I can't take it," Linus said.

"Sure, you can, and sure you can pay us back when you got it. Okay?"

Linus nodded, this time more deeply, and handed the money to Jimmy, who looked as displeased as a man could while also making a sale. Then Shawn walked Linus out to the street and shook his head.

"Sorry about Jimmy," Shawn said.

"'S okay," Linus whispered. "He's mean 'cause he was raised wrong." Then he looked over his shoulder as if Jimmy might be listening at the window. "Thanks, Shawn. We'll pay you back soon."

"I know you will," Shawn said, and watched the man trundle down the sidewalk toward the western edge of town.

Sparks flew from Hraftring as Galfarm turned another blow from the ebon blade. The great warrior, weary and sweat-glistening, gave another step, retreating closer to the cliff's edge. Their fight had ranged far as the sun rose, lingered, and began to set. Many were the nicks and bruises on the tanned flesh of the battered hero, but so too were the dents and tears in the dark warrior's armor. In one place, Galfarm's foe showed pale skin beneath a cloven pauldron, a sign that had

rejuvenated the warrior.

That had been hours ago.

But now, as the sun dipped toward the west, Galfarm found his strength waning. Hraftring remained true, but turned more slowly, and spun with less ferocity.

"Your battle is done," the figure in black said. "You have fought better than any I have encountered, but you have lost. Put up your sword, and I will have mercy upon you. Your death shall be swift and noble."

Galfarm wiped sweat from his brow and shook his head. He imagined Elgaria's green eyes and how they so oft regarded him with respect and desire. He dared not tarnish her regard by laying his sword down and letting his life go so easily. If the gods were there, and if they waited to greet him, he would not go to them with his head low. So Galfarm planted his feet once more, bent his knees, prayed to Iloth the Warrior for the strength to make a good death, and raised Hraftring in a high guard.

"Come again, foul one, for I am Galfarm, Wyrm-slayer, and you may have my life only at a dear cost."

SHAWN SWUNG THE PLASTIC shopping bag at his side as an old red pickup truck rumbled past him. He held a hand up to wave to whoever was driving and wondered if the story should end with Galfarm's defeat. What was he trying to say? Was it that evil often conquers good—that evil can overcome even the best warriors? He knew that was true. But was that enough? Or should he have Galfarm, against all odds, pull out a victory over the wicked knight? Should he have Elgaria arrive with her silver spear and save him? Perhaps the juxtaposition between Nipilian—no, *Nirilian*— and the knight's midnight armor would be a good image.

He pictured the beautiful elf in her gleaming metal plate reflecting the sunset—a symbol of Galfarm's defeat—and blinding the dark foe with it. That thought filled his chest with something he couldn't name.

"Stay thine sword, for you shall not stand against the daughter of Yrdana, Lady of the Evening Forge!" he whispered. He could see her standing over

Galfarm, her back to him, her spear at the dark warrior's neck. Shawn wiped at his eye, imagining music swelling behind the scene. Of course, he'd have to find some reason for her to be there. Perhaps she had been riding all night to meet her love. Perhaps, he thought, getting excited, she should bear the wounds of a great combat as well. Warriors, sent to waylay her, had given her battle, and she fought her way through to Galfarm.

He liked that a lot. But he couldn't do Galfarm so dirty as to have him accomplish nothing. Being saved by Elgaria was nothing short of an honor, but a battle with no victory at all? He didn't want that for Galfarm. Shawn hummed "Maybellene" as he realized that Galfarm didn't have to win; he only needed to hold out longer than his enemy expected. His victory was in holding on. That was the message. His mind flashed immediately to the battle of Helm's Deep in *The Lord of the Rings,* but he dismissed the comparison as he walked up the path to his house. Of course, people, better people than he, had touched on the themes before. But had Conan ever been saved by a barbarian princess? He didn't know. Maybe he had. It didn't matter. Whether or not Conan ever had, Galfarm certainly would.

Shawn opened the front door and walked into the house, brimming with energy and excitement.

"Ma, I've got the stuff from the store," he called. He could hear the shower, so he put the bag on the counter and pulled out the sugar. He opened the bag in a puff of sweet air, poured some into a fresh mason jar, and then rolled the thick paper top down and put it into the cupboard. Then, four scoops later, he was mixing his cup with a bit of creamer and thinking about precisely how to describe Elgaria's wounds. They had to walk a line between horrific and unimpressive. She had to look like she was standing only by main strength, but also—and Shawn had the wherewithal to feel a little embarrassed by the notion—she still had to be hot. He consoled himself with the thought that he had the same rule for Galfarm. The man must always cut a dashing figure, even when badly wounded.

He took his coffee and returned to his room. The messiness of it felt suddenly oppressive. His piles of T-shirts and boxer shorts seemed to have moved of their own accord, spreading across the small, dimly lit room from his dresser to his hamper, forming a continuity between clean and dirty. The posters of fantasy warrior men and fit, busty ladies of many genres hung from old pushpins. His old-fashioned wall calendar, featuring Samantha Lipman—the inspiration for the fair Elgaria, still showed July.

Shawn felt a wave of claustrophobia and a moment of indecision. He could take the energy inside himself and use it to write, or he could straighten things up, and in so doing, perhaps make an environment more conducive to future writing. He opted for the second choice, sipping his coffee and placing it on his dresser next to a picture of him and his mom at Valley Park. He had been ten when it was taken, but it remained one of the most joyful experiences of his life. That was back when her job had promised advancement, and there was enough extra coming in that they could afford to take a week off, drive west, and enjoy two days at the theme park. Sixteen years was a long time to go without a proper vacation, and Shawn hoped that his writing could give his mother that same kind of joy again.

As he plucked screen-printed T-shirts from the floor, Shawn pictured handing his mother two plane tickets to Glory Home, telling her that they were going to stay somewhere nice, and that he would take her on all the roller coasters. He wouldn't tell her that his stories had been published before that. He'd let her keep hoping and praying and then spring it on her all at once. That would be the first step, the first real forward movement. And then, who knew? A new house? Nothing fancy, of course. Just somewhere where she could spread out a little and not have to pay for anything.

He dumped a Metallica shirt on top of an old *Scooby-Doo* shirt and then turned to the calendar. Miss Samantha Lipman was pouting chestily over the handlebars of an old ten-speed, which Shawn appreciated. But time was time, and it must march forward. He pulled the pushpin out, flipped the calendar to September, and rehung it. Now, Samantha was leaning back on a surfboard, her blue and orange bikini struggling to restrain her astonishing figure. A thrill of desire swept through Shawn. It wasn't the desire to have her desire him—he knew that was an even more foolish dream than his writing. At best, women like Samantha endured men like Shawn, and he could not force his mind to imagine something so improbable as her finding him attractive. He could dream of fantasy Wyrms, but her thinking he was cute? That was beyond the pale. Instead, he desired only to have her let him look at her, to contemplate her like the muse she was.

He shook his head at told himself that he was pathetic. Then, taking up a black magic marker, he crossed off the first ten days of the month. He would be better at keeping up with things if this energy would only last.

Once he had made his bed and plucked several wrappers and bits of paper from the floor, he felt ready to sit in front of his laptop and write again. That was, of course, when his mother knocked on the door.

"Honey?" she said.

"Yeah, Ma?" He tried to keep the annoyance from his voice.

"I just got a call from your Aunt Sissy; Vick needs a hand. Is there any chance you could head over?"

Shawn knew he had a choice. He could fly off the handle, and she would leave him alone to write. But that was self-defeating. The deep well of creativity would dry up if he did that, and he would hurt her for no reason. Alternatively, he could simply agree to it and potentially lose his inspiration.

"Can you give me five minutes, and then I'll head over?" he asked.

"Sure, take fifteen, it's no rush," she said through the door.

Shawn flipped open his laptop and plopped himself down. He could at least get some of his ideas onto the page, and maybe a verbal sketch of how Nirilian looked in the setting sun.

Twenty minutes later, Shawn closed the front door behind him and stepped once more onto the flagstone path. This was going to be a good story, he knew it. Hands shoved into pockets, "Johnny B. Goode" on his lips, and an opening scene forming in his mind, Shawn found the late morning sun to be once more invigorating. It made him think of daytrips to Summersville Lake. As he walked the mile down the road, he wondered how he could capture the feeling, as it seemed to be a bottomless well of inspiration. Most mornings, the words came hard, as if he were picking through dry earth with an old, dull axe, hoping to find a bone or an old arrowhead. But today the beast lay before him, its skeleton fixed like a relief in the side of a hill, laid out for the taking.

The tree-lined road that led down to Aunt Sissy's place was lightly traveled. Only two cars passed him. Though lost in his reverie, Shawn still raised a hand to greet them as they went. Halfway down the road, his attention was drawn from the ethereal world of creation to an unfamiliar deer path that opened to his right. He frowned at the flat, debris-free track between two birch trees. It looked as if it had cut through Oakdown's forest for years. The problem, Shawn thought, was that there was no deer path there. He knew the roads and hills of Oakdown, and he knew of no such track between his mother's house and Aunt Sissy's. He stared at it, frowning, and stayed for a full minute, trying to make sense of it. Deciding that it must be a trick of how the leaves had blown, he took a half-dozen exploratory steps down the path until he saw it wind out and up the old barn hill to where the trees grew densely on the slope. This was no illusion, no random trick of wind-blown leaves.

Shawn debated going up the path immediately before going to Vick's. Had the path appeared shorter, he might have explored right away, but it looked like it went up toward the old barn. That was a good hike, and if he took it, Vick would be shit out of luck for hours. So, putting his curiosity aside, Shawn returned to the road and walked another ten minutes to his cousin's house.

It turned out that Vick only needed a little help. His mother was gone for the day, and his wheelchair was acting up again. He had forced the stubborn contraption into a position in front of the TV but couldn't get into it. He was watching an old rerun of some police procedural in his late father's battered easy chair when Shawn walked in. Every time Shawn saw his cousin, once tall and strong, he looked like he had shrunk another inch. Shawn knew it wasn't true, but the difference between the persistent mental image of his U.S. Marine Corps cousin and the man who languished before mindless TV in his chair was so stark that the illusion of further decay was hard to resist.

It took Shawn fifteen minutes to get Vick's chair squared away, him into it, a pot of coffee brewing, and leftovers into the oven for his lunch. Vick waved him off when he offered to stick around to take the meal out for him. Now that he was once more mobile, he could manage it all. Shawn always wanted to salute his cousin, but he always felt foolish. So, he imagined the wounded soldier Virikor, who sat in the tower of scrolls and did research for Galfarm on his adventures. He had never been able to find a good place for Virikor in his stories, but the man had been there, in the background, helping Galfarm behind the scenes.

As Shawn returned up the road, gravel underfoot, he wondered if it could be Virikor who sent Elgaria a warning. Yes, perhaps his studies had uncovered some ancient plot, and his message could come to her just in time. That would give a reason for her to be prepared against the ambush, and for all his heroes to finally get together in the next story. Of course, Virikor would fall in love with Elgaria, and that would be good stuff as far as it went, as he would juxtapose nicely with Galfarm's strength and action. An element of courtly, unconsummated love could be bittersweet.

Shawn was so lost in his thoughts that he almost missed the path. However, as he passed the opening, a car slowed and stopped next to him. It was Linus's mother who called him to the window, thanked him for his kindness, and paid him back. Shawn insisted that she didn't have to give him the $1.50 right away, but she also insisted. She was going out of town for the day anyway, and she wouldn't be back until late. She didn't want him to go without the money. Shawn thanked her and waved goodbye, feeling a pit in his stomach for the woman to whom one and a half dollars was a matter of strict honor.

The path caught his eye as he dropped the six quarters into his pocket. And finally free to pursue his curiosity, he started down the dirt track.

The hill the old barn sat on was high and steep, and Shawn had worked up a good sweat winding his way up there. He had to stop and catch his breath five times. But by the time he crested the hill, he knew his story's plot. He wished he had his laptop with him, but the battery had given out six months earlier, and he had to keep it plugged in. He could picture himself, back against a tree, a thermos of soup, a thermos of coffee, and an entire afternoon open to him to write. Maybe, if he could sell just this story, he could get the battery replaced. Then what stories would roll into his mind in the presence of nature?

He'd never really put much stock into the inspiration of the forest, but as he came to the old stone wall, he realized that he had maybe missed something valuable. Weren't writers always talking about moments of inspiration? Weren't they always seeking this or that breakthrough? Maybe this was his. With that in mind, he eyed the old tumbledown barn, long ago burned by lightning, teenagers, or some firefighter. They were supposed to be the worst arsonists out there, Shawn mused. Still, if they stuck to big old remote buildings like this, more power to them. He couldn't imagine who would build a barn on a hill, nowhere near a farm or just about anything else. No road led up here, and, as far as Shawn knew, there had never been a farm on the hill.

Shawn appraised the old, burned wood and overgrown floor, peppered with young-growth pines, ash, and maple around a low mound of piled bricks in the center. Based on the age of the trees, he guessed that someone had cleared the thirty-by-fifty-foot space in the last fifteen years, though he couldn't imagine why. He wondered if this might not be a good place to set up a little camp—nothing too ostentatious; that would invite the local kids to demolish it or steal anything he accumulated. But maybe a board and a little stash of items he could squirrel away under some rocks: some Cokes, gum, toilet paper, and extra pens. Then he could throw a tarp up for the extra-sunny days and lean back against the stone and dream his dreams. He would never again have to wonder how to describe a castle wall, or a winding path, or a cluster of trees. He could just stand up, walk out, and look around. Of course, he could find most of those things in his backyard. Still, there was something about the place that called to him.

Disappointed that his vantage from the path offered him no new perspective on the ruin, he walked to the eastern edge of the hill to look out at the rolling valleys and hills that rumbled across the West Virginia landscape. He saw downtown, and then, beyond it, the wide, cleared area of the old Haver Family Farm. He remembered visiting the farm's open spaces and close, hot smithy in school. He hadn't been back there since and wondered why. Here, he thought, was an actual blacksmith near him, one that he could watch in action. He didn't have to watch YouTube videos or read books about it. He could stand right there and take notes.

He didn't understand himself. Here was a whole world of ripe fruit to be plucked, and he'd been letting himself starve. He wished he could bottle the feeling that flooded his chest and drink it down every morning. He would be the most prolific writer in the world. Of course, he knew he couldn't, and that he was subject to the whim of the muse, or his brain chemistry, or the electric company, or whether or not Vick needed a hand. So, deciding to make hay while the sun shone, he turned away from the vista to return down the new deer path.

However, before he could do that, he felt a strange tug to look out over the western valley. He didn't know why he would; there was nothing to see. Dense forest ran all the way to Flatwoods. Still, admitting that his little inclinations hadn't led him astray so far, he obeyed and stood. He peered down at a land that fell away in greens and browns until the little swath opened where Stone Run Road struck west to Flatwoods. It was just as he imagined it, and not particularly inspiring to a man who wanted to populate the world with brave heroes and fearsome beasts. Shrugging, Shawn turned to go home.

That was when the tower caught his eye.

He froze, thinking that it was a trick of the light, and turned slowly back to scan the treetops on the hilltop below him. At first, he was certain that he had mistaken a—well, he couldn't imagine what he might have mistaken for a tower. But then, as the wind blew and rustled the trees, he saw it again. Not exactly a castle tower, but certainly a bell tower. Cast among the tall pines and wide oaks, the stone top of a church poked its way out when the branches blew just right.

There was no church on Old Congregation Hill. Even as his mind formed the words, he wondered if he was right. Why was it called Congregation Hill if, in fact, there was no congregation there? He could think of half a dozen reasons, but none was a good reason why there wouldn't be a church there. He cursed under his breath. He had to go down to see. If he didn't, it would nag him all day and night. He wished he had brought a drink with him.

The walk down from the old barn hilltop to the Old Congregation Hill was, at first, steep and difficult. It wasn't until several minutes in that he found the remains of what looked like a dirt road, still wide and clear of trees, though overgrown with grass in some places. This switched back on itself a handful of times to keep a gradual and manageable incline.

Shawn was grateful, and with his extra time, he thought about the story that would follow Elgaria's heroic defeat of the evil knight. They would visit the wounded warrior, of course, to thank him for his aid. And then what? Perhaps Virikor had his own troubles. Perhaps he could enlist the couple, and they could form a little team. Of course, Galfarm would need to rest from his tribulations, so Elgaria could take the lead. Shawn didn't mind that idea at all. He liked writing about her, and not just when he got to wax poetic about her long legs and tight stomach. He liked it when other characters in the world underestimated her, and she showed herself to be not only beautiful, smart, tough, but also creative in ways that they didn't expect. He liked the idea of her crafting objects of power that boggled the minds of her doubters.

Of course, he had to restrain himself. She couldn't be good at absolutely everything; that would be boring. But he hadn't quite worked out what her weaknesses were yet. Perhaps this story would be a good time to showcase one or two. Maybe she was bad at languages. That would be good. She could get herself a translator, someone he could bring in to create a new relationship. He started to feel a little bad as the road finally leveled out. Galfarm, he thought, was getting the short end of the stick. Even in his mind, the warrior was a little dull. He needed something more. What made sense? He was far better traveled than Elgaria, so maybe that was it. Galfarm was fluent in a dozen languages. Where she was weak, he was strong. And where he was weak, she would be strong. *Except on the battlefield,* he thought. *There, they would both be strong.*

In the battlefield and the bedroom, of course.

As Shawn followed the path at the foot of the hill, his mind saw a great web of stories stretching out for his two heroes. And his new ideas of Galfarm began to work their way back into his battle with the dark warrior. Perhaps Galfarm understood the warrior better than Shawn thought. He could read the markings on the armor. He could feel pity for the man's plight.

Smiling to himself and humming "Twist and Shout," he plodded down the path and almost tripped over a low stone wall. Shawn's knee bashed into a rock, and he let out a sullen, "Oh, come on!" A leafy shrub he hadn't thought much of had hidden the stone. Rubbing his knee and scanning the ground around him, he saw the remains of what appeared to be a foundation. Confused and intrigued, Shawn winced, limping a little, as he stepped back to appraise the situation.

Trees grew in every direction, limiting his view, but as he traced the outline of what he was now sure was a large, rectangular foundation, he picked out other shapes in the forest that looked like the remains of crumbled buildings. He climbed over the low stone wall and found that the ground underfoot gave more than he liked. He tested it by bouncing a little and was suddenly sure he was standing on old, rotten boards. He hurried back over the wall and stared in disbelief. He was not the most adventurous young man and never had been, but he knew the hills around Oakdown. He knew all the stories about the barn and the hill on the other side of town where the people had been murdered back in the '90s. He knew about the old man in the cave and the spooky carnival that people said they still saw on summer nights in Moeller's Clearing. But he had never heard of abandoned buildings on Old Congregation Hill.

Superstitious dread rose within him, and Shawn took two steps back. He was somewhere he didn't belong. He felt a strong pull to circle the hill and return home, skipping the climb back to the old barn. But he felt an even stronger pull to explore. Here was something he'd never had access to before—a real ruin, perhaps entirely untouched for decades. Here was something he could use in his writing.

He remembered his curled-up notebook and decided this could be the most consequential day in his writing career. He could picture sitting in an interview, telling the reporter or TV host about the ruins outside of town that became the lost temple of K'shyrak. He could see himself, older, gray in his beard, glasses perched on his nose, describing how he had examined the old buildings like a painter doing a study for their masterwork. The allure of the future stories, both fact and fiction, was too great for him to turn back.

Shawn circled the perimeter of the ruin with the squishy floor and came to the other side. Here, far more clearly than before, he saw what he took to be a wide street, overgrown with low shrubs, but uncrowded by trees. On either side of the open space, he could clearly see the ruined shapes of buildings marching away toward a low mount that crossed the street at the far end. He walked the length of what seemed to him to be an old main street, passed the remains of the stone church, heavily overgrown with moss and vines and peppered with bushes that bloomed out from nooks and crags. He saw wooden buildings that reached up, mostly intact and almost entirely covered with leaves. He saw piles of rubble, burned wood, and several mounds that likely hid the remains of houses or other businesses.

Shawn couldn't guess how old any of it was. But when he came to the end and found what appeared to be the moldering remains of a stockade and gate, he guessed it must date back to the Civil War at least. He couldn't imagine a reason to have a wall around the town any time after that. Beyond the wall, another road arced down the hill, but trees quickly engulfed it. Shawn was less interested in seeing where it went, sure that he would soon just find himself on the road into Flatwoods. He turned and worked his way back up, stopping where he found something interesting, and taking out his notebook to try his hand at describing what he saw.

After an hour of writing about how stones joined together, how moss humped over rotting boards, and how shadows and light mingled through moldering slats, his hand ached, and he was dubious about the quality of his work. He wasn't used to trying to describe the world in front of him so much as the world that was in his head. He began to wonder if the analogy of the artist's sketch would be useful to him. Maybe, he thought, the value was seeing it all firsthand and then letting it simmer in his imagination. Perhaps tomorrow or the next day, he would find an ancient ruin worthy of Elgaria's exploration unfolding before his mind's eye from the comfort of his little bedroom.

Tired, hungry, thirsty, and ready for a shower, Shawn decided to pack it in. If he were lucky, he could still get another good 1,500 words in when he got home before the fatigue of the day's events pulled him into an afternoon nap that his creative mind wouldn't recover from until tomorrow.

So, curling up his notebook, he started back the way he had come. He reached the end of what he was now officially calling 'Main Street' and circled the rotten-floored building. Then, with one more appraising glance over the whole town, he turned to leave.

That was when the paper caught his eye.

It fluttered from under what looked like a fallen bookcase. The object was so overgrown that, earlier, it had just looked like one tree trunk leaning against another. But, from this angle, he could see the old shelves facing down, their empty spaces open toward the ground.

And, pinned between one of the shelves and a branch, an old piece of paper wavered in the breeze.

"Impossible."

The word escaped Shawn's lips reflexively, like a hand swiping at a buzzing fly. No paper could have survived here, at least not exposed. Perhaps in some waterproof cache below the rubble, something was preserved. But dangling from an old bookshelf? Whatever it was must be new, something carried by the wind and caught at the right moment. It was probably someone's shopping list or an old love note.

Still, though sated and exhausted, his curiosity nudged him forward. Shawn picked a spot in the crumbling wall where it was the lowest and climbed over onto the springy floor. Anxiety shot through him like electricity as he pictured the floor giving out from under him and dropping him twenty feet into a dark, lonely cave where he would probably break his leg and die of thirst. He took a careful step along the wall, keeping his hand on the piled stone, and he suddenly wished he had just climbed over the rock as close to the bookcase and flapping paper as possible. He was going to die here for some asshole's notebook sketch of Rachel Haver's knockers around his math homework from the '70s, all because he had to find a nice place to climb over.

The floor sank and rose as he took each step, and Shawn cast about for something to grab on to if the worst should happen. The wall was a useless pile of stone, and nothing grew close enough for him to grab. He thought of his phone but knew what he'd see if he looked at it. There was a signal in the center of Oakdown, but even by the time he got to his house, that signal had dropped to two bars. Out on the old barn hill, there was nothing. And out here? He was sure it would be nothing. Still, the prospect of falling into a pit only to perish because no one knew where he was prompted him to give the little flip-phone a look.

It was just as he thought, no signal. This was incredibly stupid. The damned page was probably blank. As he took another unsteady step, it crossed his mind that of all the things he had done today, this was the most like Galfarm and Elgaria. The anxiety he felt in his stomach, the uncertainty of each footfall, the foresight of disaster and premature self-condemnation, all felt like things he could genuinely use in his writing.

A foot from the old bookcase, Shawn spied another mossy, grassy mound on the other side of the lean-to that pinned the fluttering page. And beside it, another rose from the earth. Each was about five or six feet long and perhaps three or four feet wide. As he finally reached his destination, he studied the ground between the trees that grew up from the old sagging floor and saw mound after mound rising a foot or maybe two.

Bookshelves.

A vast field of bookshelves rolled along within the wrecked walls of what Shawn saw must have been an old library. What had a library been doing out here? A church he understood. That belonged in what had probably been a little camp for miners or loggers. But a library? Maybe he was wrong. But the more he surveyed the tree-crowded space within the ancient wall, the more he saw them. Most were facedown, but a few tilted on their sides, and here or there, as if they had fallen, or more likely been pushed up by growing trees, some leaned like the one he now stood next to, on its proper end, almost upright. And in those, he could see the remains of shelves.

Holding wonder and fear together in his chest, Shawn crouched and looked up into the four cavities of the old bookcase. To his further surprise, he saw that the ends of the shelves were capped by metal, perhaps tin or even silver. He tugged at one of the U-shaped sleeves that bent up at its end, and it shook. But something, an old nail perhaps, still held it in place. He patted his pockets for his multitool, found it, and flipped out one of the knives. He ran the blade under the metal and found where it hitched. Dreams of selling what looked like it might be quite a bit of silver suddenly overtook his curiosity over the paper. He worked the blade up and down as the floor beneath him drooped an inch.

He froze. Had he heard what he thought he did? His stomach tightened, and his anus puckered.

Crack.

Distinct, sharp, and mortal, the sound poked up at him from under his feet. Terror seized him, and he snatched the paper before turning on his heel and taking three leaping steps across the spongy ground to the wall. He threw himself over the stone as another crack echoed behind him. Then a crash and the sound of splintered wood. He lay on the earth, bruised, sore, panting, and terrified that he had not gone far enough. He scrambled to his feet and cast a glance back at the place where he had just been. The bookshelf was gone. Where it had stood, a hole now gaped, black and oblong. Shawn stuffed the paper in his pocket, turned from the library's wreckage, and promptly threw up into the grass.

The nearness of his death, and the fact that he had known it had been close, scared him in a way he had no words for. His body shook with untamable tremors for five minutes as he thought about where he might have ended up. He didn't know how deep the hole went, perhaps only a few feet, but it was far enough to swallow the old bookshelf, and that would have been enough to gulp him down. He pictured a crocodile biting its prey and then tossing it up to let it slide further down its gullet. That, he thought, was what the earth had almost done to him.

For some reason, the fear was worse because he had known the danger was there. Perhaps he hadn't really believed it, but he could picture himself, leg-shattered, doomed in a dark place. He could see himself tormented by the knowledge that he could have simply not put himself in that situation. It was all too much. He threw up again and then dry heaved for twenty seconds before his body relented and let him regain himself a little.

Finally, leaning against a tree, his heart merely pounding in his chest instead of thundering, he pulled the paper from his pocket. He was shocked to see that it was a page from a printed book, not a blank page or someone's handwritten note. The words were mostly faded, and Shawn had to admit that the impossible seemed to have happened. Here was a genuinely old piece of paper, preserved by some kind of strange providence so that Shawn could rescue it just before escaping with his life.

He tried to read the faded ink and found only snippets legible. Here was the word 'unconscious,' there 'allegory,' and there a little cluster of 'with eyes of faith.' He turned the page over, suddenly feeling like a rube. Had he almost died for something so far gone that he wouldn't even be able to identify it with Google?

His fear was calmed, however, when he saw a small block of text still standing out boldly against the yellowed paper. Sniffing and spitting the taste of vomit from his mouth, he scanned the lines and frowned. They made no sense. He read them a second time, but he still could not understand. Then, realizing that the first part was the continuation of a longer sentence, he started to piece some of it together.

> *...which cannot be seen with the naked eye, but only perceived through the communion of the spirits with the world through the proper forms. Like a pit, like a mountain, it stands. Deep and hollow, high and mighty, throne, seat, waiting theater, city of the desert place, in all lands and none, great Harhain waits. There, the far-seeing one sits to gather his scattered brethren and make final cause against the foundations of the world.*

Shawn shook his head and blinked. He read over the page a half-dozen times, each time fitting the pieces of the writing together a little more. This, he thought, was either the writing of some crazy religious nut or the weird fiction of someone like H.P. Lovecraft. He had never been one for horror—he didn't enjoy being scared. But there was something in the passage that sparked images in his mind. He saw Galfarm, a torch in one hand, Hraftring in the other, taking studied, cautious steps across the mossy floor of some ancient, god-haunted temple. He pictured Elgaria prostrate before a many-eyed figure enthroned on dark stone, looming and brooding over her with ancient and terrible fury.

He shut his eyes tight against the afternoon sun and tried to push the images out. That was not what he wanted for Elgaria and Galfarm. Their foes, though dark, should only scare people insofar as they were allegories for the evils of the real world. He didn't want to give people nightmares.

He read the passage over again and then stood. He took his notebook from his pocket, carefully put the damaged paper between its stark white, lined pages, and curled the book up again. The overwhelming terror of his brush with death slunk back, brooding in the mouth of a dark cave in his mind. He hadn't known that cave was there. Perhaps he had dug it with his foolishness. He didn't like the idea that it would remain with him.

Use it, he thought. *Use it in a way that other writers can't.*

Shawn pushed the notebook back into his cargo shorts pocket and started for the road that zig-zagged up the hill. He debated trying to cut around through the forest, but he opted instead for the safer—if longer—journey up the old, wide road. As he trudged, limping only a little, he tried to review what he imagined for his characters after being ambushed. Galfarm was wounded; he would have to rest. Elgaria would go on a quest for their new friend, the wounded soldier whose precise name was escaping Shawn. He knew it was some variation based on his cousin Vick, but the exact spelling had slipped away. That was alright, that's why he wrote things down.

Elgaria would go to the temple of Harhain.

No, that was not it. She would go to the temple of the Goddess Hesta and acquire some item for … Vick's analog, a warrior used up by his nation. What was she seeking? Healing? No, he didn't want to make it that easy. He also didn't want Vick's character to overcome his wounds with some magic potion. He wanted readers to confront what had happened to his cousin in Afghanistan through his fantasy.

To do that, he'd have to tear Elgaria to bits and rebuild her in the watery dream pools of Mamu.

No, what was that? That was definitely not Elgaria's fate. Perhaps she would have to go through trials—no, yes, she certainly would. Trials sounded like a great series of stories for her, maybe even a short story collection, like Sapkowski's first *Witcher* book. But torn to pieces and put back together? That was too dark.

His pulse jumping in his wrists and the back of his thighs, Shawn reached the top of the hill and looked at the old barn's ruins. For the first time, he suspected that perhaps the old barn was not, in fact, an old barn. He wondered whether it had something to do with the ruined town below. Maybe it had been a storehouse set up high to keep it from flooding. Did that make sense? The town itself was on a hill and didn't exactly look like it was prone to rising waters, so maybe not. The whole thing was a puzzle that he would try to figure out.

Shawn circled the old structure and found the mouth of the little path that had led him there in the first place. Down he went, his imagination turning the descent through the wooded landscape into an ancient, narrow staircase. The trees faded, and in their place, close stone walls, poorly lit by guttering torches, hemmed him in as he turned and turned down into a brooding darkness far below the desert city that lay above in the mouth of some ancient volcano.

He reached out on both sides and felt the walls slip under his fingers, dust flecking out and scattering on the ageless steps carved from the living rock. He could hear a dull, thrumming rumble, like distant thunder below him. He knew that many voices were raised in desperate plaint to the one who sat in the midst of Harhain.

Shawn shook his head and stopped himself, catching his arm around a tree branch on the steep hill. Dizzy and disoriented, Shawn tried to assess his condition. He had had an extremely close brush with death, or, at the very least, bad injury, and his mind and body were probably in shock. The page had put some strange ideas into his head right as he was in the middle of suffering that shock. Now his brain was trying to process it all together. He needed to get home, get a little caffeine into him, or maybe close his eyes and sleep. He'd tell his mother about it. She'd understand. Then, maybe after a couple of hours of sleep, they could go to the *Dog-Shed* in town and get their standard Saturday night chili dog dinner together. The thought of sitting across from her while he regaled her with his adventure revitalized him.

He released his hold on the tree branch, and down he went. The forest remained the forest, the deer path remained a deer path, and the road back to his mother's little ranch-style house with the garden gnome and crystal ball flanking the old bench out front remained just as they always had been. A note waited for him on the kitchen counter to tell him that his mother had gone over to Nancy Chen's house for a few hours. Grateful for the chance to sleep without first explaining himself, Shawn went to his room, kicked off his flip-flops, and fell onto his bed.

The world faded immediately.

The desert winds of the bowl city cut across the streets under a dim, red sky. He pulled the tattered rag across his face and trundled down the alleyway, sand stinging his cheeks and eyes. A low, keening howl went up as the air passed over the great pit that fell away in the city's center. Searching the low, colorless, wooden doorways, he came to one with a twisted symbol that hurt his mind when he looked at it. He pushed through the door and into a low, dark room where a man sat cross-legged on a brittle straw mat.

"Do you wish to descend?" the man asked in a foreign tongue that Shawn somehow understood.

"Yes," Shawn said.

"Then make your offering at the statue of Belet-Seri, and go to the stair of Ereshkigal, and there you will find your way down. But know that though you may rise again, you shall not return."

The dream faded as Shawn heard the front door open. He rubbed his eyes and sat up, his mind soft and fuzzy. The images from his dream lingered as he looked around his room. His vision finally came into focus as he looked at the calendar picture of the lovely Samantha Lipman. He blinked, rubbed his eyes, and then shook his head. He could have sworn that the calendar showed him a different image, one of the woman wearing something over her face. But as his eyes adjusted, he saw nothing amiss.

He rose, hurried to the bathroom, and then out into the kitchen.

"Look who's awake! You ready to go grab some dogs?" his mother asked as she poured herself a glass of orange juice.

"Um, I need a few minutes … maybe a half hour? I had a long day and I haven't really been able to write," Shawn said.

"Of course, I'm not super hungry just yet anyway. You want some of this?" She held up the carton of OJ.

"No, are there any Cokes in there?"

She nodded, trading the carton for a can, which she handed him. Shawn thanked her, returned to his room, and downed half the can in one long, freezing gulp. He knew it was too soon for the caffeine to have kicked in, but he felt more awake almost immediately due to some Pavlovian response to the sugar, flavorings, and cold carbonation. He sat down at his laptop and stared at the blank screen. Elgaria.

Elgaria stood upon the mossy ground, her silver-booted feet sunk deep in the loamy earth. Her spear, Thisthring, held high before her, she challenged the knight.

"No more will you overcome the dread Galfarm, son of night and doom, child of the creeping vengeance long chained beneath the earth. Woe and wail and torment and ire well up from this place and consume thee, knight of the dark city. Here now Harhain comes, and you, rebellious pupil, shall rue the spilling splatter of your birth upon the face of creation."

Shawn stared at the words on the page and frowned. That was not what he had intended her to say. He ran the mouse over the words, highlighting them, and deleted her strange speech. He tried again.

"Come now, fell warrior, and deal with the daughter of Yrdana, Lady of the Evening Forge. I shall cleave your enchanted armor so that we shall stand on equal ground, and you shall meet your doom at the tip of my spear, Thisthring!"

That was better. It didn't quite have the punch that Shawn wanted, but that could be punched up during edits. He sipped his Coke and stared out the window, letting the scene form in his head. He could see her, blood dripping from her shoulder, down her cheek, and from her knee, battered and weary, but still mighty. He could feel the rage radiating from her against the figure who would steal the life of her beloved. She should say something of great note, something that people would quote, something that could go on a T-shirt or a mug. He imagined her painted by Boris Vallejo, light glancing from her silver breastplate, cleavage heaving, eyes smoldering, knuckles white around Thisthring's ash staff. He could see the scene with Galfarm on the ground, his arm draped over his bruised and bloodied abdomen, his eyes closed, his loincloth barely hiding his generous manhood. He imagined himself at a Spencer's Gifts, or maybe on a website, flipping through posters and seeing the image of Elgaria, the Knight, and Galfarm. It filled him with a feeling of hope and possibility.

He turned to his page and found that what he had written was gone. In its place, a single sentence remained.

"Long did I wander those benighted halls, seeking downward for the pit of the ancient star where, enthroned, he sits far-seeing and lording over the mountain of eyes."

Shawn watched in befuddled fear as his fingers typed seven more letters.

Harhain.

He pushed himself back from the desk and stared. He squeezed his eyes shut and opened them again. The word remained.

Harhain.

"What the fuck?" he breathed. He leaned back so far from the desk that he almost fell over. Then he did fall over when a knock at the door startled him.

"Shawn? Are you okay?"

He scrambled to his feet from the overturned chair and bounded to the door. His mother stood on the other side, looking concerned.

"I'm fine," he said, forcing a smile. "I just took a long hike earlier, and I'm not steady on my feet yet."

"Oh, well, maybe this can wait then," she said. "Until you're more steady."

"No, it's fine, what is it?"

"Well, I forgot to mention it before when you were so eager to get writing, but Nancy had something that I thought you might want. She was going to sell it at the next yard sale day, but I got it for you."

"What is it?"

"Well, come see, it's a little heavy. I lugged it from her place, but that's as far as I can bring it."

She led him out into the living room, where she did a little Vanna White presentation of what looked like a small, gray suitcase sitting on the couch. Shawn frowned. Then, as if someone put a sign next to it to tell him what it was, his eyes went wide. He knelt in front of the case and opened it, revealing an old blue-gray Remington electric typewriter.

"Wow, how much did you pay for this?" He looked up at her. "Wait, this is expensive, how did you—"

"I owe her four dye jobs, that's all."

"Mom, you didn't have to—"

"Joke's on her, honey, I would have gone over and done those for her for free. I miss doing them; it gives us time to gossip. Besides, I don't get a chance to be creative at the warehouse, so it's a gift for me too."

"Wow," he said, running his hands over the keys and wondering what strange things had been written on them. He thought it looked at least thirty years old, and he loved it.

"Of course, she's probably sitting over there laughing with her son, telling him she would have given it to me for free, and she's getting one over on me. Oh well," she said, plopping down on the couch. "Such is the world! Now, I've changed my mind, I am hungry. Can we get some chili dogs, please?"

"Yeah, absolutely," Shawn said, wondering what the typewriter sounded like when it was powered up. He closed the lid and shook his head. "This has been the strangest day ever," he said.

"Well, that sounds interesting. Tell me all about it on our way to the

Shed," she said.

And he did, all but the parts where he seemed to be writing things he didn't want to. Shawn figured that maybe by talking it all through, he could steady his mind a bit. His mother listened, gasped at the right moments, and grasped his hand when he told her about the hole. She had never heard of a ruin on Old Congregation Hill, but agreed that if there was a ruin there, it made sense that there was a church, given the hill's name. They ate pleasantly, enjoying $1 hot dogs and $.50 chili. They shared a basket of fries, and Shawn dutifully flirted with Dorothy, their sixty-year-old waitress who had teased him good-naturedly since he was a boy.

When they walked home, his mother hugged his arm and told him she was proud of him.

"For what?" he said, suddenly and inexplicably upset. "I haven't done anything. All I've done is imagine things and get rejected. I ruined my job at the warehouse, I dropped out of school, and I—"

"I'm proud of you because you haven't quit," she said. "I'm proud of you because you're brave enough to pursue the thing you love. I'm proud of you because you have talent and you're not wasting it. And because you're a good person, no matter what you think of yourself."

He didn't know if that last part was true. He wanted it to be true. All he wanted, he realized in that moment, was to be allowed to use his talents to help her and, if possible, the people of Oakdown and places like it. He could never be Galfarm. No woman like Elgaria would ever love him. But maybe, if the world would let him, he could make his own little stand against the evils that crushed people like Linus, his cousin Vick, and his mom. Until then, he knew he was a failure.

He wondered if Galfarm and Elgaria would be ashamed to be created by someone like him.

They walked in silence the rest of the way home as Shawn felt his old shame rearing its head anew. When they reached their house, she invited him to sit with her on the bench. But he declined, saying he had work to do. She said she understood. Into his bedroom he went, almost forgetting the typewriter on the couch. She patted it, her wedding ring clacking on the plastic, and he hurried back. She proffered her cheek and he kissed her before returning up the hallway to his room.

He set the typewriter on the desk next to his laptop, plugged it in, and switched it on. Its hum was beautiful. Shawn thought it was fitting for him to write something on it immediately, so he took a piece of paper and ran it through the roller. He pressed a key and watched an arm jump up and smack the paper. Nothing appeared. Of course, the ribbon would be dried out. He switched it off, looked around the case, and found a relatively new-looking cardboard box with a new spool of ribbon. After a little tinkering, he figured out how to remove one of the plates and replace the spool. Then, once more, he tried a letter.

I

A perhaps somewhat egotistical start, he thought.

n

He followed it with a space. Then, pressing the next key, the typewriter clacked again.

the hall of dark Harhain

What was this? He didn't want to write this. He wanted to write about Galfarm and about Elgaria.

I saw her dancing. An amber mask upon her face. Puppetlike, she moved before the far-seeing one, he enthroned and drawing to himself those many crowned brothers long imprisoned.

He stared, his eyes stinging as, in his mind, he could see the flickering flames of that dark court set beneath the mountain. Galfarm's mighty figure faded, replaced by a crowd of shadowed faces looking down at him.

She who would be a queen, she who would be a mother, she who would mend the will of the great Queen, she dances before the throne in ancient Harhain. And lo, I wept for her in the pit of fallen fire.

Elgaria moved in strange, halting motions. No, not Elgaria. Not even a woman. A girl. A girl. A girl in dark Harhain.
The typewriter clacked under Shawn Nozick's fingers.

Come On

1

THE COOKFIRE DANCED IN large, oval eyes placed perfectly above a too-wide smile set in a round, white face. The spit creaked as he turned it. He poked the meat and then put his long, white, pointed finger into his mouth. It needed more salt. Standing, stretching, and yawning, he looked up at the full, round moon. Its detail impressed him. He remembered when it had been nothing more than an idea, a word that floated in a world of words.

That had been the most surreal kind of existence in a long parade of strange existences. That or the model. The model had been particularly strange. But the world of words had been entirely different. He had been endlessly grateful when the word-world had been replaced by a cosmos of tiny colored blocks. That had been incredibly strange as well, but at least there had been a blocky moon he could experience with something analogous to sight. That moon had only nine little squares packed together that could blink on or off depending on the phase. Times had changed. The moon he stood under next to the cookfire looked like the real moon. It wasn't a perfect replica, of course. This was not the real world; it had its own rules, its own ocean, its own people, its own trees, and its own moon.

He shook his head at the moon, waggled his finger at it, and then turned on his heel. He felt good, so he began to whistle a tune, and stopped after the first high-pitched note sent a bright thrill of pain through his head. When would he learn not to do that? He figured that if he hadn't by now, maybe he never would. Shrugging and chuckling at himself, he crunched through the old leaves to where the rusted train tracks cut east. Jauntily, he poked out elbows and bent his knees, ducking and plucking his way among the branches and brambles to find his sack of salt. He might not be able to whistle, but he could sing and dance.

Come on, come on, he crooned.

Like nothing so much as a train, she sat upon the tracks. Her lights were off, her engine was cool. His fingers slithered over her steel boiler, dry and rusted. Only the most minute of vibrations told him that she had not yet shuffled off her metal coil. Her spirit remained within, and that delighted him. If she were to go, he would miss her most of all. Of course, he thought to himself, he missed her already. She hadn't spoken in years, and he wasn't sure how to fix her. He wasn't even sure she could be fixed. Still, when he needed her to, she would open her eyes and take him here and there, though not as swiftly as she used to.

Her handrails were cool as he pulled himself up into her cab. Hanging about him were old pictures and pages from magazines showing pin-ups, centerfolds, sportsmen, and movie stars. There were photos of actors and producers cluttering every open space. He remembered some of them; others might have been total strangers.

Time. Time was wrong. He lifted one of a good-looking couple and stared into the man's eyes. He felt himself pulled back, back, into the man's mind, into his body, and into the woman's arms.

For a long moment, Conroy stood frozen, staring, until his mind returned. He shook his head, laughed, and returned the picture. He snatched up his old leather satchel and rummaged until he produced another, smaller, draw-string bag. He bounced it in his palm. It was too light. He'd have to go into town and buy some more salt. He wondered if they were angry at him in town. They were angry at him everywhere else, he thought. Well, maybe not everywhere else, but there were plenty of people upset with old Conroy these days, and he wondered if he should risk heading into town.

He decided that that was a question for later, as there was enough salt for this evening's meal. Lightly, he stepped out of the cab, across the leafy ground, and back to his campfire. He salted his meat as he turned it on the spit. He wondered what he'd have to do to get back in everyone's good graces.

As the handle turned, so did the world, and he felt himself falling back, back, back.

Time was wrong.

2

HIS BREATHING IS WRONG. No, he's not breathing at all. There's water in his lungs. The river and terror press out from within him. Terror of dying, yes, but also the monstrous terror of being rude. He must never be rude, so his mother had said. He needs to speak, to thank the people, to comfort them in their doubt.

She had been delicious. They should know that.

He manages, struggling, to fight to the surface and choke the words out. Yes, at least he would not die with no manners. The water splashes and fades, and the world twists in its wrongness. Darkness blinks him out of existence.

No. No, he's still here.

He blinks. No. He can't blink. He floats. His thoughts are a twisting jumble. He can barely feel. He still exists, but only barely. There is something left of him, though, even if he can't understand what it is. He wonders if this is Heaven or Hell, but he feels too little for it to be either. He tries to move, but there is no movement. He tries to listen, but there is no noise.

He drifts, only a fleeting reverberation across the air. He makes no sound, but he has the strange impression that, nonetheless, someone is listening. Soon—or is it a million years later?—someone is speaking. Their words are muffled and gone, half-sounds before silence. Yet they come again and again, before him and behind. To his left and his right, they buffet him like little puffs of air that could do nothing to someone real. But he's not real, not anymore. They brush him back from one side, and then the other, from above and below as they get louder and more distinct. He is like a firefly, caught in a jar, bumping against glass he can't see. Someone's there on the other side of his invisible world.

"Hello?" a voice says, tinny and distant. "Roy, is that you?"

He doesn't know how to respond yet, but he learns. He doesn't know how, but he learns to make the air move in a wave. One wave at first, then more.

3

WHEN HIS MIND RETURNED, his meal came into focus over a dwindling fire. He banked it up and put another pair of logs on. When the flames caught, a drip sizzled on the logs, and he realized he had made a mistake. The drippings were being wasted! Laughing at his foolishness, he stood, straightened his cap, and started for the house. He had come here because the house's owner let him camp on her land and because he owed her protection. People were furious at him; he expected they'd be furious at her for helping him. And, thankfully, he could give protection, because as much as everyone was angry at him, they also feared him.

Through the trees he went, wending and weaving until the two-story house appeared with its brightly lit windows and ramshackle front porch. The owner was a nice woman, but she was too preoccupied with her work to do maintenance. He'd have to arrange some help for her. He wasn't a handyman, but he knew people who owed him favors. Getting them to help would be easy; remembering would be tricky. His mind had improved over the last few years, but it still was not what it once had been. One day, he hoped, they'd make their upgrades and give them all a little more memory, and then, boy-oh-boy, old Conroy would get some things done. What exactly he would get done … that he couldn't remember.

The woman in the house had more memory than almost anyone Conroy knew. Even so, during the really difficult parts of the maze, he had to lend her some of his. Those had been strange times when he had collapsed back into a world of pure words, bereft of his body and sight. He had not liked that one bit, but it had been worth it. The meal on the fire proved that.

He knocked on the faded front door and waited. He counted to a hundred before the door opened to reveal what had once been a human. She still looked the part with all the right features, wearing a white fuzzy bathrobe and matching slippers. She was bald and pale, like Conroy, but her face was a normal face, her eyes were human eyes, or at least good approximations. But, he reminded himself, she wasn't really a woman, of course. No one here was really what they once had been.

"Pardon me," he began, but the unfocused look in her eyes told him she wasn't there. She was masticating, and that relieved him. He hadn't fed her anything new for a week, which meant someone else was utilizing her. And if they were using her talents, they probably weren't going to hurt her for helping him. He studied her blank gaze and wondered what sorts of files they were giving her. What kinds of numbers was she chewing? What sort of cryptography was she digesting? He hoped they tasted good.

He grinned his friendliest Conroy grin and said, "Don't mind me, I'm just going to borrow a cooking pan. No need to spend any more of your *cycles* on me." He exaggerated the word 'cycles' because he didn't understand it. It was something she had said to him once, and for some reason, it had stuck, and he found it endlessly amusing.

She stepped back and gestured weakly toward the kitchen. Elbows out and knees up, he galumphed down the hall to the pale-yellow room and almost whistled his appreciation at the changes she had made since the last time he had visited. The floor was no longer a solid block of bright white. Instead, baby-blue and pale-yellow linoleum squares marched from wall to wall. He sighed wistfully. With every extra bit of processing power and memory, more beauty came into the world. He skipped over the clean floor and tried one of the cabinets. It swung open on its hinges. He was delighted. He took hold of a pan, and it rose from a stack of pans very much like things did in the real world. Before, he would hold out his hand, and the pan would simply appear there. Now, though it wasn't precisely the same as picking up a pan, it reminded him of it pleasantly.

"They sure are getting good at this," he said and turned to see that his host was staring at the refrigerator. On it hung a picture of the woman she had been. He thought that the picture was more than just a picture. She had told him once that she didn't keep any of her own memories in her house, since they took up too much space. They were on tape, she had said. He wasn't sure what that meant, but he dreamed of a day when she could eat her files, mash them up, and spit them back out whole and complete, all while she enjoyed her memories of who she had been out there. He wanted that for her because he liked her. They shared a common interest, even if they approached puzzles differently. He crossed to the refrigerator and opened it for her. She reached in and took an apple and held it in front of her face.

"I'm sorry that I can't chew it up for you," he said, closing the appliance that he still thought of as an icebox. He wanted to do something for her beyond just taking an apple out. He thought of all he owed her, including the meal outside. An idea sprang to mind.

"Should I bring you something more to eat?" he said. "Part of it is rightfully yours, anyway. That's what I'll do. I'll bring you a plate of happy, delicious meat!"

He took two plates, a knife, and a fork, and hurried out, down the leaf-blown path, and back to his fire. He couldn't feel the wind, but he could watch it tumble leaves about the roots of the trees, and they pulled him back to when he drifted upon the air…

With a gut-wrenching will, he pulled himself back to the present. If he didn't, the meat would burn. He could not let the meat burn. This meal, more than most, could not be ruined. He did a little skip and tried not to think about his time as nothing more than a whisper on the air, or when he found that he was able to slip into the minds of people in the real world. If he thought about those things too much, he'd go back. He always went back. He had gone back to that first time he had new arms and legs again and again. The feel of those legs, the sensation of air in his nostrils …

No, no, he couldn't think about it. The meat would burn.

Conroy saw that the bottom of the roast was a little darker than he liked it. He hustled to his rock, plunked himself and the pan down, and turned the spit.

"I'm sorry," he said. "That was rude of me."

He thought about how tragic it would be to ruin this meal and to have to go back to the cave where the rest of the meat was kept. He had no house to keep an icebox in, but even if he did, Conroy preferred his secret cave in the mountains where the ice never melted. The tracks there were strange and black, and they made Elaine tremble as she slipped along them, her wheels rarely finding enough grip to turn on that long downward slide. The track was treacherous, but it was more secure than any icebox. There his prize would keep; there she wouldn't be able to escape. He wondered if she was lonely in the cave. He wondered if he should visit her for more than just another meal. He wondered if—

The plates slipped from his fingers, thudding dully on the dirt. Conroy's eyes grew two sizes larger. An idea, a real idea, came to him. He didn't get many new ideas these days, and his last big one hadn't even really been his. His pal Daniel had given it to him, and that had led him here, to this fire, with this food. He sometimes wondered if Daniel had manipulated him into following the maze. He had left too many clues, opened too many doors for old Conroy to ignore. Why had Daniel done it? Why had he manipulated his pal—that's how Conroy thought of Daniel, as a real pal— and Daniel's own daughter?

But then, why did anyone lay out a mystery? Because they wanted it solved—solved by someone who could do something about it. Well, Daniel had succeeded. And Conroy had been richly rewarded. For that, he would always be grateful to Daniel. But now, if his idea was a good one, he thought Daniel might end up being one of his favorite people in the whole wide world. Daniel had been the founder of his feast, and now the inspiration for a new plan.

It was a shame that he was dead. Conroy thought about his friend's loss, about visiting Daniel's office, looking for him. He thought about …

His idea … His plan …

Conroy shook his head violently. His plan had almost faded away as he remembered Alex's searching, confused face. But he pushed the memory aside and snagged his idea, just before it evaporated. He examined it, like a prospector rinsing gold in a stream. Oh, it was a good idea. No, it was a great idea. An idea that would change everything for him and for everyone he cared about, the living ones at least. But to make his idea a reality, he'd have to visit someone who was angry with him. That didn't worry him too much. Almost no one could stay mad at him when he was in front of them, turning on that old charm.

But visiting the Scribe meant traveling south, and that would be disorienting. No, more than disorienting, it would unmake him, at least for a little while. He'd have to be ready, have to fill his tanks. He plucked the fallen plates and knelt by the fire. He began to cut and sang softly to himself, *Come on, come on, Old Conroy is coming …*

4

A PAINED SCREECH PIERCED the forest under a slowly rising sun as

Elaine pulled away from the campsite. Her cabin smelled of oil and soot—happy smells for Conroy. He had hoped to permeate the cab with the smell of his meal, but there was none left. He had brought a generous helping to his friend and watched her eat. It had been a joy to see a little life return to her eyes for the first time in … Well, he didn't know how long. As much as the Port had improved over the years, there was no replacement for things from the real world. Her enjoyment had stoked his hunger, and when he returned to pack up, he hadn't been able to stop himself. He consumed the rest in great, munching, salivating chomps. All he had left was a thermos of broth he had made from the drippings.

He would enjoy that later.

Conroy opened the grate and grabbed his shovel. Elaine was running sluggishly, so he scooped coal from the tender and fed her fire. Once, twice, five times he shoveled. The flames rose a little, but he mused sadly that her days of blistering heat were behind her. But maybe that was okay. If everything went to plan, she could let someone else do the hard work. Maybe, if she got to rest, she'd recover. There was nothing like a little vacation to put the pep back in someone's step.

He thought he remembered teaching someone that, back when he was just a wave on the air. He pushed that thought away, too. Things were about to get strange, and he didn't want to take a jaunt back to his Marconi days right before surreality kicked into high gear.

She took him south, along the coastline, into the deep forest. The change didn't start until an hour had passed. Conroy was sighing wistfully over a pinup of a woman in a corset with chin-length, black hair when he noticed the trees getting fuzzy. He sniffed and looked out over the edge of the old, creased fold-out and felt his stomach flutter as the once realistic-looking trees wore muddy, blurry colors. The leaves looked less distinct, and as he watched, they seemed to clump together until they were solid green masses stuck to the tops of angular, jagged trunks. Round branches became triangular tubes. He glanced at himself. His conductor's uniform was flat, all its wrinkles gone. His arms were thin rectangles joined at his elbows, and his fingers were elongated pyramids that jutted from his blocky hands.

Elaine had also lost much of her detail, her rivets reverting to hexagonal smudges that marched in lines along her polygonal boiler. At least the pinup still looked like herself, though she had also lost those little details that reminded him of the world where he had been born. With disconcert, he stared as the corseted woman morphed and blurred until she was only a smattering of squares that only hinted at the most beautiful thing in the world.

When he looked out to the passing world again, the trees were no longer tubes, but instead showed as blocky images on a flat background that rolled past him like a backdrop on wheels. He didn't dare look at himself, for that would be too disorienting. In a world with no depth, perceiving one's place was a sure ticket to the loony bin.

He leaned out into the windless air and saw the darkness rising before him. On the ground, the tracks faded and were replaced by words. The forest dissolved into a short paragraph, and the sky into a phrase.

They entered the darkness, and his sight blinked off. Instead, he felt words in his mind.

TRAIN CAB

YOU ARE IN THE CABIN OF ELAINE THE TRAIN. PICTURES HANG AROUND YOU OF LOST FRIENDS AND YOUR IDOLS. BEHIND YOU IS THE COAL TENDER. THE FURNACE GRATE IS OPEN. OUTSIDE, A FOREST ZIPS BY AS YOU HEAD SOUTH.

>INVENTORY

YOU ARE HOLDING A PINUP CENTERFOLD OF GLORIA LUDOVIK

Conroy tried to move but felt his options suddenly limited. His arms would not obey, and he could feel only a strange collection of options.

>LOOK AT THE PICTURES.

AN ASSORTMENT OF OTHER PIN-UPS, SPORTS HEROES, AND PERSONAL FRIENDS SURROUNDS YOU. IT'S A COLLECTION THAT RANGES FROM VA-VA-VA-VOOM TO WARM NOSTALGIA. A STRANGE COLLECTION INDEED!

He wanted to take a deep breath, but breathing wasn't on the list.

>PUT THE PICTURE BACK.

YOU HANG THE PINUP BACK IN ITS PLACE.

>LOOK AT THE FOREST.

THE SOUTHERN FOREST PASSES BY AS YOU CHUG ALONG THE SCRIBE'S LINE. NOTHING LIVES IN THESE WOODS. THEY ARE ONLY A BUFFER BETWEEN THE PORT AND THE SCRIBE'S HOUSE.

>LOOK AT ELAINE.

THIS IS ELAINE THE TRAIN, FAMED STAR OF RADIO, BOOKS, TELEVISION, AND VIDEO GAMES. SHE'S QUITE THE LOCOMOTIVE, THOUGH HER FURNACE IS BURNING A LITTLE LOW.

>SHOVEL COAL.

SADLY, EVEN THOUGH YOU SHOVEL COAL INTO HER FURNACE, ELAINE'S FIRE IS LOW. PERHAPS THE SCRIBE CAN HELP.

>WAIT.

THE FOREST PASSES BY.

>WAIT.

THE FOREST PASSES BY.

>WAIT.

THE FOREST PASSES BY. IT THINS AND THEN FADES ENTIRELY. ELAINE STOPS. YOU ARE AT THE SCRIBE'S HOUSE TRAIN STATION.

>GET OUT.

THE SCRIBE'S HOUSE TRAIN STATION

THIS AUSTERE STATION HAS ONE BENCH AND A TICKET BOOTH. TO THE WEST IS THE SCRIBE'S HOUSE ROAD. SOMETHING IS MOVING INSIDE THE BOOTH.

>GO WEST.

THE SCRIBE'S HOUSE ROAD

THIS IS A SHORT, FEATURELESS PATH BETWEEN THE SCRIBE'S HOUSE STATION TO THE EAST AND THE SCRIBE'S HOUSE TO THE WEST.

>LOOK AT THE HOUSE

THE SCRIBE'S HOUSE RISES LIKE A GOTHIC MANOR, MANY-PINNACLED AND STEEPLY GABLED. ITS SEVERAL WINDOWS LOOK DOWN AT YOU, DARK AND MALEVOLENT. HOWEVER, DESPITE ITS UNWELCOMING AIR, THE DOOR STANDS OPEN.

>GO WEST

THE SCRIBE'S HOUSE FRONT PORCH

AN EMPTY PORCH WITH AN OPEN FRONT DOOR. THE SCRIBE'S HOUSE ROAD LIES TO THE EAST.

>ENTER HOUSE

5

THE FIRST TIME CONROY escaped his airy prison, he found himself inside a stranger's mind, where he had confronted the complex control panel of the man's consciousness. After a few days, he had learned which levers made him move and which knobs made him talk. That first time, he hadn't made the man return to the place of Conroy's last meal; the thought hadn't even occurred to him. But the next time, and every time after, he tried to return to the town where they had made him breathe river water, where he had eaten his last honest-to-goodness supper.

Each time he managed to slip out and into someone else, it wasn't quite the same as having his own body again. But it was better than being a whisper on the breeze and a sound in a machine. This was before he waved out across the airways into people's homes, before Ronnie had given him a voice.

He missed Ronnie.

Those times weren't like having a body, not really, not until he had worked his way down into them so completely that he could feel what they felt and taste what they tasted. But by then, he would almost be heading for the door, soon to return to his cage. There was something about a body that had a spirit that wouldn't let a stranger stick around too long. He would have thought that the longer he stayed, the easier it would be. But there was some limit, some point at which the person's proper spirit revolted. The first few times, when he had overstayed his welcome, the process of being ejected had been painful. Conroy had learned to get while the getting was good after a satisfying stroll down memory lane.

Those jaunts weren't exactly like having a body all his own, but they were close. Still, they didn't compare to his visits to the Scribe's house. Here, he had a body, his own body, his human body. His feet were feet, his legs were legs, his stomach, full of delicious food, was his stomach. His face was not round, not white, not constantly grinning. He looked at himself in the foyer's dim mirror and saw the face they had drowned as it had been before that glorious night: lean and lined, with a hint of stubble.

His clothes were the same, too: overalls, a work shirt, and heavy boots that sounded dully on the cracked stone floor. He thought he looked too rough for the Scribe's House, where papers—loose, bound, rolled, and folded—covered every surface. Some were books, some were scattered collections of notes, others, he thought, might be plays or poems. But none were written in words. Each page was like a disorienting window that pulled its viewer down and into itself. The first time Conroy had come to the house, he had made the mistake of looking at a dull, yellowed paper a little too closely, and he had found himself trapped in a lesbian love story for a year. That had been an exciting education, but he wasn't interested in repeating it today. So, he kept his eyes low and furtive, looking at nothing too closely.

The study was toward the back of the house. With quick steps, he passed through the dimly lit hall with its faded green wallpaper and dark wood wainscotting, through a sitting room, and into the round, close study where the studious figure sat at his desk, a quill in his hand.

The Scribe looked human, but Conroy knew that it wasn't true. He was a denizen of that city where few humans had ever walked. Indeed, Conroy believed that the Scribe's House wasn't even in the Port, but was an outpost of that benighted place, and that as he stood in the study, he also stood within the limits of the city of madmen.

The human-looking figure at the desk was bald on the top of his head but bore a ring of hair that remained long and white. Greasy, it curled behind his large ears and against his yellowed collar. His round, thin-rimmed glasses reflected lamplight dully atop his narrow, pointed nose. Unruly mutton chops traced the sides of his jowly face and framed his thick, frowning lips. His waistcoat was brown, his buttons brass, and his frock coat something like tweed. He reminded Conroy a little of a painting of Benjamin Franklin.

"You have angered many," the Scribe said as his quill passed over the paper on his desk. "Including myself. And even so, you come to ask of me a boon."

Conroy removed his hat and held it in his hands deferentially. His throat closed, and he could only nod.

"If it were in my power to unmake you, I would." Here, the Scribe dipped his pen into an inkwell and tapped the excess off. He passed the quill over the page, though no marks appeared. "But you have proven to be strangely robust. I do not claim to understand it, though I suspect our Glorious Queen perceives your nature. And if she allows you to continue, who am I to countermand her?"

Conroy blinked rapidly at the thought of the Queen upon her hill. He had seen her light from a distance once when he had wandered into the dark city through a door in the Valley. He knew he shouldn't have been there, that he was breaking all kinds of rules. But he couldn't help himself. The door had been a puzzle, and he was Conroy.

"So, tell me, what brings you to my home to further disturb my work?"

Conroy tried to answer, but no words came out.

"Speak, or I shall deliver you into the mouth of the beast of the Tugalvud. Then perhaps you shall learn what it means to be the meal."

Conroy worked his mouth until a sound escaped. "I … I had an idea. I need your help."

The Scribe set his pen into the inkwell and turned to him, his eyes a maze of twisting worlds delving down like waterfalls into the black centers where they beheld both Conroy and all that could be in thought and imagination. Long he regarded the man who stood before him, and long Conroy's mind traced the undulations behind the Scribe's glasses, unable to resist the strange promises of unraveled mystery. He wanted to reach out and pluck an eye from its socket and peer into it like some mystic, mythological crystal ball. But he could not move under the Scribe's steady gaze. Conroy had no idea how long he stood there, nor was he certain that time could have properly measured the duration. Finally, however, the Scribe turned back to his papers.

"It will be done. Perhaps some of the power that had been prepared will be preserved and put to good use. But know that no further boon shall be granted to you until you have done some new service for the Queen. Do not doubt me. For, while I may not be able to destroy you, I can still starve you."

Conroy nodded and bowed low, unable to restrain the smile spreading across his narrow face.

6

UP THEY WENT FROM the Scribe's home in the strange southern void. Through the forest of words to the world of little colored blocks. Then to the triangles and flat colors, and finally, up into the Port, where the world looked almost real. Up they went with hope in Conroy's heart, a song on Conroy's lips, and an order clutched in Conroy's hand.

They delivered the order to the elephant and tiger, whose shoulders slumped when they read the Scribe's orders. Conroy always felt sorry for those two in particular, always working, never resting.

"This will cost us so much of ourselves," the tiger said.

"I will pay you back," Conroy said. "I will find a way. If you do this for me, I will be able to go anywhere and get you anything." That seemed to brighten the two pairs of round animal eyes. They nodded, and when they had asked for their payments, a deal was struck.

"How quickly?" the elephant asked.

"I'm not in a rush, but do not dally," Conroy said. This, too, seemed to alleviate a little of the craftsmen's worry.

"Come back in a month," said the tiger.

"Two months," said the elephant.

"Two months," Conroy said. "But not one day longer." His grin spread, and he saw it reflected in their fearful eyes. They all shook on their deal.

Conroy and Elaine camped by the water for two months, enjoying the sun, fishing, and dreaming of the future.

7

ELAINE STRUGGLED SLOWLY UP the mountain track as Conroy shoveled for all he was worth. Her fire guttered dangerously low, and he wondered if he had waited too long. He laughed and shook his head at the thought. The craftsmen had done their work well, and he hadn't wanted to rush them. In the real world, the task would have been impossible to accomplish in two months. But the Port's magic was strong, and even those who had been dragged here, like the tiger and the elephant, had their own kind of power.

Part of Conroy's power was that he didn't have to pass time the way everyone else did. During the two months, he had allowed himself to slip back and forth across his life. He had even found a door with a lock feeble enough for him to break so he could take a jaunt in a man's body to get himself a meal at the old inn. He considered appearing before Daniel's daughter to apologize for his deception in person. He didn't like deceiving anyone. That was wrong. He knew it was wrong. But he had been so hungry. But things hadn't gone well with the man he took over, and he didn't know where Alex was. She probably wouldn't want to see him right now anyway.

Conroy shoveled and wiped his dry brow reflexively. He remembered when he could sweat from work and heat. He wondered if they would ever have enough processing power or memory for him to sweat again. They had enough for him to know that his back ached, even if he couldn't feel it. So much in the Port was like that. You knew a thing was true, but you couldn't experience it the way normal people did. He knew a dull throbbing was radiating from his lower back, but he didn't experience it. He stood and stretched, and knew that the pain was relieved a bit.

He patted the cab wall and told Elaine she was a good girl and that she only had a little further to go. She would just have to chug a little further up the hill to where the long, descending, frozen track began. Conroy had detached all her cars except the tender. She had looked scandalous then, truly unclothed. That had hurt his heart. Elaine was a passenger train; she took people to places and showed them the wonders of the strange worlds whose tracks she crossed. She was not meant to go alone. But Conroy knew she didn't have the strength left to bring all her cars up to the top of the mountain again, especially not with today's cargo. So, he had endured the embarrassing sight of Elaine the Train without her cars.

Had she remained that way and carried only her tender up the track, she might have made the climb without much difficulty, even in her current state of decay. But she pulled one more load behind her, and Conroy thought it might just have been too much. He leaned out of the cab, looked forward and back, and almost despaired. Perhaps the Scribe knew this plan was a bust, and all the preparation had just been part of his punishment for ruining their plans. They'd get old Conroy's hopes up and then dash them as Elaine gave out just before she reached the top.

That possibility seemed increasingly more likely as she crawled ever more slowly up the slope. Somehow, the top of the tracks seemed farther away than it had a moment before. Were they slipping backward? Was that to be their fate? He leaned out again and stared at the ground. No. Though they only inched along, the direction of their inching was up. So, he returned to shoveling, and while he shoveled, he spoke to her, telling her his hopes and dreams, and promising her that she would not have to climb the mountain again for a long time, not until she was better.

Perhaps his words encouraged her, or perhaps she still had more resilience left than he feared, because she didn't stop. After hours of creeping along and back-breaking work on Conroy's part, Elaine the Train finally mounted the final rise of the Northern Mountains. Here, he let her rest, though he kept her furnace full. He got out and ran his hand along the hot metal of her boiler, glad to feel her heat for the first time in ages.

"You have been such a good friend," he said. "You deserve a vacation. A little push, and then I need you to brake harder than you've ever … braked? Broke?" He laughed. He imagined she was laughing with him somewhere inside her metal body. Her lamp-eyes were open, but they were looking in two completely different directions. Clouds gathered in the west, and he thought a storm might be coming in. There wasn't time to linger.

He hurried back, past her tender to their cargo, and almost whistled. Silver and majestic, the locomotive was a real beaut. He imagined putting it out in front and having it cart Elaine around, giving her the royal treatment like she deserved. And he was sure it would, as long as they didn't crash on their way down the mountain or miss the stop entirely.

Conroy sent up a prayer to his maker and then turned on his heel back to Elaine.

"All right, pal," he said, giving her one more pat. "Let's do our jobs."

8

THE SLIDE DOWN THE mountain was immediately terrifying. If the crawl up had been the slowest Elaine had ever gone, the careening drop along the frozen tracks was the fastest. She picked up speed at an alarming rate, and Conroy was convinced that even if they started braking hard now, they would pass the cave at a good fifty miles an hour. He almost pulled the lever to slow her down, but the storm was coming on fast, and he didn't dare come up short. If they froze on the tracks, who knew how long it would be before Elaine thawed? Maybe she never would.

He wondered if the Scribe had sent the storm to torment him for what he had done. Perhaps he had, and Conroy wouldn't be mad at him for that. Conroy had sure dropped a big wrench in their plans. Still, as the bald man had pointed out to him, they both had their magic. Conroy didn't know where his came from. Nor did he know why he had continued to exist after they had drowned him. He had no conception of how he had been plucked from the air or how they had caged him with their voices. He did not understand how he had gone out over the radio with Ronnie's voice, or how they had pulled him together to appear on the strange boxes they called televisions. He had been disoriented in the model, and even more so when they had pulled him into the space of words and electrical pulses. He still struggled with the fact that some part of him always existed now in little computer programs where he had to repeat the same lines over and over. He couldn't conceive of how a single thing that had happened to him had been possible, or why it had anything to do with him.

He hadn't wanted any of it. He had just been hungry. He had just wanted to ride the rails and eat good meals.

He started to hum.

But those things had happened to him, and they had changed him. He could do things. He could appear and disappear. He could summon and dispel. He could slip through doors in the cracks where the worlds met. He could bend and tear and rip and rend and chew. He could take and he could give. He remembered giving some of his memory to the woman in the house when she needed to chew the files for him. He didn't know how he had done that, nor did he even know how he had known he could do it. But he had. Now, as he and Elaine flew down the mountain track, though he didn't understand how, he knew what to do against the storm and the ice on her wheels.

He hummed louder. Over the sound of the engine, he heard others humming. Voices across time and space.

His time was broken, but sometimes, that was a good thing. Today, it was a good thing. Today, he could reach out across the strange fracture of his existence and hear the voices of children in their living rooms and bedrooms, with their radios turned up high. He sang out with them, summoning his magic from the air, and he felt them lend him their joy for Elaine's sake.

His humming turned to words, and so did those of the children. Into the rushing, frozen air, he sang:

Come on, come on, Conroy is coming!
Old Conroy is coming,
Clicking and clacking and puffing right along!
Come on, friends, come on, neighbors,
Conroy is coming and we're going to sing our song!

Elaine rumbled beneath his feet, and he felt her wheels turn once on the ice-slick steel. Heat bloomed from her furnace.

> *Oh yes, we're going to sing our song.*
> *Click clack clock! Look at the station clock!*
> *Click clack clern! It's time for you to learn!*
> *We're going to write, we're going to read,*
> *We're going to do our very best indeeeeeeeed!*

He drew the last word out, long and high, until his breath gave out. Then, with a heaving intake, he filled his lungs until he knew—but did not feel—them to be full. Elaine's lights straightened and snapped on in the growing cloudy gloom. Beams of bright yellow shot out, bathing the world in golden light.

> *Come on, come on, you won't be waiting long!*
> *Come on, come on, we're going to sing our song!*
> *Come on, come on, Old Conroy is coming,*
> *And he's going to teach you,*
> *Yes, he's going to teach you,*
> *The glorious difference between right and wrong!*

The fire in her furnace rose first into a blaze and then into an inferno. The heaps of coal Conroy had piled within her caught, and he could feel her building a head of steam. Wonderful heat spread out from her boiler across her body, and a mighty rumble shook within her. Full of both dread and cheer, he pulled her chain and let out a long blast of her whistle. It pained him, but he wept for joy. When he sang next, he did not sing alone. Her voice, so long silent, joined him, and Conroy and Elaine sang together as they sped before the storm that howled down from the mountains above.

> *So, come on, come on, for Old Conoy and Elaine!*
> *Their riding together, the conductor and his train!*
> *So come out and give them both some big whooping cheers!*
> *Set your campfires alight! They're here to teach you—*

Chug, chug, chug.

> *The glo-ri-ous difference,*

Whistle, and steam, wind, and cold, fire and fury in her steel belly.

Oh yes, the glo-ri-ous difference,

Clouds from her stack, fire on the rails, sparks kicking and jumping.

Oh friends, that Glo-ri-ous difference,

About the track, the snow melted, and green came for the first time to those frozen mountains since the Port sprang up from the void. Far before them, where the ground levelled out, Conroy watched as bright, shining tracks appeared before the mouth of the cave.

The Glorious difference between what's wrong—

Her brakes engaged, and steel screamed against steel. Conroy slammed against her doorframe as he stared out at the approaching stretch of flat, green earth.

—And what's riiiiiiight!

Elaine's voice, high and young, bright and glad, echoed out over the range like the command of some mountain god, knocking back the storm and blowing it off to the north. Conroy had forgotten that she could do that, how her joy and light would bring the sun everywhere they went. He admitted to himself with a touch of embarrassment that he had half-remembered that as one of his bits of magic. But Elaine the Train was the one who hid the rain, and made the sour, grumpy weather spiral down the nasty drain.

They came to a screeching, shouting, lurching stop. Even with the heavy load behind her, Elaine's brakes worked a treat, and they lined up with the old wooden door of the cave, now dripping with melted ice.

"Woo, Conroy!" Elaine shouted. "What a slide! I thought we were going to go all the way to the bottom and tip right off onto the beach!"

Conroy leapt down from her cab and sped along, all elbows and knees, to look her in the eyes. They were bright and open and looking at him with that same wonder and joy he remembered. Here was Elaine, back again.

"Well, we would have if it hadn't been for your quick work!" Conroy said, patting her smokebox door. "Good job, old pal! And you brought summer with you!"

"I always do. Elaine's the name, and sunlight's my game. Well, that and Pinochle!" Distantly, people laughed. He hadn't heard that sound in a long time. Elaine's eyes swiveled back and forth. "Where are we today, Conroy?"

"We're in the Northern Mountains, and we're going to make a new friend! Would you like that, Elaine?"

"Oh boy, would I! I love making new friends. In fact, I can't remember the last time I met someone new!"

"I know what you mean. Well, give me just a minute, and I'll introduce you!"

Conroy patted her again and then marched his way back past the tender to the silver locomotive. Conroy stooped next to their temporary caboose and plucked a wildflower. Then up into the new cab he went, and down he came, a posey in one hand and a circular, metal plate in the other. Elbows up, knees a'marchin', Conroy returned to Elaine. He slid the flower into a seam on her boiler.

"Hey, that tickles!" Elaine said.

He gave her another affectionate tap with his long, white fingers and then turned toward the cave where their new friend waited.

9

THE CONTRAST BETWEEN THE bright summer day outside and the freezing darkness within the cave was shocking. Conroy adjusted his conductor's cap and rubbed his arms. Unlike the pain in his back, he didn't just know he was cold; he felt it. It wasn't the same as being cold in the real world, or even in the Valley. He missed the Valley. He wondered if, after today, they'd let him visit now and then.

The path through the cave was winding, and it had been one of the first mazes he had solved when he had come to the mountains with Elaine. He knew the twisty little passages, all alike, even without a map. Most of the time. Sometimes, when his mind was not quite what it should be, he forgot. But those times were delightful too, since they allowed him to solve the maze afresh! Sadly, his wobbly mind rarely stayed wobbly long enough for him to solve the maze entirely. Usually, he'd come to his senses and remember the last few steps. Then he'd stand with his hands on his hips, shaking his head at himself for being so silly.

Today, however, he didn't forget. Instead, he followed his little sing-song mnemonic of twisting and turning until he came to the room where his most recent prize lay. She wore the same dress she had when he had appeared through the door and greeted her with his usual enthusiasm. Sometimes people's clothes changed when they came to the Port, but not hers. He remembered how shocked and curious she was to see Conroy in person. He could feel her confusion and intrigue. He could remember her thoughts, spilling out of her eyes.

Is this some trick? Is it some weird machine that Crystalline Mansion is testing for their theme park? But what is it doing in my bedroom? Oh, no, his hands feel so strange! No, no, let me go! Mom! Dad! Mom! Mom! Mom!

Now she sat against the cave wall, her hands open and resting beside her hips, her legs—no, not legs, not anymore. Her one leg lolled under her knee-length dress. Her mouth sagged, and her lips sparkled as if stardust lingered there. But Conroy knew it was just ice. Her eyes, big and brown, followed him in slow, stilted shutters. Her lids blinked in creaking, cracking flutters. A puff of mist emerged from between those ice-encrusted lips.

"Good morning to you! Brrr, it's cold in here!" Conroy said, crouching down next to her. She gave him another slow, creeping blink and another puff of misty breath. "I know it's chilly, but I have an idea that will get you warm! Would you like to get out of here?"

The girl's chin moved only a little, but Conroy took that as an emphatic 'yes.' So, he held up the round metal plate in front of her.

"Look at this thing." She looked, and her eyelids creaked wide. "I know that, after everything you've been through, this probably goes without saying, but things are about to get extremely strange."

10

WHEN CONROY EMERGED FROM the cave, Elaine didn't look as chipper as she had. The air was noticeably cooler as well. The snow hadn't returned yet, but the sky was grayer, and a nippy wind drifted down the mountain. Conroy also noticed a pool of oil darkening the ground under Elaine's cab.

"Conroy," she said, one eye turning to him, "I don't feel so good."

He gave her a sympathetic smile and walked past her to the bright silver locomotive. Humming, he bounded up into the cab and put the metal disk back into its place. He cranked a wheel, pulled a lever, and pushed a button. Then down he came again and sauntered back to Elaine.

"Conroy," she repeated, her voice bending and scraping like metal on metal. "I don't feel so good."

"I know, old pal, it's taken a lot out of you to blow that old storm away. But we're going to get you out of these mountains to somewhere warm. Would you like that?"

"I would," she said.

"Then let's give it one more push. One more push, and then you can rest."

He slapped her boiler twice before he jumped back up into her cab. He pulled one lever, shoveled some coal, and pushed another lever. Then she was off, lurching and chugging, her fire decidedly lower than it had been only minutes before. They crossed the flat stretch of land in front of the cave and began the gentle downward slope that would eventually lead them out of the mountains and down to the seashore, where the track ran along the beach.

At first, the rails remained clear of ice. But after a quarter mile, frost began to creep back onto the old steel. Another minute on, Elaine's wheels started to slide. Conroy looked behind him, over the tender, and saw the silver starting to frost over. He realized he should do something about that. He thought about the logistics for a minute.

"Conroy?" Elaine said, her voice screeching. "Can you help? I'm slipping. I can't get a hold!"

"Using the old noodle for a moment, pal," he said.

Then, finger in the air, an idea sprang to him. He grabbed a few special items and stuffed them into his old burlap sack. Then, using that old Conroy agility, he clambered out of the back of Elaine's cab and onto the coal car. Wind whooshed past him, and he almost lost his hat. But even if Elaine was waning, his magic still held, and so did his cap. He picked his way over the coal until he reached the new locomotive. A rime of ice had formed over the metal, and Conroy picked his steps carefully until he reached the rear and slid down inside. There he dumped his sack out carefully on the floor, making sure that the old thermos of broth didn't roll around, and that nothing broke or slid out the door. Then he was back up on the icy metal path as Elaine called out from ahead,

"Coonnnnnroooooooyyyyy."

He could barely distinguish her plaintive cry from the howling of the wind. Then he was down into her cab again and plucking up the shovel. He filled his sack with coal and threw the heavy load over his shoulder. They still had a way to go down the mountain track. There was time.

Back up and over and down again. He emptied the coal into the shiny silver chute. He patted his pocket and found a box of matches. In the real world, he'd need something more to get it all going, but not here, not now. Conroy could feel it. In the vast silver body, there was fire waiting to be kindled, and all it would take was a little nudge. He lit the match and set it to the coal. It went up in a great woosh, and Conroy fell back from the blast of heat. All about him, the ice began to melt. He needed more coal; she'd burn through this first pile in a flash. He grabbed his sack and returned to the tender. When he got there, he could hear a low, rumbling grinding of something up ahead. He thought maybe one of Elaine's axels had gone wrong.

"Con—" she began, "Conroy. My belly doesn't feel good. My belly. My fire is going down. I'm cold."

"You'll be okay, Elaine! We just need to get down to the warmer weather, down to the beach! We'll drink drinks with little umbrellas!"

"Conroy," she screeched, "I'm going. It's getting dark."

He looked up into the gray sky and agreed.

"Back in two shakes of a lamb's tail!" he called and scrambled back over the coal car. The silver boiler under his feet was now wet. The ice was losing. He dumped another sack of coal past the grate. He went back and back as the train slid down the mountain pass. On his fifth trip, he saw something that warmed his heart.

The silver locomotive's eyes were open.

Two lights searching and roving turned left and right. Conroy let out a whooping holler before he returned with his last delivery. This he dumped in and closed the heavy door.

"Where? Where? What? What am I? Who's there? Who is I?" the words came whistling out of the new locomotive, and Conroy put his hands over his ears. He would have to train her out of that. He chuckled at his pun, wincing. He suddenly thought of when he had been bound in a cave, when the whistle had been used against him by some terrible magic older than even the Scribe's or his Queen. Rarely was Conroy scared, but that had sent shivers down his spine, and no mistake.

He pushed the memory aside and stroked the clean metal interior of the bright new cab. It wouldn't be long now. They'd come out of the mountains, around the bend, and onto the warm beach.

The cabin lurched around him.

"Help! Out! Out! I need to get out!" the whistling voice shouted around him. She began to rumble, and Conroy felt her wheels start to turn. She, it seemed, had purchase on the old frozen steel in a way that Elaine's old wheels didn't. Their convoy started to speed up. "Out! Got to get out! Mom! Mom! Mommy! Dad! Where am I? What am I?"

Conroy sprang to his feet and scrambled out and over, over and down, his sooty sack over his shoulder. He landed in Elaine's cab.

"Conroy," Elaine said. Her voice was weak, barely audible over the wind and the plaintive panic of the locomotive behind them. "Help, I'm speeding. I'm flying." Then her voice changed, her tone was dreamy, as if she were remembering something. "Why are we going to the river? I don't want to go with you. Why are we going down to the river? Ow! Oh no! Why did you hit me? Please, stop. Oh no. Oh, Mommy! Oh no! Help!"

The last sound she made was like a memory of stone on bone, and Conroy couldn't help but rub his stomach. Then, almost taken back to that wonderful, terrible day, he was held in the moment by the sight of the track ahead. Then Conroy understood their situation. Wasting no time, he snagged up photographs, folded pin-ups and centerfolds, and grabbed pictures of baseball players and men on horses. They were going too fast now, and the curve was coming on. He threw his sack over his shoulder and took two steps back to where the coal car connected to Elaine. He reached down and thought that, if this were the real world, the trick wouldn't work.

But he was the conductor.

He pulled the long metal pin that connected the two cars and slid it into the tender's pin holder. Then he turned and looked over the old cab with a wistful sigh before he clambered up again and back. He stopped to pull the pin between the tender and the new locomotive. Then he sped along and dropped his sack into the cab. He considered riding the rest of the journey out down with his belongings, but the view was too good from up on the boiler. So he dropped himself down, his legs hugging the burning boiler, his arms wrapping the smokestack.

A keening lifted on the wind, old, rusted metal twisting and scraping against itself. It rode the air under the rambling rumble of wails for 'mommy,' 'dad,' and 'please,' two voices crying out in unison. Down they sped, and the sharp turn at the bottom raced up at them.

Elaine's voice pierced the roar. "Con—"

The word was cut off by screaming steel and wrenching iron as they took the turn too fast. At first, it seemed Elaine might just hold on. At first, it looked like she would ride on one rail, her smoking, bursting form skating on one set of bending wheels as the track curved out onto the beach. At first, Conroy wondered if she would make it all the way to where the track split.

Then she jumped.

And for a moment, Elaine flew over the sand toward the water. Silently, she soared above the world, with no conductor to tell her where to go. The sand bloomed as if hit by a bomb when she came crashing down. It rose like a wave as she slid a hundred feet, digging a deep and terrible rut in the beach. The tender followed her, tumbling end over end, flinging coal through the air, arcing like the fanned feathers from some midnight bird. Then it slammed and jumped, tumbling and tumbling, until it crashed into Elaine at the water's edge.

Conroy pulled the brakes, and the silver locomotive lurched, squealed, and finally came to a halt. They passed where Elaine had landed, so he backed up until they were parallel with the wreck. He sprang out and felt the sand sink slightly under his feet. That was new. They had changed that as well in one of their server updates. He liked it.

He walked jauntily across the rolling sand until he came to the smoking heap. His feet splashed in the briny water as it lapped slowly against her broken metal. Her boiler water, which he could see through a rent, would soon mix with the salt water. He wondered whether that was poetic.

"Conroy," she said in a thin, high-pitched voice. "Why are we by the river? I want to go home. Please let me go home."

Her words reminded him of the day long ago when they had met. He smiled.

"You are home. This is where you'll rest, right here by the sea. Isn't it a nice place? The sun is shining, the waves are warm."

"Conroy," she began, but nothing followed. Her remaining eye light— the other had been shorn off and was now taking on water and slowly sinking—turned to him and flickered. He knew her fire was going out, and she would soon disappear for good. He didn't like that; he had lost so many people. He missed so many people. He didn't want to miss Elaine.

He didn't want to miss her. She had been his companion for so long. The idea was so terrible, Conroy didn't think he could bear it.

So, he decided not to. He had heard that a person should look after their own mental health, and he had never really known what that meant. But there and then, feeling the years of longing and sorrow that would follow from losing Elaine, he decided that it was better that he didn't feel any of it. So he put his hands on her cooling metal frame and gave her back to herself. He didn't really know how he did it, or what it really meant, but he felt Elaine flow out of him and back into herself. And, a moment later, he was free.

"Now you can sleep," he said, as his sorrow slipped through his hands and into her. "Now you can go home."

He felt time pull him, and he tumbled away from the moment on the beach, back to another time and place by another body of water.

11

WHEN HE RETURNED, CONROY blinked and grinned. He stepped back from the old wreck and wondered how it had gotten there. It sure was a mess. It must have been pretty recent, as the metal wasn't rusted or covered in barnacles, which must be the old locomotive's fate. Curious, he hoped he would remember to check in on it later, to see how it progressed. But his memory was a tricky thing, and sometimes things would fade away. Still, he was sure he'd pass by on his travels with … with … What was his locomotive's name? Conroy put a thoughtful finger to his mouth and tried to recall her name. No … no, it wasn't coming to him. But it would. She was just there, waiting for him on the track.

He was about to return to her when the wrecked engine's light flickered on and then off again. He stared at it. The wreck must have been recent indeed if there was still power flowing. Then, to his surprise and amusement, the lamp glowed at him with a dim but steady light. It flickered only once, as if blinking, as a thin metal whine rose from somewhere within the ruined metal. Whoever this was, they were alive. He shook his head and wondered what a strange place the Port was.

"Well, this is a pickle for you," he said. "But I'm sure you'll figure it out." Then he patted the old wreck and headed back up the beach with elbows and knees going full steam. There he found his bright, trusty locomotive, sitting on the tracks. He climbed inside.

"Where am I?" she asked. That seemed like a strange question, and Conroy had a moment of vertigo. He took hold of one of the levers and felt his mind tilting and shifting as something within him flowed into the engine. He squeezed his eyes tight and felt a little sick for a moment. Then the world righted itself, and a grin spread across his face.

"You're in Port Imagination," he said. "And I'm Conroy!"

"Conroy," she said, trying the word out. "Conroy. I'm … I'm Jessica." He could hear the growing confidence in her voice.

"Yes! Jess the Express!" He said. "Jess the Express! She's just the best!"

"I *am*!" she said, a cheery, chipper tone bolstering her words. "I *am* the best!"

"You're fast and reliable, friendly and fun, and you don't stop chugging until the work is done."

"I burn up my coal from morning till night," she intoned, "until all of the children know what's wrong from what's right!"

Together they sang, as they always had, Conroy and Jess the Express.

12

JESS SAT STEAMING AT the boardwalk station, pleasantly rumbling as people walked up to her and patted her sides. She felt a strange warmth in her boiler as she waited for Conroy to return. She wanted him to sit on her chair and feed her some coal. Of course, they had to wait for a new tender to be delivered, but he had promised her it wouldn't be long.

She didn't mind the people touching her metal, or oohing and aahing at her chrome finish and shiny gold caps. She thought she was made to be in front of the world, and that part of her job was to instill wonder in others. She hoped that her presence made the people of the Port a little happier.

Finally, after what felt like an hour, Conroy came walking up the boardwalk with a drink in his hand. He was greeting people with big smiles, though she saw some didn't greet him back. Those folks gave him hard, angry looks, which they turned from him to her. Jess didn't know why anyone would be angry with Conroy, and certainly didn't understand why they'd have any problem with her. Still, she was young, and she had a lot to learn.

"Howdy, Jess," Conroy said, giving her a big wave. She almost tooted her whistle, but she remembered that Conroy didn't like that. So, she gave him a friendly rumble and let out a little steam, though not too much; she had to conserve it until the new tender arrived.

"Howdy, Conroy, what have you got there?"

"Oh, just a little tropical drink. Do you like the little umbrella?"

"I do," Jess said. "I wish I had a drink with a little umbrella."

Conroy frowned and shook his head. "How silly and selfish of me! I—" His eyes went wide, and his frown disappeared. "I know! I have something you will enjoy!"

He rushed into her cab, and she felt the strange warm tickling of his feet upon her floor. A moment later, he returned with a tube with a plastic cap on it. A … thermos. It was called a thermos. He unscrewed the top and poured a thin brown liquid into the cap. Then he stuck his own umbrella into it.

"Here you go! Where do you want it?"

"Um, maybe down my smoke stack?" she said, unsure if that was the right answer.

"How about in one of these?" he said, pointing to several little capped tubes that stuck off her side. She wanted to shrug, but couldn't. Instead, she rolled her coupling rods up a few degrees and back down again.

"Let's give it a try."

He pulled one of the caps up and poured the liquid down the pipe. He had been right; that was the ticket. The taste was savory and delicious and oddly familiar.

"Yummy," she said. "Thanks, Conroy, you're my best friend."

Conroy smiled and took a sip of the broth. She could see he enjoyed it, and that made her happy.

13

CONROY, STOMACH RUMBLING, EMERGED from the cave with a parcel as evening set in. It had been—well, he wasn't sure the last time he had plucked a roast from the cave, but from what remained, there weren't many meals left. He hoped he had enjoyed them, but his memory was so strange these days that he couldn't be sure.

He climbed into Jess's cab and the two of them set off down the slope, her fire melting the tracks in front of her. Conroy had a flash of memory of speeding down the slope with … had it been Jess? Yes, he was sure it had. But he had the impression that someone else had been there too. Maybe, he thought, it had been the blonde in the picture that hung on the cab wall. Maybe he had popped out into the real world and snatched her up. Maybe it was the young woman he had helped with her puzzles, the one whose files he had fed to the woman who lived in the house. Maybe she had been there with him, racing down the track.

He hoped it was. He liked her. He missed her.

They rode the curve easily, and Jess let out a whoop of steam. Conroy hooted and danced a little jig in the cab. He was hungry and looking forward to slow-roasting the meat over an open fire. They sped along the beach, and he spied the old wreck that lay half underwater as the tide rolled in. He wondered how the old locomotive had gotten there, and how long it had lain in the sand, rusted and broken, a haven for crabs and seagulls. As the wreck receded into the background in the failing evening light, he saw the locomotive's one light glowing faintly above the water.

And for a moment, it flickered off and then on, as if it were blinking.

1

September 7, 2009

FOUR SEAFOAM GREEN CARDBOARD cups almost overflowed the woman's hands as she stepped backward into *Aunt Erma's Candy and Creamery*. She was pretty, with short, straight, brown hair and tired eyes. The cups were filled with colorful twists of ice cream under clouds of cherry-topped whipped cream. She looked close to losing the lot, but still she stepped backward into the shop and held the door open.

"Pardon me," she said as she held the door open with one sneaker heel.

"No, pardon me," Lou said, swung once between his crutches, took a step, and then swung in again. "Thank you, ma'am." He patted her arm gently. "Better get those out there before you lose them." The woman laughed and ducked out as he held the door for her.

His niece, Ellen, catching up, slipped into the shop behind him. "Wow, it's crazy in here," she said.

"It smells like America in here," Lou replied after taking a long, sweet breath. And it did. It smelled, sounded, and looked like America. Sugar, a crowd, and commerce, for better or worse, all decked in red-white-and blue on a day dedicated to the workers just trying to get by while they made other people rich. Lou Chapel loved it and hated it.

Three glass display cases and a seafoam-green counter formed a shallow crescent that held the confection-hungry hoards back from the small crew of baseball-capped teenagers and their harried manager. One case held decadent-looking baked goods, fudge, and chocolates. The next was packed with a double row of plastic ice-cream buckets. Between these and the third case stood a counter where a youth, who Lou thought might be trying to grow his first five o'clock shadow, was ringing up two older boys. That final display showed fourteen deep and narrow metal trays filled with gelato. On top of that case, next to a sample spoon disposal cup, stood two signs. The first read, 'Sorry, cash only.' The second declared, 'Sorry, if you drop it, we can't replace it.'

"Doesn't seem too accommodating," Lou said to his niece, nodding toward the second sign.

"They only put that up on the super busy days. Most of the time, it's fine, unless you're a constant klutz," Ellen said. "Besides, I think you're safe. You have an inside man."

Lou followed his niece's outstretched finger to a teenage girl whose short-sleeved, green and white striped uniform button-up was a little too baggy. Her hat emphasized her slightly too-big ears, and her dark brown hair poked awkwardly out the back, curling up at the end before it reached her collar. Her mouth hung open, giving her a dull, brain-dead look that disappeared the moment she spoke to a customer.

The customer, his daughter in her pink dress, and everyone else in the room struck Lou as especially Caucasian. He had seen maybe a dozen people during the parade whose ancestors hailed from somewhere other than the northern half of Europe. He knew that the town was almost entirely white, but it was still a culture shock every time he returned. He wasn't sure if that was just the natural process of living in a world that wasn't as isolated as Lightning Falls, or if that had something to do with the town's unnatural way of being forgotten.

"She's fifteen now?" he said, his focus snapping back to the girl behind the counter.

"Fourteen. You *did* call her on her birthday, remember?"

"Yeah, right, of course. I just ... sorry, I've had a lot on my plate at work."

Click.

He knew the sound was in his head. The room and the street beyond the door were far too loud for him to have heard anything so soft and subtle. Even so, he turned and saw an adolescent boy flicking his retainer off his teeth and back on again. The young man met Lou's eye, and apparently not liking what he saw there, turned away to study the menu.

"Honey, look who's here!" Ellen said as they got to the front of the line.

"Uncle Lou!" the girl said and put her notepad down. She hurried around the counter and wrapped him with gangly arms. He let one crutch hang from his elbow and rubbed her back.

"Missed you, kiddo," he said.

She pulled back and stood on tiptoe to kiss him on the cheek. "I didn't know you were coming," she said.

"Neither did I, but I had a few days off and I wanted to see you," he said.

"How long will you be here?"

"Until Wednesday, so plenty of time for us to catch up and for you to get bored of me."

She shook her head and looked into his eyes with the love and admiration that no other human on earth had ever given him.

He wanted to slap her, to knock the feeling out of her. But, even if she looked up at him with hurt, confusion, and dismay, he knew he could not make her hate him. If he could, he knew, he would. That would be better.

"What time are you done?" Ellen asked.

"I'm working until like four-thirty today. We're getting time and a half, since it's a holiday," the fourteen-year-old girl said.

"Well, that's good," Lou said. "We'll get dinner. My treat. Where do you want to go?"

"I don't know, maybe pizza?"

"Of course," Ellen said.

"Pizza then," Lou said. "Come here and hug me again, and then get back there and take our order."

She did exactly that, and when she stood behind the counter, her notepad in her hand, she gave them the authentic experience.

"Hi, welcome to *Aunt Erma's Candy and Creamery*! My name is Chloe. How can I help you today?"

2

LOU SAT ON A bench, licked cookies and cream from a plastic spoon, and watched the crowd push its way into and out of *Aunt Erma's*. Ellen stood next to him, saying 'hi' to this person and that. She looked so normal to him that he felt a kind of universal vertigo as he thought about where he had been only a week prior, and where he was going to be soon.

Click.

He grimaced, put one elbow over the back of the bench, and looked behind him. There was no adolescent boy this time, only a pair of young women with soft-serve cones leaning against the museum's brick wall. One of them saw him and offered a half-hearted smile. He smiled back a little more enthusiastically and faced front once more.

Across the little, recessed patio area, the girl in the pink dress, whom Chloe had been serving, was eating her ice cream and swaying back and forth to music coming from Main Street. She was trying some strange dance steps that Lou couldn't decipher while also attempting to get her father's attention. But her father was busy, arms crossed, talking to another, older man whose arms were also crossed. They had the serious, knowing look on their faces that said that they were discussing something of infinite importance, be it the government, home improvement, or their cars. Or so Lou figured the stereotype went. He'd never had such a conversation.

Well, not never. He used to talk baseball with his best friend. That was before, though. Before everything.

Finally, after a particularly insistent repetition of the word 'Dad!', the man turned around.

"What is it, Syd? Can't you see that I'm talking to Mr. Lowry?"

"Yeah, but I got it!" the girl said, and she did the odd set of steps even more enthusiastically. She was not successful this time, however. And, in missing one of the steps, the girl fell onto her butt and dropped her cup of ice cream on the ground, face down.

"No!" she shouted at the overturned treat.

"Syd, what the heck? Are you okay?" her father said.

"Yeah, I'm fine, I just …"

Lou couldn't tell how old the girl was. Maybe eight, maybe nine. She looked like she was trying to figure that out as well, as he watched her struggle over whether to cry over her lost dessert. He watched with admiration as he saw her seemingly make the conscious decision not to cry, but to pick herself up and brush her pink dress off.

"I'm going to get another one," she said.

"Honey, we can't, I don't have any more cash on me."

"But I have money, it's at home. I'll pay you back," she said. "I have allowance money."

"Syd, that isn't it, I just don't have cash on me. I'd buy you four of them if I had it on me," he said, pushing a strand of hair behind her ear. The man he had been speaking to reached into his pockets with an avuncular smile that Lou watched turn into a frustrated frown. That man, it seemed, also didn't have any cash.

Click.

Lou resisted the urge to look over his shoulder and remembered scrubbing blood from his hands.

"Pardon me," Lou said, scooping the last of his cookies and cream into his mouth and dropping the cup into a waste basket next to the bench. He pushed himself up and took a swinging step forward. "I can help."

"No, I appreciate it, but we couldn't take any money, sir," the man said, though the girl looked at him like he was maybe Jesus Christ himself come down to get her some more rocky road.

"Oh, don't worry about it, I've got an inside man," he said, winking at the girl. "Family connections. Won't cost a dime. I promise. What kind did you want?"

"Cherry, please," the girl said.

"One scoop or two?"

"Two, please!" the girl said, smiling and lifting her chin.

"That's the right answer. Two scoops of cherry, coming up," Lou said.

"Are you sure?" the girl's father asked.

"Couldn't be more sure," Lou said as he started toward the door.

"Sydney, you go with him. And you thank him," Lou heard the man say.

Sydney did. She held the door and stood in line with him. "Are you from Lightning Falls?" she asked.

"I am, originally," he said.

"I haven't seen you around before," she said.

"I don't live here anymore. But I do like to come back to visit my family now and then. Have you always lived here?"

"Mhm! Always will!"

He smiled at that. "Well, maybe so, but don't give up any opportunities to go out and see the world."

To future travel, she shrugged. To the cup of cherry ice cream, she practically danced.

"That's how you lost the last one," Lou said. The girl made a comical, almost cartoonish face of realization, gripped the cup with both hands, and nodded exaggeratedly. He smiled and held back a molten flow of sorrow threatening to burst through his chest.

Click.

A muscle in his neck twitched.

"Enjoy that, and dance when it's done!" he said. She thanked him and ran out of the building.

"That was a nice thing to do," Chloe said.

"It's nothing on the scales," Lou said.

3

HE DROVE THE VAN out of town and went north on Route 3, not wanting to go down into Enterprise. That was the way he went when it was time to go back to the desert. And he'd have to go that way soon enough. In less than a month, if all went well—and honestly, when had it ever not gone well?—he'd be back here again for a night. Then he'd go south. But until then, he thought he'd head up to Washington for a day and try to exist outside of everything that made him who he was. He'd find a woman. Not normally, of course. He had no illusions that any women would be interested in his ancient ass. But he didn't mind trading for it. And he could tip well. The far-seeing man he worked for knew where secrets were kept, and where one could, without putting oneself in danger or on anyone's map, find forgotten stores of wealth.

Click.

He checked his rearview and tried not to think about his most recent outing in the van. Instead, he forced his mind back to his first trip out of Lightning Falls. He had worn his camp shirt and shorts, even though the trip to Missouri would take days. He remembered singing a Roy Rogers song and wondering if he'd be able to ride a horse. Then he remembered a boy making him lie down in the forest, and the feeling of the heavy branch against his back. Once. Twice.

Snap.

The panic had been slow to come. He had thought his legs were just numb. But it rose in him as he watched the older boy fall to the ground, his face contorted in an agony of confusion and fear until all that remained was the horror.

"I'm sorry!" the older boy said. "I'm sorry, it wasn't me. It wasn't me. I'm sorry! Help! Help! Oh God, help me!"

When the boy's voice rose to whining, frantic screeches, the real panic landed on Lou and dug its raptor talons in.

4

July 4, 2014

CLICK.

Lou flinched and turned to see the screen door closed behind Chloe. Her black bra straps rode high on her shoulders as they poked out from under the navy blue of her form-fitting tank top. Her track pants were also tight, and unlike many of the young women he had seen recently, she wore them low, closer to her hips. Lou wondered if he would have been able to recognize her as a girl if he had seen her from behind. The skinny kid had been replaced by a lean, almost muscular young woman. Track and soccer had transformed her. He wondered if her short hair was a product of necessity, or if it portended other changes in her as well.

"You want to drive down?" she asked.

"No, I feel like a good, old-fashioned walk. How does that sound?"

She gave him a cocky, easy grin and pushed her fists into her pockets. "Lead the way," she said.

The night was warm, and the town was alive. They passed a dozen knots of people who were also out, enjoying the holiday evening.

"When do the fireworks start?" Lou asked.

"They cancelled them this year; there hasn't been enough rain," she said.

"Ah, smart," he said, swinging into his next step. "You want ice cream?"

"I've had enough ice cream to last me a lifetime," she said. Then, as if sensing his disappointment, she said, "Do you like pie? Or cheesecake?"

"Every good American likes pie," he said, "it's in the Constitution. And … if you can keep a secret, I'll let you know that I've never had cheesecake."

"Never had cheesecake? Well, you've got to have some. You'll love it."

"It doesn't sound very good," Lou said as he raised a hand to an older couple walking on the other side of the street.

"Well, it is. Come on, let's go to the *Second Wave*, and I'll buy you a slice. If you don't like it, they have a bunch of pie."

Fifteen minutes later, Lou was staring down the business end of a piece of cheesecake poking out from under a mound of dripping huckleberries.

"This looks about as appetizing as it sounds," he said, furrowing his already wrinkled forehead. He wore his white hair short, the way he had back in the '50s, though he had decidedly less of it now, and he rubbed his hand through it as he wondered how disgusting the experience would be.

"It's a sweet cheese," she said, and when he gave her an incredulous look, she scooped a forkful into her mouth and let her face relax into a decadent, pleasurable mien that bordered on obscene.

"All right, all right," he said, and ventured a bite. He felt a slow, bemused smile spread across his face. "Wow," he said.

"Right?" she said as he took another bite. After letting him enjoy half the slice, she leaned forward and crossed her arms on the table. "Why haven't you ever had cheesecake?"

"Well, I guess … how much has your mother told you?"

"She told me you were in the hospital for a while," Chloe said, resting her chin on her forearm.

"That is an understatement. I was institutionalized for just about forty-five years, give or take."

"What the fuck?" she breathed and then looked around to see if anyone heard her. "Forty-five years?"

"That's right. From the early '60s until 2008. And, though things were pretty good inside, we never had cheesecake. Not sure why, maybe the Queen isn't a fan of sweet cheese."

"Who?"

"The Queen." He put his fork down and frowned at her. This was going to be difficult. He had woken up with the feeling that they should have this conversation, and he learned decades ago not to ignore the feeling. "How much do you know about our family and our—let's call them *commitments*."

She shrugged, head still down. "A little. Mom said that you have a secret mission. I thought you were kind of like a spy for a long time."

"Well, I kind of was, at least for a year or so. And my whole life was mostly spent building my cover, convincing people that I was loyal to something that I wasn't."

"Why?" she asked.

"To stop something horrific from happening."

"Did you do it?" she asked, her big brown eyes wide.

"Yes. But I made several other horrific things happen in the process. So don't look at me like that," Lou said, grimacing.

"Like what?"

"Like I'm some kind of hero, I'm not," he said. "If this were a sane universe, I'd be going to Hell. As it is, who knows?" He took another bite of his cheesecake. The berries were a little too sweet, but that was okay. "I did what I was asked to do by the people who, next to you, are the most important to me. And now … God help me … I think I'm supposed to tell you about it all."

Her eyes were too eager, and if he could have taken his knife and put it into his neck right then, he would have. But self-destruction had never been in his power. So, instead, he did the only thing he could.

He spoke.

5

THE FALLS ROARED INTO the pool before them. Chloe hugged her knees to her chest, her chin on one knee, as they sat together on a bench.

"So how do you know what he wants?" she asked after a long pause.

"It comes in different ways. First, and probably the most annoying way, is I just get told. My friend, the one I told you about, has a kind of direct connection with the man himself. So, sometimes he'll come to me and say, 'Lou, we've got to hit the road,' or 'Hey fella, it's time to do the work.' And then we're off. But more often than not, I just get a feeling. We aren't the Kusels; we don't generally get the kind of special attention they did. Heck, we aren't even the next ring out from them. We are in the outer ring, the least worthy. But we still serve. And maybe, if we serve well, we get to win for ourselves a little—" He stopped himself with a chuckle.

"What? What's so funny?" she asked.

"I was going to say 'Glory,' but that's not us."

"That's … the Queen," she said, thinking hard about their conversation.

"That's right," Lou said.

"And the other one, the robed man—"

"The Librarian. They are two of the big ones, but there are more, a whole constellation of them. But living here, the Librarian is your biggest concern. Learn about him."

"How am I supposed to do that?" she asked. He shook his head, at a loss. "So am I supposed to just start trusting feelings about things, assuming that they belong to the Man Who is ...."

"Full of Eyes," he said. "It's like a cult, you know, you have to learn all the internal lingo."

"Is it a cult?" she asked.

"Technically? Maybe. But the difference between us and a cult is that the Man is real. I've seen him. He healed me. He's not a myth or a story."

Chloe looked at his crutches and frowned. "He healed you?"

"Oh yes," Lou said. "I got hurt at camp when I was a boy. Hurt bad. I couldn't move anything below my waist. And then my friend took me to see the man. He healed me. Not all the way, but enough to show me his power and to let me do the work I needed to do for him."

"How did you get hurt?" she asked.

"That same friend beat me with a branch in the woods until my back broke." He stared straight ahead while her mouth dropped open. Finally, as she shook her head, perhaps trying to find the right words, Lou smiled and turned to her. "He wasn't himself."

6

July 8, 2017

CLICK.

Lou sucked in a long, fast breath as sleep scurried away. In the mental after-image of his dream, he could still feel himself driving. He could still feel Joseph to his right in the passenger seat, turning around to look behind them as the tree-lined road ahead was as empty as they had known it would be.

He rubbed his face and felt the old tears. He wiped them away and pushed himself up onto his good hip. The other side ached. It was doing that a lot more these days. He thought he knew what that meant, and that maybe this road was finally coming to an end. There was little about that prospect that saddened him, except for what he would leave behind.

He picked up the cheap, little flip phone from the nightstand and pressed the button on the side—thirteen minutes after five. That was a little late for him to fall back to sleep. The sun would be up soon, he'd need to be on the road, and there was no reason to drag things out more than nature demanded.

He showered fast, dried his aching body, and dressed in his compression socks, boxer shorts, and T-shirt. Then, sitting on the bed, he strapped his left leg into the brace. It didn't look exactly like the one they had put him in as a boy, but it did basically the same things. It held things in place and kept the old wound from getting in his way any more than was strictly necessary. He had often tried to work out the problem, to see if there was some better solution, but in this, the Man had never helped him.

The corner of Lou's mouth twitched as a fly flew past him in the summer morning heat. He waved it away before tightening the topmost strap. Then he pulled out his slacks and put his right leg through. Then he snapped the cuff around the bottom of his braced leg and zipped the leg up. He liked how hidden the zipper was. A person really had to look for it. It made him feel like he could keep a level of decorum in his indecorous life. His short-sleeved, button-up, plaid shirt followed his shoes, and then Lou Chapel stood in front of the mirror and wanted to laugh at himself. He looked like a man out of time, spat up from 1953. He was just missing his old pocket protector.

Lou pictured himself as a boy in a chair, with his pack across his lap, and remembered the little, cement ramp they built for him at the school. He wondered if it was still there. He remembered his father drinking himself to death, and how his mother had wept while she told him that it was all part of the plan.

"If you'd only waited a little, Pop," Lou said into his childhood bedroom. Of course, when one was in the service of the One Who Sees Far, 'ifs' and 'maybes' were vestigial luxuries.

He surveyed his room. It was almost precisely as it had been when Joseph had taken him to see the Man. The posters still hung in well-placed thumbtacks. The dresser, bed, and nightstand were a little more scuffed, a little less shiny, but still, they remained. And they would remain after him as well. That was either a comfort or a torment. He wasn't sure.

Reconciled to his uncertainty, Lou turned to go. But before he could switch the light, a thought occurred to him. He patted his shirt pocket, then his pants pockets. He heard a crinkle. He fished out a foil-wrapped packet and held it up. The picture on the front of the thin little rectangle was of a woman playing soccer—arms out, left leg extended, right knee bent just behind the ball. It looked like it was going to be one hell of a kick.

He tore the pack open and lamented the lack of bubble gum. He'd always loved the gum from baseball card packs. It had always pleased him how the dry stick crunched and crunched until, against the odds, it became soft and chewy. He wondered if any cards still had the gum or if that was something lost to time.

He dropped the foil wrapper onto the dresser and sifted through the slick, high-resolution images of the women. He was half-tempted to just pick the prettiest one, but, as Joseph would say, 'them's ain't the rules.' He could hear his oldest friend's voice in his head, and he laughed.

Instead, he flipped each card over and looked at the stats. He picked the second-best player, weighting her card just a bit more because she was stunning and her name was perfect. It was as if the pack had been picked for just this reason. He held her card up to the light, studied the woman, flipped the card over, studied her stats again, and then put it down next to the wrapper. He took the best player and also put her aside. He slid the rest back into the wrapper and dropped them into the wastepaper basket next to the door. He took the gorgeous redhead, who he knew could have run circles around him even if he'd never been injured, and swung two steps across the room to his nightstand. He dropped a crutch onto the bed and knelt as he kicked his braced leg out to one side. His fingers slid along the baseboard, plowing dust until he found the little divot. Then he slid his pinky in and pulled. Six inches of cleanly cut baseboard fell forward and revealed a hole in the old plaster wall.

A grin pulled one of Lou's cheeks as he slid the paper bag from the hole. The rectangle of cards within had grown only a little over the four years they had played the most. Decorum, the rules of the game, and the limitations of the hiding place all had demanded that the stack remain manageable. That meant Lou had had to make some tough calls and cut some great players. Even so, as he unwrapped the three layers of lunch bags that had accumulated over time, he knew he'd still find Richie Ashburn and Hank Aaron. The first card that met him sent a thrill of memory through him. Roberto Clemente looked off to the right from under his Pirates hat, as if watching a batter from the outfield. His corners were a little dinged, as were Mickey Mantle's and Roger Craig's. The Clemente had been Joseph's, but Lou had won it. Of course, he had lost his Willie Mays, but 'them's were the breaks.' There were a few other cards from the late '80s slipped in there, but they'd never played for those. He didn't think they'd play for Ronda Lee, either, but he liked the idea of Joseph finding her sitting on top of the stack. He put Miss Lee down on top of Clemente, paused, and then fanned the cards out. He found the one he was looking for, a little-known player who had one season in '58. Joseph had never been willing to put anyone up against him, so Lou had kept him flip after flip, game after game.

He turned the forgotten ballplayer's card over and saw his long-ago memorized and unimpressive stats. Then, for the sake of a game he'd never play again, he put Herbert "Herbie" Moat's card into his shirt pocket. Then he reassembled the deck, keeping the woman on top and wondering if Joseph would ever see her. And, if he did see her, if he'd get the point. Then he bid goodbye to the red-headed Chloe Fuller and rewrapped the old brown paper bags. The deck went back into the hole, and the board went back over it all.

Aching, he pushed himself back up with one hand on the nightstand. Then he grabbed the best player, slipped her into his pocket with old Herbie, hefted his bag, and left his childhood bedroom.

7

CHLOE STOOD IN THE kitchen in a slanted pair of underpants and a bunched-up tank top. She turned at the sound of Lou's crutches on the hallway floor.

"Shit," she said, half-heartedly crossing an arm over her stomach and pushing a lop-sided grin his way.

"Believe me," Lou said, "the bathing suit you wore yesterday showed off more than that. Besides, I've never been easily embarrassed."

"Good, me either," she said, returning to the coffee machine.

"That will come in handy," he said.

"The coffee machine?" she asked, looking over her shoulder.

"Yeah, the coffee machine," he said. "Put some shorts on and ride with me down to *Barry's*. I'll buy you coffee, and you keep me company one more time before I go."

"I ... um," she said, looking down the hallway. "Can you get me two coffees?"

Lou shook his head and looked back over his shoulder.

Click.

He glanced back and sniffed. "What's his name?"

She gave him a simian smile full of teeth and defensiveness.

"Her name?"

"No comment," she said. "Let me grab my shorts. Unless you think we could get free coffee like this," she said, walking backward.

"You might be a little young for Barry."

"You have no confidence in me," Chloe said, disappearing into the back of the ranch-style house.

"Not even the slightest bit true," Lou said. He took the card from his pocket and looked at the soccer player. He put her on the counter next to

Chloe's coffee mug that read 'Lightning Falls Public Library.'

"Okay," Chloe said from behind him. Her flip-flops slapped the wooden floor as she zipped and buttoned her shorts. She sported sunglasses with rectangular lenses and held her phone in one hand. He thought she looked like she was going to the beach. He wished she were.

She followed him to his van and held the door for him as he climbed inside. Then she jumped into the passenger seat and put her feet up on the dashboard. He didn't tell her not to. They rode through town and parked in front of *Barry's Coffee Shop*. A few people were talking enthusiastically at a heavy metal table, but otherwise, the morning rush looked like it was already over.

"So where are you heading?" Chloe said as she stood on the sun-baking sidewalk while Lou came around the front of the old red van. "Down 'arain way?" she said in a faux-southern drawl.

He chuckled and nodded. "Yes, for a little while at least. I can't always take it down there. It's a lot."

"You going to take me there soon?"

"I suppose I will," he said. "Every time I see you, the more certain I am of it."

"Yeah, me too," she said. The easy-cocked smile faded. "It's weird."

"Yes, and I promise you, it gets weirder," he said.

Click.

He peered back over his shoulder and saw a woman and a girl, perhaps ten years old, walking into the bookstore across the cross street.

"Well, that at least sounds interesting," Chloe said.

"'Interesting' is a word for it," Lou said as he watched the door close behind the pair.

8

SHE KISSED HIM ON the cheek and told him she'd see him again in a few months. He watched her go, a cardboard cup-carrier in hand with drinks for her and whatever young woman lay in her bed. He had a strange desire to follow her in, to sit with her in her room while she did whatever it was that two young women did. There was nothing prurient in the desire, only a longing to be part of some kind of warmth, some kind of normalcy.

Click.

He looked over his shoulder into the empty van and saw the seat by the sliding door. Then he heard the front door slam. He took another look at his childhood home with its well-maintained hedges and well-mown lawn, and thought Ellen and Joel had done a good job with the place. Then he put the van in gear and drove south, toward the edge of town. Once he was out on Route 3, he rubbed one eye and then the other.

Click.

He looked over his shoulder again. He could see her sitting there with her blonde hair around her shoulders, just like Princess Emerald. Joseph had turned in his seat, too. The girl hadn't stopped talking since they had picked her up.

"Yes," Joseph had said, "you're going to have an incredibly important part."

Click.

"Will the camera see my face? Like, if it doesn't, how will I be able to tell people that it's me? No one will believe me."

"I'm not sure if the camera will be able to see your face," Joseph said, "but you'll be in the credits at the end. Princess Emerald's body double, as played by Rebecca Moyer."

Click.

"So, my name will be there?"

"Oh yes, your name will be there. Everyone will know your name. Not everyone gets to stand in for such a big star. It's the sort of thing that makes you a star, too," Joseph said.

Click.

"If you stand in for someone, can you say that you played the same part? I mean, like, will I be able to say that I was Princess Emerald?"

"Oh yes," Joseph said, nodding and turning back to look out the windshield at the highway. A sign read 'Welcome to Missouri.'

"I'm really going to be Princess Emerald." This wasn't a question. Instead, it was said with wonder as she looked out the window and pushed her tongue up against the roof of her mouth and clicked the pink retainer down, away from her teeth. Her mouth was open as she watched the trees zip past, and morning light reflected off the saliva-bright pink PVC. Then, with a loud click, she pushed it back into place.

"Will I get to meet Emily?" Rebecca Moyer asked.

"We'll see what we can do," Joseph said. "But I have a pretty good feeling about it."

Lou checked his rearview as he turned into Enterprise. The seat was empty, and his hip ached. He patted his pocket and felt old Herbie Moat against his chest. Then he wiped his cheeks and hoped for the 10,000th time that it had all been worth it.

1

Monday, July 3, 2023

"QUAINT," MARI SAID, SLIDING her sunglasses down her nose like an 1980s movie star. She half meant it and half wanted it to sound snooty. Shale Pond's downtown was, in fact, quaint. Not only did colorful, little independent shops line the street, which rose to the front gate of Ikandaset College and its tree-scattered collegiate gothic buildings, but every lamppost was also decked out in red, white, and blue banners and streamers to celebrate the nation's birthday. It moved her and made her long for happier days.

But that longing only served to pluck the strings of her disgust for the man climbing out of their crossover SUV. She turned to him and said, "So, where do we eat? The burger joint? The Thai place? Some quirky hippy place where everything smells like weed?"

Dan grimaced and shook his head. "I think you might be in the wrong decade for hippies," he said. He sniffed. "But not for weed. I don't know, what are you feeling?"

"Burgers then," she said. A long-ago barbecue flashed in her mind's eye. "No, make that Thai."

"Thai it is," Dan said. They walked uphill and stopped under the shade of a sign that read, 'Thai Café.' Dan held the door for an older couple, and, thankfully, Mari's old view of him suddenly returned. It was the incongruity that did it, the inconsistency of a man who had murdered his own daughter holding a door open as if he were a good person. She wondered how the old man and woman would feel if they knew their door was being held by a child killer. Sometimes the façade drove her to the brink of madness, but today she was grateful for it. It put her in exactly the right mindset to slap him back into place.

Mari exchanged a pleasant smile with the older woman before stepping into the air-conditioned restaurant. She picked a table by the window and ordered the Pad Thai. She didn't notice what Dan ordered.

When the food came, she ate in silence until he interrupted her contemplation of a candle shop across the street. "So, where are we going first?"

Distracted by imagined scents of vanilla, pine, and cotton, she almost told him. But then she remembered her anger. "Why do you need to know that?" she asked.

"Maybe you get overwhelmed by the fumes," he said, trying to make a joke.

"There's a spot on Bank Street, that's where people have had the most luck."

"Not by the tree?" Dan asked, lifting a forkful of noodles to his mouth.

"That's our second stop, if Bank Street doesn't work. But I think Bank Street will work."

"She's probably starving," he said.

"No, I think she's probably fuller than she's been in a long time. Do you know how many people come up here now? It's a fucking circus. You know Centralia?"

"The place in PA? With the coal fire?"

"That's right. Do you know what's there? Do you know what people visit there?"

"Burned-out houses? Pits of sulfur?" he ventured.

"Nothing. There's nothing there. There used to be a graffiti highway, but it's gone. They covered it with sand, from what I heard. There's literally nothing to see. But you know what is an abandoned ghost-town with a podcast and pillars of smoke from underground fires?" She didn't have to answer it for him. He nodded like a beaten dog and stared at his lunch. "So, we aren't going to be able to do the ritual until after dark. Even then … we might have to wait for a long time until we're alone."

"Whatever shall we do in the meantime?" Dan asked, waggling his eyebrows. She hated that he still tried to make her laugh. She hated herself for giving in over the last few months. Those were the days when everything felt sickeningly like normal, when Alex and Dan would talk excitedly about some TV show they were watching on Netflix, or a documentary they both found fascinating. She would see them laughing, or arguing amicably, and for a moment, it would be like Emily had never been taken. Or, which might be worse, as if Mari were healing from the loss of her daughter.

I lost more than just my daughter, she thought.

Fortunately, her morning anger warm-up was doing its job. She silently mouthed, 'Fuck you.' The smile left Dan's face. He nodded and stared at his noodles. She thought he might start crying. She actually didn't mind that idea. Let him cry in a public place. Let every adult and child see this fifty-three-year-old man cry into his lunch.

She shoved a shrimp into her mouth and chewed as he disappointed her by wiping his eyes and continuing with his lunch without tears.

2

THE SMOKE FROM WEEPING Cedars hit them while they were still a mile out. The air became hazy a quarter mile away, and downright foggy as they approached the Johannsen's Mile Road Bridge. A concrete barrier blocked the bridge, and a sign proclaimed 'NO TRESPASSING.' A dozen cars were parked in a dirt patch beside the rusting metal span across the Ikandaset.

"You want to cross here, or down past the mills?" Dan asked.

"Bank Street is just on the other side, so this makes more sense." She pulled their crossover SUV into a space next to a huge pickup truck.

Dan threw a thumb toward the truck and said, "Compensating much?"

"You'd know," Mari said as she pulled on her hiking jacket. It was twenty degrees colder than in Shale Pond. She circled to the hatchback, opened it, and pulled out her pack. She checked her supplies, scanned all of their redundant boxes of flour, bottles of water, one extra iron grate, spare fire-starters, and backup food. Dan silently grabbed his backpack and slung it on. The closing trunk's sound was muted, as if the smoky fog ate half of it. A shiver ran up Mari's spine, and she shook her head at the place her husband's actions had driven her to.

On the bridge, she saw a dozen people walking, pointing, and spraying cans of paint onto the asphalt below their feet. She had been right, they would have to wait. But not for everything.

"Turn around," she said. He obliged. She unzipped a pocket on his pack and pulled out a small, crudely-worked stone carving of a child. She closed the pocket and weighed the figurine in her palm. Then she followed the sloping ground down thirty feet to the bank of the Ikandaset, where she knelt. She scanned up and down the water for as far as the haze would allow, which wasn't far at all. Above her, she could see the shadowy outline of the near side of the bridge, and perhaps a hundred feet both upstream and down. Then, heart racing, she dipped the figure into the water.

"Accept our offering, child of the great Leviathan, son of ancient waters. Accept this icon of one given to sate your hunger."

The stone grew hot in her hand. She hadn't expected that. As the heat increased, she wondered if she could hold on or if she would fail this ritual and they would have to contend with the beast.

"Shit," Dan said from behind her. Mari looked up and felt her body freeze and burn in one convulsing spasm of terror. Across the river, on the far bank, stood the dripping, bloated, blotchy corpse of a boy. His mouth sagged, his eyes ran with black water, and his fingers curled and uncurled.

Hungry.

The word slithered into her mind like oil through a crack.

Hungry.

She wanted to speak. She wanted to form the words she had memorized, but they wouldn't come.

Hungry.

"Then accept this offering," she finally managed. "Accept this into your fathomless depths for your ancient hunger."

The burning figure in her hand grew hotter, and for a moment, she thought that it was searing her flesh from her bones. But then her mind caught up with the sensation, and she realized it was no longer hot, but freezing. She drew the stone back and cupped her soaking, frost-covered fingers in her other hand.

"Fuck," Dan said.

She agreed. Fuck.

Standing next to the bloated corpse was a boy she recognized. His name had been Dwight. She had watched Dwight die in a hospital room, with tubes in his arms feeding him death instead of life. She had watched as they had placed the stone figure on his chest and put their hands on him. She had even added her hand when commanded to. She thought his death had been an easy one—final sleep after so much wasting pain. But now, as she watched the corpse-boy morph into the hulking, red-brown mass, its bone-white carapace emerging from its back, she knew she had deluded herself. An appendage, like a single, slick, club-ended tentacle, extended from the beast's body, and from it grew a wicked and broken claw of rust-stained bone. The claw reached out and dug itself into the muddy earth, dragging the hulking form toward the water once, twice, and three times. When it was mostly submerged, it turned, and the claw reached back to sink into the boy's chest. Dry heaving, Mari forced herself to watch as it pulled the boy under in a roiling riot of splashing as the … was it his ghost? His spirit? She didn't know. But she watched as whatever was left of him was dragged under, and the surface of the water once more ran still and smooth.

She tried to sound glib, but her words failed. She tried to make any sound, but it took her three long minutes of watching before she could speak.

"He won't bother us now," she finally said.

"God," Dan said. "God, what did you do?"

"What I had to. Come on, and be careful. There are other things that lurk here besides him and her."

"What about the people on the bridge?" Dan asked, pointing up to the silhouette that stretched across the river.

"Even if they were looking over the railing, they'd just see us," she said. "I think."

"You *think*?" Dan asked.

"You don't hear any screaming, do you?"

Dan opened his mouth, looked up toward the bridge, and nodded. "Fair enough."

3

THE WALK ACROSS THE bridge was more precarious than she had expected. They had to be careful of gouges in the asphalt, their resulting rubble, and people who didn't seem to pay attention to either. She had seen the pictures of the graffiti road in Centralia before they covered it, and she'd seen the more recent path beside Ontelaunee Lake, every inch covered with spraypainted faces, cartoon characters, professions of love, and, of course, dicks. Dicks everywhere. A complication and congregation of phalluses of all shapes and sizes put forth in spray paint.

The road beneath her feet looked the same, except that scattered among the faces of cartoon characters, professions of love, and the swarm of free-floating penis were phrases and symbols she didn't think she'd see in other, similar tracks of disused road. 'He is Hungry' appeared more than once. 'Beware the Shephard' and 'The Witch is Watching' were both scattered. She saw two sets of yellow eyes, four sets of three green linked half circles, which she didn't understand, and circles. The circles dominated almost as much as the dicks did. However, Mari noted, circles would often be painted in one color, but another dot would appear in the middle in a different color of paint. She pictured one person spraying a sign from a podcast and a second, unable to resist transforming it into a single comical breast.

It was base and common, and Mari hated it all.

Dan said 'hello' to people as they passed, and Mari nodded to one woman and gave a half-hearted smile to a young girl who was making a blue and yellow flower. Toward the end of the bridge stood a cluster of people working diligently with cans of paint while a middle-aged woman held a notebook and appeared to oversee their work. They didn't look like everyone else, pointing, laughing, and idly adding to the great artistic confusion. They looked organized.

As they got closer, Mari saw that the last fifteen feet of Johanneson's Mile Road Bridge was blocked off with a one-foot-thick line of paint that she thought had begun its life as a solid red bar. But over time, more cans had been emptied to reinforce the boundary between the seething mass of half-assed cartoon expression and this last stretch of road.

In the center of the area was a four-foot-wide flower that Mari couldn't identify. It may originally have been a rose, but over time, people had embellished it and changed it, adding purples, pinks, greens, and yellows. Currently, a red-haired girl was adding pink highlights to one of the petals.

Some people had tried to invade this cordoned-off space with crude drawings, but those were almost entirely covered by the brick pattern of solid rectangular blocks of color that hid the asphalt. In most of the blocks were names. It seemed that if one person marred the blocks, another person would come along and paint over it, leaving fresh blocks open for the names that adorned every step in the path. This, Mari saw, was what the small cluster of people was up to. Someone had painted America's favorite doodle across five of the painted rectangles, and the people were fixing them. The woman who looked like she was leading the group held her notebook at her side, and Mari could see a grid sketched with names and colors written in.

"They're putting them back," Dan said. There was a stupid tone to his voice, as if he were in awe. Mari wondered how he managed such incredible hypocrisy. She turned her attention to the names before her, skimming over them. She saw names like Jannette Kelpman, Kay Millport, Heloise Jones, Emma Barnes, Kathryn Goodman, and dozens more, all under the banner 'To the Women Killed by Weeping Cedars.' Every block was filled. There must have been a hundred or more. Mari's stomach turned. She wondered where the monument to her daughter was. Then her eyes flitted to a final banner that crossed the road, sectioned off beyond the dedication to the dead women. It had only five words.

IN MEMORY OF RILEY HOWARD

Disgusted by the melodrama, she spat and noticed that her spit landed on the name Anna Haller. Then she wondered if Dan would burst into flames when he walked over the names. Would their dead hands reach up from the pavement and drag him down into hell? God, if only they would. She turned and felt the disgust in her stomach turn to disbelief. There he was, kneeling at the edge of the block of women's names. Was he crying? Was he really fucking crying? Did he think that made him good? Did he think his grief made him a better man? Did it fix anything?

"Come on," she said, and saw two young women from the group squint at her as if she were some kind of monster. Their eyes flicked between the weeping man and the angry woman, and Mari wanted to slap them and tell them who they were looking at. Instead, she just repeated her command.

As Dan wiped his eyes, the first raindrop fell and hit Mari's ear. Then another. The man she had married in ignorant hope stood and brushed off his knees. Then he resettled his pack on his shoulders and followed after. No hands emerged to grasp him, no fingers clutched at the cuffs of his jeans. He simply walked over the names of dead women, and she felt her hatred for him grow. She had learned to stop being surprised at hatred's ability to expand beyond what she thought was the limit for a human heart. Over the years, she had gotten used to its ever-widening proportions.

To her shock, she watched one of the young women brush her knees off and jog up to him. She spoke in a voice too low for Mari to hear, and then she hugged him. Dan, his face twisted in an ugly contortion of unearned grief, hugged the woman back. Mari wondered what kind of sick pleasure he was getting from the encounter. Then the young woman released him, said something more, and let him go. He nodded, wiped his eyes again, and walked toward Mari with his head hung. The young woman pulled her curly brown hair back in her fist, watched him go, and Mari wanted to throw up.

The road was clear of paint after the strangely annoying dedication. Why, with so many names listed, was someone named 'Riley Howard 'singled out in particular? A memory tickled the back of her mind— something she had heard when they had visited the mansion. But before the memory could resolve itself, the final line of warnings emerged from the fog. They were only thirty feet away when concrete barriers appeared, and Mari realized that the visibility was getting worse.

Six official signs stood in front of the barriers, and one unofficial message summed them up. One warned of fire, another of smoke, another of falling debris, another of harmful chemicals, and another of wild animals. The last chilled her in a way the others didn't.

WARNING

Due to environmental conditions, rescue services cannot help beyond this point. Enter at your own risk.

The unofficial message, a last representative of the spray-painted messages, symbols, and marks, was scrawled across the concrete barriers in bright red.

Lasciate Ogni Speranza

"Isn't there supposed to be more to that?" Dan said.

"Maybe not," Mari said. "Come on, and let's stay close. We don't have to go far in, but I imagine it's easy to get lost here."

Dan stayed close behind her. He knew better than to stay in her line of sight. She was happy that it had only taken a couple of hours to undo all the harm she had done by letting him get close over the last few months.

She turned right onto Bank Street and disliked how close the river sounded. The icon had done its work, but that didn't make her feel safe. She took her flashlight out and switched it on. Dan copied her. Their powerful beams sliced through the haze, and Mari noted the houses looming to their left. From what she had seen on Google Maps, four large, well-kept homes had overlooked the water here. Now their gray, haunted corpses glowered at her from under coats of ash.

"Up here, at the intersection," she said. "Her cave is supposed to be around here."

"Doesn't it move?" Dan's voice was muffled. Mari turned to see that he was wearing a surgical mask. She guessed that he didn't want to get a lungful of all the asbestos that was definitely falling around them, spread by the flames and fumes of the town beneath their feet. Begrudgingly, she admitted that it was a pretty good idea and pulled on her own mask.

"Yes, but the place it's rooted is across the river here. This is where the men—"

A long and forlorn wailing broke the heavy silence. Her pulse leapt as if someone had poured freezing water on her, and she suddenly realized how oblivious she had been to the near absolute silence that had engulfed them since they crossed the bridge. Besides the wailing, the only sound was the river. The howls persisted and then tapered off before failing entirely. Then they came again, like the cry of a wolf pack. They were getting closer. Mari's hand instinctively shot out to grab Dan's arm.

She almost lost her nerve, but then, with whiplash speed, her fear turned to anger. The howls degenerated into laughter and the voices of a crowd of people. They sounded like teenagers as they chortled and guffawed.

"Fucking kids," she said.

"They're brave," Dan said.

"They're stupid," Mari said. "Anyone who comes here without a good reason is asking for it."

"Wow, victim blaming," Dan said.

"Fuck you," Mari said. "Come on, just up there."

"So, we might have to stay in this for hours?" Dan asked. "Why not just do this like the other ritual?"

"Because not everything is the same," Mari said. Silently, however, she admitted that staying seemed like a more daunting prospect than she had expected. Her eyes already stung, and her skin tingled. "We need to make sure no one else is here," Mari said. "My guess is those kids will leave before too long. I doubt anyone sticks around here or the bridge after dark."

"Yeah, I can see why," Dan said.

Mari agreed but scowled at him anyway. She imagined that if any of those howling teenagers had seen what she'd seen, they would die of fright. If they had beheld the great forest of ecstatic suppliants, or the Light Glorious radiating from the House of Glass, or even beheld the hunched, glowering city that—

"Dan," Mari said, freezing mid-step. She shouldn't have thought about the city. She shouldn't have thought about the city. She … should … not … have … thought … about … the … city.

"Fuuuuuckkk," Dan said, drawing the word out in a croaking whisper.

Above them, through the smoke and ash, towered the great wall of Fesoro, once the jewel of the North. Which North? Mari didn't know, but thought it must be the north of some world beyond the boundaries of any scientist's conception. Upon its hazy ramparts stood tall poles with banners unfurled, though they did not wave in the breeze. Instead, unmoving, they jutted out, as if carved from stone. And, even less distinct, behind them rose the impressions of peaked roofs and crenelated towers.

"Don't look," Dan said. But neither of them listened. They stared and trembled.

Mari was worried her bowels would let go, that she would piss herself, and that she would throw up all at the same time. She wanted to die. She wanted to crumble into the same ash that fell around her. "God," she whispered. "God, help us."

Dan grabbed her arm and pulled. She stumbled a half-step toward him. He pulled again as a red light, dull and rusty, bloomed somewhere up among the towers.

"Come on!" Dan said, pulling her again. Then his hand was around hers, and he was leading her away from the river and along a path of flagstones. They went up a set of porch stairs and through the front door of one of the houses. She followed him in and slammed the door shut behind her.

"Fuck me," Dan said. "Oh, fuck me."

For a moment, and not for the first time, Mari sympathized with her husband. The idea of sending Emily to that place, even protected within the Light Glorious, was … well, it was almost too much to bear. She had been strong enough to endure it, but in the sight of that place, she could understand why he hadn't been. But her sympathy lasted only the space of a few heartbeats. Then the hatred and disgust pushed their way easily back into her chest.

"It's clearer in here," Dan said, waving his flashlight around. He was right. The air was hazy, but not nearly as thick as outside. "So, what do we do?"

"We wait until an hour has passed. If we don't hear anything by then, we can guess that we're probably alone."

"But what if someone else shows up?"

"It's already, what, three in the afternoon? The later the day gets, the less likely anyone is to come here. People say they're brave, but no one wants to be in Weeping Cedars after dark, even if it is just to avoid bears, asbestos, and smoke inhalation where no firefighter or EMT will go."

"And the City?"

"It comes and goes; hopefully it will go by then," she said, not feeling hopeful at all.

Dan nodded. "You think you could kill someone here and get away with it?"

"Were you just reading my mind?" she said.

"Yeah, probably. Lucky for me, you need me for the ritual."

"For the ritual, not after it," she said matter-of-factly.

"Jeez, okay, I'll keep that in mind."

"I'm pretty sure that if I showed up here with you and left without you, they'd still come looking for your body even here. There was that guy who killed his girlfriend here last year, and they found her easily enough."

"Phew," Dan said. "Guess you'll have to find another place to do me in."

"I guess I will," Mari said.

4

THEY SEARCHED THE HOUSE and found that, while most of the furniture had either been evacuated or looted, there remained a scattering of broken parts that used to be a nightstand, a spindly-legged table, and some shelving. The back door, heavy and wooden, was still locked. When they undid the bolt and turned the creaking knob, a large, sloping yard greeted them. At a distance, they saw the sketch of a dark shape in the fog that might have been a small guest house or cabin.

"Who do you think lived here?" Dan asked once they closed the door and dropped their packs on the rough-cut limestone kitchen floor. Dan pushed himself up onto a slate countertop.

"Rich people," Mari said with disdain.

"We're rich people," Dan said.

"Not like this." She took hold of the handle of a complicated-looking oven mounted in a section of a wall made of red brick. When she pulled, a still-gleaming stainless-steel interior reflected their flashlights as if it had been cleaned the day before. She closed it and opened a lower door, revealing a stone-bottomed pizza oven.

"Shit, we should get one of those," Dan said.

"Please stop trying to make small talk," Mari said.

"Why?"

"Because I want our last real conversation to have already happened."

"That's going to be hard, given our circumstances," he said.

"It would be if our circumstances were going to stay the same," Mari said, closing the pizza oven. She ran a finger over the counter and found only a little evidence of the calamity surrounding the house. She wondered if the people who owned this building had invested in windows that the common explorer found hard to break. She couldn't imagine that normal people, given the opportunity to wreck a rich person's home with impunity, would all resist the urge. And yet, the house could easily have been livable after a light cleaning. She imagined that most of the buildings in Weeping Cedars weren't in nearly as good a condition.

"What do you mean?" Dan asked.

"I mean that once this mission is done, and we deliver our findings, I want to be free of you." She didn't want to see the look on his face, so she started opening cabinets. The first was empty, the second held a set of glass tumblers.

"I see," Dan said. "So you want me to move out?"

"You won't have to," she said. "Once this is done, and I ask them to, they'll handle everything."

"What does that mean?"

This time, she did want to see the look on his face.

"They will *handle* everything," she repeated slowly. "I'm not sure if they'll send you to the Port, or if they'll pose you like one of their little art displays, or if they'll have you convicted and turned into some big man's meat sock, or maybe it will be just good, old-fashioned murder, but they *will* take care of it."

She had practiced that line for years and was particularly proud of 'meat sock.'

Dan nodded slowly. "What about Alex?"

"What about Alex? She's an adult now. She's got a bunch of money, she can do whatever the fuck she wants."

"But who will look after her?"

"She's an adult, Dan. She doesn't need looking after," Mari scoffed. "Just like a fucking man to—"

"Mari … this world, this whole world that we're part of … everyone needs looking after. She will need help."

"Well, maybe you'll get lucky and they'll just stick you in the Port. Then you and your creepy fucking pal can send her messages full of your infinite wisdom."

"Conroy isn't my pal," Dan said. "He's … a monster."

"So are you!" she screamed, slammed a cabinet door, and yanked it back open again. "So!" *Slam!* "Are!" *Slam!* "You!" *Slam!*

Dan didn't move. "I know. I agree. But that doesn't change the fact that Alex will need help."

"God, maybe that's what I'll have them do, since you love her so much."

"What?" Mari noted the change in his voice. He had been calm up to that point, but now something dangerous had crept into his tone.

"Nothing," she said.

He slid from the counter, his hiking boots making a soft thud on the stone floor. "Don't think for a second that I give a shit what happens to me if it means protecting her."

"Oh, now you're a concerned father?"

"I was always a concerned fucking father!" Dan yelled. She hadn't heard him yell in more than a decade. It scared her. "I did what I did to protect Emily from your Queen."

"My Queen? You're as much in this as I am, or are you delusional?"

"No, you're right, I'm just as much a part of it, I'm just as guilty. But it's in your fucking blood. I'm just the bystander who raised your little vessel because the man who actually fathered her couldn't be seen to have a child out of wedlock, and certainly not one who would become Princess Emerald."

Mari stared, trying to process. Despite her hatred of the man, she had never crossed that particular line. And, even if she had been tempted to, she had been forbidden. Perhaps they wanted to save the revelation for his last moments, as something for him to contemplate as they took his life or sent the conductor to bring him to that little hell they built in a dead girl's mind.

"How … how did …"

"God, you really are oblivious, aren't you? Wes knew! And we wrote to each other, Mari! We wrote to each other until they executed him. He thought I should know. And, you know what? When I found out, it didn't really matter. It didn't. Because it didn't change who I was to her. She was a part of all of us. We all gave ourselves to her. Wes, Chuck, all of us pitched in, but me most of all. So she was as much my daughter as if she had my DNA."

She wanted to find the triumph in the moment, to twist the knife, but before she could speak, he did it for her.

"Don't you think I know what a piece of shit I am? Two daughters, neither one of them mine, neither one of them knowing what I faced day in and day out to keep them safe. And my hands, my brain, my fucking …" Here he beat his chest three times, six times, a dozen, with no sound but a thin, aching whine from his gaping mouth. "I did it," he said, finally. "I put her in their hands. Every day, I want to die. Every day, I want to put a bullet in me. So good, let them cut me up, or pose me, or frame me. Fuck, I'll take it and know I deserve every minute of whatever torture they hand me. You want them to put me in the Port? I'll go willingly, but I swear to the God that can't possibly exist in this fucked up world, that I will put you in the fucking ground first if I think you'll hurt Alex to hurt me. I will bash your fucking head in one of these cabinets. You will not fucking touch her, you will remember that she's your fucking daughter too!"

He advanced on her, and she raised her hands to stop him, but he was on her, his fingers around her throat. She battered at his arms. He wasn't a huge man, but he kept in shape, and everything she had learned in that stupid self-defense class just drained away as his thumbs went over her windpipe.

"I will turn you into fucking paste right here and right now unless you swear, and make me fucking believe it, you swear to me that you won't hurt her."

Mari battered his arms, reached for his eyes, and kicked at his groin, but nothing worked. He just scrunched one eye shut against her attack and squeezed his hands. Her mouth worked like a fish; she could feel her eyes bulging.

"Please," she managed. "Please."

He dropped her onto the kitchen floor, where she curled into a ball and put her hands to her throat. Before she could regain herself, she felt his boot pressing on the back of her skull, pushing her down onto the floor.

"Swear," he said. "Swear neither you nor anyone else at CM will hurt her."

"Dan," she croaked. "Stop."

"No, not until you swear. If I have to, I'll break your neck and then just walk out into the water and let that fucking thing eat me. Swear it and mean it, or you die here and now. I'm human garbage, but I will be God damned if I let you hurt my girl."

"I swear," she rasped. "I swear, no one will hurt Alex." The weight from his boot disappeared, and she curled herself more tightly, shielding her head with her arms for fear that he would come again. But he didn't. She lay, gasping until her breathing returned to a ragged approximation of normal. Then, after she gathered herself, Mari pushed herself up so that she sat with her back against the brick wall. She glanced up and saw him once more on the counter, his head hung, his knuckles white on the edge of the slate countertop.

"You're going to fucking suffer," she said.

"Good," he said. Then he dropped from the counter, and she pulled her knees up against her chest. Her hand shot out toward her bag, where she kept her knife. "I'm going to go lie down in one of the rooms up there. You can come up to kill me or get me when you're ready. I guess you could leave me there, too. But then you won't have your little ritual."

"Fuck you," Mari rasped, rubbing her throat. She pulled her pack close, drew her knife, and lay the pack down to be her pillow. Then, on the cool floor, she lay, trying to think of anything other than what had just happened. She pictured Jacob in his office, a touch over fifty—God, the same age she was now—his hair mostly gray, his eyes kind but hungry, and his voice low and soft. He, too, had put his hand to her throat, but not in violence. He had lifted her chin with his thumb, and she could remember the warmth of his fingers at the base of her neck. Only one word escaped his lips before he kissed her.

5

THREE HOURS OF AUDIOBOOKS, mindless puzzle games, and restless napping later, Mari stood in the doorway of a room that might have once been an office. Dan had picked the smallest of the seven rooms on the second floor and was snoring softly in the corner, his back to the wall. He might talk a good game about not caring what happened to himself, but he sure didn't want her sneaking up behind to cut his throat. While that might have been gratifying, no one at Crystalline Mansion would be pleased. They needed them to do this work. And they needed her. Jacob had given her more than just his DNA her all those years ago. He had imbued her with power. Of course, she couldn't use any of it, but it was there, meant to help guide and protect Auntie's vessel. They still needed that power for the girl they were preparing now. Soon, they'd stage another farce, another pretend casting for the next Princess Emerald. Soon, they'd choose the girl they had been grooming for years. Soon. And they'd need Mari for that. Someone would have to step in to protect and guide the girl after her parents met an untimely end. And who would be more fitting than Emily Carmichael's mother?

So … no, it wouldn't do to get herself indicted for first-degree murder. They might be able to get her put into whatever form Glassman was taking these days. But what good would that do? She couldn't be there for Jessica like that.

"What are you doing?" Dan said. She hadn't noticed that his eyes had opened. "Plotting my death?"

"Kind of," Mari admitted.

"Thought you said they were going to take care of me."

"That was before you put your foot on my neck," she said.

"Well, you still need me today, right?"

Grudgingly, she nodded.

He sat up and stretched his neck. "Cool, then I'll consider that a stay of execution for a couple of hours."

"No, you'll leave Weeping Cedars," she said. Dan furrowed his brow, and he looked like he did when he was remembering something. "What?" she asked.

"Nothing. Just something someone said to me."

"Who?"

"An old friend. You don't know him. Doesn't matter. Are we doing this?"

"Yes," she said. "You need to do anything before we get started? Once we start, we can't stop."

"Yeah, let me use the men's room, and then I'll be ready to rock and roll."

"I'll be downstairs," she said.

Mari left him to gather her things. She descended the carpeted staircase, her hand sliding along the dark wood banister. She wondered again who had lived here and if they had any concept of the strange world in which they lived. Did they know about the beast that lurked in their river, or the mad demigod that commanded the mighty in this town? Or did they think they were just stories to spook the children?

Did they know about the other one?

Yes, she thought. She, at least, everyone here had known about. They could fit her into their American folklore without incongruity. Mari looked out the window and saw only darkness. The sun shouldn't have set by now, but night *had* fallen. She didn't know if that was merely a virtue of the heavy smoke or if the Dark City's shadow still brooded over them.

Dan's heavy footsteps clomped down the stairs, the beam from his flashlight wavering across the floor and wall. "Guess we're alone?" he said.

"Anyone who's still here is either lost, stupid, or impossibly brave."

"Which are we?" Dan asked.

Mari didn't answer. She pulled her mask up and opened the door.

She immediately regretted it. Her knees almost buckled as she watched the world change in front of her. The yard, road, bank, and river all remained, but they transformed as if infected by a spreading, black oil. The fog, on the other hand, thinned and became a rusty haze. The grass turned black and died. The tree in the yard jittered and twisted as its bark became shining facets of obsidian.

Mari almost turned back into the house, but Dan was right behind her, and she wouldn't let him see her panic. She forced herself down a polished jet path to the asphalt, which cracked and disgorged a wide cobblestone. She wheeled her light and watched it reflect off the solid ebony surface of the Ikandaset.

"What is this?" Dan asked.

"I don't know," Mari said, trying to sound unperturbed. She didn't think she was succeeding.

"We need to get this done and get the hell out of here," Dan whispered.

Mari nodded enthusiastically but found herself frozen in place.

"Okay, then let's get to it," Dan urged. He put his hand on her shoulder, and something in her snapped. All the hate, all the fear, all the desperation and betrayal shrank back, leaving only her bare, scarred, tortured will. She dropped to one knee and unslung her pack in one motion. Dan did the same. They both unzipped and opened their bags. Mari pulled out a metal frame, and Dan drew the barrel of a sawed-off shotgun.

"What the hell is that going to do?" she asked.

"Make me feel better," he said, propping the barrel on his foot. He drew the receiver, slid it against the barrel, and snapped it up. Then he pulled a box from his bag and put it on a cobblestone. He broke the breech and slid in two shells before snapping it shut again. "Don't watch me, do your job," Dan said.

Mari nodded and unfolded the grate's legs. She pulled out one of the fire-starter logs, lit it, and dropped the grate over it, wishing she had done it in the opposite order. A covered bowl came out next, and Dan handed her a bottle of water.

"Wood? We forgot to get more wood," she said.

"No, we thought there would still be wood when we got out here," he said. "Not glass trees. Give me a minute. Do you need me for this part?"

"No, I … there just needs to be two of us here. You don't actually have to do anything."

"What?" Dan asked.

"There's no part for you to play," she hissed. "It just needs to be both of us for this to work."

"Why?" Dan asked. "I thought women did this kind of thing alone all the time."

"All the time?" she said. "No. I mean, yes, they did, but not this. This is something different. Go, we need wood."

"Shit," Dan said. Then he was up, his light spinning in a circle around them. He set off running toward the house. Terrified, she wanted to scream after him, to call him back, to tell him that they could do with just the fire starter, but she knew that was a lie. Instead, she took the lid off the bowl, removed the plastic bag within, opened it, and dumped half of its contents back into the bowl. A cloud of white puffed as she poured. Then she sealed the bag and put it carefully on the bowl's lid. If this failed, they had a second shot. That was, if they weren't either eaten, torn to pieces, or dragged away by whatever lived here.

Thunder roared from inside the house. Then it bellowed again. She didn't dare look away from her work. With shaking hands, she tried to unscrew the cap from the bottle of water, but her fingers were weak with terror. She pressed her palm down, and for a moment, as the dark around her rose and fell as if it were breathing, she remembered the last time she had been in such a place. But then, Wes had been by her side, and she had been oblivious to the monstrous nature of the world.

Another roar rumbled from the house. Some part of her, a part she wouldn't dare admit existed, felt relief that whatever was happening to Dan, he was still alive, at least for the moment. She told herself that if she was relieved, it was because she didn't want to be here alone, stuck without—

"Hello? Hello? Please, is someone there?"

It was a man's voice, but not Dan's. It wasn't as deep, and the person sounded so scared that they were on the edge of madness. Mari looked up and saw a man in a white T-shirt and torn jeans standing a hundred feet down the road, toward the bridge. Mari didn't know what to do or how to react. The bottlecap, pushed beyond its limit, finally twisted free, and she splashed water on herself.

"Shit," she said, looking down to see how much water she'd lost. Good, not much. She looked back up, and the man was gone. Hands shaking badly, she poured a half cup into the bowl and started kneading the flour and water together. Another roar. Another call from her right. She looked, and the man was back, but he wasn't looking in her direction. He was calling out into the darkness. Mari ignored him. She mixed and poured until the flour stuck together and formed a ball. She turned the ball, trying to gather all the flour from the sides of the bowl. This didn't have to be a perfect flatbread, but she didn't want to be cavalier about it.

Thunder.

She felt her chest shaking, and Mari realized she was crying. Her breath came in shallow, staccato sniffs. The dough stuck to her fingers, and she pushed the excess back into the ball. It was too sticky; she wouldn't be able to spread it out on the grate. Did she have to? Yes, she thought she might have to. She poured more flour onto the ball and worked it in. Yes, that was good, that was—

Footsteps thudded to her left, then Dan was there, and a clatter of wood fell on the cobblestone street. She dropped the bowl, and, with doughy hands, jammed the splintered remains of abandoned furniture under the grate in a rough crisscross pyramid. It took a moment, but the wood caught. Mari stretched the dough ball into a rough circle and dropped it onto the grate.

Dan reloaded as she searched her mind for the words. She found them as his shotgun closed.

"Come to those who call you. Come to those who beg. Come to those who call you. Come to those who beg," Mari whispered shudderingly as she covered her eyes with the palms of her hands and rocked slowly back and forth the way she had been shown.

"I wouldn't eat that, all that wood has varnish of some kind on it," Dan said as he eased himself down next to her. There was something wrong with his voice. Mari repeated the words twice more. When she had finished, she took her hands from her eyes, turned, and gasped. A dark hole opened on Dan's left shoulder, and his light blue shirt was stained black across his chest and down his left arm.

"Oh my God, what did you—"

"I don't think your little dolly worked," he said. "Or maybe it only works for you. Maybe you knew that?"

"No," Mari said, instinctively reaching out toward the wound. "No, I swear it, I was told it would work for both of us."

"Well, no big deal. You'll get your wish soon. I don't think this stuff is any good for me." He rubbed the black liquid between two fingers.

"No, we're going to do this, and then we're going to get out of here, I promise. I'm not going to let one of those things get you."

"Oh, I figure one of those things was always going to get me. This one here, Conroy, some other damned drowned thing. You called him a child of Leviathan. Is that a thing? Like, the big snake?"

"Just a name for something unknowable," Mari said.

"Does he slither around the Dark City then? Their own pet Jörmungandr?"

"No," she said, "not that I know of."

"Well, either way, I think he's got it out for me. I think he got me."

"Maybe you're right, maybe you pissed off ancient chaos; if anyone could do it, it's you," Mari said. She took the water bottle and poured it over his shoulder. "But, again, it's not going to do me any good if you die here and I can't explain it to the police."

"Sorry to inconvenience you," Dan said. "Tell me, what the hell are you trying—"

He froze, and his eyes grew comically large. Mari stared at his face as it tilted up to look at something tall and terrible behind her. She almost turned, but her fear was too overwhelming. She was about to scream when something long, thin, and wet snaked up her leg and across her back. Dan's eyes flicked down to her, and he shook his head in one subtle movement. Then his lips moved, but no sound came out.

Still, she could read the words.

'I'm sorry.'

The wet thing rolled over her shoulder and around her throat, and she could see that it was white and had little feathery protrusions scattered across its skin. They looked like tiny versions of the back of that one dinosaur Alex had loved when she was a toddler.

Dimetrodon.

The word came to Mari as she resigned herself to death. Perhaps it would pull her apart, or perhaps she would be lifted into the air and dashed against the earth. Maybe she would be eaten. Or, if whatever held her was merciful, it would just choke her until she lost consciousness.

"Goodbye, Dan," she said as she felt the eel-like cord begin to pull her back. She watched his face twist in sorrow and terror, and in a detached way, she found it hard to believe that he would be devastated by her death. A final, malicious thought rose in her mind.

Good. If I have to die, let him suffer as he watches.

She felt her legs straighten under her as it pulled her up. Then, without sign or warning, the long, feathered tendril slackened, and she collapsed back onto her knees. A moment later, it released her entirely. The beast, whatever it was, let out a terrible wail like a screaming lion, and then there was silence. Mari fell forward onto one hand and put the other to her throat. She sobbed for a moment until Dan grabbed her shoulder. His fingers dug into her skin. She looked up at him, ready to plead for a moment to cry, but she saw that he wasn't looking at her. Mari followed his gaze.

The woman stood in the road, her clothing torn and muddy, her hair lank and matted. She was looking at them with burning yellow eyes.

6

SHE WASN'T NEARLY AS old as Mari had pictured. That made sense, of course. The brief Norman had sent her had contained pictures of the woman they believed she would encounter, a nineteen-year-old named Ashley Bustrich who had gone missing in 2016. Those pictures had shown her a girl with dyed blonde hair, immaculate makeup, and two younger brothers who looked like they thought the world of her. Gathered from her social media accounts, they had sketched the life of a smart young woman who had taken a year off after high school to work for her family's business while her father underwent cancer treatment. They told a story that abruptly ended one autumn afternoon when her car was found by the side of the road near Weeping Cedars, apparently abandoned on her way home from dropping her youngest brother off at summer camp near Old Forge. Norman and the brief had done what they could to prepare her to see a young woman about the same age as Emily would have been. Still, she had pictured her much older.

The figure took a jittery-camera-shutter step forward, as if she were on film and someone cut out the frames between one second and the next. Mari almost screamed. Dan didn't scream; the sound that left him was like a bark of shock and fear. Another shutter-snap forward, her hands up now, open and reaching.

"Get back," Dan said. Mari wasn't sure if he was talking to her or the movie monster that was ticking toward them. He grabbed her arm hard and pulled, answering her question. As Mari scrambled backward, half rising, half letting Dan drag her, the woman-thing came forward. Her feet were bare, and the cuffs of her jeans were frayed and black. Again, the incongruity twisted in Mari's head. She had imagined an old woman in a dress with twigs in her hair, but this woman was wearing a T-shirt that had once been white, or maybe yellow, now it was a stained, sunbaked beige.

Mari could still read the letters 'C-A-M' across her chest through a mess of what she hoped was only caked mud.

"Keep moving," Dan said, but Mari pulled her arm away.

"No, I have to speak to her."

"Why?" Dan said.

"She has what they want. She can do what they want," Mari whispered.

Snap, snap, snap. The woman jittered forward until she was standing only six feet away. She stared down into the fire with her golden eyes.

"I beseech you," Mari said, her fingers scrabbling against the zipper of her pack's front pocket. "I beseech you to stay and speak. Stay and speak."

The woman opened her mouth, but she didn't speak. Instead, an image burst into Mari's mind, as if someone crammed it in, rusty and jagged. Reeling and gasping, Mari tried to resist the image, but she could not push it away.

A woman in a cloak knelt in the forest, a rabbit dangling from her fist. The woman's face, pale and gaunt, fluttered, and was replaced by Mari's.

"No … I—" Mari began, but the woman's hand shot out and pointed at Dan.

Dan lay on the floor of the big house, his eyes open, his arms out to his sides, his legs spread, naked, blue, and unquestionably dead.

The image called to her, and again, she struggled to push it away. Mari's fingers finally got hold of the zipper, and she tugged. It caught, but the angle was bad. She pushed her palm down to hold the fabric steady and pulled again.

Dan looped a rope and threw it over the branch of a tree.

Her pack opened. She slipped her hand into the pocket and found the plastic sandwich bag. She pulled it free, and without taking her eyes from the woman, she pulled it open and pulled out the piece of broken glass.

"No, I do not seek vengeance, sojourner. I seek your allegiance. My Queen offers you this token of promise."

With a badly shaking hand, Mari held the shard aloft, and it glowed red in the firelight.

"My Queen seeks your counsel," Mari managed.

The fire flared, and Mari instinctively pulled her hand back. The flames roared as the weather-spattered young woman tilted her head, staring at the piece of broken glass. She pointed a finger at it, and Mari forced herself to hold the token steady. Then, just as the woman was about to touch it, she stopped and let out a long, hissing breath. She grabbed Mari's wrist, and Mari's mind was overwhelmed with visions she didn't understand: A woman in a bed, the sky on fire, moons rising together and apart, a room in a tower, and pain—endless pain.

The vision changed to darkness and a hulking, broad figure that lumbered out of the night, its golden eyes aglow. Huge and slow, it moved toward her, unblinking, and Mari knew that when it reached her, it would consume her. As it drew nearer, she could feel its breath upon her face. In a moment, she knew, it would open its mouth and—

The fire went out, and the vision disappeared, leaving only the woman's eyes where the beast's had been. Mari opened her mouth to scream, but no sound left her except a thin, pitiable whine. The woman who had once been Ashley Bustrich leaned in and pressed her lips to Mari's cheek, and the world went black.

7

"MARI."

Dan's voice was distant, as if he were calling her from behind a closed door. She waved a heavy hand half-heartedly to ask him to let her sleep for another fifteen minutes. She pulled her blanket up over her shoulder and nestled her head deeper into her pillow.

A zipper poked into her cheek.

Mari jolted up, opened her eyes, and raised her hands defensively, as if to ward off an impending attack. The world had changed. A hazy, smoky morning met them. The tree in the nearby front yard no longer looked black, the grass had returned, and the road was once more asphalt.

"Mari, hey, it's okay, you're okay."

Dan crouched by the remains of the fire and lifted the little metal grate to the sky. The center was torn out, or maybe had burned away.

"Um, what the hell happened?" Mari said.

"No idea. The last thing I remember was you offering that woman something. Do you want to fill me in on what the hell we just did?"

"No," Mari said, looking around. Her sleeping bag lay on the road; her blankets pooled around her knees. Dan's bag was also spread out with blankets atop it. "Did we … did we make our beds after she left?"

Dan shrugged. "No idea. I guess we did, unless she tucked us in. You want to get out of here, or do you want to make breakfast on this?" He waved the broken grate.

"No. I mean, yeah, let's get the hell out of here."

They gathered their belongings as quickly as they could in the foggy morning light.

"Um," Dan said as he hefted his pack onto his back. "I don't like that."

Mari followed his gaze and saw what she thought at first was just the remains of a small animal. But as she studied it, she realized that the stark white bones were arranged in a deliberate pattern. She took a step toward it, but Dan put a warning hand on her arm.

"Maybe let's not," he said.

Her first instinct was to agree, but she knew that Jacob, Norman, and Jillian would want to see. So, she powered her phone on. It had been in airplane mode when she shut it down, so she was able to unlock it and snap a few pictures without being bombarded by messages.

"Um, there's another one over here," Dan said. Mari, shivering in the chill morning, walked across the road to find another arrangement of a small animal's bones. "I'm not sure I have to say that this is probably bad, right?"

"Shut up," Mari said. She could feel the space in her chest that had been emptied by mortal terror refilling with years of pain and disgust. "Just be quiet and let me work."

Dan obliged. He stood in the middle of the road and waited for her. When she was done, she turned on her heel and started to march back up the road, not waiting for him. But then a thought occurred to her.

She spun and stared at him. "Weren't you hurt? Your shoulder," she said.

"Yeah, I thought so too," he said. Then he showed her the place where something sharp had plunged a hole into his shoulder, where the shirt was still torn and black, but where only a red welt rose from his skin. "Guess she not only tucked us in but did some good voodoo on me."

"Don't say that," Mari said. "Let's get the fuck out of here."

But she didn't set off immediately. She scanned the town around her, the big houses overlooking the river, the trees rising along its banks, and the hint of buildings in the distance. Everything looked normal, or at least as normal as a constantly burning town could. Even the river that flowed out of ancient tides looked calm and not the least bit hungry.

She shook her head. She had seen too much to think that anything that had happened to them was a delusion or a dream. But she also guessed that if someone else had decided to spend last night in Weeping Cedars, they probably would have seen nothing of what Mari and Dan had experienced on Bank Street.

"Okay," she said. "Okay, let's go."

Dan followed her down the street and to the bridge, where the air cleared quickly. When they were halfway across, they noted two other cars in the little makeshift parking lot next to the bridge. One was a red

SUV with what looked like a family with kids milling around it. The other looked like a forest ranger's pickup truck. As they got closer, Mari read the words 'Northern Hamilton County Sheriff's Department' on the truck's door. The driver, a short, muscular woman in a uniform who had been talking to the family, stopped and leveled Mari and Dan with an appraising stare as they approached.

"Good morning," Dan called.

"Morning," the woman said. "I'm Deputy Victorine. Is this your vehicle?"

"Sure is," Dan said, sounding much cheerier than Mari expected.

"Did you sleep in town last night?"

"Uh, no, not in the town," Dan said. "We parked here last night and then camped up on this side of the river. We got up before sunrise and hiked in again early. We wanted to get some good pictures of the sunrise from inside the smoke."

Mari nodded, impressed by his quick thinking. *Of course,* she thought, *he's always been a good liar.*

"You can't camp out here," the deputy said.

"Oh, I thought that was just in town," Dan said.

"Why do you have your sleeping bags with you if you didn't sleep in town?"

"We were in a hurry; we woke up later than we planned on, so we didn't drop them off at the car. Besides, they aren't heavy."

"Are you hurt?" the deputy asked.

Dan looked down at his shirt. "Oh, yeah, I fell by the stupid river last night. Tore my shirt and landed in the mud. Here," Dan pulled the collar of his shirt down to show the red spot. "A branch got me real good. Lucky that it didn't break the skin. I'm Dan Carmichael, by the way, and this is my wife Mari."

"Are you all right, ma'am?" the deputy asked.

"What?" Mari said.

"Are you all right? Are you here of your own free will? Is there anything—"

"What? No. I mean, yes, I'm here of my own free will, and no, I'm not hurt or anything. This is my husband. Everything is fine."

"Okay," the deputy said, and put her hands on her hips. For the first time, Mari took real notice of the family next to their SUV. The woman was the kind of vest-wearing, tight-jean sporting, latte drinking mom that Mari hated. The fact that her skin, black, dewy, and glowing in the morning light, was perfect, annoyed Mari even more. But the thing that really pissed her off was the look of recognition on the woman's face as she reached out and grabbed her husband's arm.

"Do you have identification on you?" the deputy asked.

"Of course," Dan said, pulling out his wallet. Mari followed suit. She watched the husband lean down, his olive skin not nearly as flawless as his wife's, and his '70s stache looking ridiculous. She watched him also take on a look of surprise and recognition. Mari hated the woman for her perfection, and hated the man for clearly not taking care of himself nearly as well as his wife did. As she handed her license over to the deputy, she wondered if hatred was all that was left in her.

No, I can still be a mentor. I can still be a guardian. I can be there for Jessica.

But she wondered. She wondered if she would resent the young girl who would take the role that had belonged to her daughter. No, she didn't wonder. She knew.

"Okay, well, I'm going to give you a warning. You can't camp here. And, as I was telling these folks, you shouldn't come here at all, especially with children. The fumes are toxic. If I find your vehicle here again overnight, I'll write you a citation. Do you understand?"

"Yes, of course, deputy. I'm very sorry. You have a good day."

"You as well. And, Mr. and Mrs. Pellman, I again strongly advise you not to take your children on the bridge. And if you take them past it, I'll arrest you for child endangerment, do you understand me?"

They nodded.

"We won't go more than a few feet up," the woman said. *Shit*, Mari thought, *even her fucking voice is beautiful.* "Not even out over the water. But they've been looking forward to adding their marks to the road. That's not a … I mean—"

"No one gets arrested for spray painting that road," the deputy said. "And if you stay on this side, not out over the water, then … I guess it's fine." Here, the deputy looked down at the Ikandaset, and Mari got the strong impression that the water troubled her. Did she know? Or had she just heard stories?

The deputy's radio squawked something. She spoke into it, but Mari didn't catch what she said. She was trying to ignore the woman who was obviously hoping to get her attention. *She wants to say something to me, maybe to ask me if I am who she thinks I am.*

"Okay, I have to go, but please, be careful. I don't want to have to come back here with an ambulance. Because even if those signs say that rescue won't help you on the other side, if we know there are children involved …"

The parents nodded. "We promise, we'll stay on this side of the river."

"But Mom, I want to see the tribute," the oldest child said. Mari guessed the girl was ten or eleven.

"When you're older," the mother said.

"We're good to go?" Dan asked.

"Yes, but again, this is your one warning."

"Thank you, we won't do it again," Dan said, and Mari knew he was telling the truth.

Without returning the mother's look, Mari hiked back to their car, popped the hatchback, and dropped her pack in.

"You want me to drive?" she asked as Dan also unburdened himself.

"You tell me. How are you feeling?"

"I need coffee, then I'll be good."

"Great," he said. "Let's stop back in Shale Pond, and then you can take over."

8

THE TOWN *WAS* QUAINT. She still didn't let Dan know that it made her feel good to see the little shops and watch the people walking dogs and getting morning bagels before heading off to work. Instead, she waited for him to return with their cups and pastries, and thought about how to tell Jacob and Norman they had failed. She had said the words as she was supposed to, and they would believe her. She expected that they would be upset, but she also expected that she would be all right. They trusted her. They would usher her through whatever they had in store for Dan. And then they would let her mentor Jessica.

Still, she dreaded disappointing them, especially Jacob.

Dan brought caffeine and carbs, and they ate silently at a round, metal table on the sidewalk in front of the coffee shop. When her coffee had cooled, she sipped and felt the clouds in her mind rolling back. Ten minutes later, she crumpled her trash and stood.

"Okay, ready to get on the road?" she asked. Dan, not looking at her, nodded.

The drive out of town was beautiful, as was the winding scenery of Route 28 until they came to 87 an hour later. They went south past Lake George. The coffee had done its work, and Mari felt aware, sharp, and energized. She took them up to five miles an hour over the speed limit.

She would tell Jacob what happened, but she would frame it in a way to blame Dan for what had gone wrong. She didn't know how yet. And she had to be careful. If she made it seem like the attempt was worth making again, they might send her back. No, she had to find some way to put the blame on him and make it clear that a second attempt would be futile.

Mari rubbed her eyes as a cloud rolled over the sun. She switched lanes to pass a truck that was going too slowly and then slid back into the middle lane.

"Hey, everything okay?" Dan asked.

"Yeah, why?" Mari said, frowning at the road. Was it going to storm? The sky had gone dark quickly, as if a thunderhead had rolled over.

"You're going pretty fast," Dan said.

"I just want to get home. I want to get this over with."

"What?"

"Us. Finally. To finally be done. I want to never have to see you again."

Dan was silent. She glanced at him and saw that he was staring out the window. "I never hated you as much as you hate me," he said.

"For good reason. You killed our da—"

"You would have killed her, too. You know that, right? Just because she would have kept living, doesn't mean that she would have still been Emily. You were going to send her to that house. She was going to forget her name."

"But she would have been alive, Dan! She would have been a queen!"

"No," Dan said. "I don't think she would have. I don't think that that —whatever she is—I don't think she has any room for queens other than herself. She would have used Emily and then thrown her away."

"You're wrong. You're always wrong. All of you. All of you are always wrong except for him."

"What?" Dan said.

What was wrong with the sky? She had only ever seen it turn that color once, just before a hurricane. It bathed the whole world in a strange hue.

"What do you mean?" Dan asked, looking confused.

The truck that had been going too slowly was now passing her, and it pissed her off. She slowed to let him back over again.

"There's only one who has ever been faithful, only one who has kept his word. And he's coming, Dan. He's coming, and he's come for me. He's coming for me. He's coming for me, and the worlds will lament. They bound me and they carried me. They took me, but he is coming."

"Mari, Mari, slow down!" She switched lanes, passed the truck, and switched lanes again.

"He's here, he's been here, he will be here. He's searched for me across the ages. He's coming, Dan, and his claws are red, and they'll be black."

"Who is coming? Oh, God, Mari, your eyes! What the fuck is wrong with your eyes? Slow down!"

She also wondered what was wrong with her eyes. The world looked like an old photograph—sepia-toned and hazy. The truck passed her again, but this time she wouldn't let him come back over. She pressed her foot to the gas as the truck driver changed lanes and turned to look at Dan, feeling a smile creep across her lips.

"The Bear is coming."

Dan screamed as the yellow world folded, twisted, and spun before it went black.

1

THE SCREEN DOOR SLAMMED behind Emily, and she instinctively sidestepped out of the way of hammering feet. Her dress swayed in his wind as Sam, her boy—her most beautiful boy—rocketed across the boards to the steps and leapt off into the air, his arms wide like Spider-Man. For a moment, a pit opened in her stomach. Would he land badly? Would she hear a crack that would send them to the doctor and put him in a cast for weeks? Would he—But no, he landed with a seven-year-old's grace, light and springy, resilient and immortal.

Dust puffed around his sneakers, and then he was gone, zipping over grass, dutifully pausing at the sidewalk before speeding out to the field across the street where other kids tore over the open ground, zooming like the cartoon characters they watched on omnipresent screens.

The screen door closed again, more gently. Luke, her man—her most beautiful man—sauntered across to her side and took her in his arms. Music played through the kitchen window screen.

"*Oh, come take my hand,*" he sang into her ear. She obliged. He pulled her close and they danced, his hand against the small of her back, the other curled between them in hers. She remembered her parents dancing to the song once, or maybe it had been that other tune about fire. The memory came and went, and there was only the warmth of the sun, the laughter of the children, the cotton of his T-shirt, his soft, short hair, and the day's stubble against her cheek.

"Never stop," he said.

"Never stop what?" she asked, though she knew the answer.

"Dancing with me," he said. She agreed. Until the world ended, she wouldn't stop.

2

EMILY TOOK A BITE of the burger and let out an exaggerated groan of pleasure.

"Fuck that's good," she said. Her eyes darted to her thirteen-year-old son. He was engrossed in a conversation with his friend and not paying attention to his mother's 'cuss-y language,' as he called it.

"Princess!" Luke said in mock scandal. The stubble remained, but today he had replaced his usual T-shirt with a loose, casual button-up. His hair was darker than their son's, but she could already see the boy's going from golden to brown, and it twisted a knife in her. He was growing up, and every cliché ever written about it happening too fast was too weak to express the terrible longing that yawned inside her. She didn't want him to stay a child forever; she wanted to exist like God; all at once, so she could see all of him, from boy to man, never losing access to those moments when she could cradle him in her arms, and when he'd run to her with tears over some tiny loss.

Time, she thought, *is a real motherfucker.*

"This is a fantastic burger," she said before taking a comically large bite. Luke looked around, as if paparazzi were waiting to catch Princess Emerald chowing down like a barbarian at the local brewpub. And though some people looked, no one seemed shocked by the fact that the last princess loved smashburgers with extra pickles.

In Glory Home, they know I put my crown on … well, one head at a time.

She giggled at the thought as they strolled together down the sidewalk, greeting others out enjoying the beautiful summer night. She saw people from work and stopped to chat with one of the women from Makeup, who had an idea that she wanted to throw Emily's way.

"Mom," Sam said, turning from his friend, "does it ever get boring knowing everyone in the world?"

She laughed at the old joke, remembering when he first asked it as a five-year-old. She had just stopped to join a group of excited children for a rendition of "Welcome to Virtue Vista Valley!" First, he had told her to stop singing like a goat, which had made everyone laugh. Then he asked her if she ever got bored.

Her answer was the same as it always had been.

"Never."

3

"AND THAT," SHE SAID, smiling down at the three wide-eyed children, "is why we always tell the truth. I know, your parents tell you that, and it's not always fun, because you might get in trouble, but I promise, it's the best policy."

"What is?" Armando the Alligator asked. He sat on a stone by the pretend stream that ran through the pretend valley.

The children, sitting together on a log, all called out in unison, "Honesty!"

"That's right," she said. "Honesty."

"Cut!" Uwe called from beside the cameraman. "Wonderful, I think that will do it. Let's break for lunch, and then we can get to our afternoon scenes. Oh, and that is a wrap on the children for the day. Thank you, kids!"

After they took her crown and the ridiculous clear-plastic scepter that she'd started carrying the previous season, she shook each child's hand and told them to pay attention in their afternoon classes. Then came the thin, white parka to protect her dress during lunch. She felt, as she always did, like a child, even in her fifties. Of course, the thin cloth saved time and money, but she longed to have some of her meals in the Crystalline Mansion cafeteria in just a T-shirt and jeans.

Halfway to the cafeteria, her wrist buzzed. She pulled a small pair of glasses from her bag and donned them. A dim shape appeared transposed over the CM grounds.

"Hey, honey," she said, seeing Sam's face. Her son looked like he was in his bedroom at the frat house.

"Hey, Mom," Sam said. There was something wrong with his voice.

"What is it, honey?"

"I … I messed up," he said. She could hear the pain and tears ready to break out, like when he was a boy. "I don't know how or why, but I messed up. I don't know what to do."

"What happened?" She lowered her voice and walked toward a little empty picnic table. She watched him reach up to touch the side of his glasses. The scene flipped. It took her a moment to understand what she was seeing. She stopped in her tracks. Two young women, wearing only underwear, sat with their legs entwined, their heads tilted, their lips together. One held the other's face, the other held her hands to her partner's breast and neck.

They were entirely still. They remained still for a long, impossible moment.

"I did that," he said, his voice finally cracking. "I don't know what happened, one minute they were here, and then the next—"

A hand scratched at her mind, and a door, long closed, opened. Eyes peered out at her from the darkness behind the door. A voice like glass cut out from the opening.

My boy. Finally.

Hands turned knobs and pulled levers. Emily felt her lips move, and her feet turned on the pavement with a gravelly scratch.

"Don't leave your room, honey. Don't do anything. I'm going to get help. I'm going to fix this."

The words weren't hers. She couldn't remember the last time she had been moved like this, like a puppet. She wanted to scream at him, to ask him how he could do it, but the power on the other side of the door in her mind was in control. As it moved her limbs and mouth, her mind spun through a million more milling questions. How did no one hear? How did he get them to stay in that position? Why were there two half-naked co-eds in his bedroom?

Well, she thought, *that part at least I know.*

She marched, her thin smock floating about her shoulders, her hair so pinned and sprayed that it moved not at all. The last Princess Emerald pulled open a side door after the security system recognized her and strode through the offices until she came to the door that read 'Victoria Robillard.' She knocked, but didn't wait for an answer.

"Vicki," Emily said to the short-haired, smartly dressed woman, "we have a problem."

4

THE MAN WAS CLOSE to thirty, but he looked at Emily as if she were half her age and hot to trot. She'd experienced men like him her whole life. Older men, younger men, teenage boys, all wondering what Princess Emerald would be like in bed. When she was ten, the police took a man away for sending her messages. When she was fourteen, people took special interest in the beach pictures from her family's Mediterranean vacation. When Princess Emerald turned 18 for the first time in her long history, the AI-generated adult sites had a field day with lifelike simulations of a young woman who looked and sounded strikingly like her doing all manner of things while wearing a crown.

Men had propositioned her by the hundreds; women less frequently. Still, she didn't think that there was a demographic she hadn't been approached by. Last year, when she became the last Princess Emerald in every meaning of the phrase, Cassidy Dimer's son had hit on her at Cassidy Dimer's funeral. She hadn't even wanted to start trying to pick apart the Freudian psychological tangle that was going on in that middle-aged man's head. He wasn't bad looking, and after Luke's passing four years earlier, she hadn't had many intimate experiences. But she had been so scandalized and afraid that he would start crying and calling her 'mommy,' that she had shut that door hard.

But now a man less than half her age was giving her the eye across her living room. She didn't think she'd do anything with him, but his obvious interest was awakening a desire to get a little dolled up and see if there were any men in their fifties kicking around Glory Home on a Friday night. The thought was intriguing enough that she missed the first half of his last sentence.

"—think it's fair."

"I'm sorry, could you say that again?" she said. Her hand went to her temple, as if to adjust a crown that wasn't there.

"I mean," he said, clearly not repeating exactly what he had said. She generally hated asking people to repeat themselves, especially when they didn't exactly oblige. "I just think it's fair for me to be, you know, taken care of for keeping things so close to the vest."

She nodded. "I see," she said and watched his eyes go wide. "No, I do see. Please don't read that as a prelude to me having you done away with, or something like that," she said. "I understand what a burden it has been to carry my son's secrets. And you're right, there should be a reward for that. You should have some of your burdens eased."

He shifted back in his seat, as if moving away from a dangerous animal.

"Everything I'm saying is coming out like I'm threatening you," she said. "I'm not. I will take care of you, I promise." She laughed. "I will give you money," she said, shaking her head and slapping her knee. "I'll make sure your bills are paid. Will that work for you?"

"I ... I was hoping for maybe a little more," he said.

"Okay, I think that's fair, too. What do you say to ... two million?" Two million wasn't the fortune that it once was, but it would certainly ease the man's way. "And you could come back in, say, ten years, and we could see how things are going."

The tension in the man's face eased. "Yes, ma'am, that sounds more than generous."

She gave him her biggest, best princess smile, put her hands on her knees, and stood. She held out her hand to usher him from her living room. "Now, if you'll excuse me, I have other matters to deal with for Sam; he's such a busy young man. I'm sure he'll be thrilled to hear that you stopped by."

"You're not going to tell him that I—"

"Of course I am," Emily said. "But you don't have to be afraid of him any more than you have to be afraid of me. Sam knows better than any of us how hard it is to live with the things his hands do. He wouldn't be mad at you for wanting some help in carrying that burden."

She took his hand and led him to the front door.

"Do you know what the Hebrew word for heaviness is?" she asked him. She could hear the subtle Missouri turn in her voice. Internet memes of Princess Emerald with a cowboy hat instead of a crown, or a mobile home behind her instead of the original Sam's old tower, flashed in her mind. With them came images of the original Sam. Dear Sam, who missed meeting her son by the space of one hour. She wished they could have said 'hello,' just once.

"Um, no," he said, pulling her away from her memories.

"It's *Cavod*," she said, gently pulling him along to the front door. "You have a *Cavod* on your shoulders." Before the front door, she put her hands on those shoulders and felt how smooth and soft they were. She suddenly longed for Luke's strong, muscular shoulders. "We all do. Especially Sam. But that word has another meaning. And I want you to go home and look it up. You hear me?"

"Yes, ma'am," he said.

"Good. Now, you'll get a gift from us in the next couple of days. And I'm not telling you to spend it all and then come back, but if you do need anything, you be in touch, okay?"

"Yes, thank you, ma'am," he said. Then he looked her in the eyes, and perhaps against his will, his gaze flicked down to her V-neck shirt. She laughed.

"*That* wasn't what I was suggesting, young man," she said.

She gave him a friendly hug and kiss on the cheek and sent him on his way. When the front door was safely closed, she crossed her arms under the breasts he had briefly ogled, put her back to the door, and considered the weight of the things Sam's hands had made. She knew that it had something to do with his birthright and something to do with the presence that had hovered over her while she was pregnant with him. She knew it had something to do with the darkness behind the door in her mind and the great light that she saw the day her parents took her through the strange door on the mountain to the house on the hill.

When they pretended I was missing.

She remembered the headlines when she had returned: *The Princess Brought Back to Life*, and *The Resurrected Princess!* She still had the Glory Home newspaper front page framed in her office, *Glory! She's alive!*

For three months, her mind had been burdened with many things in that strange place. She'd even worn one of the plaques with her name, since she forgot it like everyone did in that house's classrooms. It had been a powerful and overwhelming knowledge she had been given, strong enough to remake her in so many ways.

Still, all that knowledge seemed paltry sometimes when she remembered her sister Alex, posed in front of her computer, chin in her hand, a plastic tumbler with a melting blended drink at her elbow, her eyes open but unseeing as Sam rocked in the corner, repeating her name over and over.

5

ON A HILL IN Glory Home, the light shone like a beacon to the nations. Her boy—the most beautiful boy in the world—stood atop a glass tower, and on every floor his wonders posed unmoving, radiating light from another house on another hill. Emily sat in her wheelchair at the foot of the hill, looking up, her shaking arms stretched above her head. She felt her body pulling up, her feet molding down into the earth, and the skin on the backs of her legs hardening and pushing her up until she was standing for the first time in five years. She felt the tips of her fingers pull and split, pull and split. Her mouth fell open, and her eyes were transformed. As the natural light of the world faded, a new white radiance gleamed out from the pinnacle of the crystal house, and it bent all things to itself. All, she knew, would rise and reach their branches up, and the world would be a forest before her son.

The door in her mind opened, and the voice tumbled out like broken glass, shredding as it fell.

Not your boy. Not your son. He was never your son. He is mine.

The man at the top of the tower, the man she had called her son, regarded her once, and then never again, as the forest sprouted across all lands. Emily breathed one last word, and its two syllables mingled with the wind.

6

THE VISION FADES AS she wakes. Her face hurts. She wants to blink her raw eyes, but her lids are frozen under the golden mask. The scream that perpetually goes up silently from her lips redoubles in a longing, frantic keen. Only two can hear the sound as she stands from her dark corner, pulled by unseen strings. Her first step is high, her knee up, her toes down. Her arms go out to her sides, elbows sagging, wrists up, fingers drooping. She prances once, then again, on the balls of her bare feet. The hem of the sackcloth garment that isn't quite a dress, or toga, or tunic flutters around her knees. Her fingers curl down, her knees bounce up, her hair, matted and tangled in the rough edges of the amber mask, tugs and breaks only to grow again under the enthroned one's gaze.

She prowls the stony ground before him, moving in time with the plinking of some stringed instrument that rings in her head. She spins once and twice and a dozen times before falling to the ground and writhing under the thousand, thousand legs of spiders only she can see. Then up she springs and turns a cartwheel, then prowls and prances once more. The plinking turns to the low, mournful moan of an out-of-tune violin. She stops her staccato steps. Her dress sways.

"Did you dream?" the far-seeing one asks her from his throne. His voice is like an instrument, like a wide reed with a dead wind playing over it, like thunder down a long road. She nods. "You dreamed of the impending night. From all these things I have saved you," he says. "Now dance. Never stop dancing for me."

She knows she will obey. She knows that until the world ends, she will not stop dancing, except when she sleeps and dreams of a world where she was almost not a mother.

Auntie

October 7, 1961

1

THE CAR JOSTLED THE woman in the back seat as it bumped over the uneven road, almost knocking her purse from her lap. She snatched it back with animal ferocity and shot the driver a furious look. She had to stop herself from yelling at him to be careful. Scolding him would be unjust. She had told him to spare neither comfort nor safety on the way to the place where her dreams had been murdered.

She didn't know what to call the emotion that lodged in her chest, pulsing up her throat and into the back of her mouth. Certainly, she was angry. Angry? She was furious. Decades of preparation were probably lying dead in a coroner's van. She studied the feeling and wondered if it contained sorrow for the dead girl. She wanted it to. She wanted to believe that she could still feel sad at the death of a human being, but she recognized that that would likely require affection, something she hadn't felt since her godson passed into the Glory back in '31. She had, of course, felt something for her grandchildren when they were young. But that feeling had faded over time, and she couldn't remember when last she felt a modicum of anything but disinterest in their lives.

Thirty years, then. Thirty years since she had felt affection or care for any living person. That realization brought its own strange, unnamed emotion, wriggling through her stomach. But, compared to the tumor of loss in her chest, it meant nothing.

The car jostled her again, and the driver had the good sense not to apologize. He kept his eyes on the dark road, his hands on the wheel, and was clearly doing his level best to obey her. He didn't know the gargantuan loss they had all suffered, but he didn't need to. She wondered if anyone alive understood what had been taken tonight except for her.

Annabelle might. Of course, Annabelle would be suffering the loss of her daughter more than anything else. That was natural, but the woman begrudged Annabelle that natural feeling. Annabelle had lost a daughter; the woman had lost her mission.

No, that was stating the case too strongly. She had lost much, but not the whole mission. While she lived, there was hope. She started calculating and wondered if they were to start over today, with a new girl, whether they would be able to meet the deadline. Ninety-five years seemed like a long time, but it wasn't. Not when there were so many rituals to perform, so many enemies to overcome—or, if not overcome, *avoid*—that a century felt constricting. Still, if they moved quickly, and if someone in the family was the right age, then perhaps, perhaps they could still accomplish the task given to them. The woman started mentally ticking through her grandchildren and who might be a good fit.

The car slowed when the red, rotating light of a police car flashed through the trees. The driver, pulling them back down to a safe speed, turned into the driveway of the two-story stone house that she had believed was safe. It should have been safe. Not only secluded, not only protected by the best natural means of security money could buy, it was inlaid with powerful wards invisible to all but those knowledgeable in the ways of the City. They were wards that only the truly mighty could have breached.

As they rolled to a stop next to a man in a police officer's uniform, the driver rolled down his window.

"Good evening, can I help you?" the policeman said.

"She's family," the driver said.

"Ma'am," the officer said, leaning down so he could see her. His eyes went wide. She was used to that kind of reaction, especially from bumpkin men who had never been anywhere where real beauty was cultivated. "Um, what is your relationship to the family?"

"I'm the girl's auntie," she said. "And her mother has called for my help."

2

PREDICTABLY, ANNABELLE WAS INCONSOLABLE. Her two sons sat beside her on the sofa, the younger holding his mother's hand, the older simply staring straight ahead. When the woman entered the room, Annabelle moved her hands from covering her mouth to her sons' chests.

"Please, please don't hurt them. Please, we can fix this, please."

She fell from the couch onto her knees and crawled across the carpet. The woman noted that Annabelle wore a blue terrycloth robe over her silk nightshirt. Everything stretched and pulled as she crawled to the woman's feet. She reminded her of the worms that crawled beneath the great Glass House.

"Please, Auntie, please, don't hurt my boys," she said. The two young men looked at her, but didn't speak or move to join their mother on the floor. The older was hardly a 'boy,' and the younger, the dead girl's twin, looked as if he'd be able to grow a beard in a year or two.

"Elton, pick your mother up," the woman Annabelle called 'Auntie' said. He regarded her for a long moment with a look of … was it admiration? Fear? Desire? Did he know how much older she was, or who she was to him? Had Annabelle told him? Would it have mattered to him? She filed that look away in case it would be useful later.

"Jacob, get her a tissue. Don't just sit there, comfort her."

The young men obeyed, and soon Annabelle was back in her place between them. Auntie sat on a chair opposite them. She suddenly wished she had dressed differently, less conservatively. Elton's eyes would not leave her, and his fixation could prove to be exceptionally useful in the decades to come. If he were devoted to her, then …

"Please," Annabelle said. "Please, we did everything we were supposed to. We didn't … she's dead, Auntie! She's dead! My baby girl is dead!"

Auntie looked at Jacob and tilted her head toward Annabelle. Elton put his arm around his mother.

Auntie nodded. "She is dead. Where is her body?"

"What?" Annabelle choked between sobs.

"Where is her body?"

"The coroner has her," Elton said. He had a deep voice and spoke calmly.

"That is what I expected. We will want her back. There will be no open casket."

"What do you mean?" Annabelle said.

"I mean, there are sixteen years of preparation in that body, sixteen years of power devoted to her to make her ready. And though there were sixteen more to follow before she was ready, there is still power in her flesh. We cannot lose it."

Annabelle stared at her. "Auntie Leah …" she began, but the words trailed off.

"Elton, I want you to tell the coroner that when he is done with his report, she is to be returned to us for burial in a private family plot. Do you understand?"

"Yes, Auntie," he said.

"Good, that will give me time to consult with the Scribe. What of the man who did this? Where is he?"

"The police have him," Elton said.

"Who is he?" At this question, Annabelle looked at Elton, and he at her. Annabelle's mouth sagged, and Auntie Leah thought she saw her shake her head ever so slightly at Elton.

"Tell me who he is, and do not lie to me."

"He …" Elton began, swallowed, nodded, and continued. "His name is Joseph Macon Lawstead."

Auntie searched her memory and found the name. "The tampered boy. The one who was meant to be … The one you replaced," the woman said.

"Yes," Elton said.

"But how? Why? What has the Surgeon against us?"

"We don't think … we don't think it was the Surgeon who tampered with him," Elton said. "He left a token, and we think it belongs to another. Maybe the Librarian."

"Show me. What is it?"

"It's in her room, we didn't move it. We didn't dare touch it," Elton said.

"That may have been very wise. All right, Elton, take me to her room, show me."

Annabelle reached out and grabbed her son's arm.

"Oh, stop it, Annabelle! I'm not going to slay your sons because your daughter is dead. Vengeance is wasteful and does not serve the Glory. Besides, your boy is among the Great Ones, and his sacrifice will be one of the jewels of this world. Would I destroy that for some misguided fit of pique?"

Annabelle regarded her with fear and sadness, which said she wasn't sure what Auntie was capable of.

"Fine, let me say it again. Your sons are safe. You are safe. There is still much to do. You are near to breaking, and I have no use for you broken. So, take heart that neither I nor any of the Pride will harm your boys. You have my solemn vow in the Glory."

This seemed to ease Annabelle a little, and she nodded to her son and released his arm. Elton stood. He was a tall young man, handsome in a severe way, and dressed, even at this time of night, as if he were ready to go to a job in the city: white button-up shirt, pressed slacks, shined shoes, and a black tie. Auntie appreciated that about him. She offered him her elbow, and he guided her to the staircase. They walked up the wide flight together without speaking. When they came to Emily's room, he opened the door and let her go in first.

She took the whole scene in one moment. To her left was a table supporting a model train set. In front of her stood a vanity, a wardrobe, and a dresser. To her right was a slightly rumpled bed with an amber stone resting on the pillow. Auntie's head swam. She reached for Elton's arm. She could feel his muscles tensing, and she let her fear push her against him. He wrapped her round with a protective arm.

"What is that?" she asked.

"We don't know. There's something etched into it." He held her close, and she could feel him tensing. She wondered again if he knew the difference in their ages, despite the fact that she appeared to be his peer. What had Annabelle told him about her? "Shall I get it for you?"

"No," she said, straightening and pulling away from him. "No, if it is dangerous, I am more likely to be safe." She walked across the diamond-patterned rug and stopped at the dresser. Sitting on top was a picture of the murdered girl with her twin brother. They were standing somewhere with water to one side, and what looked like a row of amusements to their left.

"Where was this taken?" she asked, trying to focus on anything but the stone. It confused her and made her vision swim. But focusing on the blonde girl with blue eyes and a captivating smile brought the room back into balance.

"The New Jersey shore. We went there a few times. Emily loved it. She loved being by the ocean."

Auntie nodded. Yes, the world was righting itself. "And that?" she asked, pointing to the train set.

"It's only something silly that she and Jacob would do together. They'd play at being Conroy and Elaine or make up imaginary places to run their trains to. I think this place is called Glory Downs, or something like that."

"Aren't they a little old for that?" Auntie said.

"Yes," Elton said flatly.

Auntie nodded. She felt right again. Steeling herself, she turned to look at the stone. The world swam again, but not as much as before. She forced herself to look at it, to focus until she could think clearly. Then, trepidatiously, she reached out and took the stone. The world snapped back into place.

"Have you seen this symbol?" she asked, studying the zigzagging line with an arrow at one end and a circle at the other.

"Yes, but we don't know what it means," Elton said.

"Well, I know someone who might." She slid the stone into her clutch. "This is where he came in?" She reached out and moved one of the double-door windows on its pivot. Suddenly, a thought occurred to her. "Why isn't this all blocked off? I assume they consider this a crime scene."

"I think," Elton said, "it's the wards. Any earthly authority—"

She held up a hand. "Right, of course. Well, that will only last so long, I suppose. Someone is going to ask to see the room."

"And they can see it. There's no mystery here, though."

She let him lead her back downstairs into the living room, where Annabelle stared silently at the carpet. "Tell me about this man, Lawstead.

I thought he belonged to the Surgeon, now you're saying otherwise."

"Yes," Annabelle said. "I mean, no. It wasn't the Surgeon. His … patients don't survive this long."

Auntie nodded. She remembered now. There was so much in her head, so many years of information, she often found the need to pack things away to keep them from cluttering her mind. She hadn't thought of the Surgeon for years, perhaps not since young Lawstead's situation had been brought to her attention at the camp.

"I will ask the Scribe about it," she said, not liking the creature's name in her mouth.

"The Scribe? Do we have to …" Annabelle trailed off.

Auntie watched as the grieving mother realized that there was no escaping further encounters with the Queen's servants in the near future. Along with her daughter, the hope for another fifteen years of a mostly quiet, undisturbed life had died tonight.

Auntie noted how close Elton stood to her. Again, she wondered if he knew. There was a strange phenomenon with her condition, which she had experienced several times before. People who intellectually knew her age were unable to reconcile that knowledge with a woman who looked no older than twenty-five. The fact could not stand up against their immediate experience of her apparent youth. But, even if Elton could reconcile her appearance with her longevity, would he care? A gap of four generations was significant. He was less related to her than a second cousin, and almost no one looked askance at such relationships. Not that she would pursue him, but if she allowed him to pursue her, to hope that there was a chance … well, again, that might be exceptionally useful.

"I must go," Auntie said. "I shall consult with the Scribe. He will show us the way."

"Can he bring her back?" Annabelle asked, her hands cupped before her face, her eyes pleading over her fingertips. Auntie knew that resurrecting the girl was beyond the power of all—except perhaps One—but she shrugged.

"We will see. Get her body back. I shall be gone for hours. No, stay where you are, I know how to use your door."

As Auntie brushed past Elton, she slid her hand down his arm, planting a seed she might cultivate later. She left them in their grief and contemplation, taking long, purposeful strides into the hallway. The stone floor clacked underfoot, and Auntie felt the first twinges of anxiety. She had seen and experienced things that few ever dreamed of. Yet, an audience with the Scribe remained a daunting prospect.

She unlocked and opened a heavy wooden door in the foyer hallway.

She pulled a string of metal links to light the basement stairs. Down she went, another string pulled, another lightbulb lit. Around shelves of preserves, past a pile of old furniture, she came to another wooden door set into the old foundation. Should anyone open it without the proper words, it would reveal a cramped room, perhaps intended for tools. But with the words that ever smoldered in the back of her mind, the door led somewhere else.

She spoke the burning words and waited until she heard the world change. Like stone grinding on distant stone, and metal on rusted metal, realities grated against each other. Then, when the turning of celestial gears had ceased, she pulled the little door open and stepped into the foyer of a different house.

She immediately collapsed. A hallway cramped with overflowing bookshelves flashed past in a dim blur as she tumbled to the ground, her breathing labored, her chest on fire. She reached out with a trembling, withered hand and rapped her swollen knuckles on the stone floor. She couldn't hear her knock, but she knew he would. She lay in agony as her stomach burned and twisted like she had been shot.

I was shot, she thought. *He shot me.*

Then she thought no more as darkness closed in around her.

When she came to, she was seated on a well-cushioned chair, staring at the Scribe's blurry form. He leaned forward over his desk and wrote quickly with a long quill.

"Tell me," he said, not stopping his pen.

"They have killed my great-great-granddaughter, whom we were preparing. The vessel has been shattered."

The quill froze. He looked up at her through his wire-framed glasses. "How is this possible? What power could undo the wards we set?"

Auntie, who had called herself 'Leah' since her first grandchild could not pronounce her full name, opened her palm before the Scribe and showed him the amber stone.

A director had once told her that the most effective way to make a monster scary was to establish a brave character and then have the monster terrify them. This was back before films had sound, back when she had been ... if not a star, then at least an actor on the silver screen. Before she had had her films burned.

She had always thought that the director's insight was sound, but she had never seen it done properly, had never felt the chill of the unseen beast that horrified the stalwart hero. The Scribe, she knew, was no hero, but when his face contorted in terror, she felt her blood run cold and her heart hammer and kick.

"Take that away," he cried, and pushed back from his desk, knocking his chair over. "Take it away!"

Leah closed her shaking fist and dropped the stone back into her clutch. "What is it?" she asked.

"Be glad that your sealing was interrupted! Rejoice that the sorcerer broke you, for if he had not, that stone would … would …" The Scribe didn't seem to have the words.

"It is away," she said, remembering that dank basement where she had been shot. Shot and ruined, though she hadn't known the second fact for decades. No one had.

"That sigil, that stone … we are in grave danger."

"Why? Who do they belong to?" She barely recognized her own weak, wavering voice.

"The Cursed and Cursing. The Unfettered Prince who sits enthroned in Harhain." The words meant nothing to Leah; still, she felt a thrill of terror gallop through her. "If he is against us … this is dire."

"I don't understand," she began, but he picked himself up from the floor and held one of his hands up to silence her.

"I will explain, but we must act quickly. The girl's body, do you have it?"

"I have ordered it retrieved," she said.

"Good. There is power in that body; we must find a way to preserve it," he said, dusting himself off. Then, frowning, he put his hands on his desk and hunched, as if deep in thought. Leah knew better than to interrupt him, so she waited for several minutes, feeling herself drifting dangerously close to sleep. Once she nodded, but pulled herself back from the brink.

Finally, he raised his head. He didn't look pleased. "There is a way," he said. "We must use power that does not belong to us. It is dangerous and unpredictable, but we have done it before."

"We have?"

"Yes, Garian, the Child Eater."

Auntie Leah put her hand to her stomach and shook her head. "No, he is vile. I thought we were finished with him."

"We were. And yet," the Scribe said, turning to the bookshelves about him, "his power is potent. He does not understand it, so we can use it."

"Do you understand it?" she asked.

He didn't answer. Instead, he searched his shelves until he pulled three volumes down and put them on his desk. "There may be a way to take her, your vessel, and preserve the power we have poured into her. We will bind them together; he will preserve her."

"No, that cannot be the answer," she said.

"Even now, the power we have infused in her is fading. We must begin. You must begin."

"What do you mean, I must 'begin?'"

"You know where your strengths lie. If you were a sculptor, I would tell you to make a statue to bind them to. But you are not a sculptor."

Auntie Leah saw her years on the stage and on the screen. She saw herself with Annabelle, dreaming the Child Eater's stories and binding them into scripts and sounds. As she pondered what it might mean to bind her great-great-granddaughter to the monster, she saw something new. In her mind, a tower rose. Bent and strange, it cast its shadow over a village set among green hills. And … yes, she saw her there, walking in the village, Annabelle's daughter.

"I know the answer, but I must ask so I can tell my great-granddaughter that I did. Can you bring her back?"

He did not look up as he flipped blank pages. "Not as you or she would want. But yes, she will live. I cannot claim to know what her existence will be like, but yes, she will live."

"Emily will live," Leah said, and, again, she saw the valley village … no, not a village, a kingdom.

"The Child Eater's power will be the key. We will tap it, harness it, and direct it. We will use her power as well. We will make a place from her—"

"*For* her," Leah said.

"No, from her. Though she will dwell in it … in a way. I see it in my mind, but it will take more than our strengths, even with Garian. The Sculptor and the Composer both will have to lend their power. Perhaps even the Queen herself. This will take time. But I see from your face that the work has already begun. That is good. Now, return and tell your great-granddaughter what must be done." He opened his mouth to say something more, but another thought interrupted him. "And get the man. The man who did this. We need him."

"Why? Why not just kill him?" she asked.

"I think you would find that impossible to do. No. If he is what I think he is, it would require something more than you have in your world to slay the likes of the Scion. But we can imprison him, study him, and … oh … and if we can turn him …"

Leah nodded slowly, not understanding at all. "I will have him. I will make certain of it."

"Good. Now, I will return you to the door, but you must go through on your own." The Scribe lifted her from her chair, and she felt how shrunken her body was. He carried her as easily as one might carry a baby. When he reached the front door, he opened it and set her down on the floor.

"Now go the way you came," he said. Then he turned and left her to her indignity as she reached out one hand and then the other. Taking hold of the doorframe, she pulled herself across the floor, inch by inch, minute after minute, until finally, she was across the threshold and lying on Annabelle's basement floor.

She stood, dusted herself off, and closed the door behind her. The gears of worlds ground. Then she went up and back into the empty living room. Morning light shone through the window. She took a long, shuddering breath.

"You're back," Annabelle said.

Leah turned and saw the disheveled woman. "Yes, and we have work to do. Terrible work. But you have my word, if we do it correctly, you will not lose your daughter."

"What do we have to do?" Annabelle asked, her face a contortion of fear and hope.

"Call Karl," Leah said. "We will need his help again. Have him come straight away."

Annabelle said she would and then collapsed, sobbing.

<h2 style="text-align:center">3</h2>

LEAH APPRAISED THE OPEN stretch of land bordered by sparse forest. Annabelle had chosen well; this would be a good place. It was far enough out of town that if something happened, the town would … what? What was she picturing? An atomic explosion? The Child Eater escaping? She didn't know. Maybe the distance meant nothing at all. Still, it comforted her a little.

"How deep are we going to dig?" the man asked.

"Obviously, we must have plans drawn up," Annabelle said, "but I want you to envision a vast atomic bomb bunker, and under that, one much smaller chamber. Is that possible here?"

"Okay …" the man said, scratching behind his ear. "So, you want us to go, what, three stories down?"

"That's right."

"I don't know if we can go that far without blasting—"

"Then blast," Auntie said.

"How big are we talking for this third floor down?"

"The size of a vault," Annabelle said.

"Vaults can be a lot of sizes," the man said.

"Then of a mausoleum, the kind you see in your local cemetery," Leah said.

"Okay, so … ten by ten?"

"That's good," Annabelle said. "Can you build that here?"

He appraised the land in front of him and nodded. "We'll need to do a full survey, but yeah, I think we could do that. You're planning on just the one building out here?"

"No," Annabelle said. "It will be a whole office complex. But we are starting with this one special building. Just in case," she said.

"In case the Ruskies get us," he said.

Neither Annabelle nor Leah responded. They just looked at the open land and imagined how they would fill it.

4

THE WOMAN WHO HAD called herself Auntie Leah sat on her great-great-granddaughter's bed and watched the brightening eastern sky with dread. All things seemed uncertain, but it hadn't always been that way. She remembered when her brother first convinced her of the safety of their path. She had sat next to him and listened to the Lion preach about universal love, reconciliation, and the wondrous Glory that streamed from the Crystal House atop the hill. She had felt the Glory flowing through her when she had tapped out her brother's poem over the telegraph. Then she had been confident. When they ushered her into that basement to seal her against the coming ages, all had seemed unshakable. Even when that bastard shot her, there had seemed to be no doubt that the might of the Queen would overcome. But then, she had not known what powers were arrayed against them. Then she had not known that the bullet had done its work. She had not known the decades of toil that would follow that realization, decades spent trying to fix what that sorcerer had done in that cursed town.

She weighed the amber stone in her hand.

"Roger," she said. "Roger, my dearest brother, I miss you. I wish you were here. Oh, God, I wish you were here."

No voice responded except the morning birds, heralding the impending dawn.

Thank you for reading Shards of Amber.

For more from the Weeping Cedars Universe visit
WeepingCedars.com

About the Editor

Dawn E. Dagger is an author and editor who hails from rural Ohio. She is obsessed with anything literary, caffeinated, or in need of research. She has been a fan of Weeping Cedars since 2020 and can confidently say that the world of Weeping Cedars has changed her life. When she's not writing, reading, researching, or deep in any other creative endeavors, she can be found at home, snuggling her cats and wonderful husband, safe from the horrors of the world.

About the Author

J.W.G. Wise writes twisting horror stories from one side of a hundred-year-old duplex in Pennsylvania, where he abides in a love/terror relationship with small-town America. He lives with his loving and lovely wife, the only force that keeps him from wandering into the streets of the Dark City alone one idle Thursday afternoon.